Darkest Before Dawn

Katie Flynn has lived for many years in the Northwest. A compulsive writer, she started with short stories and articles and many of her early stories were broadcast on Radio Mersey. She decided to write her Liverpool series after hearing the reminiscences of family members about life in the city in the early years of the twentieth century. She also writes as Judith Saxton. For the past few years, she has had to cope with ME but has continued to write, albeit more slowly.

Praise for Katie Flynn

'Arrow's best and biggest saga author. She's good'
Bookseller

'If you pick up a Katie Flynn book it's going to be a wrench to put it down again'
Holyhead & Anglesey Mail

'A heartwarming story of love and loss'
Woman's Weekly

'One of the best Liverpool writers'
Liverpool Echo

'[Katie Flynn] has the gift that Catherine Cookson had of bringing the period and the characters to life'
Caernarfon & Denbigh Herald

Darkest Before Dawn

KATIE FLYNN

arrow books

Published by Arrow Books in 2005

1 3 5 7 9 10 8 6 4 2

Copyright © Katie Flynn 2005

The right of Katie Flynn to be identified as the author of this work
has been asserted by her in accordance with the Copyright, Designs and
Patents Act, 1988

First published in the United Kingdom in 2005 by William Heinemann

Arrow Books
The Random House Group Limited
20 Vauxhall Bridge Road, London, SW1V 2SA

Random House Australia (Pty) Limited
20 Alfred Street, Milsons Point, Sydney,
New South Wales 2061, Australia

Random House New Zealand Limited
18 Poland Road, Glenfield
Auckland 10, New Zealand

Random House (Pty) Limited
Isle of Houghton, Corner Boundary Road & Carse O'Gowrie,
Houghton, 2198, South Africa

The Random House Group Limited Reg. No. 954009

www.randomhouse.co.uk

A CIP catalogue record for this book
is available from the British Library

Papers used by Random House
are natural, recyclable products made from wood grown in
sustainable forests. The manufacturing processes conform to
the environmental regulations of the country of origin

ISBN 0 09 948697 0

Typeset by Palimpsest Book Production Limited,
Polmont, Stirlingshire
Printed and bound in Great Britain by
Bookmarque Ltd, Croydon, Surrey

For Melvine Holland with many thanks for your help and constant cheerfulness . . . and for having such a wonderful family!

Acknowledgements

First and foremost, grateful thanks to David Holland, who gave me the idea for this book and explained the mysteries of signalling on the railways, and to Brian Holland, who told me all about the Settle to Carlisle line. Also, many thanks to Fred Seiker, whose book *Lest We Forget* is invaluable to anyone investigating the infamous Thai–Burma Railway in WWII.

Chapter One
Autumn 1938

It was a fine day. The pale September sunshine made the streets of Liverpool look almost beautiful, but Seraphina Todd, leaning over the Houghton bridge and gazing into the canal, thought wistfully that not even the sunshine, or the gentle warmth of the day, could reconcile her or her younger sisters to living in this great sprawling city.

They had been here now for three months, inhabiting a dreary flat above the grocery store in which her mother worked. At first, the flat had seemed large to them, used as they were to the narrow confines of a canal barge, but when the family had lived aboard the *Mary Jane* they had spent most of their time out of doors; someone had had to lead old Gemma, a mighty Percheron mare, when it came to crossing bridges or negotiating a path pitted with water-filled puddles, or made treacherous by builders' rubble, illegally dumped on the towpath.

Glancing sideways, Seraphina saw that her sisters were gazing as wistfully down at the canal as she was herself. Evie, the baby of the family at ten years old, looked as though she might burst into tears at any moment. Seraphina felt pity well up within her. Evie was a tough and feisty child, not given to tears; she was not given to regrets for that matter. Seraphina knew her youngest sister hated living in the city and longed for the freedom she had once enjoyed, but she also knew that Evie was unlikely to confess to such feelings.

Usually, she tightened her mouth and made of things; it was only rarely that her feelings allowed to appear.

Seraphina was about to put a comforting arm round her when Evie, sensing that she was being watched, stuck a grimy forefinger up her nose and began to forage about purposefully. Seraphina hated nose-picking and leaned forward to slap Evie's hand down instead, but she was not quick enough. Evie dodged and ran behind Angela, pulling a face at her eldest sister once she was safely out of reach and remarking as she did so: 'Nyah, nyah! Got you goin' then, didn't I, Fee?'

Seraphina smiled reluctantly. 'You're a dirty little beast,' she said reprovingly. 'Why can't you use the handkerchief our ma gave you, like a Christian? If Dad knew the way you behaved . . .'

'Well he don't; and he won't 'cos you're no tale-clat, Fee,' Evie said. She gave a little skip and tugged at Angela's skirt. 'Oh, don't I wish we were aboard the old *Mary Jane*, heading for the Pennines!'

Angela turned her large, dreamy blue eyes on her little sister. 'The truth is, queen, that we all miss the canal horribly, even Ma and Pa,' she said gently. 'But Pa was right, you know; living and working on the canal, we were never in one place long enough for us girls to get work. Fee here is eighteen and I'll be fifteen in a few weeks. And it weren't just work, either. Pa said we never met anyone for long enough to get to know 'em, an' though he liked canal folk well enough, same as we all did, he says the future for bargees ain't what it was, now the railways an' big lorries shift goods so much quicker than we could. Because we're so much slower, the pay's a deal poorer, and though she never complained Ma was findin' it more 'n' more difficult

2

to feed and clothe all of us. But now, with the *Mary Jane* and both the butty boats let out to Jimmy and Hetty Figgins and with Ma and Pa both earning a proper wage, we're laughin'.'

Seraphina gazed at her sister with some awe; Angela was quiet and gentle and this was quite a long speech for her. Even so, her explanation did not seem to satisfy Evie, who made a derisive noise and scrambled up to sit astride the parapet of the bridge, gripping the grimy stones with her knees, as though she were riding a horse. 'Laughin'? I bleedin' well ain't laughin',' she said, pushing a lock of her straight brown hair out of her eyes. 'Why, Fee, you was real fond of that Toby, the one who worked in the bakery and taught you how to snare rabbits when you were a kid. And anyway, we ate well enough, didn't we? An' who cares about clothes?'

'Toby was a friend to the whole family, but, even so, we didn't see much of him once he was in work,' Seraphina said, looking long and hard at the youngest Todd. She had personally supervised Evie's washing and dressing that morning and had thought her neat as a pin when she had left the flat. Yet somehow Evie had managed to get extremely dirty – the palms of her hands were black – and there was a three-cornered tear in her faded blue cotton dress. Seraphina sighed. 'It's pretty plain that you don't care about clothes, even if Angie and myself do,' she said resignedly. 'What a dirty little toad you are, Evie Todd! And if our pa was to hear you swearing and talking so badly . . .'

'If he was to hear me swearing he might change his mind about a proper school being the right place for me, 'cos I learn all me swearing off of the kids there,' Evie said triumphantly. She giggled. 'I heared one of me teachers say t'other day that there were members

3

of her class who cussed worse'n bargees, and it's true, Fee. Some of the kids, particularly the boys, can't say a whole sentence without a bad word in it.'

Seraphina smiled; she couldn't help it. Evie always had an answer for everything, that was the trouble, and Seraphina knew the uselessness of lecturing. As soon as you started to reprimand Evie she would be off, skimming down the street in her dirty old plimsolls and probably taking them off and tying them round her neck with the laces as soon as she was out of sight. So Seraphina just said: 'Never mind what other people do, Evie. You're the daughter of a lay preacher so you ought to be above reproach. Let the others swear if they want to, but think how it would upset Ma and Pa if they heard you cussing. I know we all miss the barge, and the canal folk, but Pa has always wanted a steadier job and to give Ma the sort of life she deserves. So don't you go spoiling it.'

Evie sighed and actually looked almost contrite. 'Well, I won't spoil it then,' she said. 'But oh, Fee, however are we going to stand living all cooped up for the rest of our lives? It's not so bad for you because you'll probably get married soon, but I'm only ten so I've got years and years before I can escape.'

Seraphina sighed. Because of their changed circumstances, she was to enrol on a teacher training course, and though she liked the idea of such a career she did not relish spending all that time still dependent on her parents, with no earnings of her own. Angela had already had two job interviews and thought herself fortunate to have gained a position as a sales assistant in Bunney's department store. The wage was small and the hours long but at least Angie would have money of her own. However, Seraphina had always been the brainy member of the family, soaking up her mother's teaching and going eagerly to any local school when the opportunity arose. She had taken – and passed with flying colours – her School Certificate the previous year and knew in her heart that her parents were right; once she was in teaching, she could command a decent wage and probably get work anywhere in the country, whereas poor Angie would have to struggle, perhaps for years, and have to live in the city for the rest of her life, unless she married a countryman, of course.

Seraphina was about to remind her small sister that she herself would be tied to the city while she worked her way through college, when the chimes of a nearby clock gave her pause. It was eleven o'clock and Ma had sent them out to buy greengroceries, something the shop in which she worked did not stock. What was more, she had bidden them visit the market stalls on Great Homer Street, where fruit and vegetables were a good deal cheaper than in the shops, and here they were, on Burlington Street, wasting time gazing at the canal and wishing themselves far away.

Seraphina had been leaning on the bridge but now she straightened and bent to pick up the new marketing bag which her mother had recently purchased, saying that the old stained sack they had used aboard the *Mary Jane* was not suitable for city life. 'When we mainly bought from the farms we passed a sack was better than a marketing bag because the vegetables came complete with dried-on dirt,' her mother had said.

Evie slid off the parapet as soon as Seraphina stood up, but Angie continued to lean on the wall and gaze dreamily down at the greasy water below, so Seraphina gave her a nudge, quite a hard one. 'Come on, goose; didn't you hear the clock strike eleven?' she asked. 'Ma will be waiting for her messages so that she can start a stew simmering. Can you remember where she said we were to buy the meat? From which butcher, I mean.'

Angela straightened up reluctantly, pushing both fists into the small of her back. 'I don't know as Ma said any particular name,' she remarked. 'Since it's only for a scouse, though, I dare say it'll be the cheaper the better. I'm powerful fond of an ox tail, myself, but if we can't get one of them, I'd go for best end o' neck – that's mutton – or a nice piece of stewing steak – that's beef. Pig's cheek is all right and don't cost much, but it's not really a stewing meat, if you know what I mean.'

Seraphina nodded her understanding. Of the three of them, Angela was the only one who was truly domesticated. She loved cooking and cleaning, and other housewifely tasks, and had kept the tiny cabins of both butty boats neat and sweet-smelling. It was she who had learned from their mother how to skin and joint a rabbit, how to pickle onions and red cabbage and how to make jam from hedgerow fruit. Angela was the one who made all her own clothes and was subsequently better dressed than any of them. She could turn a collar, sides to middle a sheet, and create a decent little frock, or a man's working shirt, from odds and ends of material purchased for a ha'penny from a rag trader, so now Seraphina decided to let her sister do the actual buying when they reached Great Homer Street. Angela might be sweet and easy-going – well, she was – but she would not allow herself to be cheated, and tradesmen soon realised that the gentle girl, with her soft voice and friendly blue eyes, was quite capable of going elsewhere if she thought their prices too high.

Great Homer market, when they reached it, was crowded with traders and customers, and the noise of bargaining, arguing and a good deal of laughter was enough to make Seraphina want to put her hands over her ears. However, the three sisters plunged into the mêlée cheerfully enough, and were soon beginning to make their purchases. They found a butchery stall and bought the coveted ox tail, then moved on to a farmer's wife who was selling her own vegetables quite a bit more cheaply than vendors at other stalls. Consequently, there was a long queue of would-be customers, and Seraphina had been waiting patiently for ten minutes when she discovered that Evie was missing. She nudged Angela. 'Where's Evie?' she asked, peering anxiously into the crowd. 'She was with us at the butcher's stall, and at the apple lady's, because I saw her nick a couple of those bright red apples when she thought no one was looking. That child is turning into a right little gypsy, if you ask me.'

The queue shuffled forward and Angela turned a placid blue gaze on her sister. 'Oh, she'll 'ave met a pal from school, or just got bored and wandered off,' she said. 'But you shouldn't call her names; there's folk who call us – bargees, I mean – water gypsies. Besides, every kid on the canal, and most of the grown-ups as well, would dig up a few turnips or some potatoes from a farmer's field, and think no harm. Why, even our ma picked up windfalls and helped herself to the odd swede or mangold to make Gemma's supper more filling. So why should our Evie think taking a couple of apples is stealing?'

'Angela Todd, I'm surprised at you. What would our pa say if he heard you talking like that?' Seraphina said virtuously. 'Stealing is stealing, which means taking something which isn't yours. Oh, I know what you mean about spuds and turnips and that, because everyone did it – everyone except our pa, that is – but somehow taking stuff off a stall is different. Perhaps

7

it's because someone had picked the apples off their own tree and polished them up with a cloth to make them look all shiny and bright, and carted them in from the country and set them out in a lovely pyramid on the stall . . .'

'All right, all right, I know what you mean,' Angela said hastily. 'And I know you're right, really. The trouble is, if we were still on the canal and our Evie fancied a bite, she'd just nip ashore and pick a mug full of blackberries, or look for wild plums. It's different here, I know, but she is only ten . . . did you pay for the apples, by the way?'

'Yes I did, because the woman saw her take them,' Seraphina admitted. 'And she charged me a penny, which I'm sure was far too much. But since Evie had skipped off – and eaten a good half of the first apple – I didn't have much alternative.'

The queue shuffled forward once more and Angela gave a crow of triumph. 'So she didn't steal them, because you paid for them! Well, that's all right then. Can you see those big carrots, just behind the pile of turnips? I reckon if we buy two bunches of them and two pounds of turnips, and a string of those big brown onions, it will make a grand stew. Oh, and what about potatoes? They're so heavy to carry, but they're really cheap, so if we could manage a stone between us . . .'

Seraphina agreed reluctantly to buy all the things her sister suggested, though her arms ached in anticipation of the weight they would be asked to carry back to the flat. Presently, hefting the marketing bag between them, the two girls turned for home. Seraphina kept a look-out for her small sister, though she had very little hope of spotting her amidst the crowds. What was more, she had a shrewd suspicion that Evie would not appear until they were extremely close to home, for she hated carrying and usually managed to evade a marketing trip. If, as Angela suspected, her sister had met a pal from school, then they would be lucky to set eyes on her again before the next meal; Evie would certainly turn up for that since, despite her small and skinny stature, she was always hungry, eating enough to satisfy your average ploughboy, her father often remarked.

So Seraphina was not surprised when her sister had failed to put in an appearance by the time the two girls dragged their purchases up the narrow stairs from the yard at the back of the grocer's shop and dumped them in the small kitchen, with sighs of relief. 'Ma is going to be pleased with us,' Angela observed, unwrapping the ox tail and putting it into a saucepan. She gestured to the worn black leather purse which Seraphina had placed in the middle of the kitchen table. 'We've brought back quite a lot of change, much more than we would have if we'd simply shopped locally.'

'Ye-es, but we've come back without her ewe lamb,' Seraphina pointed out, tipping vegetables into the sink. '*We* know she's perfectly safe, but Ma will worry, or she would if we told her Evie had skipped off. As it is, by the time Ma comes up for dinner, Evie will probably be back. I don't think she has ever missed a meal except by accident. Are you going to give me a hand with the carrots, queen? They'll need scraping and I've got all the spuds to scrub and the turnips to peel.'

There was no sign of their father, so when the girls had finished preparing the family's evening meal they decided to go out again, to discover what was showing at the Forum. It was just possible that their mother would wish to lavish some money on them that afternoon because they had shopped so successfully, and a visit to the cinema was always a treat.

*　　　*　　　*

9

Martha Todd was serving a customer, carefully selecting the goods required from the shelves and placing them in a large cardboard box, when Mrs Wilmslow called. Martha hesitated, glancing around her. Usually, Mr Wilmslow would have gone through to see what his sick wife wanted, but today he had gone round to the warehouse to pick up some provisions and might not be back for an hour or more. Saturday was always a busy day and the grocery was well situated and popular with local housewives, so Mr Wilmslow employed two Saturday girls. They were sisters, Molly and Annie, but they had gone off to Rhyl for the day and Mr Wilmslow had taken it for granted that Seraphina and Angela would stand in for his missing employees. However, he had failed to warn Martha so she had sent the girls shopping, which placed her in a dilemma. Mrs Wilmslow was unable to do much for herself, and Martha would have liked to go straight through to the back to see what the older woman wanted, but with no one to watch the till, a large order only half made up and the shop full of would-be customers, she simply could not leave her post.

Upstairs, Harry would be pottering round, doing nothing in particular. He had been suffering from a shocking cold earlier in the week and Mr Bister had sent him home on Thursday with orders not to return to work until Monday, and Martha knew he would be down in an instant if he knew how things stood. However, she dared not leave the shop to run up the outside stairs and ask for his help. The woman she was serving, Nellie Proudfoot, was not easy to deal with but she was one of Mr Wilmslow's best customers, spending most if not all of her housekeeping in the shop. If Martha offended her, her employer would not be pleased, and though she had only worked for him for twelve weeks or so she already knew how important his business was to him. What was more, he had let them rent the flat for a very moderate sum provided she worked for him for an even more moderate one, so Martha had no desire to get into Mr Wilmslow's bad books.

Mrs Wilmslow called again and the next customer in the queue leaned across the counter. She was a fat, untidy woman with a bush of grey hair, a round and shining red face and a jutting, whiskery chin. Martha could not recall her name but knew she was another regular customer. 'Eh up, missus, where's old Wilmslow gone then?' she said, drawing down the sides of her mouth. 'Want me to give you an 'and whiles you nip back to see what she wants? I done it before, when the old skinflint found hisself wi'out an assistant . . . afore your time, that were.'

'Oh, Mrs – Mrs . . .' the name came to her in a burst of happy inspiration, 'oh, Mrs Bunwell, thank you ever so much.' She eyed the woman's bulk rather apprehensively. 'Only – only I really could do with some help and Mr Todd would be down in a trice if he knew the fix I'm in. I wonder . . . could you possibly . . .'

'Mrs B. won't never gerrup them steep old steps of yourn,' another customer remarked. 'I'll nip up for you, missus; 'twon't take but a minute.'

'And I'll serve Miz Proudfoot here whiles you go an' see to that poor dear woman,' Mrs Bunwell said, surging round the counter. She beamed at Martha, adding comfortably: 'Don't you fret yourself, queen. Ol' Wilmslow would be the first to say I'm reliable; ain't that so, gels?'

There was a murmur of agreement from the assembled customers and the young girl in the stained apron and raggedy dress, who had offered to go and fetch Harry Todd, turned to grin as she went out through the open doorway. 'It's true as I'm standing here; ol' Wilmslow used to nag poor Mrs B. something dreadful because she were a bit slow like, but he trusted her or she'd never 'ave got be'ind that counter. Shan't be a tick.'

She disappeared and Martha watched for a second as Mrs Bunwell began to take the various goods on Mrs Proudfoot's list off the shelves and place them tenderly in the cardboard box. Then she went through the curtain which separated the shop from the back premises. Once, she knew, the Wilmslows had lived in the flat upstairs and the back rooms had been used for storage. But when Mrs Wilmslow became bedridden, her husband had converted the back premises into quite a respectable dwelling with a kitchen, a stockroom and a sizeable bed-sitting room. Mrs Wilmslow spent her days in the bed-sitting room, in a large double bed, and now, as Martha popped through the curtain, the older woman sighed with relief. 'Thank the Lord you heared me at last,' she whispered. 'I needs the WC.'

Martha knew that Mrs Wilmslow meant she wanted the chamber pot which was kept in the bedside cabinet, for the invalid could no longer manage the journey to the privy in the back yard. Nodding her comprehension, she produced the large, flower-decorated utensil and helped Mrs Wilmslow to move across the bed; she always got out on the far side so that, should anyone come through the curtain at an unfortunate moment, customers would not see her performance.

'I heard someone clacking up them stairs just now,' she said as Martha helped her to climb back between the sheets. 'Mr Wilmslow told me the Sat'day girls were off for the day, idle little sluts, so I suppose it were one of your gels givin' a hand like?'

Martha blinked at the unexpected spite in the older woman's voice. Molly and Annie were good girls, hard-working and honest, never complaining when Mr Wilmslow kept them late, or expected them to cart heavy sacks from the back premises into the shop itself. Now that he lived downstairs, if his wife was having a restless night he slept on a camp bed in the stockroom, no doubt soothed by the scents of cocoa, coffee beans and dried fruit which surrounded him.

However, there had been a query in Mrs Wilmslow's tone, so Martha decided to ignore her unchristian remark and tell her what she wanted to know. 'Actually, Mr Wilmslow didn't tell me that Molly and Annie weren't coming in today, so I sent my daughters off to do some shopping for me,' she informed the other woman. 'But when I heard you call, one of the customers said she'd run up and tell my husband that I needed him downstairs. He's not busy, and—'

Mrs Wilmslow interrupted. 'I hope you've not left the shop unattended,' she said querulously. 'I know I'm a scouser meself, but Mr Wilmslow comes from Chester and he says all scousers is thieves and vagabonds. If one of them women gets her fingers into our till . . . well, that'll be you out on your ear, Martha Todd.'

'I left Mrs Bunwell in charge,' Martha said quietly. 'It was either that or leave you to your own devices, Mrs Wilmslow. I didn't have much choice really, wouldn't you say?'

As she spoke, she was settling Mrs Wilmslow back amongst her pillows, wrestling with a strong desire to tell her employer's wife where she got off. But when she looked at the older woman's thin, pain-racked face, she merely gave her a cheerful smile. It was probably the pain speaking, she told herself, rearranging Mrs Wilmslow's faded pink bedjacket and preparing to carry the chamber pot through to the back yard. 'I'll put the kettle on while Mr Todd is keeping an eye on things; then you can have a nice cup of tea.'

Mrs Wilmslow sniffed. 'I wouldn't mind a cup of tea,' she admitted grudgingly. 'And when them gels of yourn come back, you tell 'em they ain't to go off in future wi'out they asks permission first. Mr Wilmslow told me what rent you pay, so I reckon we've every right . . .'

Martha gritted her teeth and sailed out of the room, feeling the heat rush into her cheeks. That's the trouble with being a redhead, she reminded herself, pushing the back door open and crossing the cobbled yard: your temper sometimes gets the better of you and you don't just blush a pretty pink when you're cross, you go the colour of a beetroot. So I'll rinse out this here jeremiah and splash my face with cold water before I put the kettle on. By the time I return to the shop, no one will guess how cross I felt.

When Martha returned to the Wilmslows' bed-sitting room, she heard her husband's deep tones mingling with those of the customers and smiled with relief. She checked that Mrs Wilmslow was all right, then went back to the shop. Harry was standing behind the counter, alongside Mrs Bunwell, writing down each item she had placed in the cardboard box and checking the shelf stickers for the appropriate price. He turned as Martha entered and grinned at her. He was a tall, spare man, his hay-coloured hair just beginning to turn grey at the temples, and he was still very tanned, his skin leathery and deeply creased from a lifetime on the canal, for Harry's father and grandfather before him had been barge masters and until three months earlier his entire life had been spent aboard the *Mary Jane*. He greeted his wife cheerfully but looked rather helplessly at the customers waiting to be served. 'I'm afraid I'm a bit slow like, because I don't know where the things are kept,' he said apologetically. 'But Mrs Bunwell and meself have teamed up; she fetches the items off the shelves and I write down the prices. It seems to work pretty well.'

'Right. Well, you two get on with the orders and I'll serve customers who don't want stuff delivered,' Martha said briskly. 'Mrs Wilmslow fancied a cup of tea so I've put the kettle on, but until it boils I'll get on here.'

The three of them worked frantically for the next twenty minutes, but as soon as a lull came Martha hurried into the tiny back kitchen, turned the gas off under the kettle – the room was full of steam though she had left the back door ajar – and made a pot of tea. She poured a delicate porcelain cup for her employer's wife and filled three chipped mugs for herself, her husband and Mrs Bunwell before carrying the teacup through into the bed-sitting room and putting it down on the bedside table. Mrs Wilmslow gave her a reptilian glance. 'Where's me biscuits?' she rasped. 'It's eleven o'clock, ain't it? I allus has two Marie biscuits and a squashed fly for me elevenses.'

'Sorry, Mrs Wilmslow,' Martha said with forced cheerfulness. Why couldn't the woman simply ask for the biscuits? She must know very well that it was Mr Wilmslow who normally brought her elevenses. She went into the kitchen and flung open the pantry door. She found the biscuits in a tin and put three on a plate, carrying them back into the bed-sitting room and placing them tenderly alongside the cup of tea. Mrs Wilmslow reached out a trembling hand and took one of the Maries. She held it close to her eyes as though she suspected it might be a fake, then took a very small, very unenthusiastic bite. Crumbs cascaded down the front of her cotton nightdress and she chumbled the small mouthful half-heartedly, then returned the biscuit to the plate and picked up the squashed fly, submitting it to the same inspection as the first. 'They're perishin' well stale,' she muttered. 'I'm a sick woman, I don't have much pleasure out of life an' he saves all the stale biscuits for me elevenses. Why, you could bend them Maries into a hoop if you'd a mind.'

Martha longed to tell the other woman that if the biscuits had been truly soft she would not now have crumbs all down her front, but knew better than to say so. Instead, she turned away, saying over her shoulder: 'I must fly. The shop bell has pinged twice since I came to get your tea; we don't want to lose customers, do we?' She did not wait for a reply but returned to the kitchen, snatched the three mugs of tea and went back into the shop with an inward sigh of relief. What a wretched, miserable woman Mrs Wilmslow was! The local nurse came in three times a week to 'see to her' as she put it and had given Martha to understand that the job was one she did not relish, but this was the first time Martha had been called upon to 'see to' Mrs Wilmslow herself and she understood completely how the nurse must feel.

Back in the shop, which was quiet for a change, the three of them sipped their tea. Martha was just beginning to wonder whether her employer's frequent nastiness could be laid at his wife's door when Mr Wilmslow staggered into the shop, his arms round a large sack which he deposited on the floor with a hefty thump. He was as tall as Harry, but pale as milk, with a fringe of gingery hair round a monastically bald pate, a long spade-shaped chin and a Roman emperor's nose. His eyes were a very pale brown; Martha thought them angry eyes, as though their owner had a grudge against the whole world. He did not greet them, or even look at them properly, merely saying in a high, nasal voice: 'Fetch in them sacks what's piled up on the cart outside and gerra move on. I hired the cart and the driver by the hour, so the sooner it's unloaded the better I'll be pleased.'

Martha half expected Harry to tell Mr Wilmslow that he would do no such thing, was not his employee, but though she saw a slight flush rise in his tanned cheeks he merely gave an almost imperceptible shrug and went briskly out of the shop. Mrs Bunwell gave Martha a gap-toothed grin but stayed where she was. 'I'll mind the till,' she said genially. 'I ain't humping sacks for that old skinflint what won't even give me a word o' thanks for helpin' out this morning, lerralone a couple of loaves of bread or a few pennies for me trouble.'

Martha pulled a wry face; she knew it was true. Mr Wilmslow grudged parting with so much as a penny and would claim that, since he had not personally authorised Mrs Bunwell's assistance, any money – or goods – given to her must come out of Mrs Todd's own pocket. Martha needed every penny she earned, for though Harry's job as a warehouseman was well paid they had had a good few expenses when they moved into the flat. They had had to buy beds, chairs, a couple of tables and even linoleum for the floors, for Mr Wilmslow had taken everything out, even the curtains, and anything he could not use in his new quarters he had sold down at Paddy's market, though his new tenants would have willingly bought such things from him.

Martha reached the cart just as her husband strode past her with a heavy sack over each shoulder. He caught her eye and slowed. 'Get back to the shop, love,' he said quietly. 'I'll not have you straining your back trying to cart these things. It's man's work . . . and besides, there's only half a dozen left.'

Martha knew better than to argue, but as she turned back into the shop she said under her breath: 'You shouldn't be doing it either, Harry. Why, he never even asked you to give a hand and I bet he won't thank you either. Dump those two and then get back to the flat; you're supposed to be off sick.'

Harry did not reply, and Martha returned to the shop in his wake to find Mrs Bunwell about to depart. Mr Wilmslow was shrugging himself into the brown overall which he wore for work and taking up his position behind the counter once more. Mrs Bunwell addressed him, her tone firm. 'I been workin' here for the past half-hour, Mr Wilmslow, givin' Mrs Todd there a hand, 'cos there weren't no one else who could help out. I dare say you won't want to pay me, bein' as you didn't ask me yourself, but I'll take two tins of conny-onny and a small loaf and we'll call it quits, awright?'

Mr Wilmslow opened his mouth to object, then seemed to think better of it. 'One tin of conny-onny,' he said briskly. He turned to Martha. 'And since your gals were supposed to give a hand today, you can pay for the bread.'

'My husband has also been helping out, Mr Wilmslow,' Martha said coldly, choosing a small loaf and wrapping it in tissue paper before handing it to Mrs Bunwell. 'I think you could say his time – and strength – is worth rather more than the price of a small loaf.'

Mrs Bunwell smothered a chuckle as she let herself

out of the door, holding it open for Harry, who was carrying the last sacks into the premises. 'That's right, luvvy,' she said, giving Martha a broad grin and a wink as she spoke. 'An' don't forget, if them gals of yours had helped out, they'd have wanted more'n a word o' thanks. Gals these days . . .'

But at this point a group of housewives entered the shop, and Martha, smiling despite herself, moved forward to serve the first of them whilst her employer, rubbing his long, big-knuckled hands together as though he were trying to remove something sticky and disgusting from his fingers, asked the next customer what he could get her. Business resumed. Harry returned to the flat and Martha continued to serve the remaining shoppers and to sip her cooling tea whenever she had a free moment, though she had heard Mr Wilmslow mutter that it were too bad; he only had to turn his back and not only did his assistant help herself to a hot drink, but she handed cups of tea round to all and sundry. Martha decided to ignore the remark. For the time being at least, she had little choice. She thought she could have got a better paid job almost anywhere but the flat was cheap and convenient and she had no desire to start yet another search for accommodation. So she continued with her work in silence and presently Mr Wilmslow said, irritably, that he supposed they had both better go and get themselves something to eat. 'I'll only have a sandwich though, since we're short-handed, so don't you be long, Mrs Todd,' he said, crossing the shop and twisting the 'Open' sign to read 'Closed'. 'If Molly and Annie were here there'd be no need to close, but I dare say you'll want to feed that husband of yours, and them gals too, if they've deigned to come home by now.'

'That's right,' Martha said shortly. 'See you later,

Mr Wilmslow.' She was not sure whether he expected her to cut short her own dinner hour, too, and did not intend to enquire. Instead, with an inward sigh of thankfulness, she left the shop and headed for the flat.

Harry was at the cooker when he heard his wife come running up the outside stairs. He was more than capable of toasting cheese on four rounds of bread, for anyone living on a canal barge had to be able to do all the various tasks necessary for the smooth running of the vessel, and Harry had frequently cooked the meals whilst his wife went shopping in the nearest village, or foraged in woods and fields for nuts, fruit, mushrooms or berries, whichever was in season.

When Martha entered the kitchen he swung round to greet her, noting her flushed cheeks and the angry sparkle in her eyes. He wondered how long it would be before she lost her temper and told Mr Wilmslow what to do with his job, for though she had frequently called her employer mean and crotchety Harry had not personally had anything to do with the man until today. Having seen Mr Wilmslow in action, if only for a few moments, he realised how selfish and demanding the other man was. Martha was a hard worker, as were all the women on the canal, but she had never worked for someone else before. He thought she would have taken to it well enough had her employer been a pleasanter person, but he doubted her ability to put up for much longer with an ungrateful, greedy old man, who despised his employees and did everything he could to reduce their wage at the end of every week.

Martha, however, greeted him cheerfully and began to set the table, saying as she did so: 'I'm taking an hour off for my dinner whatever that old devil downstairs says.' She reached up and put an affectionate hand on the back of her husband's neck. 'Bless you, Harry. There's nothing I like more than toasted cheese with some pickles. I don't know whether the girls will be in, but if they are they can make their own food.' She walked across to the larder and presently emerged with two large ripe tomatoes. 'I'll fry these up and we can have them on the side. And we'll have a nice piece of apple pie for afters – I baked yesterday.'

Harry nodded. Since moving into the flat, Martha had had to bake in the evening, since Mr Wilmslow kept her busy during the day. Harry was an easy-going man in many respects, but he would not have dreamed of allowing his wife to work on the Sabbath. He was usually preaching at one church or another in the city, but when he was at home he spent the time reading the Bible or writing sermons.

On the canal, things had been different. Sometimes, of course, he managed to moor near the church at which he was to preach, but quite often this was not possible and the family had a long trek between parishes. Harry was no killjoy and in summer, particularly, the walks had been delightful, with the girls playing tag, or skipping, or picking flowers to decorate the boat. Even in winter the walks could be pleasant, for the girls would collect holly and long strands of gleaming ivy which they would wind round the chimney pots of the *Mary Jane* and her butty boats.

It had not been easy for Harry to make the decision to leave the canal and the *Mary Jane*, but he had done so for two overwhelmingly important reasons. The first was simple enough: he meant to retire one day, as many bargees did, to the small village of Burscough where his father, and grandfather before him, had owned a cottage alongside the canal. Normally, such a cottage passed from father to son, but Harry was the third in a family of boys and his elder brother, Edmund, had sold the cottage and taken a job as a merchant seaman sailing from the port of Liverpool, which meant that Harry had no home to which he could retire. He had made a living on the canal, sufficient to keep him and his family fed and clothed, but after twenty-five years his savings were pathetic. So when a friend had told him that Payton and Bister were looking for a truly reliable and trustworthy man to take charge of a huge canalside warehouse, he had been very tempted. The wage was far in excess of the sort of money he was earning on the canal, which would mean his savings could increase with some rapidity, and of course the family would have to move into a permanent home in Liverpool. This would be a good thing because it would help with his second reason for accepting the warehouseman job: both he and Martha wanted something better for their daughters than a life on the canal. Seraphina, with her great sheath of dark gold hair, was not only unusually beautiful, but also extremely clever. Harry knew she took after her mother. He and Martha had met – and indeed married – very young, when Martha had been a pupil teacher at a school in Leeds. She had never completed her training and Harry had often felt guilty because Martha had loved her work and would, he thought, have made an excellent teacher. So when he saw Seraphina taking after her he was determined that, unlike Martha, she would be given a chance to have a proper career in education. Whilst they lived on the canal, however, this would not be possible, so the job offer seemed a heaven-sent opportunity to give his eldest daughter a chance to better herself.

Then there was Angela. She, too, was a very pretty girl, though nowhere near as clever as Seraphina, and her parents were sure she would marry and be happier bringing up a family than having any sort of career. However, she was not physically strong and Harry wanted her to meet young men other than those employed on the canal. He wanted to see Angela in a pleasant home of her own, with a garden to care for and children at her knee who could go to a school round the corner and get a proper education. The schooling of all three of his daughters had suffered from the nomadic nature of the bargees' lifestyle.

He did not worry overmuch about Evie, who was a tough little creature, not beautiful like her sisters but inventive, self-assured and full of energy. Besides, at only ten years old, her character was still unformed and he had no idea whether she would take after himself or his wife; he rather thought neither. Both his elder daughters missed the canal and their lives aboard the *Mary Jane*, though they were beginning to settle down now; Seraphina would start at teacher training college in a few days and Angela was working at Bunney's. Suddenly Harry realised with some surprise that he had no idea how Evie felt about their changed circumstances. Oh, she missed the freedom of life on the canal, grumbled about the boredom of having to be in school every day during term time, but she seemed to have a dozen unruly little friends with whom she had spent most of the summer holidays.

The toasted cheese was done and Harry dished up, then put the plates on the table and reached for the frying pan in which the sliced tomatoes sizzled. Neatly, he covered the toasted cheese with the slices, then stood the pan on the draining board and lifted the hissing kettle off the gas. He spooned tea from the caddy into the brown teapot just as Martha re-entered the room. 'The girls are coming,' she remarked, taking her place at the table. 'Thank you, Harry. This smells delicious.'

The two began to eat as the girls clattered up the stairs and burst through the door. Harry saw that Evie was not with them but did not worry overmuch; Evie was a law unto herself and would magically appear once her food was on the table. He smiled at his second daughter. 'You cut the loaf, love, and slice the cheese; Seraphina can do the cooking for once, since it's so simple.' He turned to his wife. 'Are there any tomatoes left?'

Martha shook her head. 'No, I'm afraid I used the last,' she said apologetically.

Seraphina sighed. 'If we were still on the canal, we'd be able to pick some of our own tomatoes,' she said, rather reproachfully. 'Or if we were near Micklethwaite we could cadge a bagful from Toby Duffy's ma.'

Harry said nothing but he shot a quick glance at his eldest daughter under his lashes. So he had been right. Toby Duffy was a pleasant enough young man, a village lad who had been a friend of Seraphina's when they were young. Harry had thought – hoped – that the two might grow apart, but they did not seem to have done so. He thought Toby a nice enough lad but, if the truth were told, simply not good enough for Seraphina, and he did not want to see her tied to a baker's apprentice without ambition or much thought for the future. Toby was one of a large family and when Seraphina had first brought him aboard the *Mary Jane* had been barefoot, dirty and clad in trousers and shirt which were little more than rags. Now Harry admitted that the strapping young man that Toby had become had clearly attracted Seraphina – but she knew so few young men. Yes, I did the right thing in taking the girls away from the canal – and away from Toby Duffy, Harry decided. After all, Seraphina's only eighteen; she's got years ahead of her before she need consider whom she wants to marry.

'I wonder what Toby's doing now?' Angela said idly. 'Oh, no! Seraphina, the toast is on fire!'

Chapter Two

When the Todd family had decided to desert the canal and live and work ashore, Toby Duffy had thought it would make very little difference to his relationship with Seraphina. After all, he had always had to put himself out to spend time with her and had walked miles so that he could have a few hours in her company whenever the *Mary Jane* was in the vicinity. Mr Todd was both kind and good-natured, and as soon as he realised how much it meant to both Seraphina and Toby he generally tried to moor the boat within reasonable distance of Micklethwaite, the village in which Toby lived. This had not always been possible, so sometimes several weeks had elapsed during which Toby and Seraphina had not met.

When Mr Todd had first mooted the idea of living ashore, however, Toby had taken it for granted that they would move to Leeds. At the time, he had been working there as a baker's apprentice, and it would have meant that he and Seraphina could have seen a lot more of each other. But Liverpool was different. It was a great deal further off and completely foreign territory to Toby. He knew that the Todds were living on a street called Scotland Road, but had no idea where that was. Seraphina had said she would write and she had done so, but Toby was no hand at correspondence and though he had dutifully replied to her long and lively letters, his answers had been dull and short. The trouble was, he had known within days that he would never willingly remain a baker's apprentice. He hated the terrible heat from the huge ovens, the constant bickering of men forced to work in such uncongenial conditions, and the fetid smells of yeast and sweat. He started work in the early hours of the morning and was too tired and dispirited to do anything other than fall into his bed at the day's end, so he could think of nothing interesting to write. Had he and Seraphina been able to meet, though, it would have been a different matter.

But now, at last, he had something really interesting to tell her, for whilst he was with the bakery he had been in digs in Martin Terrace, quite near Wellington station, and had become friendly with a junior porter who was sharing his lodgings. Frank, a real railway enthusiast, had taken him to the station, and Toby had gradually realised that life on the railways was infinitely preferable to life as a baker. He told Frank that he was interested in any work which meant he could be outside, and then, a couple of months back, Frank had said that a junior porter was wanted, by the LMS Railway, at a small and very remote country station. Toby had applied and got the job, had moved there a month previously, and was now beginning to realise that he had fallen on his feet. The work was far harder than he had anticipated and by the time he had paid his landlady he had almost nothing left over, but he thoroughly enjoyed it, and when he had time off the beauties of the countryside, which he had missed horribly whilst he was in Leeds, were there for the taking.

Had he stuck to his job as a baker's apprentice, he would have had a foot upon a ladder which would have led, eventually, to well-paid and regular work. He knew his parents thought he had been a fool to take the porter's job, but they were an easy-going couple – his father was in the Navy, so not often home – and when he had told them of the conditions in which he had worked in the bakery, they took his decision philosophically, though they could not help him financially for Toby was one of half a dozen children and had been given his chance.

When he had lived at home, Toby had not realised how hard his mother worked because she never seemed to hurry. She was, in fact, extremely efficient and she had delegated many jobs to the older children – Toby had set traps for rabbits, stripped the hedgerows of nuts and blackberries and worked in nearby fields for a bag of potatoes or a few large swedes or turnips – but even with such help, she had had a good deal to do. She took in washing, occasionally worked as a scrubbing woman at the big house, and always baked her own bread in the old-fashioned oven set beside the fire. To be sure, the children were frequently dressed in rags, but they were seldom actually hungry and with eight mouths to feed Toby realised, now that he was a man, that this had been no mean feat.

Now, he sent money home, knowing that his elder brother and sister did the same, but took little part in the affairs of the Duffy family. It was a cross-country journey of nearly twenty miles from Wateringford to Micklethwaite, and anyway there was no longer any room for him in the tumbledown cottage where he had been born and brought up.

He was very happy in his new lodgings. His land-lady, Mrs Marks, was a widow and a motherly soul whose own children had long ago left the nest, and consequently she treated Toby like a son. She cooked his favourite meals, did his washing and ironing and even lent him her late husband's old bicycle so that he could go off into the surrounding countryside when he was not on duty.

Right now, Toby was digging in the long flower bed which ran from the station entrance to the end of the platform. Mr Tolliver, the stationmaster, had decreed that some form of floral decoration should front the long bed but that behind the chrysanthemum plants which Toby was now setting winter greens should flourish. Toby loved gardening and looked with satisfaction at the long vegetable plot. There were sprouts at the back, because they were tall and leggy, and then several rows of drumhead cabbages, small and leafy as yet, but they would have firmed up nicely by the time the first frosts arrived. And the chrysanthemums were already in bud so they would make a brave show as autumn drew on. Mr Tolliver had commandeered the small walled plot of his own front garden to grow on plants for his station, so the chrysanthemums had been basking in the September sunshine, protected and cosseted, until Mr Tolliver decided they were strong enough to withstand life on the more exposed station platform.

Toby set the last plant, firmed it down and stood up, regarding his work with satisfaction. The bed looked grand; he was sure Mr Tolliver would approve when next he came on to the platform, and it was nice for the passengers to see the neat, well-tended beds as they got on and off their trains. Toby thought of the big Leeds station he had visited so often, the cigarette ends scattered on the platform, the cast-down papers which the wind twirled into piles, the soot and dead leaves which gathered in every corner. He would not have been anywhere near as happy working in such a place, even though he would have had other young men – and young women too – for company. Here, he was the only junior porter on duty and the long list of instructions which was pinned up daily in the office had at first completely floored him. There was so much to do! He worked from half-past seven to five, or half past ten to eight, and how he worked! His normal, everyday duties were to clean the waiting room, lay and light the fire, clean the ticket office and the stationmaster's small lair, clean and mop down both the ladies' and the gents' toilets, brush the platform, clean all the windows and keep everywhere tidy. Then there were the additional jobs such as posting bills, carting mail bags, getting milk churns on and off the trains and, of course, helping any passenger who needed assistance, running errands for the engine drivers and opening and closing train doors at the appropriate moments. On top of everything else came the deliveries. Anything sent to the station by rail had to be hand-delivered to its ultimate destination, and this could be as far as eight miles away. Toby blessed his kind landlady and her husband's old bicycle, for though he had to push it up many steep hills he could also coast down the other side, and it undoubtedly saved him a good deal of time.

In addition to these tasks, it was a junior porter's job to fill the signal lamps with paraffin and take them to and from the signal box, and thus it was that Toby became friendly with John Giles, the signalman at Wateringford. Sometimes, John and Toby would sit in the cosy box and John would show his new friend how to work the levers. Toby loved his work but thought that it would be just grand to be a signalman and decided that, if the opportunity ever occurred, he would apply for such a job.

Now, Toby bent to pick up the empty trug in which he had carried the last of the chrysanthemum plants and turned back towards the station buildings just as his ears caught a faint and distant whistle. He did not need to glance at the clock above the waiting room to know that he was hearing the approach of the ten–past eleven express, and because he was still interested in the glamour of the mighty engines he stood where he was, pushing his cap to the back of his head with one earth-smeared finger, to watch the train as it thundered through.

As soon as it had gone, its tail disappearing round the bend, he turned and made his way back to the small shed where Mr Tolliver kept the gardening equipment. Toby was not on duty today but had chosen to come in to do the flower bed. His replacement was Joe, who was presently engaged in cleaning out the waiting room. Joe did not care for gardening, though he was quick enough to help a passenger with heavy luggage because this invariably meant a tip and Joe was saving up to buy himself a new bicycle. Though he disliked manual labour, he was by no means lazy since he pedalled everywhere at a good speed. He belonged to a cycling club and during his summer holiday had cycled all the way down to Land's End in Cornwall. That was the main reason for his wanting a new bicycle, for the existing one had barely made it back to Joe's cottage, and though Joe still used it for work you could hear him coming a hundred yards off, squeaking and rattling as he forced the poor old machine to do speeds for which it was never intended. Joe had a lady friend who worked at the nearby hall as a kitchen maid and she had promised Joe a small sum towards his bicycle fund when his birthday came round.

Toby stacked the tools in the small shed, having first cleaned and oiled them thoroughly, for Mr Tolliver was fussy about his gardening implements. Then he strolled over to the stationmaster's office. Thinking about Joe's young lady had reminded him of Seraphina and remembering Seraphina had put him in mind of the fact that he had still not told her about his change of job. She would write to him care of his landlady in Leeds, and though he had asked that lady to forward any letters which might come for him, he was beginning to doubt whether she had done so. Seraphina usually wrote weekly and he had not yet received any correspondence from her. I really have to make the effort and tell her all about my new job and how happy I am to be back in the country, he told himself. Oh, I know Seraphina's only eighteen, same as me, but I've always thought she and I would make a go of it, one of these fine days. I know she's beautiful and I am not, I know she's clever and I am not, I know she's going to have a career in teaching whereas I am just a railwayman and will probably never rise any higher than portering because I don't believe I'm very ambitious either. But Seraphina never seemed to care what I did so long as I was happy. So I can't let us grow apart just because I'm no great hand at letter-writing and the job here simply eats up all my time. Well, it's my day off today so I'll go back to the house, borrow some paper from Mrs Marks, grit my teeth and write Seraphina a really good long letter. It won't just be about my new job either; I'll tell her how dreadfully I miss her, how I long to see her again . . . perhaps I might even tell her I like her better than anyone else I've ever met. One day soon he would visit her because cheap fares were one of a railwayman's perks; he would tell her that too.

But oh, it was such a glorious day! September was almost at an end and in the woods and lanes, copses and hedgerows the leaves were beginning to turn and the berries, shining and scarlet, or richly black, were changing the countryside into a scene of such beauty that even five minutes shut up in the house would be a penance. His free time was rare because he used a good deal of his time off in the station garden and in his landlady's vegetable plot. I could write this evening, he told himself, because today might be my last chance to get right away from the station and enjoy the fine weather. Sometimes October brought gales which sent the glorious multicoloured leaves whirling from the trees to lie in great rustling mounds in every corner and crevice. Then he would be busy at the station, barrowing the leaves away to the far end of the platform where he would pile them into a great heap interspersed with broken branches, old copies of magazines and newspapers left behind in the waiting room, and any other suitable material. He and Mr Tolliver would choose a calm day and then they would light the bonfire; already he could smell the sweet country smell of burning leaves, hear the crackle as the flames caught a dry branch, see the blue hazy smoke rising into the clearer blue of the sky. He could almost hear Mr Tolliver adjuring him: 'Add some more leaves over here, boy . . . give her a poke, she's only smouldering round this side . . . fetch out them old dried pea haulms and chuck 'em on top . . .'

Toby remembered the little lake set deep in the heart of mixed woodland only a short bicycle ride away. He rather thought it was private property because through the trees, if you looked really hard, you could just make out an old house, grey-stoned, slated, but with windows so grimed that he was pretty sure the place must have been abandoned years ago. So far as he had been able to make out, the trees had encroached on the house so that it had reminded him of Sleeping Beauty's palace. And there had been fish in the lake; he had seen them all right, clear as clear through the limpid brown depths. Trout perhaps? The lake had had a stream running into it from the direction of the house and running out of it on the other side to dive under a small road bridge. He had discovered the lake by following the stream and had meant to return with his fishing rod to see if he could bag a trout or two, which his landlady could cook for them. He could go today – why not? The evenings were still quite long; he could write to Seraphina as soon as supper was over. He could describe his fishing trip to the lake; he could make a point of fighting his way through the briars and brambles and discover in what state the house had been left. Yes, he would do that.

Toby headed for the stationmaster's office. It was only polite to tell Mr Tolliver that he was leaving now even though he was not actually on duty. He poked his head round the office door. Mr Tolliver's large booted feet were neatly crossed at the ankle and lodged on the desk, whilst the rest of him, eyes firmly closed and mouth agape, clearly dead to the world, was slumped in his leather chair, which was balanced precariously on two legs.

Wickedly, Toby cleared his throat in the manner of Mr Fellowes, the regional director. In one swift, though horribly uncoordinated gesture, the stationmaster's feet – and those of the chair – descended sharply to the floor and Mr Tolliver surged upright. His tiny gold-rimmed glasses were so crooked that only one eye could see through the lenses and he appeared to be trying to swallow half of his walrus moustache. He was still trying to straighten his tie, button his jacket and prevent the chair from falling backwards when he recognised Toby. 'You young bugger!' he said wrathfully. 'Tryin' to get my job, are you? Thought you'd scare me so bad I'd die of an apoplexy . . . well, not this time, you young devil. Why couldn't you come round the desk and wake me gentle, like?'

'With a kiss?' Toby said innocently. He had just been thinking about Sleeping Beauty so the comment came readily to his lips. Mr Tolliver gave a reluctant grin, unbuttoned his jacket again and sat down in his chair.

'No, *not* with a kiss, you horrible little heathen,' he said reprovingly. 'With a gentle touch on my shoulder or – or a quiet word.'

'I only cleared my throat,' Toby pointed out virtuously. 'I don't see why you've got in such a taking, honest I don't. And I only popped in to tell you I'm off now. It *is* my day off and there's a lake . . . it's such a grand day I thought I might try for a trout or two.'

Mr Tolliver glanced towards the window through which dusty sunshine slanted. 'Aye, when I were your age nothing would have kept me hanging round the station on such a day,' he said, with all his customary generosity. 'Get the missus to put you up a few sandwiches and an apple or two. You're a good lad so I guess I needn't ask if you've planted out all the chrysanths.'

'Thanks, Mr Tolliver,' Toby said gratefully. 'An' I've finished the chrysanthemums; I spaced 'em out so they've gone from one end of the bed to the other. They'll make a grand show when they're all in bloom in a couple o' weeks.'

'Off wi' you then. Good luck wi' the fishin'!'

Harry was making his way to work through the early morning streets. To his own secret surprise, he found he enjoyed his work at the warehouse. To be sure, there had been some initial unpleasantness from one or two members of the staff under him because they resented the fact that their old boss had been sacked. Harry, however, had recognised that the sacking of Herbie Hughes had been unavoidable once the owner had discovered that the man was a crook. Mr Hughes had had a neat scheme going whereby he had somehow managed to sell off large quantities of goods and put the money in his own pocket. If he had behaved a little less greedily he would probably have continued to get away with it, but unfortunately with every successful swindle he had grown more self-confident, more sure that no one would ever question the accounts which he handed in.

It had started long ago when a case of tinned salmon had slipped off the hoist and burst open upon the warehouse floor. Mr Bister, who owned three large warehouses, had taken Hughes's word for it that the tins were too badly damaged to be sold on. Herbie had put them into a skip but had returned that night with a handcart, on to which he had loaded not only the tins which had fallen from the burst-open crate, but also a sack of sugar and another of hazelnut kernels. He planned to say that both sacks had been damaged – torn open – when the crate had burst, and had wheeled his trophies off, probably in a state of some agitation, since this had been his first attempt to cheat his employer.

Mr Bister had suspected nothing. A good deal of stock went missing between the ships and the warehouse because the men working on the docks were, in Mr Bister's opinion, a fair set of rogues. So when his head warehouseman had filled in his receipt sheet with nine sacks of hazelnuts instead of ten, and nineteen sacks of sugar instead of twenty, he had assumed that the sacks had never even appeared at the warehouse.

He had signed the sheets and asked no questions so, as he told Harry, in a way he had almost encouraged theft.

This had gone on for some time, but eventually, of course, Herbie Hughes had gone too far. It was partly because he had begun to sell some of his ill-gotten goods to respectable shopkeepers who began to talk amongst themselves, but also because one of the other employees at the warehouse had realised what was going on. He was a young lad and had begun to fear that, as the last person to be employed, he might be blamed, for even he had seen that the thefts were becoming more and more blatant. Herbie was taking anything he fancied, anything he felt he could sell for a profit. He had even handed stolen goods to some of the workers under him, assuring them that they were his perks for work well done and thus ensuring, he had believed, that none of them would split on him.

However, he had reckoned without the new young lad, and also he had reckoned without his employer's diligence. Mr Bister, who made a point of checking through each month's work, had been struck by the rising number of missing crates, sacks and boxes of goods. He had decided to keep an eye on the warehouse for a couple of nights, for though he employed a night watchman the man was old and was chiefly concerned with preventing break-ins. If the head warehouseman let himself in with his keys and helped himself quietly to goods which he had placed as near the staff entrance as possible, the night watchman would be unlikely to realise that he was no longer alone on the premises, or that a theft was taking place.

Mr Bister had watched for two nights and had been mortified – and furious – to realise that he was actually employing a thief. On the third night, the police had watched with him and Herbie Hughes had been caught red-handed. Mr Bister had sacked him and had then questioned the rest of the staff, most of whom had avowed total ignorance of what had been going on. Only the new young lad had spoken up.

Mr Bister had told Harry the story but he had not prosecuted his head warehouseman because he saw no point in doing so. He knew that without a reference Herbie Hughes would not get another decent job, and thought that was punishment enough. Harry, however, was rather uneasy about some of the men now working under him. He kept a close watch on all of them and knew they were not stealing at present, but he also knew they resented the checks he kept upon everything entering and leaving the warehouse and wondered, uneasily, how long it would be before one of them decided to chance his arm.

However, the recent fate of Herbie Hughes was still very much in the forefront of their minds and Harry hoped that the fact that he checked and double-checked would discourage malpractice. Mr Bister certainly believed it would do so, for, as he had said, only the head warehouseman held keys to the premises. He had explained to Harry that every warehouse suffered from petty pilfering and that this was not what worried him. 'You can't blame the fellers for taking the odd jar of jam or pickles,' he had said. 'It's when it gets to being a crate of jam or pickles that I have to put my foot down.'

Harry had quite seen the justice of this; though he had never done so himself, he knew that most of those who dwelt on the canal, and their families, thought it no particular sin to take a bag of potatoes, a couple of swedes or a good, big armful of hay from a farmer's field. The men snared rabbits for the pot or shot a couple of fat wood pigeons, and if a farmer's hen laid astray, they would collect the eggs as their children collected blackberries or hazelnuts. The warehousemen under him were the same. For the most part, though, they were careful to take only damaged goods. Harry knew that in a good many cases they damaged the goods themselves, coming to him to show a cracked jar or a dented tin before quietly pocketing it, and he supposed there was no harm in it.

At this point in his musing, Harry reached the warehouse and banged cheerfully on the door, which was the signal for the night watchman to start packing up. Then Harry produced his keys and let himself in. Immediately, the many and varied smells of the warehouse invaded his nostrils. He sniffed appreciatively; coffee beans, cocoa, the country smell of grain, the soft sweetness of sugar – they all blended into a smell which he was beginning to enjoy because there was no doubt that he really liked the work and knew himself to be very good at it. The most important thing a head warehouseman has to do is to see that every inch of available space is put to good use whilst making sure that those items which are needed on a regular basis are stacked where they can be easily reached.

Mr Bister knew a thing or two about barges since he owned a fleet of them. He knew how important it was to load the goods they carried correctly and had guessed that Harry, used to the far smaller space available aboard the *Mary Jane* and her butty boats, would find the stocking of a warehouse both familiar and yet a challenge. He had been right; after only a few weeks in the job, Harry had worked out the best place for everything. He could look at a gap and gauge with considerable accuracy how many crates, boxes or sacks he could wedge into it, and he moved his stock around with complete confidence, knowing that as fast as he moved goods out from the floor on to the delivery vans, more would be coming up from the docks. Harry was neat by nature and he enjoyed the challenge the warehouse represented, though he had made mistakes; everyone did. Once, he had stacked a large quantity of tinned goods against the back wall of the warehouse, only realising after it was walled in by other commodities that the stuff was needed urgently by a wholesaler on the other side of the city. There had been a good deal of swearing and a good deal of laughter as the men worked frantically to get at the tins, but it had taught Harry a lesson. Since then, he always kept his paperwork handy and consulted it before choosing where to place each consignment.

'Mornin', Mr Todd, sir.' Mr Fuller, the night watchman, hefted the old canvas bag which contained his sandwich box and his flask – both now empty – over his shoulder, and shambled across the warehouse, a good-natured grin splitting his craggy, unshaven face. At night time, he had the run of the place and brewed himself many a cup of tea in the little kitchen behind Harry's office. But his wife made his sandwiches and filled his flask as though he were still employed down on the docks where there had been no facilities for making cups of tea. And no nice comfortable chair in which an old man might snooze peacefully when the night was quiet. He had a fat black mongrel bitch, far too rheumaticky to chase a rat, let alone catch one, but she would give tongue immediately if a stranger entered the warehouse, or she heard someone acting suspiciously outside the building.

Herbie Hughes had disliked dogs – or said he did – so Mr Fuller had not brought Bessie with him whilst Herbie had been head warehouseman. No doubt, had

Bessie been around, she would have warned the old man when Herbie entered the building, so both Mr Bister and Harry had gladly agreed to the old man's bringing his companion with him, and now Bessie grinned up at Harry, and butted his knee with her head.

'Good morning, Bess, old lady. Morning, Mr Fuller; anything to report?' Harry said, bending to fondle the dog's silky ears.

'No sir, us had a quiet night, though Thomas caused a bit of a stir by catching a rat,' Mr Fuller said, with a chuckle. 'That young cat is going to be worth his weight in gold; I'm thinking Mr Bister ought to pay him a regular wage 'cos that's the third rat he's caught this week.'

'Jolly good,' Harry said, trying to infuse his voice with enthusiasm. Rats did not only infest warehouses. They were quite capable of getting aboard canal boats as well, and, as a young lad, Harry had met one face to face when fastening a canvas cover to the combing. Unwisely, he had crawled forward, expecting the rat to flee, but instead it had jumped at him and bitten his chin. He had the scar still and felt a revulsion for rats which he could not quite conquer, though he was continually impressing upon others that rats were still God's creatures and should be dealt with as quickly and as painlessly as possible. Now, he looked around him, a trifle uneasily. 'What have you done with the body? It's not in the office, is it?'

Mr Fuller chuckled again. 'I purrit just inside the main doors. Thomas broke its neck, just like a terrier does, so it's crouching there, lookin' real lifelike. I hopes as it'll give Baldwin a turn, since he's the one as told the boss I must be in league with old Herbie.'

'But Mr Bister knew that wasn't true,' Harry

protested. 'I suppose I ought to move the corpse . . . but I don't think I shall. Heaven knows, the lads have played enough pranks on me.'

The night watchman cocked a knowing eye. 'Pranks? Oh aye, I s'pose you could call 'em pranks. But you wants to watch that Baldwin; if anyone was in league with Herbie, it were him. Oh, don't worry, I reckon he's learned his lesson, but he's a spiteful sod and I reckon he's missin' the little extras he got because he were Herbie's mate, like. Still an' all, he's in work which is more than you can say for a lot of poor devils.'

'True,' Harry said. 'Is the kettle over the flame, Mr Fuller? I'm that parched I could drink the canal dry. Want to join me in a mug o' tea?'

'I wouldn't mind,' the old man said, turning back towards the kitchen. 'I put the kettle on 'cos I know how you are – allus thirsty.' He grinned up at Harry, his watery eyes twinkling. 'That remark tells me you're a bargee, Mr Todd. A scouser would say *I could drink the Mersey dry*, not the bleedin' canal.'

Harry returned the man's grin as they entered the small kitchen where the kettle was beginning to hiss on the Primus stove. 'It doesn't matter what I say; one glance at my leathery face would tell you I'd spent my life on the canals,' Harry said, rather ruefully. 'You know I'm a lay preacher? Well, I were preaching away last Sunday, up in Everton, when I heard a little boy in the congregation ask his mother whether I were an African or an Indian. She, poor soul, was rare embarrassed and gave him a cuff, but not an answer, so I leaned down from the pulpit and told him I were a water gypsy, which had the poor little feller in a rare puzzle, I can tell you.' The kettle came to the boil and Harry spooned tea from the caddy into the small brown teapot and poured a judicious amount of conny-onny into two tin mugs, then left the tea to brew. 'Children say straight out what everyone else is thinking, but I dare say he'd never heard the term "water gypsy" before. But he knows it now, for I'm sure his mother enlightened him once we'd gone our separate ways.'

'Mebbe so,' the old man acknowledged. 'It's strange how some folk feel about them as lives and works on the canal. Why, you're no more like a gypsy that I am meself, Mr Todd. Save that your complexion is – is kinda tanned. But in the old days, when there was sailing ships, the seamen were as brown as yourself an' no one called them gypsies.'

Harold picked up the teapot. 'Tea's brewed,' he said. 'There's nothing wrong with gypsies and we do have one thing in common: we can't put down roots, can't have a regular place to call our own. Oh, don't get me wrong, I loved the life, but I wanted something better for my daughters. My eldest is going to be a teacher and there wouldn't be any college education for her whilst we lived on the barge.'

'Do you miss it? Life on the canal, I mean?' the old man asked curiously, sipping the hot tea. 'It must have been an adventurous sort of existence; every day different, never waking up to the same view through your window.'

Harry gave this some thought, then finally shook his head. 'I've had forty-four years of wandering,' he said slowly. 'I loved it but I didn't know anything else. Now, I'm enjoying this job and appreciating things you'll take for granted. There's cinemas, cafés, big shops, all sorts. And when you're on the canal it's all work and very little play, especially if like myself you aren't a drinking man. Some of 'em spend every evening in a pub but I never could see the point of it. Anyway, one of these days, when I've saved up enough money, I'll buy me a neat little canalside cottage in Burscough, where all the barge masters go to retire. I'll be able to relax there and so will Mrs Todd, and we'll do so with a clear conscience because we'll have given our girls a good start in life.'

Mr Fuller drained his mug, then stood it down on the table. 'I've a gal of me own and a couple o' sons, all married and away from here,' he observed. 'But as for retiring, I can't see that happening, somehow. Mrs Fuller is a dab hand with her old sewing machine; she makes curtains and cushions for one of the big stores and of course I've got me job here, which I enjoys well enough. I don't deny we could scrape by on my little pension but the money I earn here – and what Mrs Fuller makes from the stores – means we're real comfortable.' He sighed deeply and began to button up his shabby overcoat. Straightening his checked cap, he turned to leave the room, saying as he went through the door: 'I allus feel as I should bid you good night, Mr Todd, when I comes off me shift. Eh, but it's an upside down life when you're awake all night and asleep half the day. See you at six.'

Harry accompanied the old man to the staff door, which he left open for the men who would be arriving in another thirty minutes or so to start the day's work. Then he crossed to the huge main doors through which goods would begin coming presently, and glanced down at the dead rat. He gave a slight shiver although, all too plainly, the creature was dead. He told himself he ought to move it, take it out to the dustbins, but then decided against it. Baldwin shared his dislike of rats and he was an awkward employee, slow to obey, quick to grumble, and surly. Harry knew the other man was responsible for many of the small irritants which had plagued him since he had first taken on the job,

44

so if the rat startled Baldwin it might not be a bad thing.

Whistling beneath his breath, Harry returned to his office and got out the paperwork he would need once the day started. Soon he was absorbed, planning where he would put incoming goods when the day's consignments began to arrive.

Evie burst into the kitchen, her fringe on end, one half of her hair still in its bedtime plait and the other half hanging limp and straggly around her face. She was dressed in her school skirt and blouse but the blouse was buttoned in the wrong holes, and Evie looked pleadingly across to where her mother was cooking porridge. 'Mam, Mam, do gimme a hand! This perishin' blouse must have a button missing or something 'cos it won't do up straight no matter how I try. I axed Fee to do it for me but she were too busy brushin' out her old hair, and Angie said I were quite old enough to dress meself, so she wouldn't help either. Oh, Mam, I know it ain't time for school yet, but I want to be early because me an' Annie Butcher means to gerrin a game of hopscotch before the bell goes.'

Martha swung round from the stove and shook a reproving finger at her daughter. 'Why oh why d'you have to pick up the local accent when your pa and myself have always been at pains to teach you to speak properly? Your sisters don't say "ain't" when they mean "isn't" or "gerrin" when they mean "get in", so why must you? And as for "axed", well, if your father heard you . . .'

Evie stuck out her lower lip. 'I have to talk like the others, Mam, or I wouldn't have no pals. Kids don't like it if you're different. It's all right for Fee and Angie;

45

they're *old*, but I'm only ten an' if they think I'm tryin' to talk posh, the other kids will hate me.'

Martha sighed. 'That's true, my love, but it applied to your sisters when they were in school just as much as it does to you now. Your pa always used to say that children have two languages, one for home and one for the streets, though in our case, of course, it was more like one for the boat and another for the bank.' She chuckled. 'So try and speak nicely, Evie, when you're at home with us.' She pulled her daughter towards her and began patiently unbuttoning the little girl's cotton blouse, then buttoning it up correctly. 'More haste, less speed,' she admonished. 'Where's your hairbrush? And don't forget: talk nicely in the house, if you please.'

'I won't forget, Ma,' Evie said resignedly, knowing that her mother spoke no more than the truth. She adored her pa, thinking him the best man in the whole world, and it would distress him if she talked with the local accent or swore, even though swearing was supposed to be the prerogative of canal folk.

Presently, neat once more and with her hair in two pigtails, Evie sat at the table and demolished a plateful of porridge. Then she jumped to her feet, seized her jacket from the hook on the kitchen door, and grabbed a round of buttered bread from the plate in the middle of the table. 'Where's me carry-out, Mam – Ma, I mean?' she said, through a mouthful of bread and butter. 'If it ain't – isn't, I mean – ready, I'll have to go without it 'cos I promised Annie . . .'

Martha chuckled and handed Evie a small packet wrapped in greaseproof paper. 'There's two jam sandwiches and a piece of fruitcake,' she told her daughter. 'But you could always come home, you know. Your school isn't far off.'

'I know, only most people take their dinner with

46

them,' Evie explained. 'Can't stop, gorra run.' She shot out of the back door and thundered down the rickety iron staircase, then turned to hurry along the pavement towards the court, where Annie lived. As she had expected, her friend was already waiting for her, accompanied by her older brother, Gareth, and his friend Percy Baldwin. Gareth and Percy had acquired a bundle of rags tied together with string, which they were kicking from one to the other, and took no notice of Evie, so she and Annie fell into step as they made their way along the pavement. Presently, the two small girls were joined by others and they turned into the schoolyard, making their way towards the hopscotch squares and discussing who would have first go.

The game proved to be an exciting one and when the bell went there was a concerted moan from the players. Evie, however, did not repine. She was quick and neat at all games and usually won, and anyway the match would continue in their dinner break. She linked arms with Annie and the two strolled across the playground to where the children were lining up into classes. Evie and Annie took their places, Evie reflecting how strange it seemed to have all girls in her class, for in the small village schools in which she had formerly been a pupil there had been too few children to segregate the sexes, so boys and girls had been taught together. Indeed, many of those schools had had only two classrooms, one occupied by the five- to nine-year-olds and the other by the ten to four-teens.

The bell rang again and the children began to file into their classrooms. Annie and Evie sat at a double desk at the back, alongside another desk at which sat Millie and Sandra. The four girls often played together and now Millie leaned over as the teacher began to take the register and whispered into Evie's ear. 'I heared something about your dad the other day . . . well, I heared something if he's the feller what Bister had took on at Payton and Bister's biggest warehouse.'

'Oh?' Evie said, only vaguely interested. Her father spoke very little about his work but she had taken his carry-out down to the warehouse one morning and had envied him working amongst all the lovely smells, especially when he had explained how he had to plot to fill every inch of available space. Evie liked doing jigsaws and her father had made her several quite difficult ones. Evie, looking at the warehouse, had remarked that it was like a gigantic jigsaw and she thought her father had a most exciting job which must be fun as well. Now, however, she remembered belatedly that Millie had asked her a question. 'Sorry, what did you say?'

'I asked if your dad were the head warehouseman at Payton and Bister,' Millie said patiently. 'If he is, two of the fellers were talking about him. I heared them, so I did.'

'Oh,' Evie said again. 'Yes, me dad does work for Payton and Bister. What did you hear, then?'

'Well, the lads were saying that their dads were going to play a trick on him, like. I dunno why, but some of 'em miss the feller what were there before your dad took over.'

'What sort of trick?' Evie enquired, immediately alert. She knew that the men had played at least one trick on her father already because it had made him laugh when he had told the story to his family.

They had filled a sandwich with Lux soap flakes, as well as cheese, and offered it to him, hoping to see him foaming at the mouth. 'Beware of the Greeks when they coming bearing gifts,' her father had remarked, sagely, and had then explained the quotation to his

48

small daughter. He had guessed, of course, that the sandwich had been doctored and had pretended to accept it, turning his back on the giver for a moment whilst rooting in his own sandwich box. 'I'm very fond of a cheese sarnie,' he had said jovially, 'but you must have one of mine in exchange. No, no, I insist.' He had handed the cheese and soap flake sandwich back to the man and had stood over him, saying gently: 'Now don't rush off until you've told me whether you like the little addition, because Mrs Todd always puts just a tad of mustard into my butties. C'mon, man, what do you think?' Evie had enjoyed the joke hugely when her father told her how the trickster had been forced to munch down a large mouthful of cheese and soap flakes and how it had been he, and not her pa, who had foamed at the mouth. Indeed, the man, Jacob Tilling, had enjoyed the joke too, if not the sandwich, and had become her father's champion, saying that someone who not only took a trick in good part but could turn it against the trickster was the sort of feller he most admired.

So now, Evie waited eagerly for the answer. If it was the kind of prank which would amuse her father she would say nothing, because it would be a sort of cheating, but if it was an unkind or spiteful trick she would tell her father.

Millie, however, was unable to help her on this score. 'I dunno. You'd have to ask Gareth Butcher or Percy Baldwin,' she explained. 'They didn't seem to know theirselves *what* was up, just that something was.'

Evie was opening her mouth to reply when the teacher's voice was raised. 'Get out your arithmetic books please, girls. Mabel, you are blackboard monitor this week, I believe. Kindly clean the board for me and then I want someone with really neat handwriting to chalk today's date along the top of the board.' A forest of hands immediately shot up into the air and the teacher smiled. 'Ah, but which of you knows today's date?' Half a dozen of the hands lowered themselves into their owners' laps, but the rest continued to wave vigorously. 'Very well . . . Sandra Higgins, come up to the front, please.'

That night, as the family sat round the table playing a game of cards before going to bed, Evie mentioned what Millie had told her. She saw that her mother looked a little anxious and Angie rather annoyed, but Seraphina merely smiled and their father did likewise.

'They'll settle down and decide they're being foolish,' he said tolerantly. 'They've tried any number of tricks – or they did at first – but most of them seem to be toeing the line now. In fact, the only one who isn't is Reg Baldwin. He's a difficult nut to crack but he must know I'm getting near the end of my tether so far as his behaviour is concerned. He is a lazy b— blighter, too fond of tucking himself away behind a couple of tea chests while everyone else is working. I suspect he has a crafty fag, so, since smoking is strictly forbidden, the first time I catch him having a puff he'll be out on his ear. I've warned him twice, but there won't be a third time.'

Martha had been staring down at the cards in her hand but at her husband's words she glanced up, a crease appearing between her brows. 'You mean you caught him smoking in a warehouse and didn't sack him on the spot?' she asked incredulously. 'Harry, my love, I know how generous you are . . . but was that wise?'

Harry chuckled. 'No, no, you misunderstand me,' he assured her. 'I've never caught him doing anything apart from skiving, but the last time I did so I thought I could smell tobacco – burning tobacco, I mean. Luckily, though, I can move about quiet as a mouse when I want to, and next time Mr Baldwin goes missing he's going to find an unexpected – and unwanted – companion joining him in his latest hidey-hole. Most of the men are of my mind, because the less work Baldwin does the more they get landed with, so I dare say someone will tip me the wink if I'm too busy to notice that Baldwin's gone sneaking off again.'

'Oh, I see,' his wife said. But when the card party broke up and she was supervising Evie's preparations for bed, she surprised her daughter by questioning her closely as to who had been talking about her father.

'It were Percy Baldwin and Gareth Butcher,' Evie said. 'Oh, Mam, I do believe that Percy's dad works at Payton and Bister. Of course, that must be how he knows what's going on; Percy must be Reg Baldwin's son.'

Her mother's eyebrows rose and the crease re-appeared between them, then the frown disappeared and she patted Evie's nightgowned behind. 'Hop into bed, love,' she commanded. 'I don't suppose there's any harm in the tricks the fellers in the warehouse play on your dad, but I don't like the sound of Mr Baldwin. What's his son like?'

Evie sat up and considered the question thought-fully. 'I think I feel rather sorry for him,' she said slowly. 'I've seen him with a bruised face and skinned knees, and he isn't very bright so he's often in trouble at school; that's what Annie's brother says, at any rate, an' he should know since they live in the same court and usually walk to and from school together.'

'Poor lad,' her mother murmured. She moved around the girls' room, tidying automatically. 'Well, if you hear anything more, my love, I think you'd best tell either myself or your father, because from the sound of it Mr Baldwin is a violent man and I don't want to see your father hurt.'

Evie agreed fervently that she did not want to see her father hurt either and would do her best to discover what was afoot. Then her mother left the room and Evie cuddled down in bed, heaving the blankets up over her shoulders, for it would soon be October, and the nights were already growing cool. She decided that she would ingratiate herself with poor Percy Baldwin. He was always hungry, so she would beg an extra sandwich in her carry-out and offer it to him. If she did this two or three days running, she thought it would then be safe to enquire, in a jokey manner, just what his father was planning to do at the warehouse. If she played her cards right, pretending to look up to him, letting him win if they played any sort of game on their way to and from school, then she saw no reason why he should not confide in her.

Satisfied that her plan would work, Evie let her thoughts begin to drift and was soon fast asleep.

Chapter Three

Evie began to make a pal of Percy Baldwin the very next day. When the children met outside the court in which the Butchers lived, Percy was sporting a black eye, purple in the middle and rainbow-hued round the edge. It was natural, therefore, for Evie to enquire how he had got such a shiner. Percy might have replied that he had walked into a door or simply passed the question off with a flippant answer, but instead he said bitterly: 'Me bleedin' dad did it, that's what. He got hold of me mam by the hair and he were thumpin' an' kickin' her, so I went for him, and so did me brother, Ron, though he's only six. He chucked Ron right across the kitchen an' he punched me straight in the eye. Me dad's strong an' me mum ain't.'

'That's awful,' Evie said, genuinely shocked. She knew that violence occurred in most walks of life, but punching a boy of twelve and beating a defenceless woman was outside her experience. 'Was he drunk?' she asked timidly. 'Me dad's always going on about the evils of drink and I remember him saying that Stobo – he's a barge master – were meek as a lamb until the drink were in him and then his cabin were like a Punch and Judy show wi' Stobo beltin' his old woman an' Mrs Stobo beltin' 'im back. So I suppose it were the drink with your dad, eh?'

Percy nodded unhappily, falling into step beside her whilst Gareth and Annie, and a couple of others, went on ahead. 'Yes, I reckon the drink always makes him worse,' he admitted. 'But he's a bad-tempered old bugger, mean as they come, even when there's no drink in him.'

At this point, Evie pulled the greaseproof packet of sandwiches out of her satchel, peeled off the top two and held one out to Percy. She had planned to do this, but in fact it was a spontaneous gesture she would have made anyway, so sorry for Percy did she feel. It occurred to her for the first time that, despite the fact that he was two years older than she, they were the same height and build and she guessed that his father probably drank the money which should have been spent on food for his family. Percy stared at the sandwich, his eyes glistening. 'I reckon you didn't have time for no breakfast this morning,' Evie said. Then, as Percy still hesitated, 'Go on, take it. Me mam knows I gets peckish on me way to school so she usually puts in one or two extra.'

'Well, thanks very much,' Percy said. He took the sandwich and demolished it in three extremely large bites. Evie, who was about to attack the other sandwich, hesitated. She had had a large plateful of porridge and two rounds of toast at breakfast and was not really at all hungry. She waited until Percy had swallowed the last crumb, then pushed the second sandwich into his hand. She remembered how her mother had said that one must always give as though there were no merit in the giving, because the person to whom you gave might feel embarrassed by their need. But it ain't as though we're grown-ups, Evie told herself. Kids aren't ashamed of being hungry, they're just hungry. 'I had porridge for me brekker this morning,' she said rather gruffly. 'Where's Ron? Why ain't he coming to school wi' us?'

Percy finished the second sandwich more slowly and

answered her question through a rather full mouth. 'Ron? Oh, he's still at the hospital. I told you me dad chucked him across the room . . . well, he bashed his head on the edge of the door and Mam called Mr Briggs next door round and he punched me dad and knocked him out, and then Mam took Ron to the hospital. When she come back, she said Ron were okay but very shook up, so the hospital would be keepin' him in for a day or two.'

'What did the doctors and nurses say when your mam told them your dad had thrown him across the room?' Evie asked curiously as they approached the school gates. 'I bet they were furious, weren't they?'

Percy gave her a tolerant glance. 'Wharrever makes you think me mam 'ud be such a fool as to tell 'em the truth?' he asked derisively. 'Cor, there'd be endless trouble if she did any such thing. We don't want the scuffers round our house, nor we don't want to see Ron and little Emmy – she's only two – taken into one of them children's homes. The scuffers can do that, you know, if they think a feller might kill a kid when he's too drunk to know what he's doin'.'

Evie knew that such things did happen. Indeed, she had heard threats made by canal parents when their kids were being particularly difficult. 'I'll buy a red beret and send you off to that Strawberry Fields,' Evie had heard a fat barge woman scream. 'You won't find the teachers there turnin' a blind eye if you sag off school or don't help get the messages in.'

Evie had not known what she meant but Seraphina had enlightened her. 'The Salvation Army have a children's home in Liverpool called Strawberry Field, and the children have a uniform of red blazers and berets,' she had told Evie. 'It's a wonderful place, a big old house with beautiful gardens, an orchard, swings and slides . . . oh, all sorts. But canal kids have something even more precious than wonderful grounds and swings and slides. They have freedom, Evie, and that's worth more than silver or gold.'

So now Evie nodded her understanding at Percy's words. 'So what did your mam say?' she asked curiously. She knew that neither of her own parents would ever tell a deliberate lie but she also knew that other people were different. Besides, if telling a lie might keep your family out of trouble, then she supposed that even her own mother might stretch the truth a little.

'Oh, she said Ron fell downstairs,' Percy said airily. 'It's what she allus says. If she told the truth, me dad 'ud murder her, which wouldn't be much help,' he ended. 'Thanks for the butties, Evie; you're a good kid.'

By now they had reached the school gate and Percy was raising a grimy hand in farewell and turning into the boys' playground. 'Hey, hang on a mo,' Evie said urgently. 'I just want to ask you . . .'

But it was no use. A large and corpulent teacher with a huge nose and a stained waistcoat had appeared at the entrance to the boys' school. He was ringing a big hand bell and shouting to the boys above the noise he was making to get into line. Evie stood and watched for a moment as the boys scuffled and shouted, and then she made for her own gates, by no means dissatisfied with her morning's work. She was now on excellent terms with Percy Baldwin and knew that he hated his father and would not be unwilling to tell her anything she cared to ask, particularly if she continued to provide him with the food he lacked. She decided she would suggest that he might like to come back to the flat one day soon for some tea and a game of snakes and ladders, or ludo. Her mother never objected to feeding her pals, and when she saw Percy's skinny, half-starved frame would do so even more willingly.

'C'mon, Evie Todd, where's you been? I were walkin' wi' Ruthie, talking about Christmas, 'cos our class is goin' to do the Nativity play this year. Ruthie wants to be Mary, but I reckon I'd rather be a shepherd, 'cos you get to hold one o' them white woolly lambs what the teachers make. They're ever so sweet and cuddly; I wish my mam could make things like that, so I do.'

'She's gorr'erself a sweetheart,' Ruthie said mockingly. She was a fat and freckled girl with red hair and a round, good-natured face. 'She were chatterin' away to 'im . . . oh aye, they's sweet on each other, I could tell.'

'He ain't my sweetheart, he's just a boy,' Evie said dismissively. 'But I felt real sorry for him; his dad punched him in the face and he's got one helluva shiner. What's more, his little brother's in hospital, 'cos he . . .' she remembered, belatedly, the story that Mrs Baldwin had had to tell the authorities, ''cos he fell down the stairs,' she finished weakly.

Annie and Ruthie grinned. 'That's what all the mams say when someone gets belted, 'cos if a feller gets took in by the scuffers he might lose his job and then there'd be no money comin' in,' Ruthie said sagely. Evie knew that Ruthie and her brother Si were the only children of the elderly couple who kept the corner shop two hundred yards further down Scotland Road. Her parents were pleasant, friendly people and Evie was sure they had neither of them ever raised a hand to their children, but she guessed they would talk in front of Ruthie, perhaps not realising how much she took in.

'Well, anyway, Percy ain't no sweetheart of mine,' she said firmly. 'But he's nice and it ain't his fault his dad's a mean old sod.'

'That's true,' Annie said wisely. 'He's awright is Percy, otherwise me brother Gareth wouldn't be his pal. They play footie together and Gareth says Percy's the best player in the court. He says he'll play for the Reds one of these days.'

At this point, the bell interrupted them and the girls hurried to form lines, and presently took their places in class. As Evie settled into her seat, she glanced across at Millie, wondering whether to ask if the other girl had any more information about the doings at the warehouse, then decided against it. Anything Millie told her would be second if not third hand. Now that she was on good terms with Percy, she felt she had access to first-hand knowledge.

The teacher opened the register and began to call the names and Evie settled back in her seat. Before too long, she would know as much as Percy did as far as pranks were concerned.

That evening, the warehousemen met for a drink at the Bridge Inn at the end of Chisenhale Street before making their way home. It was not pay day and the pub would not give them tick, so they sat chatting companionably, each man making his mug of porter last as long as he could. The only one not to join in the talk was Reg Baldwin, who sat with both hands round his mug, gazing frowningly at the sawdust on the floor. He was in a bad mood and wanted to put off going home for as long as possible. He had only the haziest memories of the previous night, but despite his present ill humour he still felt a glow of satisfaction as he remembered his fist crunching into someone's face and the delicious swoop as he had chucked someone – someone light – across the filthy kitchen. He remembered shouting at his wife because the meal she had provided had not been to his liking, though he had no recollection of what had been on the table. His wife had bleated and wept, screaming that he was tearing the hair from her head, begging him to let her go so that she might begin to prepare a meal which he would enjoy. He had laughed at the suggestion, knowing that there would be no more food in the house. He remembered bellowing that he wanted GUINNESS, GUINNESS, GUINNESS . . .

Then, he supposed, the fight had started, not that it had been much of a fight. His sons were a cowardly couple; it had not taken him long to settle their hash. But his wife had somehow managed to sneak out of the house while he was teaching the boys a lesson and brought in that interferin' bugger Briggs. The man was huge, a docker, strong as an ox. Even now, Reg could see the man's fist raised, which was the last thing he did remember.

He had woken this morning, stiff, hung over, with a mouth as dry as a desert and a raging thirst. He had been lying on the floor, his head resting in something sticky and disgusting which proved to be his own vomit, and when he had shouted for assistance no one had come. He had managed to get up on to all fours and had crawled across to the sink beneath which – thank God – was the pail, still half full of water. He had grasped the bucket as lovingly as if it had contained Guinness and had drunk a good half of the suddenly delicious ice cold contents. His head had still been swimming after the previous night's drink, but he felt better and had crawled back to the couch, heaving himself aboard it and falling immediately asleep.

He had been woken again by someone shaking his shoulder. It was the boy, Percy, white as a sheet save for an enormous black eye. Reg had reached out for him, meaning to use the boy's shoulder as a support to help him sit up, but Percy had stepped back quickly – so quickly that the question that had hovered on Reg's lips – *Where did you get that black eye?* – became immediately unnecessary. Well, I reckon he deserved it, Reg had told himself, glancing at the kitchen clock. Oh, God, if he were to get to work on time, he'd need to get a move on. In the old days – the good old days, he had amended – the fellers would have come for him, and of course Herbie Hughes would have done the same. But ever since Herbie's dismissal, things at the warehouse had gone steadily downhill. Mr Harry bloody Todd, a right nasty prig of a feller, had somehow managed to persuade the other chaps that time-keeping was important, as was the sacredness of the goods entrusted to their care. So far as Reg was concerned, the only sacred thing in the warehouse was himself and he felt sore and sick and angry when he thought of the many little ploys that he and Herbie had worked out which had led to the enrichment of them both. Tins of pineapple and tins of red salmon were easy to smuggle out and to sell around the pubs afterwards. And then there was tea and coffee, always popular amongst the house-wives. Many a feller now drinking in the pub was glad to take home two ounces of tea for his missus, knowing that the gift would shut her mouth to his shortcomings. Luxury goods, such as Belgian choco-lates, destined for the smart shops on Church Street or Bold Street, were very popular, and in some pubs Reg had become so well known as a purveyor of cheap goods that even now customers raised their eyebrows at him and were disappointed, even angry, when he was forced to shake his head.

If only they could get rid of Todd! He had dreamed

of it ever since the man's first day as head ware-houseman. The trouble was, he was so damned good at the job. Herbie's thefts – and those of Reg himself – had depended upon the chaotic way in which goods were stored. It had meant you could check in a dozen crates of tinned peaches secure in the knowledge that Herbie would have to split them to get them into the place at all. That was the moment when you manoeu-vred a crate away from the others, perhaps shoving it into the boiler room for a day or two. If it was missed, it could be produced; if it was not, then Herbie or Reg would be at liberty to break it open and make off with the contents. However, all that was at an end, for Todd knew where every lump of sugar was stored and almost nothing could go missing without a fuss. Now, at the end of each month, the men were paid a bonus, but this did not compensate Reg for losing his standing in the community as a provider of cheap luxury items. Besides, there was the thrill of stealing the stuff, which had lent an element of danger to each ordinary working day, and made him feel one helluva good feller as he handed out the sorts of goods most people never even touched, let alone tasted.

The odd thing was, though, that apart from Mickey Platt, none of the other warehousemen disliked the new order of things. In fact they were saying, frankly, that they thought it a great improvement. 'It's made life much easier, Mr Todd knowing exactly where every-thing is, and drawing up a fresh plan each day so that everyone else knows as well,' one of the men had said. 'And you know how it is – when everyone realises that someone's at the nicking game, then you're all half afraid the boss'll end up believing it's you. Why, honest men have had the push before today and a'course the thief just chuckles to hisself and stays stumm, because a feller that'll steal from his employer won't think twice about puttin' someone else in the frame if he gets the chance.'

At the time, Reg had nodded wisely along with the rest, but afterwards he and Mickey had discussed the new order and agreed that something ought to be done to get rid of Todd. 'I'm not saying anyone else would be as bent as Herbie,' Mickey had said. 'I agree with the fellers that we don't want someone like that; far too dangerous. What we want is someone who'll turn a blind eye to a bit of pilferin' – a coupla tins o' salmon, a bag o' sugar poured off when you've split a sack, like; a tin of golden syrup to make a nice treacle tart of a Sunday . . . that sort of thing. What I'd call perks of the job, I suppose.'

So now, sitting in the pub and taking no part in the conversation going on around him, Reg began to try to think of a foolproof plan which would cause old Todd to go back to his bleedin' canal boat and never poke his nose into a decent warehouse again. By the time he had finished his porter, several ideas had risen to the surface of his mind, but they all needed cooperation from someone else, and that someone would have to be Mickey Platt. The other man was not present, having made his way straight home, but Reg knew where he lived and decided to visit him. We must strike while the iron's hot, he told himself virtuously. Todd's already had three months and he's used them to change just about everything. The next thing we know, he'll start looking into our private lives and deciding who he could do without, because there's no doubt about it, when a warehouse is run the way Payton and Bister is being run, you don't need the same level of staff. That's why I can get away wi' having a smoke in a crafty corner. Oh aye, I'll nip round to Mickey's place on me way home tonight.

Reg had done as he had promised himself he would, but had been disappointed. Mickey Platt had gone to visit an elderly aunt who sometimes gave him his tea in return for the performing of small tasks which were too heavy for her. Reg had made his way home, still plotting furiously. He had let himself into a cold and empty house, for neither his wife nor any of his children were to be seen. Cursing, Reg examined the food cupboard and found it empty. He took down the teapot where he knew his wife kept her housekeeping money, but that was empty too, and for the first time it occurred to him that the kid he had thrown across the room the night before might have been more badly injured than he had supposed. His blood ran cold at the thought. Scuffers were notoriously hard on child beaters and it would be no good explaining that he had scarcely touched the boy, that the lad had tumbled down the stairs, or tripped on one of the uneven floor tiles in the kitchen. Why, if the kid were real bad, his wife might see it as a chance to get her revenge on him for occasionally having a drink or two, and might tell the scuffers that it had been he who had punched his son and chucked him across the kitchen. You could never tell with women; they could be as spiteful as hell if they thought a feller would be thrown into the cooler and therefore unable to give them the slapping they deserved for their treachery.

He was considering what he should do when somebody banged on the front door. Reg let himself out of the kitchen and went down the short hallway, wondering uneasily who would be calling on him and hoping it was not a scuffer. He opened the door cautiously and was much relieved to see Mickey Platt standing on the doorstep.

'Eh up, Reg,' Mickey said cheerfully. 'Me old woman said you wanted to see me.'

'That's right; so I do. Come in, old feller,' Reg said, holding the door wide. He was about to shut it behind his friend when his son Percy came across the court, hesitated, and then somewhat warily climbed the steps and slid past his father, making for the kitchen.

Reg followed his friend and his son into the cheerless room, then ordered Percy brusquely to fetch water and get the fire lit. Percy looked at him resentfully, and for the second time Reg noticed that his son was sporting a black eye. For Mickey's benefit, he asked, 'Where'd you get that shiner?' and then, before the boy could answer: 'And where's your mam and the rest of the family? Gone off on the spree, I dare say?'

His son glanced across at him again and Reg saw both fear and burgeoning bitterness in the lad's eyes – or eye rather, since the blackened one was closed – but said nothing whilst he waited for a reply.

Finally, Percy spoke. 'Mam's taken us round to Auntie Nell's because her house is so near the Stanley hospital,' he mumbled. 'She told me to come round to pick up some clothes for Ron because they're keepin' him in hospital another night and the nurse said they'd only let him out tomorrer if he had some clean clobber.'

Reg glanced uneasily across at Mickey, who was following the conversation with blatant curiosity. It had taken Reg only a moment to grasp what must have happened the previous night, but Mickey was a young man who had not been married long and probably did not understand how irritating kids could be. Reg turned his shoulder on his friend and fixed his son with a threatening eye. 'Oh ah, I remember your mam sayin' as Ron had tripped an' fallen down the stairs and give himself a nasty crack on the head,' he remarked. 'You kids is all the same, always in trouble. What ward's he in? I'll go round when I've had a bite to eat an' check up on 'im. Your mam might ha' left me a note, though. I wouldn't have minded going round to Nell's place myself an' all. I dare say she'd ha' made me somethin' hot to eat.'

Percy muttered something beneath his breath and continued to busy himself with newspaper and kindling, so Reg turned back to his friend. 'Look, Mick, we've gorra do something about old Toddy. I've gorra plan, only it takes two . . .'

Percy scrumpled up the newspapers and made a wigwam of the kindling, then reached for the matches. As soon as the wood had caught and was burning steadily, he would add tiny pieces of coal until the whole thing was ablaze. Then he would perch the kettle above the flame and nip upstairs for a clean shirt and kecks for Ron, always supposing that he could find some.

The coal caught. Percy had been listening, idly, to his father's conversation, and suddenly it occurred to him that the men were talking about Mr Todd, the feller in charge of the warehouse . . . Evie's dad. They had talked about him before, but . . . oh, differently. This time his father's low-voiced comments sounded much more purposeful and this made Percy prick up his ears; it sounded as though Reg Baldwin really meant business and that could be bad news, both for Mr Todd and for his daughter.

The coals began to blaze and Percy went and filled the kettle from the bucket beneath the sink, then heaved it across to the fire. He missed some of the conversation but was back in time to hear Mick demurring. It seemed he did not wish to participate in the plan, saying it was the sort of trick which might easily backfire, and could even lead to the wrong man's becoming the victim.

At this point, Percy decided to go upstairs and find the clean clothing he wanted. He did not know exactly what sort of trick his father was planning to play upon Mr Todd, but Mickey Platt didn't seem keen and Reg had said the trick needed two, so perhaps nothing would come of it. He found the clothes without too much trouble and came downstairs very quietly indeed. He had no wish to be collared by his father and dragged back into the kitchen to make the men a cup of tea, yet he was still curious about the plan his father had spoken of. He had not shut the kitchen door properly when he left the room and now paused by the door, listening intently.

'. . . I'm the one who'll do all the donkey work,' his father was saying persuasively. 'All I want you to do, old feller, is to call Todd across when I gives you the signal. Don't forget, all I mean to do is give him one helluva scare and mebbe a bruise or two. But it mustn't look deliberate; it's gorra be somethin' real accidental. The way I see it, one fright ain't likely to send him scuttling back to the canal, but two or three . . .'

'Reg, me ol' pal, it just won't work,' Mickey was saying. 'Barge masters don't scare easy, and if it were to go wrong . . .'

'It *can't* go wrong,' the other man said. His voice was beginning to rise. 'Norrif we both work it out together. But if I'm left to manage alone . . . then, I admit, it could go wrong. An' whose fault would that be?'

'Yours,' the other man said promptly. He sounded

truculent now and Percy heard the creaking of the big old basket chair and knew that his father's pal was getting to his feet. 'You say it's nobbut a prank, Reg, but to my mind it's a bloody dangerous one. Just forget it, d'you hear me? Forget it.'

The sound of footsteps came towards the door and Percy, clutching his burden, shot up the corridor and out into the court, to make his way to his Auntie Nell's house on Orwell Road. He knew the family would not stay there long, only while Ron was in hospital probably, for the house was crowded enough with Auntie Nell's four boys and three girls. However, it was a respite from his father's uncertain temper, so despite the fact that it more than doubled his walk to school, Percy was quite pleased with the way things had turned out.

He reached the house and entered the warm kitchen thankfully, for the evenings were growing cool. His aunt had saved him a bowl of stew and two or three large potatoes, and Percy thanked her and tried to eat the food slowly. After he had eaten, he was given blankets and told to join his cousins in the boys' room, so he trooped up the stairs and squeezed, with much giggling, into the enormous bed which took up most of the floor space. As he snuggled down, Percy told himself that he would have to be off real early in the morning if he wanted to meet up with his pal Gareth on their usual corner. He hoped the girl, Evie, would be there as well. He thought he would tell her that his father had planned to play a trick on her father, but it had all come to nothing because one of the other men wouldn't agree to take part.

As he drifted off to sleep, Percy remembered that Mickey had said the trick was dangerous and wondered, vaguely, what his father had planned. But it had been a long and exhausting day and, very soon, he fell asleep.

Evie bolted her porridge as soon as her mother put the plate down in front of her. Then she offered to make her own carry-out, which made her mother laugh. 'Oh yes, and I can just imagine what a mangled wreck my nice new loaf would be if I let you get your hands on it,' Martha said. 'And not a smidgeon of butter or a scraping of jam left for anyone else, I dare say. No, love, I'll do your carry-out. Are you still wanting an extra butty and another piece of cake? Who are you feeding this time? And what do you want in your butties, come to that? There's sardine and tomato paste, mixed fruit jam, or I can spare some corned beef if I cut it thin.'

'Ooh, corned beef! Can I have some brown sauce on it?' Evie said eagerly. 'If I can have two corned beef sandwiches and one sardine and tomato paste, that'll be lovely. And two pieces of cake, Ma, if you don't mind. I've got this new pal; he's older'n me but he don't seem to bring any carry-out to school, so I reckon he'll be glad of a bite.'

Martha reached for the loaf and began cutting it into exactly even slices, so rapidly that Evie thought she worked like some sort of machine. 'And what's the name of this unfortunate being?' she enquired presently, beginning to spread margarine on each slice as swiftly and efficiently as she had cut the loaf. 'How did you get to know him, anyway? I understood that boys and girls don't mix in city schools.'

'It's Percy Baldwin; I told you about him. I think his dad's the one Pa said makes trouble at Payton and Bister.'

'Oh,' Martha said, rather doubtfully, a slight frown

creasing her brow. Then the frown disappeared. 'Well, it's not the boy's fault that he's got an unpleasant father, so you can take an extra apple as well. They're only the little red ones which you can buy six for a penny, but they help to fill a gap.'

So when Evie set off for school presently, she was fairly laden with food and looking forward to handing a good share of it to her new friend, but when she reached the corner where they usually met, a disappointment awaited her. Gareth, Annie and Ruthie, and Ruthie's brother, Si were waiting, but there was no sign of Percy.

'I dunno where the family's gone; none o' the kids nor their mam were home last night, but Mr Baldwin were there okay and I dare say the kids'll come to school as usual from wherever they spent the night,' Gareth said, when Evie asked after his pals. 'Ah, speak of the devil . . .' for at this moment Percy panted up, skidding to a halt beside them.

'Sorry I'm late, fellers,' he said breathlessly. 'Me brother Ron's in the Stanley so our mam had us all stay with Auntie Nell last night, 'cos she lives nearby. But I think Ron's coming out today, so I s'pose we'll be back in the court by teatime.' He sounded regretful but Gareth and Annie both smiled, and Gareth gave him a playful punch on the shoulder.

'That's good news; our side missed the best footballer in the team yesterday,' Gareth said. 'I dunno how come you're such a grand footballer, old feller, because you ain't even got a decent pair of plimsolls, lerralone boots. I reckon it's just natural genius.'

Evie saw that he was only half joking and that Percy was really pleased and presently, when conversation became general once more, her new friend dropped back to walk beside her. 'I heard me dad talkin' to one of the other fellers from the warehouse last night,' he remarked, almost casually. 'They were going to play some daft sort of prank on your dad, but they decided agin it. The other feller said it was too dangerous.'

'Dangerous?' Evie said, her eyes widening. 'Why would they want to do something dangerous to my dad? He's a good man is my dad. He's never harmed a soul in his whole life.'

'That's why; I reckon he's too honest,' Percy said wisely. 'They want to drive him back to the canal . . . or that's what they said, anyway.'

Evie's eyes brightened. Though she never said so, she missed the canal horribly and thought she would do almost anything to return to the *Mary Jane* and the old, free, wandering life. In her heart, however, she knew that it had been hard on both her parents, who had worked day and night for very little reward. Besides, when enough money had been saved, she knew her pa meant to buy a cottage in Burscough, and living there they would have the best of both worlds. So she said: 'They'll never do that – drive him back to the canal, I mean. Why, our Seraphina is in teacher training college and Angie's enjoying her job at Bunney's. Still, if they've decided not to do it, whatever it was . . .' She fished around in her canvas satchel and produced two sandwiches. 'Here, have a butty. And there's some little red apples . . .'

'Thanks,' Percy said gratefully, taking the sandwich. 'Me Auntie Nell's ever so generous. She give us each a big plate o' porridge, but somehow I allus seem to be hungry.' He looked at her anxiously. 'I reckon you get a good breakfast . . .' He waved the sandwich at her. 'This ain't your brekker, is it?'

'No fear; I have a plate of porridge and then as much toast and jam as I can eat, and weekends we has bacon butties an' quite often a boiled egg,' Evie said truthfully. Her parents had always insisted that everyone had a good breakfast aboard the *Mary Jane* because of the hard physical work which was necessary to get their cargoes to their destinations. The habit had lingered even now they were living ashore and Evie, looking at Percy's skinny frame, realised anew how lucky she was.

'That's all right then,' Percy said, gobbling the sandwich as though he had never so much as smelt porridge, let alone eaten a large plateful that morning. 'You going to wait for me after school? Only I reckon I'll go home to the court – the Cavvy, us kids call it – and check to see if Mam and the others are back. The nurse said Ron could come home today if he had some clean kecks an' that, so I went home last night an' picked 'em up. That was how I come to hear me dad an' his pal talkin'.'

Evie hesitated; she did not want to hurt Percy's feelings, but if he was to be her pal there were things she had to know. 'Does your dad often lose his temper, Perce? I know you said he were drunk, but he wouldn't have been drunk again last night and yet your mam kept you out of his way, didn't she? Oh, by the way, my mam asked me to ask you if you'd like to come back to the flat after school an' have your tea wi' us. But if you've got to go back to your own place . . .'

Percy's eyes had brightened at the invitation and now he spoke up quickly. 'That's real kind of your mam. It 'ud be great to go back to your place. Only the thing is, I've gorra tell me mam – if she's back in the Cavvy by then, I mean. Tell you what, you come back to the Cavvy wi' me so's I can tell me mam where I's goin' an' then we can carry on to your place. As for me dad, he – he's often bad tempered, only never in front of people what ain't family. He won't be home till seven or so – like your dad, I dare say – but if he were to come in an' find you there, even if he'd just stubbed his toe on the doorstep he'd stop cussin' an' be nice as pie. So will you come? After all, if you an' me are goin' to be pals, it's easier if we know where the other one lives.'

'Yes, I'll come,' Evie said readily. She had never actually been into Cavendish Court and thought it would be interesting to see what Percy's house was like, particularly since her friend Annie lived only a few doors away. 'Right then, I'll wait for you when school's out.' By now, they had reached the boys' gates, and as Percy turned to go inside Evie thrust one of the small red apples into his hand. 'See you later, wack,' she said in imitation of the way she had heard the big boys talk.

Percy turned and waved, then set off at a gallop to catch up with Gareth and Evie broke into a trot so that she could link arms with Annie. The bell rang and lines began to form. Another school day was beginning.

Harry arrived at work early, as he always did, and settled at once into the routine of the day. The men arrived in ones and twos, all feeling cheerful, for today was Friday, pay day, and tomorrow was Saturday, when they only worked until noon. Most of them, Harry knew, would go to one or other of the football matches, according to which team they supported, the Reds or the Blues, but a few would have various different ploys. Harry himself meant to take Martha up to Aintree. The *Mary Jane* was coming into the city today, and Jimmy and Hetty had agreed to moor up by the race course so that Harry and Martha could join them for the rest of the trip down to the wharf. Harry liked to see the old boat and make sure that everything aboard her was in apple-pie order, and he knew how eager Martha was to return to the old craft – as eager as he was himself.

Harry began to hand out the tasks which each man was to perform and soon the day's work was in full swing. He had noted Baldwin's absence and was annoyed, though the man had told him the previous day that one of his sons had been injured falling downstairs. He had not seemed particularly worried, but Harry supposed it was possible that the child had taken a turn for the worse and that Baldwin was at his bedside.

He said as much to Taffy, a cheerful little Welshman who had worked down the mines and was as strong as an ox, but Taffy shook his head. 'Nah, he don't give a fig for those kids,' he remarked. 'Likelier he had a skinful last night an' woke wi' a sore head . . . no, that ain't likely, come to think, 'cos today's pay day, so yesterday he'd be down to two brass farthings, same as the rest of us.'

Harry was about to chide the other man for being so cynical when a footfall sounded behind him and Reg Baldwin came slouching in. Harry's eyebrows shot up. 'You're late, Baldwin,' he said bluntly. 'Any reason?'

The man peered at him. 'Me old woman stayed with her sister last night so there were no one to make me breakfast an' I overslept,' he said hoarsely. 'The kid's not so good; the one I told you about yesterday.'

'Right,' Harry said crisply. 'Go up to the first floor an' stack the crates with Benny, as the hoist takes them up.' He did not believe a word Baldwin had said, having seen the way the man's eyes shifted uneasily from his own, and noticed the other men's covert grins. As Baldwin turned away to mount the wooden stair which led to the first floor, Harry added quietly: 'And don't forget what I told you, Baldwin. There's a time and a place for everything and warehouse rules aren't made for fun but for safety, all right?' The other man did not answer, and Harry sighed and turned away to get on with his own work.

Fridays were always busy and today was no exception. The man working the hoist was constantly on call to fetch some goods down and take others up. Usually, Harry blew a whistle at noon so that they might eat their carry-out, accompanied by the tea which the lad brewed up in the office, but today it was half-past twelve before he even noticed the time. He apologised for this oversight and gave the men an extra ten minutes, but then it was back to work again as the lorries, carts and vans came and went and Harry himself kept the paper-work up to the minute. It was almost four o'clock and time for another break when he realised he had not seen Baldwin for some time. Sighing, he climbed to the first floor, then up to the second. He walked quietly round a huge stack of tea chests and there was Baldwin, standing close to a tiny window, a cigarette halfway to his lips. Harry's patience snapped. All the men knew smoking was forbidden, all of them knew it was dangerous, yet here was Baldwin calmly puffing away as though he believed himself to be the invisible man. He reached forward and snatched the cigarette from Baldwin's fingers, throwing it to the ground and grinding it beneath his heel. 'Get your cards, Baldwin,' he said harshly. 'You're sacked.'

Baldwin's eyebrows shot skyward. 'For doin' what, Mr Todd, sir?' he said and his very tone was an insult. 'I just been shiftin' a load o' sugar sacks . . . what's wrong wi' that? Ain't I entitled to take a breath? It's break time, after all.'

'Break time is when I blow the whistle, and you were

74

smoking which is strictly forbidden,' Harry said, keeping his temper with difficulty. 'There's no point in arguing; you're out. I'll get your cards myself.'

Baldwin's jaw jutted obstinately. 'Mr Hughes hired me and I reckon Mr Hughes is the only feller that can fire me,' he drawled. 'Anyway, it ain't right 'cos you've gorra give me a week's notice. A'course, you wouldn't know that, bein' as you're just a bleedin' bargee what's never hired or fired a feller in his whole life.'

Harry knew a moment of horrid doubt. His own contract with the company stated that two weeks' notice must be given on either side, so Baldwin might be in the right of it; perhaps he ought to have given the man a week's notice. Yet he did not fancy having to work for another whole week with a man who constantly flouted both his authority and the company's rules. Instead, he compromised. 'You will be paid for the full week, which is up to noon on Saturday,' he said firmly. 'But you will leave tonight when everyone else does, and you need not come in tomorrow morning. Is that clear? And don't come to me for a reference, Baldwin, because I could not in all conscience say that you were a hard worker who had the company's best interests at heart.'

To Harry's astonishment, Baldwin's jaw dropped open. 'You're sacking me without a reference?' he said incredulously. 'But I'm well known in these parts as a bloody good worker. Oh, I dare say you can sack me now that Mr Hughes has left, I dare say you can do that, but I've gorra family to feed. You've gorrer give me a decent reference, else how are we all to live? Why, I heard you tell old Reddo that you didn't mean to get rid of any staff, only not replace fellers when they retired.'

Harry had turned away but now he swung back. 'I

said there's no point in arguing, Baldwin,' he said calmly. 'Come to the office for your cards at six o'clock.' And with that, he hurried back down to the ground floor, where he picked up his inventory and continued with his work, only remembering to blow the whistle for the ten-minute break when he was reminded by the young lad who ran errands and made the tea.

Promptly at six o'clock he went to the office, found Reg Baldwin's documents in the filing cabinet, and began to fill in the necessary form whilst deciding what he should say if Baldwin started on about his rights. The truth was, he had none since he had deliberately flouted company rules, but Harry was not a man who enjoyed friction of any sort and he meant to tell Baldwin that he might, after all, give him a reference. He would not lie, but he might manage to get round the reason for the dismissal without actually saying that Baldwin had been caught smoking in the warehouse.

At half-past six, Harry slammed the papers into his top drawer, locked it and reached for his cap and coat. Normally an even-tempered man, he was simmering with annoyance. Just who did Baldwin think he was? So far as Harry was concerned, the other man could now whistle for a reference. Harry certainly did not intend to take the man's cards round to whichever hovel he inhabited, nor did he intend to hand them over should Baldwin turn up the next day. He would send him to Mr Bister. It was a nuisance, because Mr Bister would have left the building by now, but Harry decided that as soon as his boss arrived the next day he would explain what had happened and give him the necessary documentation to hand to Baldwin when, or if, he came searching.

Harry was almost home when he suddenly remembered that the following day was Saturday and Mr

Bister might not come in at all. He sighed. Saturday mornings were sometimes extremely busy but he knew they would manage somehow; perhaps they would manage even better without Reg Baldwin, constantly skiving off work, constantly grumbling, constantly trying to make trouble.

He reached home and greeted Martha with a smacking kiss, sniffing the air appreciatively. 'That's mutton stew, or I'm a Dutchman, with those lovely herby dumplings,' he said, taking off his cap and coat and hanging them on the back of the kitchen door. 'You're a clever little woman, Martha Todd, because I've had an awful day and I'm hungry as a hunter.'

'Ma knows it's your favourite, Pa,' Seraphina said. She was bustling about the kitchen laying the table whilst Martha lifted the lid off a large pan and checked on the pudding boiling within. 'She's made a jam roly-poly as well, because of tomorrow.'

'Tomorrow?' Harry said blankly. 'What about tomorrow? It's going to be every bit as bad as today's been, because today I sacked a man for the first time in my life. It was Reg Baldwin, the one I told you sneaks away in corners for a smoke. I've warned him over and over, but today I caught him red-handed, amongst the tea chests of all things, having a crafty drag. I ha' no option but to sack him, only then I realised tomorrow was Saturday, and I'd be a man short. Still, I've never shirked hard work . . .'

'Pa!'

'Daddy, have you forgotten . . . ?'

'Oh, Harry, but it's your day off!'

Seraphina, Angela and Martha all spoke at the same time. Harry groaned and sank into a chair. 'Oh, Martha, love, it went clear out of my head. Believe me,

I've been looking forward to seeing the old *Mary Jane* – and Hetty and Jim – as much as any of you. Oh, my goodness, whatever shall I do? I don't know Mr Bister's private address so I can't go round there and explain the situation.' He paused, thinking. 'Tell you what, I'll go to the warehouse, same as I always do, and make sure everything's set fair. When the men arrive, I'll explain that it's my day off and see if Wilmott – he's my deputy – thinks he can manage with a man short. With luck, Mr Bister will come in early so I can get away, but he doesn't always put in an appearance on Saturdays.'

'But suppose you can't, Pa? Get away, I mean,' Angela said plaintively. 'It's taken me ages to persuade Hilda to work a Saturday for me and I just know if I try to change it I'll get into awful trouble.'

'If I can't get away, then you girls will have to go without me,' Harry said, rather sadly. He turned to his wife. 'I know you'll agree with me, my love, that we can't let Jim and Hetty down. But I'll try and join you at the wharf, even if I can't make it to Aintree.'

Martha smiled at him tremulously, and put her arms round him. 'It's not your fault, Harry, it's the fault of that awful Baldwin fellow. And his son, Percy, will be here any minute now because Evie's asked him back to tea. I'm awful sorry. I'd have made some excuse if I'd realised . . .'

'There's nowt wrong with the lad coming to tea. In fact, it's probably a good thing since Reg Baldwin has just been paid and will probably drink the lot and go home just longing to hit someone, or something,' Harry said gloomily. 'He's a bad 'un is Reg Baldwin; I pity his kids and his wife, particularly now. Well, if you don't mind, my love, we won't break it to him that his father's lost his job . . . or perhaps we should, what do you think?'

'Forewarned is forearmed,' Martha said, after only the briefest pause. 'If he knows his dad's liable to be in a bad temper, then he can get into his bed and lie low, well before closing time. Ah, I hear their feet on the stairs; I'll start dishing up at once.'

Chapter Four

Saturday morning dawned cloudy and Harry thought rain was on its way. Martha was always first up since she liked to make sure that her family had a good hot meal inside them to start the day. So when Harry entered the kitchen, it was to the good smells of bacon frying and porridge bubbling in the pot. He crossed the room and gave his wife a quick hug, and then, being Harry, his first thought was for the young lad who had shared their mutton stew the previous evening. 'Morning, my love. You know, the more I think of it, the more certain I am that we did right to tell young Percy his dad was out of work,' he said, taking his place at the table. 'I don't imagine he'll get another job as a warehouseman, but surely he'll get something? And then there's the dole . . . I *know* I did the right thing. Baldwin knew it's absolutely forbidden to smoke in the warehouse; there's notices everywhere. One spark near the tea chests and it could have been curtains for all of us.'

Martha chuckled, putting a plate of porridge down in front of him. 'You don't want to keep worrying yourself over what's already happened,' she said bluntly. 'From what you've said – and from the way we know he behaves – that Baldwin's a real bad lot. Well, for instance, think about Percy's eye. His father must have punched him with the sort of force a man uses in a desperate fight with another man. And he put the younger boy in hospital, so losing his job is no more than he deserves.'

Harry began spooning porridge. 'I know you're right and I know sacking him was right too, but those poor kids and that poor woman,' he said miserably. 'In the whole of my life, love, I've never been in a position to stop a man earning a living, and I feel sure if I'd been a better man, more experienced like, I'd have found a way to make him see what a fool he was being without actually sacking him.'

Martha snorted inelegantly. 'Rubbish,' she said roundly. 'Most men would have sacked him weeks ago, the way he went on. So stop blaming yourself and eat your porridge.'

Harry laughed. 'Oh well, I dare say you're right,' he admitted. 'But I could kick myself for letting the whole business put our day on the canal right out of my mind. Still, you and the girls will go, won't you? And I will try to get along and meet you later, honestly I will.'

Martha walked across the kitchen and peered out of the window. 'Well, we've promised Jim and Hetty so we'll have to keep our word, but it's just started to rain and judging by what I can see of the sky from here, it's going to be a really nasty day,' she said. 'Don't you bother to come along, my love, if it's raining cats and dogs, because we'll all be cramped up in the living cabin and that's no joke when it's tipping down outside. Poor Hetty means to make us a meal, so I should think she'd be downright grateful to have one less.'

She had moved back across the kitchen as she spoke and Harry heard the sizzle as she dropped a thick round of home-made bread into the frying pan to accompany the bacon and eggs she had already cooked. He waited until she had placed the full plate before him, then reached for the HP Sauce, poured a generous helping on to the side of his plate, and turned to smile up at her. 'Yes, mebbe you're right and there'll be no point in my rushing off if it's still raining hard. You know as much about the *Mary Jane* as I do myself, so you can tell me, when we both get home, if Jim and Hetty are doing right by her, and by dear old Gemma. A good horse is worth its weight in gold to a barge master and no better horse was ever foaled than our Gemma.'

Martha laughed and leaned across to give him a quick kiss before putting her own plate of bacon and eggs down opposite him and taking her seat. 'When we first married you said that no better horse had ever been foaled than Gemma's mum Molly,' she reminded him.

Harry grinned. 'All right, all right; I admit I've got a weakness for all horses, particularly our own,' he said. 'Percherons are particularly good at towing because they learn easily and are very strong.' He glanced at the clock above the mantel, reached for another slice of bread and wiped it round his plate to gather up the last smears of egg, bacon and dripping. Then he folded the bread into a sandwich, hooked his jacket and cap off the door, and turned to give Martha a kiss just as the kitchen door opened and his three daughters surged into the room. Evie, in the lead, closed her eyes and raised her nose to heaven with an expression so reminiscent of the Bisto Kids that her parents both laughed.

'Oh Ma, I *do* love Saturdays, and I do love bacon and eggs,' Evie said. 'Are you off already, Pa? Isn't it a shame that the weather's changed, though? It's been fine all week and just because it's Saturday and we're having a day out, the bloomin' rain had to come tippin' down.'

Harry, passing her, rumpled her already untidy hair.

'Never mind, Evie, maybe it'll clear up,' he said. 'Be good girls, all three of you, and help Ma. See you later!'

The girls chorused that they always helped their mother, and then Harry was outside and clattering down the stairs, his mind turning from his family to the day ahead.

The rain was so heavy that he could scarcely see across Scotland Road and the drops hitting the puddles looked the size of pennies. He hesitated for a moment, for he was wearing a thin coat and knew that somewhere in the flat were the oilskins he had worn aboard the *Mary Jane* in foul weather. But then a tram came rattling along and he jumped aboard. He usually walked to work but there was no point in arriving at the warehouse looking as though he had swum there, so he rode to the nearest stop.

Getting down from the crowded tram, Harry set off for the warehouse with the rain driving into his face and slithering, coldly, down his neck. As he sloshed through the puddles he thought, with grim humour, how much he had changed in the last four months. As a barge master, he had been out in all weathers, had scarcely noticed rain, sleet, or indeed sunshine, save as to the effect it had on his journeyings. When the canal froze over, the ice could split a boat open as easily as he could crack a hazelnut, so no barge master worth his salt ever slept, save in cat naps, during a severe frost. He had always kept a foot of clear water all the way round the *Mary Jane* and both butty boats, even though it meant staying awake all night to keep the strip of water open.

And now I'm behaving as though a heavy rainfall was a wretched nuisance and a reason to change my ways, he scolded himself. Aboard the *Mary Jane*, of course, heavy rainfall after a prolonged drought could spell trouble because planks which had shrunk during the dry let the water pour in when heavy rain came, but ashore, tiles and brick took little heed of the weather and his family would remain comfortably dry whilst they were beneath a roof.

His place of work was reached by a narrow cobbled passage, surrounded on all sides by factories and warehouses, and whilst he was in this passage Harry was out of the worst of the weather. He took off his cap and actually wrung it out, then continued on his way. He wondered whether Mr Bister would come in, then put the matter out of his mind. He would speak to his boss as soon as he could, and explain matters regarding Reg Baldwin. Until then, he would simply get on with the job in hand.

Reg Baldwin woke that morning with a splitting headache, a mouth like the bottom of a parrot's cage, and a feeling of gloom which seemed to have no definite cause. He'd had a night of it, going from pub to pub along the docks, and felt no particular surprise over his physical state. He was not even surprised to find that he had apparently bedded down on the kitchen floor because this often happened when he went on the booze with his pay packet still intact. However, he rarely felt as though something horrible either had happened or was about to do so. Often he felt aggressive, furious, even fighting mad, but not – not . . .

A small picture was forming in the back of his mind. The hated face of Harry Todd, the reproving, wagging finger, the smugness of the fellow as he had told Reg . . . what had he told Reg? Something unpleasant, no doubt. Was I skiving? Reg asked himself. Well, if I was, why not? I remember now: he were late blowin' the bleedin' whistle so I took meself off round the back of the bleedin' tea chests for a quick drag . . .

Baldwin gave a deep groan and hauled himself to his feet. Immediately, a gang of small and vicious dwarfs began to beat hammers inside his aching head. Moving at all hurt him but he had to get to the water bucket. If he didn't lubricate his desiccated mouth, dry throat and arid stomach with a great big draught of cold water, he would very likely die.

He reached the sink, fell to his knees, and drank in huge gulps, then glanced at the kitchen clock. Damn it to hell, if he didn't get a move on he'd be late for work and that wouldn't please the bloody barge master. It did not occur to Baldwin that his wife was usually in the kitchen at this hour, getting breakfast; he simply grabbed cap and jacket off the back of the door and charged out of the house. By the time he arrived at the warehouse he had remembered two things. The first was that the kitchen clock was supposed to be wound up every Friday night and that he had not done so, for in passing the chemist on the corner he realised that he was more than an hour earlier than he should have been. In fact, it was still extremely dark and there was no sign of dawn in the east. The second thing he remembered was that that miserable old barge master had given him the sack the evening before, and told him to fetch his cards. He had not done so since he had every intention of fighting his case, trying to persuade Mr Bister that he had not been smoking the cigarette but merely holding it between his lips, much as a baby sucks a dummy. He would say that Todd had never liked him, had been against him from the first, always looking for some reason to boot him out. He would tell Mr Bister . . . oh, there were a thousand things he could tell him, for he could not imagine how he could get another job in such hard times. Folks said that there was a war coming and went on saying it, despite Mr Chamberlain's 'Peace for our time', and if war did come then all the young men would go and older men, such as himself, would be much sought after. But it was no use counting on a war; no, he must speak to Mr Bister as soon as he could and tell the boss that Todd had always had it in for him. He would say the other man was jealous of the more experienced hands and wanted to get rid of them because they showed the barge master up for the greenhorn he was. He would remind Mr Bister how Herbie Hughes had leaned on him, asking his advice, giving him responsible jobs . . . no, perhaps that would not be wise. Better just concentrate on putting the boot in for the barge master and reinstating himself.

He reached the warehouse. The big doors were shut and barred so he went round and banged on the side door, and presently the old night watchman came grumbling down and let him in. Baldwin explained about his mistake over the kitchen clock and was invited to share a cup of tea with the old man. But instead, he decided to take a look around the warehouse, see whether there was any way he could work things to his advantage. After all, it was not yet common knowledge that he had been sacked; he had told no one and he was pretty sure that Harry Todd had not done so either, for when Mr Evans, who was the accountant for all three Payton and Bister warehouses, had come round with their pay packets, there had been no dark looks, no cruel jokes about making the most of this money because it might be the last he would get for some time.

So Baldwin refused the tea, saying that he might as well get on with some work since he was early anyway.

He picked up a pile of papers, stuck a pencil behind his ear and moved out of the office. The old man had always left by the time the staff arrived and had no idea of what Baldwin's position was within the firm. He probably assumes I'm standing in for the barge master for some reason, Baldwin thought, with a chuckle. Ah well, they say the early bird catches the worm, so let's see whether it's true.

Despite the tram ride, Harry was late arriving at the warehouse. As he emerged from the passage, a lorry, rounding the corner, tried to brake. The driver had not allowed for the slippery state of the cobbles, and with a hideous screeching the vehicle slid across the road and into the side of a building, spilling its cargo everywhere. Harry ran forward. The cab of the lorry had been crushed against the brickwork and though the driver was mercifully unhurt it took some time to release him. The man vowed he was fine and began trying to gather up his scattered load, but Harry told him that he would be sensible to go along to the hospital and get himself checked over. Only when the man agreed to do this did Harry make his belated way, through the still torrential rain, to the warehouse.

Several of the workers had come out when they heard the sound of the collision, but Harry had ordered them back at once and they had gone willingly enough. Now he was glad they had done so, since it gave him the opportunity to see for himself how they were managing. It looked as though they were doing pretty well. Clearly, they were loading the top storey now, for as Harry moved across the warehouse the man on the hoist was swinging an enormous crate up on to the upper floor. Harry checked with his eye that there were men up there to receive it and put it into its appointed place, and was about to return to his office to fetch invoices and delivery sheets when something about the man working the hoist caught his attention. He stopped, staring hard at the person perched at the controls. Good God, if he hadn't sacked the man himself, he would have sworn that it was Reg Baldwin! What on earth was happening? He took a couple of steps towards the hoist, and saw the other man's face light into a grin so totally soulless and wicked that he stopped in his tracks and stared. He heard a warning shout, and even as he glanced up he saw the crate plunging towards him and knew the reason for that devilish grin. He even thought, as the crate smashed on to him, that he heard Baldwin say: 'Gotcher, you bugger.'

Then, nothing. A moment of fierce and terrible pain, then darkness.

Percy woke at his usual time to hear rain sleeting down on the slate roof and gurgling along the gutters. For a moment, he imagined having to trudge to school through the downpour, then remembered that it was Saturday and got out of bed. Last night, he had gone to do the messages for his mother since there had been no food in the house – his father had clearly not bothered to eat at home whilst his family were staying at Auntie Nell's – and he had bought two large loaves, a packet of margarine and some marrow and ginger jam. If he got up now and was first down, he could get himself some breakfast before the rest of the family, gannets every one, gobbled the lot.

Moving carefully, because he did not wish to wake the others, he pulled on his old kecks and a ragged jersey, then stole towards the stairs. He was halfway down the flight when he remembered that, in all likelihood, his father would still be in the kitchen, probably sprawled on his back, snoring like a hog, for he had returned home at midnight, too drunk to mount the stairs.

The racket his father had made just opening the door and reaching the kitchen had woken the boys, but no one had got out of bed, and as soon as the shouts and yells had stopped, sleep had overcome them once more.

But now, poised on the stairs, Percy wondered whether it might not be wiser to return to his room. Last night his father had been calling down curses on Harry Todd's head, swearing revenge, shouting that he had been unfairly treated. If he woke in a mood as vile as that of the previous evening, then Percy felt he had a better chance of retaining a whole skin if he stayed in bed until his mother got up.

Nevertheless, Percy continued down the stairs and very soon saw that the kitchen door was ajar. Curious, he descended into the hall and peered cautiously into the kitchen, seeing at once that the room was empty. No enormous figure snored on the battered horsehair sofa, or slouched in the old wicker chair with its uneven legs. Percy blinked around. The fire was out and the curtains were still drawn across the window which overlooked the court. Percy crossed the room, walking on tiptoe despite the fact that he could see that his father was nowhere about. He supposed the old devil might be in the parlour, though this was very unlikely; last time there had been a money crisis his mother had sold the easy chairs and settee which had formerly adorned that apartment and his father was unlikely to have gone into a comfortless room when he could spend the night on the kitchen sofa, with the sink – and the buckets of water – conveniently close.

It did occur to Percy, as he drew back the limp and faded curtains, that his father might have staggered out to use one of the communal privies at the far end of the court, but a second's reflection made this seem unlikely. The slop bucket could be utilised without leaving the kitchen and Percy guessed that after a bout of drinking such as his father had enjoyed the previous evening Reg Baldwin would not traipse all the way down the court to use the privy.

Yet . . . where the devil was he? It seemed unlikely that he would have gone out of the house in search of food when the pantry contained the bread and jam which Percy himself had intended to eat for breakfast. The court was empty because the rain was tipping down, so Percy went back across the kitchen and checked the food cupboard, though he knew that men rarely felt hungry after a prolonged bout of ale supping.

As he had guessed, there was no sign that anyone had so much as lifted the loaves from the crock. Percy was about to begin the task of lighting the fire – it would be nice to make his mother a cup of tea and take it up to her in her bed – when he glanced at the clock above the mantel and realised immediately that it had stopped. Of course, his mother usually wound it on a Friday evening, but because they had not lived in the house for a couple of days she must have forgotten. Would his father have realised that? What if Reg Baldwin, waking in a groggy state, had seen the hands standing at twenty-past eight and thought he was going to be late for work? Smiling grimly, Percy went over to the pile of newspapers his mother kept beneath the sink and was beginning to crumple the pages preparatory to laying them in the grate when a cold and terrible feeling engulfed him. Last night, his father had been mouthing threats as to what he would do to Harry Todd when he got his hands on him. Percy remembered now that Mr Todd had sacked his father, which was no doubt the reason for the drinking bout and the subsequent threats. It also meant that Reg Baldwin should still have been in the house, since he had no job to go to. Suppose he had woken in the same evil frame of mind and had gone off to the warehouse to get his own back on the other man? Percy thought Mr Todd was the nicest man he had ever met and had envied Evie her gentle, humorous father. Mr Todd had known that Percy was the son of the man he had just dismissed yet he had been really kind, making Percy feel a real friend of the family, a welcome guest.

Percy's heart began to hammer; he remembered the conversation he had overheard in this very kitchen only two evenings ago. His father had wanted to play some sort of trick on Mr Todd but Mickey had said . . . oh, good God . . . he had said it was too dangerous . . . too dangerous . . .

Standing there in the kitchen, Percy was suddenly certain sure where his father had gone. He threw the paper down on the floor and hurried out of the house. Out in the court, the rain pelted down on him and he was soaked to the skin in minutes, but he never gave the weather a thought. He wished, desperately, that he could have afforded a tram but as it was he would simply have to run, and it was a fair way from the Cavvy to Payton and Bister's warehouses. He knew there were three of them, a couple alongside the canal and another down by the docks, but he had never paid much attention to his father's moans and groans about work, and realised he might have to visit more than one before he discovered where Mr Todd worked. Splashing through the puddles in his bare feet, he soon had a stitch like a red hot needle in one side, and the rain had blurred his vision so that twice, when overtaking a group of pedestrians, he slipped off the kerb into the gutter, bruising his feet.

He reached the nearest warehouse and panted up to the door. It took him ten infuriating minutes to get someone's attention because they were taking deliveries and there was much bustle and toing and froing. He was noticed all right, shouted at too, and eventually told that Harry Todd was in charge of a warehouse a good half-mile off. 'Thanks. I've gorrer see 'im real urgent, like,' Percy said breathlessly, setting off once more. 'It's – it's what you might call real serious.'

He reached the warehouse which employed Harry Todd and as soon as he got within ten feet of the big double doors, he knew that something was terribly wrong. There were lorries drawn up with their drivers standing in small knots, talking in low voices, but no goods were being taken in or out, and the warehouse workers were also standing about. Percy panted up to the nearest group, a hand clapped to his side. He picked out one man who looked as though he were in charge – he was wearing a navy blue suit and not a brown overall, as the other men were – and addressed him urgently. 'Please, sir, can I speak to Mr Todd? It's – it's a matter of life or death, as you might say.'

The man turned and looked down at him. 'You're too late, son,' he said, in a strained, unnatural voice. 'There's . . . been an accident.' He peered more closely into Percy's anxious face. 'Who are you? Not – not one of his children?'

'No, no, I'm a friend of the fambly . . . What sort of accident?' Percy asked wildly. 'Is – is it a bad accident? The hospital sort? Only, if so, I'd best get to the hospital, ask 'em if I can have a word wi' Mr Todd . . .'

The man hesitated, but before he could say a word, a sentence from a group of brown-coated warehousemen came clearly to Percy's ears. 'I dunno why they bothered to send for a doctor,' the man said dully. 'No one could have survived a crate that size landing on 'em. It were like a bleedin' butcher's shop in there, I'm tellin' you.'

'Shut your mouth, Reddo,' the man in the navy suit said quickly. 'This young man is a friend of . . .'

'Sorry, Mr Bister, I didn't see no one . . .' the man began, but Percy had turned away, tears pouring down his face. Even as he did so, he saw his father leaving the group of men and coming towards him.

'Sorry, Mr Bister; the lad's me son,' Reg Baldwin said. 'I telled you we were friends with the Todd family . . .' He put a heavy hand on Percy's shoulder, swinging the boy round to face him. 'Why, he'll be in a rare taking . . . had his tea with 'em last night, didn't you, lad? Though I don't know what you're doing here,' he added, speaking directly to Percy for the first time, with a world of menace in his tone.

Percy looked up and read the look in his father's mean and watery eyes. *I'll kill you if you make trouble for me,* the look said. *Don't you dare go blabbing to anyone or I'll break every bone in your miserable little carcass.*

'I – I come to tell you our Ron's not too well,' Percy said. 'I thought . . . me mam said to tell you . . .'

He was running out of words, and was mightily relieved when his father broke in, turning to address Mr Bister. 'There's nowt I can do here, Mr Bister, sir,' he said humbly. 'So if it's all the same to you, I'll go back with the lad here. Our Ron only came out o' hospital yesterday. He had a nasty fall – went from top o' the stairs to the bottom – so I reckon the doctors at the Stanley let him out a bit too soon.'

Mr Bister was beginning to tell Baldwin that he might as well leave when another man moved quietly forward and put a detaining hand on Baldwin's shoulder. 'I don't know if you realise, Mr Bister, that it were Baldwin who was on the hoist when the accident happened,' he said quietly. 'I don't think the police will be too pleased if you send him off home before they've heard his version of the . . . accident.'

Mr Bister's thin, grey eyebrows shot up. 'No one mentioned who was driving the hoist; I got the impression that it was Mickey Platt.' He raised his voice. 'Platt! Come here a minute.'

Mickey Platt came over to them and Percy saw at once that it was the young man who had visited their house and refused to take part in the 'prank' which his father had proposed. Now, Mr Platt looked extremely uneasy. His face was as white as a flour sack and his eyes rolled uncomfortably. 'Yes, Mr Bister?' he asked.

'I thought you were on the hoist this morning, but Mr Tilling here says different.'

'I – I were on the hoist, Mr Bister, sir. But about half an hour ago, Baldwin called up to me that there were a telephone call for me and would I take it in the office. He – he said he'd man the hoist while I were gone. I – I didn't see no harm in it an' I come straight back. I were the one what yelled the warning when I saw the crate come loose, but it were too late. No one could have got out from under.'

Baldwin began to try to shout the other man down, but Mr Bister said sharply: 'Quiet, Baldwin!' and Percy's father subsided, muttering.

Mr Bister turned back to Platt. 'I don't approve of my staff taking telephone calls during the working day, but I dare say it was an urgent matter?' He stared very intently at the younger man, his eyes hard and cold. 'Well?'

Platt began to wring his hands and to glance, nervously, at the faces surrounding him. The expressions were grim and Percy was not surprised when Platt's voice shook as he replied. 'I – I don't know who it were, sir. When I got to the office, there weren't no one on the other end of the line. I axed who wanted me, but there were just this brrrr noise, so I hung the receiver on its hook an' come back to the warehouse.'

Mr Bister's cold gaze swung round and fixed on Baldwin's face. 'Who wanted your workmate, Baldwin?' he said, and his voice was cold as ice. 'Come along, man, speak up.'

Percy felt almost sorry for his father. The face which had seemed so self-confident and cocky had crumpled into a grey mask down which beads of sweat were running freely. 'I – I dunno . . . I think the feller said he were Mickey's brother, needed him urgent. The truth is, sir, I been so upset over Mr Todd's death, I can't think straight, and . . .'

'You are a liar, Baldwin, and I'm beginning to remember talk I've heard,' Mr Bister said quietly. 'You didn't like Mr Todd, and you did your best to cause trouble for him. He told me himself that he'd given you an official warning because he'd caught you smoking in the warehouse. Come along, man, just what did happen? And I'll have the truth this time, if you please.'

Driven into a corner, Reg Baldwin began to mutter that he had never meant to hurt anyone, had meant merely to scare Mr Todd. 'It were just a prank, like,' he mumbled. 'Why, I were fond of the chap. He were a good boss. Oh aye, he caught me smoking once, but I were grateful he warned me, told me how dangerous it were, and didn't sack me on the spot. Honest to

God, I'd reason to thank him . . . certainly no reason to – to kill 'im.'

Percy gathered up all his courage. He was cold with fear, although sweat beaded his brow, but he knew he must speak out now or he never would. 'But Dad, Mr Todd had sacked you,' he said, and his voice came out surprisingly firmly, considering the state of terror in which he spoke. 'He sacked you last night, you know he did.'

Reg Baldwin roared, a dreadful, sub-human sound, and launched himself at Percy, but he never got near him. He was pounced on by four of his workmates and borne to the ground, and even as they struggled to subdue him, Mr Bister spoke. 'Keep a good firm hold of him, men, the police will be here soon,' he said briskly. 'This is a matter for them, not for us.' He turned to Percy. 'And you'd best make yourself scarce, lad. Or, no – on second thoughts, you'd best stay by me because you'll have to repeat the statement you've just made to the authorities. And don't fear that your father will take reprisals for this morning's work, because he'll be in no position to do so.'

Martha glanced towards the window as she laid the table for high tea. It was a grey and dismal day, but then, Martha thought, every day had been grey and dismal since Harry's death. Christmas had been the worst the Todd family had ever known and they made little pretence of enjoying the festive season, though Martha had scraped together enough money to buy each of her daughters a small, but useful, gift. Now, since it was New Year's Day, she had announced, that morning, that they would hold a conference as soon as tea was over.

The family conference had been one of Harry's

ideas. He was a great believer in letting the children share in any decision-making and had long ago inaugurated a council meeting whenever anything had to be decided.

Since his death, however, Martha had been too bewildered, too sick with loss, to consider such a thing. It was only because, in the dark days following their dreadful Christmas, she had realised they must pull themselves together or go under, that the idea of a conference had occurred to her.

As she moved around the table, laying it up for tea, she wondered how much of the terrible atmosphere that prevailed was her own fault. When she had accepted that no more would the clatter of Harry's boots be heard on the outside staircase, no more would his deep and cheerful voice begin to tell her about his day as soon as the outer door opened, she had gone out and bought a great quantity of cheap black material. She and the two older girls had cut and sewed and made themselves and Evie black blouses and skirts which they had worn right up to Christmas. It was only on Christmas Eve that Seraphina had spoken to her about the unwisdom of insisting on such total mourning garb. 'It really isn't fair on Evie to expect her to go to school dressed as if for a funeral,' she had said gently. 'As for Angie, she has to change into her shop clothes in the staff cloakroom every morning before she can begin work. And even you, Ma, put an overall on when you start in the shop. Don't you think ten weeks of wearing black is enough for folk who have their way to make and their living to earn? And you know, black is so dismal; it makes you look pale and ill even if you're not.' She had taken a deep breath and put both arms round her mother. 'So tomorrow, being Christmas Day, we're all going back into ordinary clothes,' she had said coaxingly. 'And we very much hope you will do the same, but of course it's up to you.'

Martha had given her daughter a hug and had then stepped back and smiled at her. 'You're right and I'll do just as you suggest,' she had said humbly. 'I've been selfish, and in a way . . . oh, a sort of show-off. But grieving comes from inside a person, not from what they're wearing. In fact . . . remember the red dress your pa bought me a couple of years ago for Christmas because he said it reminded him of holly berries? Well, I'll wear that . . . it would please Harry, don't you think?' Seraphina had agreed, with a tremble in her voice, and the next morning – Christmas morning – everyone had got up and dressed in their best.

They had all tried very hard to be jolly as small presents were unwrapped and admired, and then they had gone to church. The rector was a man of about Harry's age, his dark hair already streaked with grey, his face gentle. He had preached a lovely sermon, reminding his congregation that joyous though the Christmas season must be for all Christians, it was also a time for remembering those who were no longer with us. 'It is easy to say that one's loved ones are with Jesus in His heavenly paradise, but the pain of loss cannot be eased by such remarks when grief is new,' he had said. 'So temper your joy in this happiest of festivals with sympathy for those who cannot rejoice whole-heartedly, because sorrow is still uppermost in their minds.'

Now, Martha looked down at the grey and white checked dress she had put on to go to church that morning. She had worn the scarlet wool frock on Christmas Day and Boxing Day, but had changed into something more suitable for everyday wear after that.

She would have done so even if Harry had been alive; one did not wear one's best dress for any but special occasions, she reminded herself.

As it was Sunday, high tea consisted of a large plate of bread and margarine, a dish of hard boiled eggs and a Madeira cake which Martha had made that morning, upon her return from church. She had always gone to church regularly, and when Harry died had at first expected to find comfort in the place he had regarded so highly. Instead, seeing someone else preaching from the pulpit simply increased her sense of loss, but she knew how it would hurt Harry if she stopped attending, so she continued to go twice every Sunday, morning and evening, and sometimes popped in during the week and knelt for a moment to say a prayer or two. She told herself that it was too early to find the comfort she sought and glanced up at the kitchen clock, hoping that the girls would be in soon from their walk, for today they would miss the evening service in order to hold their conference, and she felt half guilty, half pleased, that she would not have to go out again into the damp, grey day.

She was just wondering whether there was sufficient food on the table when she heard the clatter of shoes on the outside staircase, and presently all three girls came into the room. Seraphina looked beautiful, her rich dark gold hair misted with tiny drops and her cheeks flushed from hurrying. Behind her, Angie was taking off the blue headscarf she had tied over her pale blonde curls and, right at the back, Evie was shedding her worn navy blue coat, shaking out her damp hair and then coming over to eye the table hungrily. 'Hey, Mam, why hard boiled eggs, why no meat?' she enquired plaintively. 'There's a tin of Spam in the pantry, I seen it when I were getting the oats out for the breakfast porridge. And what about me mustard and cress? I grew it special and you did say we could have it for tea today, I'm sure you did.'

Martha laughed and, reaching for a towel, began to rub her youngest daughter's wet hair. Evie was a bright little thing and, knowing how tight money had become since her father's death, she had started her own small business. She had cut an old towel into six pieces, soaked each piece beneath the running tap, purchased – Martha hoped she had purchased – several packets of mustard and cress seeds from Woolworths and proceeded to grow her crop. When the mustard and cress was about three inches high, she had harvested it with Martha's kitchen scissors, tied it into penny bunches and sold it, either up and down the Scottie or in the Great Homer Street market. Of course, she then had to work very hard to remove the roots from the pieces of towelling in order to plant a fresh crop and Martha often giggled to herself over her small daughter's new hobby, if you could call it that. But she had to admire Evie's dogged perseverance and had actually suggested throwing away the old towelling and buying fresh material from the market, where a ragged towel would probably cost only a penny or two.

Evie, however, would not take what she plainly considered to be the easy way out and besides, she was somewhat shy of market stallholders at the moment. By a great piece of misfortune she had been standing in Great Homer Street, selling her penny bunches, without realising that similar bunches were being sold for tuppence by a fat and dirty woman in a man's cloth cap, who stood close by. The woman had had the bunches on a tray round her neck – Evie's were carefully displayed in a shallow cardboard box – and when she pounced on her, giving her a good clip round the ear and telling her that she was ruining her trade, Evie had been both shocked and frightened . . . at first, that was. Martha had been indignant when Evie had told how she had got her bruised cheek, but Evie had shaken her head. 'No, Mam, she were right. If some little kid had fetched up along o' me selling bunches for a ha'penny, I'd ha' give her a clout meself an' sent her on her way. We've all got a living to make, d'you see? Why, when spring comes, I'm going into the country on Sundays to cut watercress from a running stream, 'cos the old feller what sells ducks' eggs and trussed chickens and bags of corn for popping says folk are so fed up eating nothing but sprouts an' winter cabbage that they'll pay threepence a bunch for water-cress, if it's fresh, that is.'

'But if you pick it on a Sunday an' sell it the following Saturday, it won't *be* fresh,' Angela, who had been listening to the conversation with some amusement, had remarked.

She clearly thought she had put her little sister in her place, but Evie was having none of it. The little girl had sniffed scornfully. 'I shall keep it in the sink, in a big bowl, and water it every day and I shan't take the roots off till the Sat'day morning,' she had announced, giving her sister a withering glance. 'I'm not daft, Angela Todd.'

And she was most definitely not daft, Martha reflected now as Evie fished a bowl out from under the sink and placed her mustard and cress triumphantly on the table. Martha was proud of Seraphina's beauty and brains, and proud of Angela's creativity, for her middle daughter sketched and painted very well indeed and her dressmaking was so good that she could have taken it up as a career. Martha also admired Angela's soft, appealing prettiness and the way she stuck to her work at Bunney's even though she found it hard, but most of all Martha admired little Evie. Her small monkey face could never be described as pretty, and no matter how well fed she might be she remained skinny and scrawny. She was not clever, her school-work being merely average, but she was quick-witted and hard-working and would, Martha found herself thinking, do very well in whatever career she decided to take up, even if it were only growing mustard and cress or running a stall at the Great Homer Street market.

Martha bustled over to the stove where the teapot waited to be filled with water from the hissing kettle. She made the tea and poured four mugs of it, then added conny-onny and handed a mug to each of her daughters, taking the last one herself. As she handed Evie hers, it occurred to her for the first time that in the old days she had always made four cups of tea and a smaller one, of milk and water, for Evie. Ever since Harry's death, however, Evie had insisted upon drinking tea and now Martha realised that this was another example of Evie's thoughtfulness. It would have been horrid to pour only three mugs of tea, because it would have been yet another acknowledgement that her dearest Harry had gone for good.

'Who's saying grace?' Seraphina said, as they settled themselves round the table. Harry had insisted that, as soon as a child was old enough, they should take a turn at saying grace before each meal.

Martha looked round the table, trying to recall who had said grace at breakfast, but Evie was before her. 'It's me, which is really lucky since it's my mustard and cress,' she said proudly. 'Mam, when I grow up, I'm going to buy a farm. Then I'll be able to send you all the eggs you want and butter instead of margarine, and lovely fresh veggies and things. Or p'raps you could give up your job with Mr Wilmslow and come and live with me? That 'ud be nice, wouldn't it?'

'Very nice; but right now you might remember that no one can start until you've said grace,' Martha reminded her.

Evie heaved a dramatic sigh but closed her eyes, clasped her hands and spoke rapidly and in none too pious a tone. 'For what we are about to receive, may the Lord make us truly thankful, amen,' she gabbled. Then she opened her eyes. 'Wharrabout the Spam, Mam?' She giggled at the rhyme. 'Though I suppose eggs an' cress go better together than Spam 'n' cress.'

Martha reached across the table and began helping herself to bread and margarine, motioning her daughters to follow suit, and presently there was silence save for munching noises and requests to pass the salt and pepper. However, by the time the worst of their hunger was satisfied, the girls were chattering once more. 'I met me pal Percy on the way back from church,' Evie remarked presently. She glanced, diffidently, up at her mother. 'I – I know you don't want to talk about it, Mam, but times is awful hard for them, with their dad in prison and no proper money coming in. Mrs Baldwin takes any job she can get, but Percy was saying folks won't give her a job because of what Mr Baldwin did.' Martha noticed that the colour had risen in her small daughter's cheeks and that her eyes were very bright, and guessed she was holding back tears. 'That ain't right, is it, Mam? Pa would have said about the sins of the fathers . . . you know.'

Martha sighed and got to her feet, beginning to clear the table. 'You've jumped the gun a bit, love, because it's a matter for our family conference,' she said. 'Still, we'll get this lot cleared away and then get down to business.'

Presently, the four of them took their places once more at the cleared kitchen table and Martha began to speak. She explained what the girls probably already knew: that without their father's salary coming in regularly, things were going to be very difficult; Seraphina would not be going back to teacher training college when term commenced. It was not solely that they could not afford the fees; they needed the extra money Seraphina could bring in if she took paid work. 'I feel awful about asking you to give up your training,' Martha said, apologetically, to her eldest daughter, 'but although we aren't at war and I hope to God we never will be, there is a factory in the city making uniforms for the armed forces and another making munitions. They pay very good money and if you were fortunate enough to get a job at either one of them, I think we could manage fairly well.'

Angela leaned forward. 'But Ma, why shouldn't I try to get a job in a uniform factory?' she said eagerly. 'I could earn much more than they pay me at Bunney's, I'm sure. And I know I could do the work. If I was earning more, wouldn't that mean Fee could stay on at the college? Only, as you say, it does seem a shame to waste her cleverness on factory work.'

Martha smiled affectionately at her second daughter. 'I don't think I actually did say that, my dear, but I expect I implied it.' She paused, not wanting to pour cold water upon Angela's idea, and whilst she hesitated Seraphina broke in.

'It's all right, Angie. I realised weeks ago – well, when Pa died – that I shouldn't be able to continue at college. Mr Quennell, the principal, realised it as well, so he called me to his office.' She turned eagerly to her mother. 'I didn't say anything at the time because I thought you might decide to go back aboard the *Mary Jane*, but you've made it pretty clear over the past few weeks that you don't mean to do that.'

'We couldn't manage aboard the *Mary Jane* without your father's strength and knowledge, and besides, I couldn't do that to Hetty and Jim – take away their livelihood, I mean,' Martha said. 'Oh, I know we all miss the canal and the barge most dreadfully, but your father decided on a life ashore for good, practical reasons and I'm sure we all agree that Pa never acted rashly, so we'll continue to follow the path he chose for his family.' She turned to Seraphina. 'Well, dearest? Just what did your principal say?'

'He said there are things called bursaries and grants which are available to intelligent young people who want to teach but cannot afford the fees,' Seraphina said, blushing brightly. 'I told him I didn't think I'd be able to apply for such a grant because you need the wages I would bring in if I got a job, but he's most awfully sensible, Ma, and really very nice. He suggested that I should leave the college now and reapply next year, putting in for a bursary at the same time and explaining our changed circumstances. He says he's certain there is a war coming and, when it does, everything will change. All the young men will go into the forces so if they are to keep the college open they will need girls to train up as teachers more than ever.'

Martha reached across the table and clasped her daughter's hand tightly. For a moment she did not trust her voice; dear Seraphina! Some girls might have insisted that they be allowed to continue their training, particularly since a grant would presumably pay for most, if not all, of her fees. But Seraphina was generous and understanding. Martha realised that when the family had first settled round the table to have their conference, she had felt sure she was the unluckiest and unhappiest woman in Liverpool. Now, she knew she was one of the luckiest, to have three such wonderful daughters. She knew there were folk on the canal who had thought that she and Harry were over-indulgent parents, giving their daughters not only love and support, but also all the material possessions they could afford. They had gone out of their way to see that the girls attended school every day during term time, even though it meant sometimes travelling quite long distances, morning and evening. Homework was always done, even though the teacher who handed it out might not see the work for two or three weeks, and whenever they were moored in a big city, Harry and Martha had seen to it that the girls visited museums and galleries – even theatres, if the money would run to it – and had introduced them to the joys of really good libraries.

And now I'm reaping the benefit, Martha thought, squeezing Seraphina's slim fingers. Fee is willing to give up her place at college; Angie, who is so shy and timid, is prepared to work in a busy factory amongst people she does not know; and even little Evie, bless her, is working away selling mustard and cress, and wants us to do something to help her friend Percy, even though his father . . . his father . . .

'Ma?' Seraphina's voice was gentle. 'What do you think? If I work for a year – well, nearly a year – and then apply for a grant, would I be able to complete my course? Or would you rather I concentrated on bringing in some money for a few years . . . just until Evie reaches fourteen, say.'

'I think we might try Angie's solution,' Martha said

thoughtfully. 'Or have I got it wrong? Can you apply for this grant right now?'

Seraphina shook her head. 'No, I think it's only possible at the beginning of the college year. That's why Mr Quennell made his suggestion.'

'Well, in that case . . .' Martha was beginning when she was interrupted by Angela, her face alight.

'Oh, Ma, then if I go for a job in the factory when Fee does, we'll both be earning good money and that should make it easier – if we save up, I mean – when Fee starts at college again next year. What a blessing it is that we've got this flat.'

Evie, who had scarcely spoken for the last few minutes, nodded her head emphatically. 'Yes, it is a good thing, because all the kids at school say rents is awful high,' she said wisely. 'Only you're not very well paid, are you, Mam? Could you do a factory job, or are you too old?' She looked hopeful. 'If you'd let me, I'd like working in the shop for Mr Wilmslow, even if he didn't pay too well, because it would mean we could keep the flat, and you could earn even more money.'

Martha and the older girls laughed. 'What about school, little monkey face?' Seraphina said mockingly. 'You don't know how lucky you are, young lady! When Angie and I were your age . . .'

'Oh, when Angie and you were my age, you walked a hundred miles to school each day, and only had bread and water for your dinners when you got home,' Evie said sarcastically. 'And the *Mary Jane* was made out of cardboard and leaked at night, and the fishes swam in and nibbled your toes. Anyway, what's the use of school? Half the kids on the canal hardly ever went because it were too awkward. And Mam could teach me evenings, or one of you two could.' She stared defiantly round the table. 'I don't see why I should be the only one not helping my family just because I shan't be eleven till March.'

Angela jumped up from her place and went round the table to give Evie a hug. 'How can you be so daft, queen?' she said. 'Why, look at the money you've earned with your mustard and cress. And you do so much for Ma – you get the messages, find some wonderful bargains amongst the market stalls, earn pennies from the neighbours by taking care of the younger kids when their mams are busy. If it weren't for you, our ma wouldn't be able to work every hour God sends for Mr Wilmslow, because Fee and I will be working a good way from home and shan't get back till late. As it is, you lay the table, peel the spuds, make up the fire . . .'

Martha looked at Evie's face, which was glowing pink. 'Angie's right, my love,' she said, smiling down at her youngest daughter. 'We'd all be lost without you, but even if I was allowed to keep you away from school, I wouldn't do it. Remember, your pa always said education was terribly important, so the last thing I would do is to keep you off school.' A sudden thought assailed her. 'And I don't want you sagging off to do odd jobs to earn a bit extra,' she finished warningly. 'Understand?'

Evie nodded, though her lower lip stuck out. 'All right, Mam,' she muttered. 'But wharrabout Percy? He says he'd work if he could, same as his mam. Only no one won't give him a chance. I thought if there were anything we could do to help . . .'

Martha sighed. She knew what Harry would have said but had to struggle with herself before she spoke. Reg Baldwin was in prison with a charge of murder hanging over his head, though everyone knew it might be reduced to manslaughter if a jury considered that the tragedy was unintentional; an accident, in fact. 'I'll go round and visit Mrs Baldwin, see if there is anything I can do to help,' she said resignedly. After all, Martha knew very well that both his wife and Baldwin's children had suffered grievously from the man's violence. The words had come reluctantly but she was glad she had uttered them when she saw Evie's face light up.

'Oh, Mam, I knew you'd help them if you could,' Evie breathed. 'I told Percy that my mam would do her best. You are good; they'll be so pleased.'

'I may not be able to do anything at all,' Martha said hurriedly. 'We don't have any spare money ourselves, chuck, though I'll take her a bag of potatoes and a slab of my Madeira cake. Then we'll put our heads together, me and Mrs Baldwin, and see if we can come up with something.'

'What about a job in one of these new factories?' Seraphina said. 'Only . . . I hope it isn't one of the factories where Angie and myself mean to try for jobs.' She caught her mother's reproachful eye and coloured. 'Sorry, Ma, that was a nasty thing to say,' she said humbly. 'I didn't really mean it. I'm sure we shall all be pleased if Percy's mother gets any sort of job.'

Martha was as good as her word. She worked in the shop as usual all day Monday and then, after tea, she set off to walk to Cavendish Court. Evie had offered to accompany her, but she decided the child's presence might be rather awkward, so she set off alone. She wore her old black coat and the dark purple cloche hat she had worn for years on the canal boat, since its head-hugging shape meant that it was unlikely to blow off, and she carried a huge black umbrella because it had rained, intermittently, all day, and clearly intended to do so all evening.

Martha walked briskly, dodging the puddles. Evie had given her explicit directions so she had no fear of missing her destination and she walked purposefully, eager to get her errand performed so that she might return to her own fireside.

It had been a funny sort of day, she reflected as she walked along the darkened street. Mr Wilmslow had sent her through to the back to help his wife a couple of times, something he never did normally. However, the nurse who looked after Mrs Wilmslow had contracted a heavy cold – possibly influenza – which she did not wish to pass on to her patients, so anyone with a moment to spare had been pressed into service. Because Mr Wilmslow was such a disagreeable sort of man, his customers resented being asked to pop into the back for a word with Mrs Wilmslow, though most of them complied. Mrs Symonds, a cheerful, red-headed woman, who seemed to get along well with everyone, had confided in Martha that long ago, before she became ill, Mrs Wilmslow had been a cheerful, chatty little body, who loved working in the shop and took a keen interest in her customers. 'Which is more than the old feller does, miserable old git,' she said. She spoke rather too loudly for comfort and Martha had hushed her involuntarily. Mrs Symonds had laughed, revealing several broken and blackened teeth. 'Don't you worrit yourself, Miz Todd,' she had said. 'He'll be in that little scullery place of theirs, mashin' the tea. But as I were sayin', old customers, like meself, remember Ruby when she were fit 'n' well, so wharrever we does, we does for her.' She had been gazing at Martha with frank curiosity, her head a little tilted to one side, like a thrush listening for worms, Martha thought, amused. 'Miz Todd, wharrever have you done to your hair?'

'I haven't done anything; it just happened,' Martha had said uncomfortably. She had never believed the stories she had heard of men and women whose hair turned white overnight after some shocking or terrible experience, and indeed, it had not happened to her quite that precipitately. But in the three months since Harry's death two wings of white had appeared, one on each side of her auburn head.

'Well, if you ask me, working for that old bugger back there is enough to turn anyone's hair white,' Mrs Symonds said, with all her usual frankness. She had caught Martha's eye and the already bright colour had deepened in her round cheeks. 'Sorry, queen; I weren't thinkin'. You've had a deal more to bear than a stingy boss. We looks in the *Echo* every night, Mr Symonds and meself, but they've not brought him to trial yet. Eh, I hope they top the evil bugger.'

Martha had opened her mouth to make some soothing, Christian reply, and had heard, with horror, her voice saying, emphatically: 'So do I.' So she was glad when Mr Wilmslow came through from behind the shop, remarking tartly as he did so that if Mrs Todd had nothing better to do than gossip with the customers, she might fetch a box of tinned peas through from the storeroom and begin restacking the shelves.

Now, Martha, who had been glancing up at the street names as she passed them, turned left into Lawrence Street and then almost immediately left again into Cavendish Court. She saw with some dismay that the houses were both tiny and tumble-down, though they were three storeys high which meant, she supposed, that despite the narrowness of the façade they could hold a family. Some courts, she knew, had rear yards which were reached via a narrow jigger, but these houses were known as back-to-backs and visitors had no alternative but to use the front door. Accordingly, she mounted the three grimy steps in front of No. 9, searched for a knocker and, failing to find one, rapped sharply on the door panel with her knuckles. There was a long pause, during which she could hear the mutter of subdued voices and guessed that the only people who came calling on the Baldwins were unwelcome tradesmen requiring payment, or the landlord wanting his rent. Martha hesitated. She was about to try the door handle when a face appeared at the window on her left; a face she knew. She stepped towards the window, then realised that the boy would be unlikely to recognise her beneath the canopy of the black umbrella and lowered it, snapping it shut and feeling raindrops dribbling down the back of her neck. 'It's me, Percy, Mrs Todd,' she said, leaning close to the glass. 'Let me in before I'm soaked to the skin.'

There was a scuffle and then the door opened a cautious inch. 'Me mam's took off,' Percy said hoarsely. 'She thinks you're a-goin' to tell her it's all her fault that Mr Todd's dead. She's rare sorry but she's so skeered that there's no talkin' sense to her.'

He would had closed the door again, was beginning to do so, but Martha was having none of it. If the canal did nothing else for a woman, it gave her strength, she told herself grimly, putting her shoulder to the closing door. 'Oh no you don't, young feller-me-lad,' she said cheerfully. 'I'm coming in and you can just fetch out your ma from wherever she's hiding because there's no way out of a back-to-back save through the front door, and I've not walked all this way, in the rain and the wind, just to turn round and go home again.'

Percy sighed deeply. 'She's in the parlour . . . in there,' he whispered, pointing to the door, firmly closed, on Martha's right. 'Don't be cross. Things is bad for us, and me mam's norra strong woman. Meself, I think we're all a deal better off without me dad, but . . .'

He stopped speaking as the knob of the parlour door began to turn. Slowly, creakingly, the door opened a short way and a tuft of faded fair hair and the tip of a pink and trembling nose appeared round it. 'Has she gone?' a nervous voice enquired in a husky whisper. 'Oh, I'm near dead of fright. I'm sorry to run off, chuck, but I just couldn't face the reproaches.'

Percy's eyes rolled wildly but before he could speak Martha had stepped forward and pushed the door wide, inserting herself into the gap so that it could not be slammed again. 'Don't you worry yourself, Mrs Baldwin,' she said gently. 'I don't deny that what happened was a terrible, terrible thing, but I reckon it was no fault of yours.' She smiled encouragingly at the other woman. Mrs Baldwin was tiny and skinny with a thin, weaselly face, fair hair going grey and a look of permanent anxiety. She was wearing down-at-heel slippers and her skimpy brown dress was almost hidden beneath a huge and filthy calico apron. 'Why don't we go into your kitchen where, no doubt, there's a nice fire burning and you can make us a cup of tea while we have a chat?'

Two hours later, Martha waved goodbye to Mrs Baldwin and set off across the court. As soon as she had entered the kitchen, she had seen that things were in a bad way. The room was filthy, the sink full of dirty dishes and the fire almost out. A line of wet washing was slung, precariously, across the room, the clothing dripping sullenly. And on the hearthrug, a boy of about six and a tiny girl played with some sticks of kindling wood. She had glanced, hopefully, at her hostess, who had gazed back with lacklustre eyes, so Martha had taken it upon herself to get things moving.

She took off her hat and coat and rolled up her sleeves. 'Percy, fetch some coal in, and a bucket of water,' she said briskly. 'Ron – I take it you must be Ron – find a brush and dustpan so I can sweep this floor while I wait for the kettle to boil.' She turned to her hostess. 'You sit in the chair, my dear, and nurse the little girl, whilst Percy, Ron and myself get things sorted out. Have you eaten yet? No? Then as soon as I've got things straightened out here, we'll settle down for a talk over a nice cup of tea and the Madeira cake which I've brought with me.'

Mrs Baldwin had uttered a feeble protest but had been glad enough to hand over to Martha, and surprisingly quickly a fire was roaring in the grate, the kettle was beginning to steam and the room, if not spotless, was at least a good deal cleaner than it had been upon her arrival. The two women had seated themselves at the table whilst Percy got the younger ones into bed. Then they had settled down to talk; Martha had been sure the other woman would find it much easier to discuss her situation if her children were out of the way.

'Now, Mrs Baldwin, you and I can get down to business. I understand you have no job at present.' Martha had glanced enquiringly across at Mrs Baldwin. Once, she had no doubt been a pretty, energetic woman, but fifteen years of marriage to a brute and a bully had shattered her nerves and given her no faith whatsoever in her own ability to so much as scrub a floor.

'No, I ain't in work right now, Mrs Todd,' the younger woman had agreed meekly. 'And I know I've let everything gerron top o' me, but it's havin' no money and Mr Baldwin always sneerin' at me . . . it takes the heart out of a woman, that sort of treatment. I used to clean a couple o' pubs, which kept a bit o' money comin' in, but then, at the beginning of December, I heared two fellers talkin', and – and next mornin' I didn't go in. They was talkin' about Mr Baldwin, an' I was just so skeered . . .'

She had stopped speaking. Martha had waited a moment and then prompted her. 'So you waited a day or two and then went back,' she had suggested. 'What did the landlord say?'

'I didn't go back for nigh on a fortnight,' Mrs Baldwin had confessed miserably. 'Christmas is their busiest time o' year, so they'd replaced me, a'course.'

'Well, it's not Christmas now and we're at the start of a new year. Tomorrow, I'll get Mr Wilmslow to give me a bit of time off and I'll go round to those pubs with you. I'll explain that you've been very poorly – they'll understand why – and I'm sure the landlords will give you a few hours. Once you're working again, you can ask around, see if anyone else needs a hand. Market stallholders are always glad of someone reliable and honest who can take over while they have a bit of a break.' She had smiled encouragingly at the younger woman. 'And you'll be a deal better when you've got a proper job to keep your mind occupied. Is there someone who could look after little Emmy while you work?'

'Oh aye, the neighbours is good; they'll give an eye to Emmy,' Mrs Baldwin had said eagerly. 'Percy was right, Mrs Todd, you're a real nice lady. An' you've give me fresh heart.'

'Can you be ready by about a quarter to twelve tomorrow then?' Martha had asked. 'I'll get Mr Wilmslow to release me from half-past eleven, but if

I'm a few minutes late don't worry, because I'll be along, no matter what.'

Now, Martha made her way through the dark and rainy streets, feeling that she had done her best. She did not much like the thought of having to ask Mr Wilmslow for a favour, but Monday was always a quiet day in the shop, and if he objected she could remind him of how often she had worked late and how willingly young Evie had helped out after school, without expecting – or getting – any payment for such work. True, Mr Wilmslow usually slipped Evie a custard cream biscuit or a couple of bull's eyes, but this was scarcely adequate payment for an hour or more spent stacking shelves, serving customers, or delivering boxes of groceries, though the last had only happened on the run up to Christmas when folk were ordering more than they could carry themselves.

When Martha re-entered the flat, it was to find Evie all agog to hear how the visit had gone. 'It's a horrible, awful ugly place, ain't it, Mam?' she enquired eagerly when Martha told her story. 'Of course, you only saw it at night, but in the daytime it's criss-crossed with lines of washing, and the brick and the cobbles are black with soot. Did you like Mrs Baldwin? I like Percy ever so much but I've never seen his mam. Is she like him to look at?'

'No, not a bit,' Martha said, taking off her coat and hat and draping both garments over the clothes horse which stood before the fire. 'But she seems a pleasant enough person. I'm going round there tomorrow, if Mr Wilmslow will give me an hour or two off, and I reckon she'll be working again quite soon.'

Evie gave a tremendous yawn. 'Thanks ever so much, Mam, for helping. And now I'm off to bed.'

Martha rumpled her youngest's hair affectionately;

both the older girls had gone off to bed already, knowing that they would have to be up betimes next morning, but Evie did not start school for two more days. 'Yes, you run off,' she said. 'And have a bit of a lie-in in the morning; it'll do you good.'

Chapter Five

'Mr Wilmslow, I wonder if I could have a word before you open up?' Martha asked as soon as she entered the shop next morning. 'I'd like an hour or so off, say from half-past eleven until two.'

Mr Wilmslow had been piling tinned peas into a pyramid, but at her words he stopped short, his greying eyebrows flying up towards his hairline, and then descending over his brows in a deep frown. 'Whatever do you want time off for? God knows, you've only just had your Christmas holiday,' he said bleakly. 'And here's me never taking so much as five minutes, always on call . . . why, even at night there's Mrs Wilmslow wanting this that or the other. So what do you want time off for, eh? I gives you an hour for your dinner, though what you do with yourself for a whole hour . . . time to eat a four-course banquet—'

The tirade ended abruptly when Martha cleared her throat meaningly. 'Monday isn't a busy day, Mr Wilmslow,' she reminded him. 'And you know I work late whenever you're busy. In the run up to Christmas, it was almost eight o'clock some nights before I got up to the flat and all I'm asking for is an extra hour or so to tack on to my dinner break. Surely you can manage without me just this once.'

Mr Wilmslow began to mutter that the hour she mentioned might well be the thin end of the wedge; that, having squeezed extra time off out of him, she might repeat the exercise whenever she felt inclined.

Martha wisely held her tongue. Protestations were useless because Mr Wilmslow knew very well that she would never behave in such a manner. And presently his monologue mumbled into silence. He balanced the last tin of peas on top of his pyramid, stepped back to admire it and knocked the top three tins of baked beans off the pyramid behind him. Martha giggled, but so quietly that she did not think he had heard until he turned and gave her a grudging smile. 'So you think it's funny, do you?' he said, rebalancing the tins of baked beans with pernickety care. He came across the shop, lifted the flap and came round the counter to stand beside her. 'Well, I dare say, just this once, I'll spare you for an hour.' He leered at her. 'So long as you ain't goin' to meet some feller . . . I don't believe in me staff havin' followers.'

Martha stared at him in blank astonishment. How could he possibly make such a stupid and dreadful remark? But then she realised that he was trying to make a joke, trying to give her the time off and ask why she wanted it without sounding too curious. So she turned to the shelf behind her and began making a space for some goods she had just brought in. 'I'm going to see the wife of one of my husband's fellow workers,' she said quietly. 'She's in need of a bit of help.'

She was about to enlarge on this statement without admitting upon whom she would be calling, when she felt a hand slide along her waist. She stiffened and turned sharply, but Mr Wilmslow had removed his hand as soon as she moved and now said testily: 'Very well, very well, I said you may have the time off, but I do think, in return . . .'

The tinkling of Mrs Wilmslow's bell interrupted him, followed by her frail but undoubtedly irritable voice.

'Arthur? I dropped me perishin' knitting and I can't reach it! Mr Wilmslow, will you come!'

Mr Wilmslow heaved an exaggerated sigh. 'This'll be the fifth bedjacket she's knitted an' never finished since she were first took bad,' he muttered. 'Oh, I s'pose I'd better go . . . I'll put the kettle on whiles I'm out at the back, since I never had time for breakfast this morning.'

Martha watched his angular back disappearing through the swinging curtain. She knew that he probably spoke the truth when he said he had not had breakfast that morning. His first job, as he often told her, was to see to his wife, and when she was in one of her more demanding moods he did not have time to get himself so much as a drink before the shop had to be opened. She wondered what he had been about to say when his wife's bell rang, but then the doorbell tinkled as a customer came in and very soon she had other things to think about, for Mrs O'Mara was a good customer who bought almost all her groceries from Wilmslow's grocery store. However, she would not buy anything new without testing it, peering at it, and shaking its container, and when Martha was weighing up flour, sugar or lentils, would insist upon such items being weighed more than once, and would then peer, suspiciously, into the bags as though suspecting that something quite different had somehow managed to substitute itself for the goods she had actually ordered.

Despite Martha's saying that Mondays were always quiet, they had a brisk flow of customers for most of the morning, and when the hands of the clock crept round to half-past eleven Martha was quite worried that Mr Wilmslow would change his mind and tell her she would simply have to stay. She was not at all sure what she would do if that were the case, but as it happened there was only one customer in the shop at the time – a woman wanting two pounds of macaroni – and Mr Wilmslow waved Martha away, saying gruffly: 'I'll deal with this. I doubt you've had the forethought to bring your coat and hat downstairs, so you'd best go an' fetch 'em, 'cos any fool can see it's mortal cold out there. And I want you back on the dot, or I'll be obliged to dock you two and a half hours' wages.'

'Thanks, Mr Wilmslow, I shan't be late,' Martha gabbled, hurrying out of the shop and clattering up the metal stairs.

It had been raining earlier but now it was simply cold and grey, and when she shot into the flat Martha was not surprised to find Evie sitting at the kitchen table, with an exercise book and several old newspapers spread out before her. She beamed at her mother as Martha entered the room. 'I'm doin' me holiday tasks,' she explained, indicating the newspapers with a wave of her hand. 'It's current . . . current affairs. Me teacher wants to know what's happening in Europe and as much as we can find out about that German feller . . . Mr Hitler, I mean.' She glanced at the clock above the mantel. 'You're early, Mam. It's not dinnertime for another hour.'

'No, and I'm afraid you'll have to make your own dinner today,' Martha said apologetically, reaching up for her hat and coat. 'I'm off to see Mrs Baldwin and when I come back I shall have to start work at once, so I'm afraid it'll have to be a cheese sandwich or something for you, my love.'

'I'm coming with you, Mam,' Evie said at once, rushing to the hook to fetch down her own coat. 'Me an' Percy can buy a penn'orth of chips 'cos I've got tuppence.'

Martha began to object but then saw her small daughter's face fall and changed her mind. She was guiltily aware that Evie must often be lonely because life ashore was so different from life on the canal. On the *Mary Jane* they were together all day as a family; Evie would lead the horse, help with the cooking, washing and cleaning, go with one of her sisters or a friend to pick berries from the hedgerows or fetch the messages. She would almost never be alone, whereas now, with her mother working full time, Angela doing the same, and Seraphina, even now, out looking for a job, Evie was frequently left to her own devices. So she smiled at her daughter whilst buttoning her own coat and said equably: 'I'll give you another tuppence, then you and Percy can have a positive feast! But we'll have to hurry; I promised Mrs Baldwin I'd be there by quarter to twelve.'

Presently, mother and daughter jumped aboard a number 23 tram heading for Lawrence Street, and were soon knocking on the door of No. 9, Cavendish Court, which was opened by a beaming Percy. He had scarcely begun to speak, however, when his mother put him gently aside and stepped out into the court. Martha saw, approvingly, that Mrs Baldwin had made a real effort to tidy herself up. Her light-coloured hair was pulled back from her face and tied into a knot with what looked suspiciously like a black shoe lace, her face was clean and she was wearing a black dress and cracked, down-at-heel black shoes. The dress, although faded and shabby, was clean, with white collar and cuffs, though Martha's keen eye saw that these were made of paper, and Mrs Baldwin had also had a go at polishing her shoes. Martha smiled at the younger woman. 'You look grand, my dear,' she said heartily. 'I'll leave Evie here, in Percy's charge, while we do our business.' She smiled at Evie. 'Stay with Percy, love, and try not to get into mischief.' She turned back to Mrs Baldwin. 'Where's Ron and Emmy?'

'Next door,' Mrs Baldwin said briefly. Martha began to move away but Mrs Baldwin stopped her, a hand on her arm and a stricken look on her face. 'I didn't get them nothing for their dinners,' she said huskily. 'I – I didn't think, money being so short an' all. What's more, the fire's gone out . . . I saves what little coal I've got left for evenings, when everyone's home. I don't reckon it's as cold during the day as it gets when darkness comes.'

'It's all right, Mrs Baldwin,' Evie said cheerfully, before her mother could speak. 'Mam gave me some money to buy chips so we'll get our dinners all right. And if we goes across to the market, we might be give a couple of orange boxes to chop up for kindling. Then we can sell 'em, a ha'penny a bundle.'

'Don't you dare go to the market, young Evie, or not until Mrs Baldwin and I come back, at any rate,' Martha said reprovingly. ' I want you here when I call for you, not gallivanting off selling chips from door to door.'

Evie giggled. 'That's odd, ain't it, Mam? You've give us money for chips, the potato sort, an' I were going to *get* money for chips by selling the wooden sort. But you'll be gone an hour or more, won't you? Tell you what, Perce an' meself will go over to the market first and see if we can cadge a couple of boxes off of someone, then we'll buy us chips to eat and come back here. We can break the boxes down into kindling while we wait for you and then sell the bundles round the houses later.'

'Yes, all right,' Martha agreed, as the four of them

turned out into Lawrence Street. She addressed Percy. 'If your mam gets some work – and I'm sure she will – then you'd best buy some coal. Do you have an old pram, or a stirring cart, or something?'

Percy shook his head regretfully. 'No, we ain't got nothin' like that. But if I get half a sack I reckon I can carry it meself.'

Martha eyed him, doubting that he could carry half a sack of spuds, let alone coals, but it would have been tactless to say so. Instead she said: 'Right you are, then. Now keep out of mischief and we'll see you later.'

When their mothers had gone, Percy and Evie eyed each other speculatively, then Evie grinned. 'When did you last buy coal, Percy Baldwin?' she asked derisively. 'My dad were a lay preacher so my mum don't know nothin' about how ordinary people live. I bet you've been nickin' coal from the goods yard ever since you were old enough to scramble over the wall and wriggle across the railings; ain't that right?'

Percy stiffened indignantly. 'No that ain't right,' he said. 'Me dad were on good money and Mam always got him to buy the coal because he could get it brung home, or even delivered, and no one could expect my mam to cart anything that heavy. Mind you, since he's been – been . . .' his eyes slid around wildly, whilst a tide of colour swept across his face, 'been away, I've climbed that wall more'n once.'

'So've I, though me mam would kill me if she knew,' Evie said cheerfully. 'The thing is, we've got nowhere to keep coal, no yard, no scullery, nothing like that. And the flat's awful small. So Mam gives me money for enough coal to last the week and sends me out with Billy – he's Mr Wilmslow's delivery boy – to buy it. Of course we does buy it most of the time, but Billy's one of eleven kids, you know, and his mam's awful hard up. Nickin' coal from the goods yard behind Exchange station is a two-man job really, so I goes along with Billy and he pops the extra coal into me mam's bag as a sort of thank you for me keeping douse while he and his brother fill their sack.'

Percy gave her a glance of considerable respect. 'I thought you were going to say you'd nicked it off of the coal barges,' he said. 'That 'ud be a deal easier than climbin' that perishin' wall.' He looked her up and down consideringly. 'You're no taller than me, you might even be a bit shorter, an' I'm tellin' you, climbin' that wall is a killer. You don't want to try it; bein' a girl, you'd probably fall an' break both your legs.'

'I wouldn't steal from a coal barge,' Evie said, sounding as scandalised as she felt. 'They're me pals, the folk on the canal. Still an' all, you're right, it 'ud be a whole lot easier. And I wouldn't mind nickin' a bit of coal from Izzy Evans, because he's a hateful, dirty old wretch, and so's his wife, and so's his sons.'

'Izzy Evans? Who's he when he's at home?' Percy said, as the two of them joined the queue outside the fried fish shop. 'Reckon you know everyone on the canal, don't you? Reckon you know everyone's cargo 'n' all.'

'Izzy Evans carries coal down to the docks from the pits up in Yorkshire,' Evie said briefly. 'And yes, I reckon I knows what cargo most boats carry. But I wouldn't steal from anyone, 'cept Izzy Evans – oh, and maybe old Fitch, because he swore at me dad once, when me pa was leggin' the *Mary Jane* through a tunnel, lying on his back with drips from the roof bouncing off him. Old Fitch wanted to pass and Dad wouldn't let him;

it's too narrow, see, and the *Mary Jane* and one of the butty boats might have been damaged.'

'Leggin'? Butty boats?' Percy said plaintively. 'Wharrever d'you mean, queen?'

'Percy Baldwin, you're more'n two years older'n me and you don't know the half of what I does,' Evie said, but she was smiling. 'When the canal boat goes through a tunnel you have to unhitch the horse from the boat so's someone can lead it along the towpath. Now most of the boats don't have engines, not if they've got a horse, that is, so the barge master lies on his back, on the roof of the boat, an' pushes the boat along by . . . by . . . walking along the underside of the bridge. You have to be real strong to do it. And butty boats are the ones which the canal barges tow behind them.' She chuckled. 'Me dad used to say it were like a duck with a couple o' little 'uns. Butty boats have a small cabin but no stove or nothin' like that. Now d'you understand?'

'Aye, that's plain enough,' Percy said, as the two of them reached the top of the queue. 'My, don't them chips smell good. I'll have lots of salt 'n' vinegar on mine; how about you?'

By the end of the day, Seraphina was worn out and cross. She had thought it would be a simple matter for a girl who had actually been in teacher training college to get a job, but she had reckoned without the after-Christmas inertia which afflicts shoppers when the festive season is over and the cold of January really begins to bite. After trying the uniform factory to no avail she had visited what felt like a hundred shops, only to be turned down in each one, though a hairdresser on Bold Street, admiring the great mass of her golden hair, had made her two offers. The first was to buy her hair, should she decide to sell it, and the next was to take her on as an apprentice. The latter would involve on the spot training and would eventually lead to her being able to either work for a good wage in a hairdressing salon, or possibly open her own business.

This had sounded like an excellent scheme until the proprietress told her that she would work for several years for a minuscule wage – and work long hours, furthermore. Regretfully, Seraphina declined the offer. Then she had tried the big department stores and moved on to smaller shops and cafés, still without success. She had walked up and down Church Street, where the really lovely shops were, and had finally decided to give up, for today at any rate. In fact, so worn out had she been that she had thought she would treat herself to a cup of tea and a bun in Lyon's Corner House.

Now, taking a corner seat, she allowed herself to relax for the first time that day, and glanced around her. The place was packed and the waitress who brought Seraphina her pot of tea and sticky currant bun was in such a hurry that she knocked into another waitress, sending her tray flying. Seraphina knew that the girls were called 'nippies' and could see why, for, without fuss, the girl who was serving Seraphina swerved round the mess, swiftly unloaded her tray, and then turned back and began to pile broken crockery and bits of food on to it before hurrying back through the swing doors at the end of the restaurant. The girl who had been bumped into made no attempt to help, but slouched off, to be stopped before she had gone far by an elderly woman in a black dress who must be, Seraphina supposed, a supervisor of some description. 'Come to my office, Miss Nugent,' she said briskly.

'This really will not do, you know. I've had to speak to you seven times in three days, and—'

'And you can stick your bleedin' job where the monkey stuck his nuts,' the girl said rudely, her voice unnecessarily loud. 'You treat us girls like bleedin' slaves, wi' never a word o' praise, and it's nag, nag, nag from the moment we gerrin until we limps off home to soak our bleedin' corns in a bleedin' mustard bath.'

Seraphina watched sympathetically as a slow tide of red blotched the older woman's neck and face. 'Very well, Miss Nugent, if that's how you feel I shall not need to tell you to leave,' she said stiffly. 'Since today is only Monday, I would normally expect you to work your week, but after the way you have spoken . . . your rudeness . . . your bad language . . .'

'I wouldn't stay if you paid me treble,' Miss Nugent shouted. 'I wouldn't stay if you went down on your bloody bended knees an' begged me. I wouldn't stay . . .'

The noise she was making was so loud that every eye was upon her and all conversation hushed, and Seraphina was not surprised when a man emerged from the swing doors at the back of the restaurant and came rapidly towards the pair. Miss Nugent turned to him and began to reiterate everything she had said, but it seemed he was having none of it. He caught her by the shoulders, whisked her round and virtually pushed her across the restaurant and through the swing doors, still protesting volubly and telling the man, who seemed to be called Mr Grundy, that it was no manner of use his trying to bully her and she would have a full week's pay in lieu of notice or he would find himself in deep trouble . . . she had friends in high places, so she did.

The older woman had followed the other two out

through the swing doors, and Seraphina half expected her to emerge from them again, seconds later, bowing, smiling and blowing kisses, as actresses do for a curtain call at the end of a show. However, nothing of the sort happened, and presently two nippies emerged with laden trays and conversation became general once more.

Seraphina began to sip her tea and then a thought struck her. The restaurant was crowded already and would be more so later, when folk wanted an evening meal. The manager, if Mr Grundy was the manager, was now one nippy short. She, Seraphina, was looking for a job. She was young and strong and fully capable of carrying out the work required, so why should she not apply immediately and offer to start work at once?

Accordingly, Seraphina finished her tea, gobbled her bun, paid the waitress and then asked her whether it would be possible to have a few words with Mr Grundy. The girl looked doubtful. 'If it's a complaint . . .' she began, but Seraphina shook her head, smiling.

'No, indeed it is not,' she said. 'In fact, I thought everyone – except Miss Nugent, of course – behaved beautifully, just as they ought. But I can see that you are going to be hard pressed, with a member of staff short, and – and I have been meaning to start looking for a job, so if Mr Grundy would consider me . . .'

The girl smiled. 'I'll take you through to his office right now,' she said eagerly. 'Miss Nugent were at the start of her shift but I'm at the end of mine and I just know Miss Peabody – she's the supervisor – will be asking me to work till closing time and I really do want to get away because my young man is taking me to see the panto at the Empire this evening and the show starts at seven. I'm Nellie Bradshaw, by the way, and you . . . ?'

Seraphina hesitated. She hated telling strangers her shame-making name and wished, for the thousandth time, that her father had not seen, in his tiny, newborn daughter, a likeness to the seraphs and angels depicted in his family Bible. Unfortunately, having christened her Seraphina, he had claimed that his second daughter, too, had the face of a tiny angel and had christened her Angela, another fancy name. In fact, Evie was the only lucky one. Her father had immediately referred to her as his little cherub, but Martha, far more practical than he, said that Cherubima, or Cherubetta, would be going too far. 'And she's got the face of a baby monkey, nothing like a cherub at all, so we'll call her . . . Joan? Janet?'

'We could call her Eve, after the very first woman on this earth,' Harry Todd had said gently. 'But I didn't mean to call her Cherubima or Cherubetta. I was thinking of Gabrielle – after the angel Gabriel, you know.'

Martha had sniffed. 'A fancy French name isn't going to get her far aboard the *Mary Jane*,' she had pointed out. 'You know how it is, Harry – everyone calls Seraphina Fee, and Angela Angie. Do you want folk calling your daughter Gabby?' Her husband had laughed and given way and his youngest daughter had been christened Eve.

But now, Miss Nellie Bradshaw was looking at her enquiringly and Seraphina took a deep breath and replied, with all her usual directness. 'My name is Seraphina Todd. How do you do, Miss Bradshaw?' Miss Bradshaw said she were fine, thanks, and hurried Seraphina along to the manager's office, where they encountered a red-faced and ranting Miss Nugent emerging. Miss Bradshaw knocked on the door, then threw it open. 'Here's a young lady, Miss Todd, what's keen to work with us,' she said baldly. 'She heard Miss Nugent being dismissed, so thought there might be a chance for her. Can I leave her with you, Mr Grundy? Only the place is filling up and what with Stoker being off with her bronchials, Miss O'Reilly takin' time off to get her tooth pulled, and Miss Nugent stormin' out, we're going to be awful short-handed this evening.'

Sitting behind the desk, Mr Grundy had looked so like a well-boiled and startled prawn that Seraphina had hard work not to smile. He was of medium height and had a great deal of spiky, sandy hair, unfashionable side whiskers, and an enormous moustache, though no beard. His pale blue eyes beneath thick and riotous sandy brows bulged, but he smiled very pleasantly at Seraphina and asked her to sit down. 'Are you healthy and strong? And why did you leave your previous employment?' he asked, shooting the questions at her so rapidly that Seraphina barely had time to consider her replies.

'I'm pretty strong and, I think, very healthy because until six months ago I lived on a barge working the Leeds and Liverpool Canal,' she explained. 'My family came ashore so that I could take a teacher training course, but – but I have been forced to abandon the course for the time being since I need to earn some money. I know your nippies have to be able to run with a loaded tray – or at least to walk extremely quickly – and I'm sure I could do that easily.'

Mr Grundy nodded, then asked some more questions, and at the end of ten minutes or so told Seraphina all about the rates of pay and the hours which she would be asked to work. 'We pay our staff more highly than any other café or restaurant, I believe, because everyone here is always having to hurry,' he told her. 'But the tips are what really keep our nippies happy, because over half of our clients are gentlemen and if you are pleasant and polite they tip extremely generously.' He eyed her up and down, then smiled. 'We will provide you with two black dresses and four frilly white aprons, caps and cuffs, which we will launder for you at the end of each week's work. And with that extraordinarily beautiful hair, I think you will find tips come fast and furious. Can I assume that you'll take the job and start . . . well, at once?'

Seraphina did not hesitate. 'Yes please,' she said. 'But – but what about uniform? If you are thinking that I might use Miss Nugent's dress, I don't think it would do at all. I'm a lot taller than her and a lot thinner as well.'

Mr Grundy smiled indulgently. 'We have a stock of newly laundered uniforms in almost every size,' he said confidently. He got up from behind his desk and went across to the door, gesturing for Seraphina to follow him. 'Miss Peabody is deputy manageress and a kind and capable person. She'll provide you with clothing and put you in the charge of one of the senior girls who will tell you exactly what to do.'

Twenty minutes later, Seraphina checked her appearance in the long mirror by the door of the staff room to which she had been led. The uniform had indeed fitted, and she thought she looked both neat and efficient. Miss O'Donnell, into whose care she had been given, smiled at her through the looking glass. 'You look as if you've been waitressing all your life,' she said cheerfully. 'But all you'll do for now is fetch and carry for me and a couple of the others; we won't let you take orders until you've had a bit more experience. All right? Ready to go?'

'Yes, I'm ready,' Seraphina said. She had got a job

and would be earning a weekly wage, and right now that was the only thing that mattered. Smiling, she followed Miss O'Donnell out of the staff room and into the restaurant.

By the time winter had changed into spring, the Todd family were beginning to settle into their new lives, Martha thought, as she stood in the kitchen, ironing Evie's new blouse. Seraphina had to work shifts but admitted that she really enjoyed the job, though it was undoubtedly extremely hard work. She had begun to have quite a social life for she was often invited out both by the other waitresses and by the young men who frequented the Lyon's Corner House. Angie sometimes went with her and was always much admired, but she was a quiet girl and seemed to have very little interest in young men. Seraphina, on the other hand, enjoyed the dances, visits to the cinema, and trips out on her day off. She still talked about going back into teacher training in the autumn but Martha secretly doubted whether her gay and ebullient daughter would actually do so when the time came. She thought Seraphina would find a classroom full of children dull work after the rush and excitement of being a nippy in a very large restaurant, particularly since, as Mr Grundy had anticipated, she always ended each day with her apron pocket full of tips. Martha looked wistfully towards the window. Outside, a gentle breeze ruffled the leaves which were just beginning to appear on the only tree within sight and she could not help thinking, longingly, of her old life on the canal. In April, there would be primroses and violets on every bank. The grass would be thrusting new shoots, bright and luscious, and the quickthorn hedges would be bursting into vivid green leaf, whilst in those same hedgerows songbirds would be courting, trilling, building their nests. Over the water meadows cuckoos, returning from their African winter, would be swooping on any insects which had emerged into the sunshine, lambs would be frisking in the pastures, and rabbits would be bringing out their young from the darkness of their burrows into the bright spring sunshine.

Dreamily, Martha allowed her mind to wander back, to imagine waking as the sun rose, blinking the sleep out of her eyes and lighting the stove in order to boil a kettle so that they might enjoy a cup of tea with their breakfast. Once she was dressed and the kettle was boiling, she would open the doors at the end of the cabin and glance around, seeing cattle knee-high in white mist, and Gemma, cropping the long grass, turning her great head and greeting her mistress with a gentle whinny. Gemma had known the routine as well as her mistress. Martha would return to the cabin and fetch out a piece of bread, a wrinkled apple or a carrot, and then she would jump off the *Mary Jane* and walk along the towpath to where Gemma was teth-ered. The great black horse would bend her neck to take the titbit and as she crunched would thrust her head against her mistress. Martha could feel the warm satin skin, the horse's soft, whiskery lips on the palm of her hand; for a moment, she could even breathe the clear fresh air of early morning, hear a distant cock crow and the muted sounds of water lapping against the hull of the *Mary Jane*.

'Mam? Do you want me to start the porridge?' Evie's voice brought Martha back to the present with much the same effect as a dousing from a bucket of cold water. She gasped and jumped, eyeing her daughter reproachfully.

'Evie, how you startled me! Can you open the window, love? It's awfully stuffy in here and I was just thinking back to a year ago.' She sighed. 'It's the spring, I suppose. The flat's been cosy during the winter, but now spring is here . . .'

Evie, busy mixing water and oats, nodded. 'I know what you mean, Mam; we all does,' she said. 'The canal is so beautiful at this time of year, with all the country for us to enjoy. But I try not to think about it because it makes me think about Dad and that just makes me miss him worse.'

Martha smiled at her youngest but shook her head. 'No, no, you mustn't ever stop thinking about your father. I certainly shan't. Living with him, talking to him, being loved by him, was the best thing that ever happened to me. I remember him every day, but not with sadness, because that's pointless. We had wonderful times, Evie; d'you remember how your pa used to get me to put up a picnic and take us all off to fish at a little lake he knew of, or to go nutting in the woods? And he loved to help at haymaking, though I know you children hated it at harvest time, when the men clubbed the rabbits for the pot. You mustn't forget times like that, nor let them make you sad, because good memories should be treasured and taken out often, like old photographs, so you can get pleasure from reliving them.'

Evie stared dreamily down at the pan she was stirring for a moment, then nodded briskly. 'You're right, Mam. But when I'm grown up I shan't stay in this place, because I want to make more memories of my own; country memories. I'll go and get a job on a farm or – or marry a farm worker – but I shan't stay in the city.' She must have read her mother's pained and guilty expression, for she said quickly: 'Oh, I know Pa had to bring us here to live so that Fee could go to college and you could save up enough money to buy a cottage in Burscough for your retirement; I understand that, truly I do, but I remember you telling us how cross your mam and dad were when you went and married Pa, and that means you made your own life, doesn't it, Mam? So I'm going to make my own life, one day, and it'll be a country life, no matter what.'

Martha couldn't help laughing at her daughter's expression, which was a mixture of anxious apology and grim determination. Poor kid, she thought, torn two ways. She wants to show me that she understands why we took her away from the life she loved and stuck her down in a big city, far from the countryside which was her birthright. And she also wants me to understand that she means to go back to it as soon as she's old enough. Well, good for her! And if I'm ever in a position to go back myself, I'll do just that. The thought of living above the shop and slaving for old Wilmslow for the rest of my life does not appeal. Aloud, she said: 'You're absolutely right, Evie; everyone has to live their own life and you and your sisters were brought up in the country and have good reason to want to go back when you're able. Or at least, that is the way you feel, but I don't know about Fee and Angie. Fee has a great many friends, both girls and young men, and she enjoys dances, theatres, nice restaurants and so on. I think she might find the country boring now. As for Angie, she never took as much interest in the countryside as the rest of us. She's a real domestic body; she loves housework, sewing, cooking, all that sort of thing. Angie will make someone a wonderful wife, but whether she will choose a countryman or a city dweller I wouldn't like to have to guess. Now how's that porridge coming on?'

She folded the last garment and switched off the iron. It was an electric one, brand new, and Martha's pride and joy. She reckoned she could do double the amount of ironing in half the time it had taken when she had had to use flat irons, heating them before the fire and having to abandon them to be reheated after only ten minutes or so. If they had still been on the barge, of course, there would have been no question of such luxuries as electric irons, electric lights or, indeed, a gas stove, which was the next thing she intended to invest in. Mr Wilmslow had one in his back scullery, and lately she had used it quite often since her employer frequently asked her to go through to the back and cook something for himself and his wife. Since it made a pleasant change from serving in the shop and she was paid just the same, Martha always agreed and really enjoyed using the wonderful gas cooker.

However, she had learned to grow wary of being in the scullery when Mrs Wilmslow was dozing or engaged with a friend, since Mr Wilmslow had taken to 'popping in', ostensibly to see how she was getting on. In the shop, he treated her as he had always done, snapping and snarling if he was in a bad mood, criticising the way she stacked the shelves and arguing that there was no need to be friendly with the customers, though one must not of course ever be rude. If he was in a good mood, he chatted quite amiably, telling her anecdotes about his younger days or about his parents, who had died many years ago. He never attempted any sort of intimacy, never called her by her first name, never asked questions about her life on the canal, or how the girls were getting on, and the same rules, it seemed, applied in the back rooms – except for the scullery.

If Mr Wilmslow came into the scullery when his wife was occupied, he would be a little too friendly, a little too jovial, and the fact that he expressed this in an undertone made Martha uneasy. He never attempted to touch her, the way he had done in the shop three months before, but Martha thought he only held back from any such gesture because of his wife's nearness. Once, Martha had been bending over the oven to take out a meat pie which she had just cooked for the Wilmslows' supper. She had been using a folded tea cloth to prevent her fingers from being burned, and with the pie halfway out the tea towel had slipped sideways. Martha had squeaked with pain and snatched her hand away, and Mr Wilmslow, who had been standing by, holding the plate upon which she would place the pie, had reached forward to take it from her, telling her brusquely to go and run the scorched finger under the tap, 'else it'll blister and you'll be no use for a couple o' days.'

As he took the pie dish from her, his hand had brushed against her arm and he had given her a very strange look from under half-lowered lids whilst his mouth had curved in a small smile. He had started to whisper something but had scarcely got more than two words out when his wife's voice had come, shrilly, from the other room. 'Arthur! Nurse has just left and the shop bell's tinkled twice. If it takes two of you to get me dinner out of the oven, then things have come to a pretty pass, and you've lost us a customer . . . that bell tinkled twice . . .'

Mr Wilmslow had shot out of the scullery like a scalded cat and Martha had gone on preparing the meal, telling herself that nothing would have happened even had Mrs Wilmslow not called out, but in her heart she was not so sure. She thought her employer a nasty, mean old man, yet she had to admit that he had a pretty miserable sort of life. Mrs Wilmslow nagged and moaned and criticised and Martha knew that their married life, for want of a better term, could not be what she would call normal. She supposed, vaguely, that this might be hard on any man, even one as pernickety and miserable as her employer.

'The porridge is ready, I reckon, Mam. I'm going to have golden syrup on mine,' Evie said. Martha had already laid the table with four porridge bowls, spoons, a loaf and a packet of margarine. Now, Evie staggered across and began ladling porridge into the four dishes. She splashed a good deal about, for the pot was heavy, but Martha thanked her and began to clear up the mess with the dishcloth whilst Evie carried the now empty pan over to the sink and ran water into it.

Martha was beginning to slice the loaf when the kitchen door opened and Angie and Seraphina came into the room. Both girls were ready for work and took their places at once, beginning to eat whilst Evie poured water from the hissing kettle into the teapot, made and poured the tea, and then took her place at the table. Martha glanced at the clock on the mantel and began to eat her own porridge as fast as she could. Seraphina started work at nine, as did Angie, but Mr Wilmslow liked his assistant to be on the premises by half-past eight at the latest, since a good few of his customers came in early when they had unexpectedly run out of breakfast cereals, bread, or 'something to put in his butties', such as a small tin of sardines or a pot of meat paste.

Martha finished her porridge, drained her mug of tea and stood up just as Seraphina did the same. However, Martha only had to descend the stairs and she was in her place of work, whilst Angie and Fee had to walk to the tram stop, get aboard a vehicle crowded with other workers, and make their way into the city centre. So now she watched as the girls donned coats and hats and prepared themselves for the day ahead. Seraphina got at least two good meals at the restaurant but Angie usually took a couple of sandwiches – cheese for her lunch, jam for her tea – which Martha prepared for her before breakfast. Now Angie snatched up the greaseproof package, thrust it into her black shoulder bag, and leaned over to kiss her mother on the cheek. 'Thanks, Ma, for making my sarnies. You are good,' she said, as she said every working day. 'C'mon, Fee. If we miss the next tram, the one after will be so crowded it might go straight past the stop.'

'All right, all right,' Seraphina said, standing on tiptoe to check her reflection in the glass face of the clock. 'See you tonight, Ma; be good, Evie.'

Martha waited until the two older girls had gone, then turned to her youngest. 'And what are you going to do with yourself today, my love?' she asked. 'There are a few little jobs around the house that I'd like you to do, but nothing else. And it's far too fine a day to spend indoors. Is Percy coming round?'

Martha knew that, during school holidays, Percy and her daughter spent a good deal of time together. She had no doubt that many of their ploys were kept secret, but she also knew that they joined together, whenever possible, to earn some money. They needed pennies for such things as the Saturday rush at the cinema, bus or tram rides out into the country, or the little extras – sweets and fruit – which children the world over enjoy when they have the opportunity. She had a strong suspicion that neither would think twice about nicking coal from the yards behind the station, fades from the fruit market, or anything from anywhere which seemed to belong to no one in particular, but though she knew that Harry would not have approved – she disapproved herself, come to that – she also remembered her own childhood and how it had seemed fair game to follow the cart carrying cabbages, in order to pick up and run off with any that fell from the load.

So now she looked enquiringly at Evie, but received only a nonchalant shrug of the shoulders in reply; whatever Evie was going to do today, she did not intend to talk about it. Martha reached down her overall from its hook and put it on; it was one of two dark brown wraparounds which tied at the back, grudgingly provided by Mr Wilmslow. Then she said goodbye to Evie, who was already clearing the table, preparatory to washing the crocks, and set off down the stairs.

By the time she entered the shop, Mr Wilmslow had opened up and was serving the first customer, a railway worker who popped in most days to buy what he termed his 'snap'. He usually bought six milk rolls, a wedge of cheese and a couple of iced buns, and now he was discoursing loudly on the contents of his newspaper as he waited for Mr Wilmslow to wrap his purchases. 'There ain't no doubt that war's coming, and coming fast,' he announced portentously. 'Them bleedin' wops walked into Albania without so much as a by your leave, and the government is going to evacuate all the kids from big cities like Liverpool into the country just as soon as that old Hitler oversteps the mark. As for that old Chamberlain . . .' He snorted. 'Peace for our time, indeed! Oh aye, there's war comin' all right, you tek my word. Even the bleedin' government can see that.'

'I'm sure you're right, Mr Brown,' Mr Wilmslow said

politely. Martha thought, rather bitterly, that regular male customers were always right, so far as her employer was concerned. 'That'll be one shilling, please, sir. Yes, I'm sure you're right.'

'Well I am; an' I'm too old to be prescripted,' Mr Brown said piously, rather spoiling the effect by adding: 'Not but what I'd dearly like to give Hitler a bloody nose, an' that Eyetie an' all . . . Musclebound, or whatever 'is name is.'

'Conscripted,' Mr Wilmslow said mildly. 'And from what I've read in the papers, the fellow in charge of the Italians is Mussolini. But I scarce dare open a newspaper these days because the news is always bad, and I don't let one near Mrs Wilmslow. She'd be that upset if she knew there might be a war . . .'

Martha slipped behind the counter as another customer entered the shop, but all the while she was serving, she was listening to Mr Brown's conversation. 'My newspaper says old Chamberlain's thrown down the gauntlet – that's a glove, that is . . . My newspaper says Hitler won't stop at the Polish border, he'll march right on, just to show old Chamberlain who's boss.'

'Aye, I dare say you're right,' Mr Wilmslow said placatingly, shooting a sideways glance at Martha as he did so. Having frequently heard her employer saying that there was no truth in such statements and that folk who said there was a war coming were just trouble-makers who deserved to be shot, Martha lowered her eyes. Mr Wilmslow knew very well that she would not give him away, and of course he had no idea how she felt herself because she would not have dreamed of admitting it. But Martha bought the *Echo* daily and agreed with Mr Brown that Britain could not fail to become embroiled in what was happening in Europe. I'm glad I've got girls, Martha thought to herself as she took her customer's money and went to the till to get change. If I had boys I'd be most dreadfully worried because I'm sure they'd be called up for the armed services – prescripted, as Mr Brown called it – and young men are foolhardy and find war exciting. Girls, thank God, are different.

Perhaps because Mr Brown had started it, however, the talk in the shop that morning was mostly concerned with the threat of war. One customer remarked, bitterly, that she saw no reason why Londoners should be given free air raid shelters whilst folk like herself would have to make their own arrangements. 'Me son – he's in the Navy, as you know – says it's because London is a port and they're certain to bomb ports, but Liverpool's a port an' all, so we're bound to get hammered sooner or later. They did ought to give us free bomb shelters as well.'

'Nah, we'll be all right,' another customer remarked. 'We're too far away from the Continent; them Boche won't be able to reach us. Oh, I saw the pictures in the papers, and the newsreels, about how they bombed Madrid, but that's only next door, so to speak. All them foreign countries is only next door, whereas us, we's an island.' The middle-aged woman who had spoken chuckled hoarsely. 'Oh aye, the old Irish Sea will keep us safe, you mark my words.'

'And the Channel,' someone else observed. 'They've gorrer cross the Channel before they can bomb old London, so maybe the cockney sparrers won't need them shelters after all.'

Mr Wilmslow was on the bacon slicer, turning the handle and obviously trying to ignore the conversation, but as he neatly fielded the last slice and wrapped the order in greaseproof paper, he turned to survey his customers. Martha grinned to herself. They were all women and Mr Wilmslow rarely allowed his female customers to get away with anything, so she guessed he would soon interrupt and waited with considerable interest, for the women who were discussing the war were not the sort to allow Mr Wilmslow to push them around.

'Well I dunno about Madrid being only next door, but I do know as the fellers say there'll be war before Christmas, and if you ask me we should've stopped them earlier – the Huns, I mean,' another woman said. 'We should've stopped 'em last year when they attacked their own people . . . what did they call it? Oh aye, Crystal Night. We should've declared war then.'

There were murmurs of agreement from other women in the shop and Martha saw Mr Wilmslow's neck redden and his thin cheeks begin to swell, and waited for the explosion. She did not have to wait long. 'Women!' Mr Wilmslow snarled. 'Anyone would think you wanted a war. Well, most of you's young I suppose and can't remember the last lot, but I do remember it. There were rationing, and a terrible shortage of food, clothing, fuel . . . everything what makes life endurable. If you were rich, you did okay, but—'

A large, red-faced woman in her sixties cut across the shopkeeper's remarks. 'Now that I do take issue with, Mr Wilmslow,' she said angrily. 'Why, the king himself said that everyone, rich 'n' poor alike, must tighten their belts and eat less bread. And that there Kettle chap – or were it Keppel – what were in charge of the king's household, he said as how the royal family had always stuck to the same rations as the rest of us. So you tek back what you just now said.'

For a moment, Mr Wilmslow looked as though he might be going to order the customer out of his shop, but she was large and strong and a regular customer;

Martha could almost see her employer thinking better of it. Instead of the angry words she was sure he would have liked to utter, he said placatingly: 'Well, what a memory you've got, Mrs Kavanagh, and you no more than a child at the time! But I weren't meanin' the royals when I said the rich, because everyone knows royals is different.' He turned to the next customer. 'Yes, missus, what can I get you?'

Up in the flat, Evie made beds, swept and dusted, peeled potatoes for the evening meal, and cut bread and marge for the snack which she and her mother would share later. Only when she felt she had done all the jobs necessary to keep the flat in apple-pie order did she head for the stairs. She and Percy usually had some scheme going and today they meant to go to the pet shops on Heyworth Street to see if the owners wanted old lettuce or cabbage leaves for their collections of rabbits, guinea pigs and chinchillas. If so – and if they would pay for such provender – then she and Percy would go to the wholesale fruit and veg market on Great Nelson Street with their collecting bag and pick up any unwanted greenery lying around.

Both children were quite aware that they were not supposed to enter the market and equally aware that their presence, if detected, would lead to their immediate expulsion, probably accompanied by a clip round the ear. But they considered it was worth the risk since they could fill the bag in two minutes flat, whereas if they went to one of the street markets, not only would it take far longer to collect sufficient vegetable matter, but they would be competing against every kid in the neighbourhood whilst the schools were still on holiday.

During term time, of course, it was different. Evie and Percy did not sag off school often, but when they did they certainly never wasted their time haunting the markets. Instead, they would skip a lecky which was going into the country – or even pay the fare and travel like Christians – and spend a blissful day picking wild flowers. At Christmas, of course, they had collected holly and mistletoe, in January and February great masses of delicate snowdrops, in March the little wild daffodils. Now, in April, it would be primroses and violets. The flowers they picked would be tied into tiny bunches and sold either from door to door or to folk queuing outside cinemas and theatres, for even the most hardened young lady would go all dewy-eyed if her young man presented her with a sweet-smelling bunch of spring flowers.

But if one made an expedition into the countryside one started early and did not return for the midday meal, and in the school holidays Evie had responsibilities which she took very seriously. Her mother took it for granted that Evie would do the housework and prepare a simple meal whilst she and her other two daughters were working. And Evie was proud that her mother trusted her and would never let her down. Sagging off school was another matter altogether, for her mother expected her to be away all day, and somehow managed to do both chores and any messages herself, knowing – or believing, rather – that her youngest was in school and would remain there till four o'clock.

Now, however, Evie meant to go round to Percy's house and pick him up so that they could make their way to Heyworth Street together. If rabbit food was wanted, then they would continue on to the market, but if not, they would still volunteer to clean out all the pets' cages and boxes, for this was a job they both loved. On board the *Mary Jane* Evie had once been the possessor of a grand ginger kitten, which she had loved devotedly. When he grew into a strong and clever cat, he had often brought young rabbits home which Martha had been glad to take for the pot, though Ginger always got the head and guts. But just before they had moved out of the *Mary Jane*, Hetty and Jim had asked if they might keep Ginger, and Evie, who truly loved her pet, had agreed, regretfully, that this might be the kindest thing. 'He's a canal cat, sweetheart,' her father had said gently, seeing the tears shining her eyes and slipping down her cheeks. 'He wouldn't be happy living in a flat over a grocer's shop, even though I dare say he would soon clear the entire neighbourhood of mice. And you can visit him whenever the boat moors down by the docks,' he had finished.

This, however, had not been possible. The first time Evie had gone down with her mother and sisters to visit the *Mary Jane*, Hetty had admitted that Ginger had stalked off the boat when they had pulled alongside the farm in which the cat had been born and had not returned. Hetty had asked the farmer and his wife if they had seen the cat, but they had not done so. Hetty, who admitted she had been looking forward to being provided with young rabbits for the pot, had kept her eyes open, but had not seen so much as a whisker of their furry friend.

Evie, imagining her Ginger caught in a trap and starving to death, or being kidnapped by gypsies, had cried herself to sleep for a week, but once again her father had comforted her. 'Ginger knows all about traps and is far too cunning to get caught in one,' he had said robustly. 'As for being kidnapped, don't you mean catnapped? He is far too independent to stay with anyone against his will. He'll have found himself a new home – and remember, sweetheart, he's a male cat. He's probably got himself a nice little wife and a litter of beautiful kittens, and he will be far too busy providing for them to think about returning to Hetty and Jim. He scarcely knows them, after all.'

So now, though Evie missed her dear Ginger and thought of him often, she no longer worried about him, and her trips to the pet shops made up, in some degree, for her lack of a pet of her own. She and Percy had discussed the possibility of acquiring a kitten; they did not mean to buy one but thought they might steal one from amongst the raggle-taggle collection of cats who moused for a living down by the docks, and produced kittens on a regular basis. However, even though she was working again, thanks to Evie's mother, Mrs Baldwin had been horrified at the thought of another mouth to feed, albeit such a tiny one, and Martha herself, though sympathetic, had said she would have to obtain Mr Wilmslow's permission before introducing a cat into the premises, and had felt that this might be easier when summer came since then the kitten could do its business outside. It had been this, in fact, which had stopped Evie from getting a cat, for where would such business be performed? The tiny yard at the back of the shop was paved, the jigger was cobbled and the nearest suitable space was St Martin's Recreation Ground. The poor little kitten would be bursting long before it reached real earth, Evie had concluded, and she had abandoned her plans to provide the family with a pet.

Now, she clattered down the iron stairs and popped her head round the shop door. Martha was weighing up broken biscuits and tipping them into a stout brown paper bag whilst Mr Wilmslow was balanced on the small stepladder, reaching up to the top shelf for a jar of candy sticks. Evie's mouth watered but candy sticks were expensive, especially if purchased from Mr Wilmslow, so she contented herself with smiling at her mother. 'I've done the housework an' now I'm off to fetch Perce,' she called. 'Want any messages, Ma? Mr Wilmslow?'

'No thanks, duck,' her mother said cheerfully, but Mr Wilmslow looked round and said that, if she were passing a chemist's shop, his wife wanted a bottle of cough mixture and a small packet of blackcurrant cough pastilles.

Sighing inwardly, Evie crossed the shop and stood against the counter. At first, Mr Wilmslow pretended that he did not know she was there, and then, when she cleared her throat and uttered his name, he climbed reluctantly down from his perch, banged the big jar of candy sticks irritably down on the wooden counter and pressed 'void' on the till so that the drawer shot open. He selected a shilling from within and handed it to her so grudgingly that she saw her mother turn away to hide a smile. 'I want me change,' he said warningly, handing over the coin. 'All of it, mind; don't you go keeping nothing back.'

'You can have the whole shilling back, Mr Wilmslow,' Evie said politely. 'I bought a bottle of cough linctus for Seraphina back in January and it were one and sixpence, honest to God it was, and the pastilles is . . .'

'All right, all right,' Mr Wilmslow grumbled. He opened the till again and extracted a half-crown, gazing down at it as though it were his first born and she were King Herod, Evie thought, with an inward giggle. He handed the coin over, then clicked his fingers in her face, causing Evie to step back hurriedly. 'Give me me bob back,' he demanded. 'Don't tell me you'll need more than half a crown for cough mixture and pastilles, 'cos that I won't believe. And I want—'

'You want your change; all of it,' Evie cut in, handing back the shilling and pocketing the half-crown. 'See you later, then.' She hastened out of the shop, eager to escape before Mr Wilmslow dreamed up another message for her to run. As she hurried down the Scottie, she thought crossly that with one thing and another it would be dinnertime before she reached Cavendish Court. Usually, she would have spread some bread and marge with paste or jam, wrapped the slices in grease-proof paper, and added anything else she could find which her mother could spare. But today she had been in too much of a hurry and had hoped that her mother would give her a copper or two as a reward for the work she had done. If it hadn't been for mean old Wilmslow, Mam probably would have handed over some cash, Evie thought resentfully now; him and his bleedin' change, and not a word about giving her a ha'penny or so for getting his nasty wife's nasty medicines.

But it was a beautiful day and Evie was beginning to cheer up and to wonder whether there was any food in the Baldwin kitchen when someone stopped in front of her and two hands descended on to her shoulders. Evie tried to wriggle free, then looked up into the face above her own and felt her heart give an enormous leap. 'Toby! Whatever are you doing here? Don't say you're working in Liverpool . . . oh, Seraphina will be so pleased! She watched the post for weeks, but . . .'

Toby Duffy smiled down at her, his dark eyes twinkling. 'I know, I know, don't you nag me 'n' all,' he said guiltily. 'I've been meaning to write, but oh, I'm such a poor hand at letter-writing. In the end, I took a couple of days off so's I could come calling. I've booked into a lodging house, just for the one night, and I thought I'd take Fee out to the flicks or the theatre . . . only I've been up and down this perishin' great road all morning and there's no sign of the number Seraphina gave me. I saw where it ought to be, but it was a shop.'

Evie giggled. 'Of course it's a shop, you idiot; Ma works for the owner, Mr Wilmslow, and we live in the flat above. But there's no one in because everyone's working. Fee had to give up her place at the teacher training school . . . but I suppose you know all that . . .'

'No, I didn't know that,' Toby admitted. 'Fee stopped writing to me . . . oh, before Christmas, I suppose. I knew nothing had happened to her, though, because . . . well, truth to tell, she threatened me. She said she'd give me a week to reply to her letter and if I didn't, then that was the last time she'd write to me. And though I did keep meaning to write . . .'

Evie sighed. She had always liked Toby most awfully, and seeing him again had reawakened all her old feelings. He was kind and funny, and easily the best-looking young man she knew; he had been her ideal for years and it was hard for her to admit that he had feet of clay. Seraphina was right, in fact, to grumble about him, yet Evie knew that if she had been grown up and lucky enough to have Toby come calling, she would have welcomed him with open arms, as no doubt Seraphina would.

She said wisely: 'I know, I know, you just never got round to it. Well, if Fee gives you a hot reception when she sees you, it's no more than you deserve. In fact I should think she'll ring a right peal about your ears,' she added frankly. 'Look, I'll tell you where she's working and how to get there, but I can't come with you. I'm meeting me pal Percy, and I'm late already. But Fee is working in the Lyon's Corner House on Church Street. If you hop on a number 20 or 21 tram and ask the conductor to put you down near Church Street, then you can't fail to find the Lyon's Corner House.'

'Thanks ever so much, Evie,' Toby said gratefully. 'What time does Fee finish work, d'you know?'

Evie shook her head. 'No, I'm afraid I can't help you there because the girls work shifts, but if you go in and ask for her, I'm sure Fee will tell you what time she leaves off today. She might even persuade someone to do an extra hour or two for her, you never know.' She grinned at Toby and pointed to a short line of people waiting on the edge of the pavement. 'Join the queue, Toby, and don't forget, you want a 20 or 21. See you later, I expect.' She took a couple of steps towards her destination, then turned back. 'If I were you, I'd take Fee a little peace offering – a few flowers, or a bar of chocolate, something like that.'

Toby grinned sheepishly. He was carrying a Gladstone bag and now he put it on the pavement and fished in it and produced a small parcel. It was wrapped untidily in brown paper so Evie could not see what it was, but Toby shook it and she heard it rattle. 'It's a jar of humbugs,' he said. 'I remember how she loved humbugs. See you later, Evie.'

Evie tried to smile brightly but it was an effort. Toby seemed to have forgotten that Seraphina was no longer a child but a young woman, and a young woman with a good many admirers. If one of her new beaux took her to the theatre, he would present her with a box of expensive chocolates, or some exotic bloom to pin to her coat; if anyone got humbugs, it would be Evie. And how nice it would have been had Toby been fond enough of Evie herself to have brought her some small gift. But perhaps I'm wrong, perhaps Fee really would prefer humbugs, Evie thought, as she entered Cavendish Court. She hoped so, at any rate, for she had always liked Toby best of all their old friends, and hated to think that Seraphina might scorn his gift.

Chapter Six

Toby jumped aboard the first tram to come along, a 21, feeling that things were going his way at last. He had arrived in the city full of hope, sure that Seraphina would be delighted to see him, but gradually, as he had trekked up and down the Scotland Road, hope had dwindled. He had begun to believe that Seraphina must have deliberately given him a non-existent address, so meeting Evie had seemed a rare piece of luck, the answer to a prayer. Then he had had another bit of luck, which was catching the first tram to come along and arriving outside Lyon's Corner House without any more ado.

He stood for a moment on the pavement, staring in through the big glass doors. The place was crowded, and since all the girls were dressed identically he had some difficulty in picking Seraphina out. In fact, he could not do so, could only guess that one of the quickly moving figures was the girl he had come so far to see. He squared his shoulders and moved purposefully into the restaurant as a group of young men came out. He spotted a vacant table for two and slid out of his overcoat, draping it across the back of one of the chairs. He was immediately joined by a middle-aged man who stared at him almost aggressively and said, 'Mind if I share your table? It's always rare busy in here, but usually I arrive early; today I were late.'

Toby thought rather bitterly that since the man had sat down before he finished speaking it would have been too bad had Toby been waiting for a friend. As it was, he simply said shortly: 'Help yourself,' and then reached for the menu.

'The roast beef is best; I allus have the roast beef,' his companion said. 'And plum duff and custard for afters. I allus has the same. The nippies know me; they know I allus have the same.'

'Oh aye?' Toby said stolidly, but he felt rather dismayed. He had not meant to have a meal, intending to order a pot of tea and perhaps a buttered scone, but looking around him he saw that almost everyone was eating a cooked dinner. Sighing inwardly, he waited for a waitress to approach. If it had not been for his companion, he would have asked the girl for Seraphina at once, but he decided he could scarcely do so when he was taking a place which would otherwise contain a proper customer. He saw a nippy approaching out of the corner of his eye, a tall, fair-haired girl, and for a moment he thought his luck was holding, that this was Seraphina, but when she reached him he knew at once that he had been mistaken. Her voice was broad Liverpudlian and the colour of her hair had clearly come out of a bottle, but her smile was friendly and she addressed them both with good humour. 'Yes, gents? What'll it be today, then?'

This seemed to give the lie to his companion's confident assertion that all the nippies knew him, but then the girl took out her pad and pencil without waiting for either of them to speak. 'One beef, one duff, one pot of tea, for Mr Cripps,' she said rapidly. She turned to Toby. 'And you, sir? What can I get you?'

But Toby was not attending. He was staring towards the back of the room where another tall and slender girl was delivering orders from a loaded tray on to a table whose occupants were four smartly dressed young men, probably in their mid-twenties. Even though her back was towards him, Toby would have known her anywhere. 'Seraphina!' he said beneath his breath. 'Oh, Seraphina!'

The nippy had moved closer to him and was leaning over as though she suspected he were deaf. 'What did you say sir?' she asked rather plaintively. 'I'm afraid I didn't quite catch what you said. Was it the steak and kidney? The roast beef is always good – ask Mr Cripps here – but there's lamb and mint sauce today as well as the steak and kidney pie . . .'

The sound of her voice jerked Toby back to the present. 'Oh . . . I'll have the steak and kidney, please, miss,' he said, speaking quite at random.

'And the duff?' the girl enquired, scribbling on her little pad. But Toby was watching Seraphina, almost unbelievingly. She was flirting, there was no doubt about it, paying far more attention than necessary to the young men, laughing, and then turning away and going off towards the kitchen with a lively step and swaying hips.

Toby could feel his hair begin to bristle like a dog's hackles when it sees another dog grabbing its bone. Seraphina had changed! When her father had been alive and they had all lived aboard the *Mary Jane*, she would never have dreamed of behaving in such a blatant manner. But of course she had not seen him, did not know his eyes were upon her.

The nippy was still there, patiently waiting for a reply to some question which he had not even heard. Toby was about to ask her what she had said when his table companion leaned forward. 'You 'ave the plum duff and custard, mate,' he advised kindly. 'It's prime, I'm tellin' you.'

'Oh,' Toby said, enlightened. 'But I don't want any pudding, thanks; I'll just have a pot of tea.'

The waitress scribbled in her pad once more, thanked both men for their orders, and left them. Toby turned back to stare accusingly at the young men with whom Seraphina had been laughing and joking, but they were engaged in the serious business of eating and anyway the distance which separated them from Toby was too great to allow his overhearing any comments they might make. But they must think she's really cheap, to laugh and joke with strangers the way she did, Toby told himself resentfully. I'm sure if her parents – well, if her mother – knew she would tell her to find herself a more respectable job. But his companion was addressing him, so Toby dragged his attention back to the other man.

'. . . steak and kidney pie is pretty good, and of course it's cheaper than the beef,' Mr Cripps was saying wisely. 'I'm mortal fond of the duff but I don't have it every day because some days they do a treacle puddin' and if there's one thing I can't resist, it's treacle puddin'.'

He waited, obviously expecting Toby to ask when the Corner House served this rare treat, but Toby's attention had returned to the other end of the restaurant where Seraphina was re-entering through the swing doors with another laden tray. Toby watched jealously as she went to yet another table, occupied this time by half a dozen young men, and began to place the laden plates before each diner, laughing and chatting as she did so. 'It's too bad,' Toby muttered. 'Folk'll start talkin' about her, sayin' she's easy . . .'

'What were that you said?' his companion asked rather querulously. 'I comes in for me tea sometimes. They does a lovely date and walnut loaf.'

Perhaps fortunately for Mr Cripps, since Toby found himself fighting a strong urge to punch him on the nose, their food arrived at this point. Mr Cripps pushed up his sleeves in a workmanlike fashion, helped himself liberally from the mustard pot, and began eating, which meant that he could no longer talk. Toby picked up his own knife and fork and began to tackle the steak and kidney pie. It was indeed delicious, but ambrosia would have turned to ashes in his mouth when Seraphina bounced back into the kitchens and the men at her table all laughed uproariously over something she said as she disappeared through the swing doors. Toby ground his teeth and shovelled the remainder of the creamy mashed potatoes into his mouth so fast that he almost choked. He had always considered Seraphina his own particular friend . . . no, dammit, if he were honest, he had always considered her his girl. He had never asked her to marry him – they were both too young – but he acknowledged, now, that he could not imagine a future which did not contain Seraphina.

Well, if that really is so, why didn't you write to her, a small, niggling voice in his mind demanded. Why, you never even answered her letters, not properly, because four ill-written lines on a page torn from an old exercise book isn't a real reply. And now you come here, and watch her at work, and criticise her, and it's just like spying . . . well, it *is* spying. And what's more, since you're so far away, you can't actually hear a word that anyone has said. It's probably all perfectly innocent.

'. . . and the tea's none of that wishy-washy stuff what you get in the Kardomah or Cooper's. I ain't denyin' they're ladies' places really, and seemingly ladies like weak tea, but I dussent. I like a cup so strong that the teaspoon can stand up in it without no help from anyone. Ah, here comes our nippy now, and that'll be our tea, I reckon.'

'I didn't hear you order tea,' Toby said morosely, accepting his own pot.

Mr Cripps smiled indulgently. 'I told you I come here every day,' he said reproachfully. 'The nippies know I finish me meal with a cuppa.'

Toby grunted. Seraphina had just come sailing out of the kitchen. This time, it appeared, she was clearing tables since her tray was empty. He poured tea into his cup with his eyes fixed on her slender yet curvy figure, and was immediately taken to task by Mr Cripps, who jumped to his feet and began energetically mopping at the table top whilst gazing reprovingly at Toby. 'Hey, hey, hey, keep it on the perishin' island, boy,' he said as he mopped. 'Tell you what, I don't reckon your mind's on the job. Why, if I hadn't shouted out, you'd have gone on pourin' until the pot were empty.' He beckoned to a passing waitress. 'Gerrus a dishcloth, there's a good girl,' he said jovially. 'Me pal here's had a bit of an accident.'

The girl was Seraphina. She came over to the table, glanced at the mess and then froze, her eyes on Toby's face. Slowly, a wide smile spread across her countenance. 'Toby!' she breathed. 'I didn't know you were in Liverpool. How odd that you chose to have your dinner in the very place where I'm working.' Her eyes shifted from his face to the table. 'Oh lor, I'll fetch a cloth. Shan't be a mo.'

Toby stared down at the table, swimming in tea. He didn't know whether he felt more like laughing or crying. She didn't realise he had come specially to see her; thought that his presence was a mere coincidence. It crossed his mind that he could tell her he had been moved from his present station to a different one many months ago, and had never received her letters, particularly the one giving him the ultimatum, but he knew he couldn't do such a dishonest thing, not really. When she came back with the dishcloth, he would explain, ask her when she finished work, suggest that they should meet and catch up on each other's news. But Mr Cripps was still jabbering away, telling Toby that he was a shipping clerk with the White Star line, asking him what he did for a living and where he was lodging, for he had noticed that his new friend spoke with a Yorkshire accent.

Toby began to explain that he worked on the railways and had come to Liverpool to visit old friends, but then Seraphina was back. She cleaned up the table incredibly quickly, told Toby that she would send out fresh tea and disappeared whilst he was still opening his mouth to tell her how he came to be in the restaurant. He told himself that it did not matter, that by the time she returned he would have planned exactly what to say, but she did not come back. Another girl brought the replacement tea and presently Mr Cripps stood up and went ponderously over to the desk to pay his bill. Toby stayed at the table for ten more minutes, staring hopefully at the swing doors which led to the kitchen, then decided that he must ask to speak to Seraphina, for it seemed that she was not going to reappear.

He got up and went to the desk and paid his money to a stout and elderly lady wearing tiny, gold-rimmed spectacles and a neat black dress, though without the white collar and cuffs sported by the nippies. When she had taken his money, and given him his change, he asked her when Miss Todd would be free. The elderly woman looked him up and down, though not unkindly. 'I'm afraid I can't give personal details out to members of the public,' she said firmly, and held out her hand for the bill which the next customer was proffering.

'But – I'm not a member of the public. I'm – I'm

Miss Todd's cousin,' Toby said wildly, if untruthfully. 'My ma – that's Miss Todd's aunt – asked me to pop in and give her something.' He produced the ill-wrapped parcel and said: 'I was to find out how she and her sisters were doing and whether my ma could do anything to help Aunt Martha – that's Sera— I mean Miss Todd's mother,' he ended.

The woman looked at him doubtfully, then her gaze moved to someone behind him and she brightened. She stood up – she was in a small glass cage to the right of the doorway – and spoke in a clear, commanding voice. 'Miss Todd, come over here a minute, will you?'

Toby swung round. Seraphina, an enquiring look on her face, was approaching fast. He stepped towards her and spoke almost in a whisper. 'When are you free, lass? I need to talk to you.'

Seraphina tightened her lips and her eyes sparked dangerously, and Toby realised, with some disappointment, that she had recovered from the surprise, even pleasure, of seeing him, and was remembering her grievance. However, she said crisply: 'I finish at six. Is that all?'

Poor Toby was dismayed by her tone and the cool look in her beautiful blue eyes, but he knew better than to show it. 'Is there a staff exit?' he hissed.

'Yes, round the back,' Seraphina said quickly. 'I must go, Toby, we're awfully busy,' and with that she disappeared into the kitchen once more, leaving Toby to make his way out of the restaurant. As he did so, he reflected gloomily that this elegant, sharply spoken young woman was not the Seraphina Todd he had known and loved. Living in the city, working in the restaurant, had changed her out of all recognition. But perhaps the change is only skin deep, he told himself, as he began to stroll along Church Street. He had planned to visit the big stores – Lewis's, Cooper's, Bunney's – and it occurred to him now that he might keep the jar of humbugs, which suddenly seemed rather a naïve present for the sophisticated young lady Seraphina had become, and buy her something more appropriate. Chocolates would be nice, or a pretty scarf, only summertime was approaching, not really scarf weather. He would choose something nice and she would forgive him for his shocking behaviour and allow him to make amends.

When Toby had left the restaurant, Seraphina went about her work in a thoughtful mood. She had been really angry with Toby. She had accepted that he disliked writing letters, but that was really no excuse for the way he had behaved. After all, most people have to do a great many things they dislike in the course of their lives, and when he had failed to reply to either coaxing or threats she had decided that not only was his indifference hurtful, it also meant that their relationship had come to an end. She had resolved to put him out of her mind and she had done so. She had banished the thought of him so success-fully that his sudden appearance in the restaurant had shocked her into smiling at him and that, she supposed, had seemed like the thin edge of the wedge to her old friend. She had gone back into the kitchen, determining not to return to the restaurant until he had left. She had peeped through the round portholes in the swing doors and had seen him go over to pay Mrs Edwards. She had then waited a further five minutes to give him time to leave before she sallied forth to clear more tables. When Mrs Edwards had called her over, and Toby had spoken to her, she had honestly intended to snub him mercilessly, to tell him to go back to his wretched little country station since he obviously found it so fascinating that he had not kept in touch with his old friends. But there was something so appealing in the glance he had shot at her that she had been unable to prevent a stirring of pity. She had pretended to think it was mere coincidence which had brought him to the restaurant but she knew, of course, that that would have been stretching even coincidence too far. He had come in search of her, probably after visiting Wilmslow's and being told by Martha where her daughter worked. She did not mean to let him believe he was anything but an old friend, but she could at least be civil, meet him after work, and take him back to the flat for a cup of tea and a sandwich, before putting him on a tram for Lime Street station and waving him off without a pang.

But as it happened, even taking him home to tea would be awkward, because one of the customers had asked her to go dancing at the Grafton this very evening and she had more or less said she would. He had given her the telephone number of his office and she was supposed to ring him some time during the afternoon to confirm that she was free to go. Now she would have to tell him an old friend from the country had turned up and risk his displeasure; if she said she was working late, he would undoubtedly pop into the restaurant and find her out in a lie, and that would never do. Roger Truelove was a well-educated young man with rich parents, living in a large house somewhere on the far side of Prince's Park. Seraphina had never visited his home but she had walked along the road and looked curiously at the big houses with their beautiful gardens and wondered, enviously, what it would be like to live in one of them.

Now, she smiled almost mechanically as she went from table to table, clearing dirty cutlery and crockery, collecting half-used sugar bowls and milk jugs, and then using her cloth to wipe every last trace from the shiny table tops. There was a telephone booth not far from the restaurant which she could use when she finished work, but even that would be awkward, because Toby would be with her and would undoubtedly want to know whom she was telephoning. However, at this point, Seraphina gave a mental shrug; why hide the truth from Toby, after all? He no longer mattered to her, did he? In fact, she decided it would be a good thing for both of them if he knew that she had other friends beside himself. Surely he could not have expected her to sit around waiting for him whilst he failed to answer her letters and generally behaved as though she did not matter to him.

'Miss! Miss, I ordered a pot of tea for two and two buttered scones a good five minutes ago and I told the young lady we were in a rare hurry 'cos we've gorra train to catch; can you see if you can hurry 'em up?'

Seraphina looked guiltily across at the speaker, a small, bird-like woman with a beaky nose and faded blue eyes. She and her companion were sitting at one of her tables and Seraphina realised that she had been so busy thinking about her own life that she had completely forgotten she was here to do a job of work. One of the other nippies must have assumed that Seraphina was too busy clearing tables to take orders and had done so for her. She bent her most charming smile on the little lady, then transferred it to her companion. The two were so alike that she did a double take which made both customers smile. 'We're twins,' the speaker explained, indicating her companion. 'We has a day out together now and then, meetin' in the city 'cos it's halfway house for us, but she's out at Southport and I'm t'other way, Chester, and we don't want to miss us trains.'

Seraphina was beginning to say that she would go and check when one of the other nippies came through the swing door and headed towards them. 'Your tea and scones have arrived, ladies,' Seraphina said cheerfully. She addressed the other girl as she began to unload her tray on to the twins' table. 'I'm awfully sorry, Liz. I was so busy clearing I didn't notice I had customers, but it won't happen again.'

Liz, a short, stout girl with a beaming smile and a gap between her front teeth, finished unloading her tray and turned to hurry back to the kitchen with Seraphina. ''S all right, Fee; you'd do the same for me if I were rushed,' she said. 'Who were the feller?'

'Oh, just a friend of the family,' Seraphina said airily. 'From the old days, you know. I've not seen him since we left the canal, but he was in Liverpool, so he decided to look me up.'

'And meet you after work this evening,' Liz said. 'Are you taking 'im to the Grafton?'

'Honest to God, no one can keep anything to themselves in this place,' Seraphina said. 'No, I'm not taking him to the Grafton. He – he isn't that sort of friend. In fact, I don't suppose he can dance. I'll take him home to tea, but that's about it.'

'But Dawson told me you were going to the Grafton wi' Mr Truelove,' Liz said as the two of them pushed through the swing doors into the kitchen.

'I think nippies are the nosiest people in the whole of England, and you're the nosiest one of all, Liz,' Seraphina said roundly. 'Actually, I'm going to have to cancel my date, worse luck. I said I'd ring him if I could go so we could arrange where to meet. So I'll do that as soon as I've finished work. Maybe he'll agree to us going out tomorrow night instead of tonight,' she added hopefully. Of all the young men who had taken her about since she started work at Lyon's, Roger Truelove was not only the most well-to-do, but also the handsomest and most charming. He was tall and broad-shouldered, with thick corn-coloured hair, amazingly blue eyes, and a crooked smile which revealed very white and even teeth. He came into the restaurant a couple of times most weeks and all the girls thought him a splendid young man but this was the first time, so they assured Seraphina, that he had asked any of them out.

'I wish he'd take me out,' Liz said wistfully. 'He's gorgeous, ain't he? And he's clever; he's got to be clever to be an accountant, hasn't he? I remember last year – before you started here, Fee – he used to come in some mornings early, get hisself a quiet corner table, order a coffee, and spread out papers all over the table, an' books an' that. Then he'd read and make notes, an' order another coffee whenever one of the supervisors came near him. He told several of us girls he was studying for his finals, and then one day he came in with a big grin on his face and a big box of chocolates, and told us he'd passed wi' flying colours. We were all ever so happy for him . . . and the chocolates was for us! So you see, he ain't just handsome, he's a real nice feller an' all.'

Seraphina, who had heard this story several times already, smiled a trifle absently. 'Well, if he's a really nice chap, perhaps he'll let me swap our date from today to tomorrow, when I've explained about Toby,' she said hopefully.

The two girls crossed to the enormous stainless steel sink where Seraphina unloaded her tray on to the draining board. The washer-upper gave them a tired smile and began to rinse the dishes and cutlery before putting them into big wire baskets which would be immersed in boiling water before being placed on the drying rack, whilst the two nippies stood the milk jugs and sugar bowls to one side for emptying and refilling.

'If it were me, I'd not lerron that it were a feller, no matter how old a friend that feller might be,' Liz said shrewdly. 'Just say an old friend . . . no, say an old friend of your mam's. It ain't a lie, it's God's truth, and you don't want to make him think you'd rather be with someone else, do you?'

'No I don't,' Seraphina said fervently. She was beginning to wish Toby a hundred miles away; how dared he ignore her for weeks and weeks and then simply swan into her life and try to claim her as of right? She had liked him very much, once, but so much had happened since then that she felt like a different person. Responsibilities and worries, which she had never expected to have to shoulder, had come her way and the carefree girl Toby had known was a thing of the past.

'Todd! You'd better get back, queen. There's a big party just come in an' Miss Peabody's purr'em on your tables. It's some sorta women's group – I reckon they're a shoppin' trip from one o' the villages, an' they'll only want tea and mebbe a plate of buttered scones, but you'd best look lively.'

'Thanks, Evans,' Seraphina said, hastily putting the last of the sugar bowls down on the counter. She flew out of the swing doors, snatching at her pencil and pad as she went. 'Good afternoon, ladies; what can I get you?' she said, smiling at the hot and flustered faces of her customers. Work began again and it would be some while now before she could even begin to think what to say to Mr Truelove. 'Is it tea and cakes for . . . sixteen? Or would you prefer scones? There's a new batch just come out of the oven.'

When Seraphina emerged from the restaurant at six o'clock, Toby was waiting. Despite herself, Seraphina smiled at him. He was, after all, a nice-looking young man, with thickly curling dark hair, a strong cleft chin and a crease in one lean cheek, which appeared whenever he smiled. But his navy suit was cheap and shiny with use and his boots, though well polished, were cracking across the toes. Seraphina realised that, since he was no longer living at home, he would probably have to pay to have his shirts laundered and his suits cleaned, and decided that she must ask after his mother and numerous brothers and sisters. She was beginning to do so when he thrust a small packet into her hands. 'It's for you,' he said gruffly. 'It's what Evie used to call a sorry present – remember? Whenever she'd annoyed one of you – and it happened quite often, because she was a naughty kid, wasn't she? – she'd take off into the woods or fields and come back with a few flowers, a handful of nuts or a couple of windfalls, and say it was a sorry present for whoever she'd upset. Well, I've behaved badly towards you, Seraphina, and I'm really sorry.' He looked down at the packet in her hands. 'Go on, open it.'

'I'll open it in a minute, but first I have to make a phone call,' Seraphina said firmly. 'You see, I had arranged to go dancing with a friend tonight, only then you turned up, so I shall have to cancel it.'

She half hoped that Toby would show himself to be a real gentleman and tell her to go to the dance, but instead he asked suspiciously: 'A feller? Well, I'm not surprised, because I saw you bein' rare friendly with them young chaps at dinnertime. But I dare say you have to be friendly with all sorts, else you'd not hold down your job.'

Seraphina shot him a fulminating look, saying icily: 'I don't *have* to be friendly with anyone, Toby, I just have to be pleasant and efficient. And if I choose to go dancing with someone, it's because I like him and enjoy his company. So if you'll excuse me, I'll just go and make my telephone call . . . unless you'd just as soon spend the evening chatting to Ma and my sisters?' she added. She tried to keep the hope out of her voice but guessed she had not succeeded very well when she saw Toby's cheeks flush.

However, he only said: 'Make your perishin' phone call then,' in a sulky voice, and held open the door of the booth for her to enter. Then he managed to annoy her a second time by not standing well clear of the booth but remaining close enough, she thought, to hear her end of the conversation. She would have liked to tell him to move further off, but then she realised that anything she might say was very unlikely to be of a private or intimate nature, and relaxed somewhat. She pushed her pennies into the slot and dialled the number, pressing button A when a voice answered.

'Hello? Mrs Truelove speaking.'

For some reason, this threw Seraphina, who had expected Roger Truelove himself to answer the phone. However, she took a deep breath and said, as steadily as she could: 'Could I speak to Mr Truelove please? Mr Roger Truelove?'

There was a short silence before Mrs Truelove answered and then her voice sounded rather amused. 'You'll be wanting my son; I'm afraid he's not home from work yet, but can I take a message?'

Seraphina hesitated, then decided that perhaps

leaving a message was a really good idea. 'Yes, if you please,' she said, rather breathlessly. 'Would you tell him that – I shall be unable to meet him this evening as an old friend of my mother's has turned up unexpectedly and I have to go home to – to give a hand.' She longed to suggest that Mr Truelove might like to postpone the date and not cancel it altogether, but felt she could scarcely do so.

'Very well, I'll pass the message on,' Mrs Truelove said. 'But you haven't given me your name, my dear.'

'Oh,' Seraphina said. 'But he'll know . . . I'm S-Seraphina Todd.'

She half expected Mrs Truelove to comment on her unusual name, but the other woman merely repeated briskly, but still with that edge of amusement in her voice: 'Miss Seraphina Todd will not be able to meet Mr Truelove this evening. I'll see he receives the message as soon as he gets home. Ah, wait a moment, I think that's his key in the lock.'

It was, and a moment later Seraphina found herself explaining to Mr Truelove how an old family friend had turned up unexpectedly to spoil their outing.

There was a short pause and then, to Seraphina's joy, Mr Truelove said tentatively: 'How about tomorrow night? I take it the *old friend* isn't going to be a permanent fixture?'

A wave of pleasure and relief swept over Seraphina so that she giggled. 'No, no, they'll be off home later tonight,' she said joyously. 'And tomorrow evening will be fine, Mr Truelove, just fine. Suppose we meet outside the Grafton Ballroom at eight o'clock?'

'I've a better idea,' Mr Truelove said. 'Why don't I meet you out of work? We could have a meal and then go on to the ballroom later.'

'I couldn't do that,' Seraphina said at once. 'I

couldn't go to a dance in my ordinary clothes. I've a special dress for dancing, and shoes – well, sort of sandals really – and I unpin my hair and wear it loose, and . . .'

Mr Truelove was laughing. 'Yes, I know what you mean; it was a foolish suggestion,' he said. 'We'll go out for a meal some other time; tomorrow, we'll meet at eight.' He paused a moment then said, almost casually: 'Just who is this old friend of your mother's? How old is an old friend?'

Seraphina's mind did a desperate jig and came up with a whopping lie. 'I suppose she's about fifty,' she said. 'But a gentleman doesn't ask a lady's age.'

Mr Truelove laughed again. 'Very true,' he said lightly, sounding relieved, she thought. 'Until tomorrow then.'

Seraphina emerged from the phone box and smiled brightly at Toby. 'There, that's done,' she said briskly. 'And now let's get back to the flat; Ma and the girls will be dying to see you again and ask a million questions, about your family, your job – oh, just about everything, I suppose.'

They had walked a few paces when Toby put a detaining hand on her arm, drawing her to a halt. 'Aren't you going to open my gift?' he said bluntly. 'You needn't, of course, but I – I'd rather you did it now and not back at your mother's flat. It's – it's kind of private.'

Immediately filled with foreboding, Seraphina unwrapped the glossy pink paper to reveal a tiny box covered in blue velvet. She snapped it open and her worst fears were confirmed. The box contained a small gold ring, set with three tiny blue stones, which glittered up at her from the bed of white silk in which the ring was held.

'I got blue stones to match your eyes,' Toby said softly. 'It ain't an engagement ring because I don't have enough money to get engaged, for I shan't be able to get married for years, not on a porter's wages, but one of these days, Fee, I'll get you a proper ring. Will you – will you marry me one day, when we can both afford it?'

Seraphina snapped the little box shut and tried to push it into Toby's hand, but seeing the crestfallen look on his face, she gave the hand a squeeze as she did so. 'Toby, you're being very unfair,' she said gently. 'You are talking of getting engaged, getting married, when for months you haven't even bothered to reply to my letters. And you must realise that when you and I were friends, I knew almost no other young men, apart from the ones on the canal, and Ma and Pa didn't want me to end up tied to one of them. You don't seem to have changed much, Toby, but I've changed an awful lot. And I don't want to tie myself down to anyone. When September comes, I'm probably going back into teacher training and shan't be thinking of marriage for years and years. So don't be offended, but just take the ring back, there's a dear.'

Toby turned a dull red. 'But it's a present to say I'm sorry, not to tie you down,' he said gruffly. 'It's not expensive, not really, and I said it's not an engagement ring. I – I just thought it were pretty and you'd like it.' He looked at her with the beginnings of anger. 'If you don't want it, chuck it under the nearest tram, because it's no use to me,' he finished.

Seraphina stared at him helplessly. If she accepted the ring, she would feel obliged to him in some way and she was determined not to do so. She said: 'Give it to someone else! Give it to your mother, or one of your sisters . . . but I can't and won't accept it, Toby, is that clear?'

Toby snatched the ring back in its small box and pushed it into his pocket. 'All right; but I shan't give it to anyone else,' he said thickly. 'I'll save it for you, Seraphina, when you're in a better frame of mind.' He took her arm, rather roughly, and began to hurry her along the pavement. But after ten minutes of walking along in complete silence, he slowed and looked down at her, giving her a rueful smile. 'Sorry, sorry; you're right, of course, as always. I should never have bought you a ring when I can't afford to ask you to marry me. Tell you what . . .' He was grinning now, standing the Gladstone bag he had been carrying down on the pavement and rooting through its contents. Seraphina watched, rather warily, as he produced another parcel and thrust it at her. 'Take this instead. It were what I brought for you originally, only Evie seemed to think . . . oh, hang it, Seraphina, I've been every sort of fool!'

Seraphina opened the paper and then, as he stood up, smiling sheepishly, she flung her arms round him and gave him a hug. 'Humbugs, my favourites! Oh, Toby, let's just be pals again, the way we were when we were kids, and saved our pennies up to buy a few humbugs. And now let's get a move on or Ma will serve the meal and we'll have to make do with leftovers.'

Evie was mashing the potatoes when Seraphina and Toby entered the room. They were smiling but Evie immediately sensed tension and her fork stopped work for a moment whilst she gazed enquiringly from one face to the other. 'Mam's just nipped down to the shop to buy a couple of tins of peas and another of baby carrots,' she explained. 'When I told her you'd come calling, Toby, she guessed at once that Seraphina would bring you home to tea. We've got shin of beef done in a casserole, with onions and carrots, and I've done extra potatoes, only Mam wanted some more veggies to fill up the plates, like.'

'That's grand,' Toby said awkwardly. 'I didn't mean to put no one out, but in the old days your mam just cut another slice off the loaf and everyone shunted up so I could sit on the end of the bench. Where's Angie?'

Seraphina had gone over to the pantry to fetch an extra mug and another plate, and took no notice of Toby's question. They've had a perishin' row, Evie thought impatiently, and she was pretty sure the row would have been of her sister's making. When she had left him earlier that afternoon, Toby had been lit up with pleasure and excitement, but now he was looking uneasy and defensive, casting anxious glances at Seraphina's rigid back. Evie wondered whether to ask straight out what was the matter but decided against it. The old Seraphina had been sweet-tempered and easy-going, but then she had just been a girl, or so their mother said. Now Seraphina was a young woman and, as such, a mystery to Evie, and probably to Toby as well, Evie suspected. She lost her temper when things went wrong, sometimes shouted, and expected both her younger sisters to do as she told them, though it was only Angie who did so. Evie had grown adept at slithering out of the way when Seraphina was being unreasonable or too demanding.

Once or twice, Evie had asked her mother why Seraphina was so difficult now, so different, too. She thought that it might have something to do with their father's death, but Martha had shaken her head. 'It isn't that so much as the fact that she's growing up and having to take responsibility for her own actions, but when things don't go right for her she's still child enough to want to find someone to blame,' she had explained. 'When we lived aboard the *Mary Jane*, Seraphina had few responsibilities and most decisions were taken either by her pa or by myself. Now she's in a responsible job, earning good money. She worries that Angie ought to be doing work which uses her talents, and she worries that I'm at the beck and call of the Wilmslows, people she despises. She wants to train as a teacher yet she's afraid that she'll find it hard to manage without her salary from the restaurant. Then there are the young men who are forever turning up on our doorstep, or waiting for her when she comes out of the restaurant at night. They make her feel she's beautiful and important, which is nice, but they also make her feel that she should choose one of them. I think part of the trouble is that Pa and I guarded both Seraphina and Angela too closely. We kept them young by making all their decisions for them, never giving them responsibility. Why, even teacher training college was your pa's idea; Seraphina just fell in with it because she was sure Harry knew best.'

So now Evie answered Toby's question, since her sister appeared not to have heard it. 'Angie will be in quite soon now,' she said. 'She often works late but she always lets Mam know and she hasn't done so today.' She turned to her sister, emerging from the pantry. 'Did you have a good day, Fee? I know you're always busy but—'

Seraphina was saved from having to reply by the opening of the door. Angie and Martha came into the kitchen together, laughing and talking as they did so. Angie's face flushed a delicate pink when her eyes fell on Toby, but she greeted him composedly and Martha was frankly overjoyed. She flung her arms round him and gave him a big hug and a smacking kiss on the cheek. 'But why haven't you written to us?' she enquired plaintively, though Evie was sure that her mother knew the answer to that question. 'Seraphina read us a couple of letters that you'd sent but then you stopped writing.'

Toby began to mumble that he was awful sorry he had been a poor sort of friend, but Martha shook her head fondly at him. 'What's past is past,' she said, with all her usual generosity. 'And fancy you coming to see us when I've no doubt you've a thousand better ways to spend your time. Evie said she sent you along to the restaurant; what did you think of it, eh? I'm really proud of the way both girls have found work and stuck to it, though I know it isn't what either of them would have chosen. And how are you getting on, Toby? And your family, of course. Do you see much of them? I suppose Ned and Phil are both in work now?'

Evie saw Toby blink as her mother fired these questions, but he replied easily that his brothers were indeed both working, one on the canal and one for the railways, that his parents were well as was the rest of his family, though he saw little of them since his job as the only porter at a small country station meant that he had little time off. 'But in fact, the reason I came to see you today was because I may not be at my station much longer,' he said and Evie saw how his glance flew to Seraphina on the words and how Seraphina would not meet his eyes, but continued to lay the table as though to make her indifference plain to the whole world.

Martha was lifting the casserole out of the oven and carrying it carefully across to the table as he spoke. She was concentrating on the job in hand and did not immediately reply, so Evie dived into the breach. 'Not staying at your station? Are they going to make you an engine driver or something, then?' she enquired breathlessly. Long ago, when she had only been four or five, Toby had occasionally given her a 'seater' on his rusty old bicycle when he had overtaken her walking into the nearest village. As they jogged slowly along, he had often told her how he meant to be an engine driver when he grew up.

Now, however, Toby laughed at the suggestion. 'No, no, nothing so exciting,' he assured her, and once again Evie saw his eyes flicker hopefully towards Seraphina. She felt really cross with her sister; surely she must be interested in the doings of such an old and trusted friend? But apparently she was not, or, if she was, did not intend to admit it. Evie sighed to herself; if this is what happens when you grow up, then I don't think I'm going to enjoy it much, she thought, and turned with real interest to Toby.

'I want to make some enquiries about the army,' he said. 'I want to know if they would teach me how to drive and service vehicles. Then, if war does come . . .'

Evie stared at him, aghast. Of course she had heard folk talking, even her teacher at school talked about it, but, so far as she knew, none of these talkers ever actually did anything. And now, she realised, Toby had got Seraphina's attention at last, for her sister was staring at him, wide-eyed. Evie began to speak, to say that the army might send him away, to Scotland, or to Wales somewhere, but Seraphina cut across the words almost before they were out of her mouth. 'There isn't going to be a war. There can't be,' she said wildly. 'I'm going back to teacher training college and I couldn't do that if there's a war on. You're just warmongering, Toby Duffy.'

Evie saw dark red colour rush up Toby's face and would have leapt to his defence, but Martha beat her to it. 'Don't be so silly, Seraphina,' her mother said tartly, with a real edge to her voice. 'Toby is absolutely right and everyone knows it, except you, apparently. It isn't a question any longer of "if" but rather of "when". Why, if you don't know that Britain can't go on letting Hitler gobble up Europe, then you must be foolish indeed.'

It was Seraphina's turn to blush. Evie waited for an outburst of self-justification, but it seemed that Martha's biting tone had had its effect, for Seraphina merely said: 'Sorry, Ma. Sorry, Toby. You're both absolutely right, of course. It's just that I hate the thought of war, and bombs falling, and maybe the invasion they all talk about. I suppose I'm a coward, really, because whenever a customer mentions war I make some excuse and move away. And I don't read the frightening bits in the *Echo*, either; I mean there's nothing I can do about it, is there? So I might as well ignore it, keep my head down and hope it goes away.'

'No, that's not the right attitude at all, Fee,' her mother said gently. 'If everyone talked like that, where would our army, navy and air force be? They'll need all the young men they can get, as they did in 1914, and young women, too, this time. Now, that's enough talking for the time being or we'll never get our food eaten whilst it's hot.' As she spoke, she had been dishing up, and now she indicated that they should all sit down and listen to Angie, whose turn it was to say grace.

The blessing over, no one spoke until Martha signalled them to start eating, and then it was Martha herself who broke the silence. 'I suppose you young-sters will want to go off to the cinema, or the theatre, when the meal is over?' she said brightly. 'Since you're working at a country station, I don't suppose you get many opportunities to go the pictures, do you, Toby?'

Toby shook his head and darted a quick look at

Seraphina, who stared fixedly down at her plate. She isn't just cross with Toby, she's cross with herself as well, Evie thought. Ma doesn't often tell her off and she's blaming Toby for showing her up. Silly girl . . . but I expect she'll unbend presently and agree to go to the cinema with him.

However, Seraphina said nothing but continued to eat steadily, so Evie spoke up. 'I'd love to go to the flicks,' she said. 'There's ever so many picture houses to choose from. What about you, Angie? You like the cinema.' She dared not ask Seraphina, though she was tempted to do so.

Martha laughed. 'You aren't going anywhere, young lady, not with school starting tomorrow,' she said firmly. 'I meant Seraphina – and Angie, of course.'

Before either girl could answer, Toby smiled at his hostess. 'It's a grand idea, Mrs Todd,' he said, and there was real regret in his voice. 'But I'm afraid I shall have to go straight to Lime Street when supper's over and catch a train back to Leeds. I'm awful sorry, but next time I come into the city, mebbe we could all go out somewhere and I'll arrange to stay over. There's cheap lodging houses down by the docks and more near the station, I believe.'

Evie stared at him, opening her mouth to remind him – as if he could have forgotten – that he had booked a room for himself for tonight, but even as her eyes met his she read the warning flickering there, and closed her mouth again. She looked down at her plate and carefully scooped some potato on to her fork, before saying brightly: 'Well, I dare say Mam won't mind if I walk to the station with you, Toby. It isn't a long walk so I can be back well before my bedtime.' She turned to her sisters. 'Do you want to come? Fee? Angie?'

'I've got homework to do,' Seraphina said shortly. Evie could have shaken her. Her sister was doing evening classes, she knew that, but they had never interfered with Seraphina's pleasure before. It was clear to Evie that the classes were just a useful excuse and that the homework was just another way of punishing Toby.

However, she said nothing, but turned her gaze on Angela, who blushed. She shot a look at Toby under her thick blonde lashes, and when she spoke her voice was hesitant. 'I – I could do with some fresh air; I'd like to come.'

When the meal was over and the time had come for Toby to leave, Martha gave him a hug, half a fruit cake and a number of messages for his mother, since the two women had always been on good terms. Then she waved the threesome off.

They were passing the shop front when there was a patter of feet behind them and Seraphina caught them up. Evie noticed how Toby's eyes lit up as he turned impulsively towards her eldest sister, clearly hoping that she had changed her mind and would accompany them to the station after all. However, this was not the case. 'I've got to go along to the telephone box to make a call,' Seraphina said breathlessly. 'It's about the homework for my evening class. So I thought I'd walk with you, just as far as the box.'

The eager animation died out of Toby's face. He tried to chat naturally to the girls as they walked, but when Seraphina left them to take her place in the short queue waiting for the telephone, Evie thought he actually looked almost relieved. Pretending not to mind that Seraphina had clearly not forgiven him must have been extremely hard for him and Evie was pleased to see how he relaxed once her eldest sister had gone. He linked his left arm with Angela and his right arm in Evie's, apologising when his Gladstone bag banged against her legs, and the three of them soon recaptured the old familiarity. Toby told them stories about his family and the station at which he worked; Evie told him some of the antics she and Percy got up to, and Angie described her friend Annabel, who shared her interest in needlework and knitting, and was coming over to the flat later that evening with a sewing pattern she had promised to lend her. In fact, so at ease did they become that Toby confessed to Angela that he had booked a room for the night in a lodging house on Great Nelson Street. He also admitted that he had intended to cancel the room and go straight home on the next train, but no longer wanted to do so if the girls would promise not to say anything to Seraphina.

'I don't blame her for being angry with me because I treated her badly,' he said. 'But I've come a long way to see you all and I hoped she might let bygones be bygones.' He looked shyly from Evie to Angie. 'Mrs Todd had a quiet word with me whilst you were getting your coats on. She said – she said I must come again and not fret over Seraphina. She said there had been so much unhappiness and upset and Seraphina was at a difficult age and worried, furthermore, about her career. She said to leave it for three or four months and then come again, and she was sure my reception would be very different. I mean to write to all of you every single week, from now on, and perhaps, you never know, it – it might help to show Seraphina that I'm truly sorry.'

Evie tightened her lips; she felt really annoyed with Toby. How could he be so feeble when Seraphina had shown him so plainly what she thought of him? And what about poor Angela? It had never before crossed

Evie's mind that her second sister had a weakness for Toby, but now she saw that this was so. Angela's eyes softened whenever they fell on Toby's curly head, and when he spoke to her and she answered, faint colour rose in her cheeks and her eyes brightened. Evie felt desperately sorry for her, because she was certain that Toby had never even considered Angela as anything but the sister of his beloved. Furthermore, she did not think that Angela was right for Toby; she was far too meek, far too biddable. And Toby must have known it. Evie was pretty sure he had not noticed Angela's admiration and she hoped that her sister would not be hurt when she realised she stood no chance with him.

They reached Great Nelson Street and Toby bade them a formal goodbye, telling them that he intended to spend the evening in the nearest cinema and saying, rather wistfully, that it would have been nice if they could have accompanied him. 'But your ma made it pretty plain that she wanted you back home for your usual bedtime,' he said to Evie. 'And if I kept you out late, she'd worry most dreadfully. As for you . . .' he smiled at Angela, 'you've already made plans for the evening. But thank you very much for walking me back to my lodgings.' He turned away from them with a cheerful wave. 'See you in three or four months and don't forget to keep an eye out for the postman. You might even drop me a line now and then, to let me know how things are progressing.'

'He's awful nice, isn't he?' Evie said, as the two sisters began to retrace their steps. 'I think Fee's real silly.' She looked up into Angela's calm, fair face. 'If I were a bit older and he liked me instead of Fee, I'd forgive him like a shot for not writing letters.'

Angela smiled. 'He really is most awfully nice,' she agreed, in her soft voice. 'Goodness, we must get a

move on, Evie, or we'll be late for your bedtime and
that would never do.'

Evie sighed but agreed and the two girls hurried on
their way back, both, Evie suspected, thinking of Toby
as they walked.

Chapter Seven
September 1939

Seraphina clattered down the iron staircase and hurried up the passage which led out on to the Scotland Road. She was doing a late shift at the restaurant but meant to spend the morning shopping for an evening dress. It was a beautiful sunny day and her young man – if he could be called her young man – had invited her to spend a weekend at his parents' country home.

When Seraphina had told her mother of the invitation, Martha had been doubtful. The country had been in a state of considerable tension for weeks now. Europe was in turmoil; Germany was threatening to invade Poland, having already reduced Czechoslovakia to ruins, and Britain had been put on a war footing. Children were getting ready to be evacuated from the major cities, men and women were joining the forces in ever increasing numbers, and Chamberlain had given an ultimatum to Hitler, saying that he must withdraw his troops from the Polish border or Britain would declare war.

'I know you've been dreading a war, my love, as indeed we all have,' her mother had said, 'but you mustn't simply bury your head in the sand, you know. Mr Chamberlain is going to speak to the nation on Sunday morning, and it's my belief that he will tell us Hitler hasn't agreed to his demands, and that will mean we shall shortly be at war. With everything so uncertain, you should be in your own home, not in someone else's.'

But Seraphina had not agreed. She had been going out with Roger Truelove for four months and this was the first time he had invited her to his home, saying that he wanted her to meet his parents. To Seraphina, this sounded as though he was serious, and more than anything, she told herself, she wanted to be Roger's wife. He was the youngest partner in his father's accountancy firm, as well as being quite the best-looking young man Seraphina knew. So she tried to explain to Martha that Roger was important to her, might even be seriously considering her as his future wife. 'A man like him doesn't take just anyone home to meet his parents,' she had said. 'As for a war coming, I still think Hitler will draw back, but even if he doesn't, why shouldn't I have my wonderful weekend? After all, Ma, if you're right and conscription comes in, then it may be the last chance I have of getting to know his parents before he's whisked away from all of us.'

So Martha had reluctantly agreed that Seraphina should go and had actually accepted that her daughter would need an evening dress, because Roger had told Seraphina that although the weekend would be informal, he would be taking her dancing on the Saturday evening.

So now, Seraphina hurried across the little back yard and down the passage, her mind playing delightfully with the possibilities of a new dress. Colours flashed before her eyes – blue? Green? A delicate pink? And she fairly shot on to Scotland Road. She rounded the corner and ran full tilt into the postman. He was a cheerful, elderly man, with a square red face and bushy grey hair, and he caught her by the shoulders, dropping some letters on to the ground as he did so. 'Well, wharra lovely greeting,' he said jovially, releasing her to pick up the letters he had dropped. 'Where's you off to in such a hurry, miss? Early shift, I suppose? Well, you can save me a trip up them bleedin' stairs by taking your post since you almost bowled me over as you came round the corner.'

'I'm awfully sorry, ' Seraphina said breathlessly, taking the letters he handed her. 'I'm off to buy myself a new dress.' She glanced at the letters in her hand. 'Oh, it's all right, there's only a couple for my mother and one for the whole family; they'll keep till I get home tonight, no doubt.'

The postman sighed and pushed his cap to the back of his head. 'You'd best give 'em back to me,' he said resignedly. 'There might be something important in one of them and it would never do if the Post Office thought I'd not pushed them through your letterbox.'

Seraphina was not an unkind girl and she knew that the postman's feet gave him gyp on the iron staircase, so she hung on to the letters, shaking her head and smiling at him. 'It's all right; I'll take them up myself. It won't take me a minute.'

'Thanks,' the man said gratefully. 'You're a good gal, you are. When you're my age, and weigh as much as I do, them iron steps seem to go on for ever.'

Seraphina chuckled and flew up the stairs, shooting into the kitchen where the rest of the family were tidying round. 'Post,' she said, slapping the letters down on the table. 'One's from Toby; I recognise his writing. Is it all right if I open it, Ma? He said something in his last letter about coming up to Liverpool . . .'

Evie looked up sharply from her task of packing her school bag. 'I don't see what difference it will make to you whether he comes or not,' she observed. 'I don't believe you've written to him once, Seraphina Todd; it's Mam and Angie and meself what take it in turns to write to tell him all our news. Why, you don't even send your best wishes!'

Seraphina laughed. 'You don't know the half of what I do,' she said teasingly. 'I might write to him every day, for all you know, and post the letters off privately.'

'Oh yeah?' Evie said rudely. 'But you don't, do you?' She sniffed. 'You think you've got better fish to fry. You think that yeller-haired twerp, with his smart suits and his drawly voice, is better'n Toby, but he ain't.'

'Evie,' their mother said warningly. 'I'm sure Mr Truelove is every bit as nice as Toby; he's just different, that's all.' She turned to Seraphina. 'Yes, Fee, you might as well open the letter, since it's addressed to the whole family, and you can read it aloud, only you'd best hurry or Angie will miss her tram.'

Angie took her jacket off the kitchen door and slipped into it. Then she ran a comb through her soft curls, took down the neat navy blue hat which matched her jacket, and perched it at a becoming angle on her head. Seraphina suddenly realised that her sister was showing much more interest in her appearance than usual, but she was in too much of a hurry to speculate on the cause. She ripped open the envelope and pulled out the two closely written sheets it contained. She ran her eyes over the first few words, expecting the usual stilted comments, then gasped. 'Oh Ma, you'll never guess what he's been and gone and done. He's joined the army – Toby's joined the army and now he's in Catterick, doing his basic training!'

If Seraphina had tried, she could not have won a more astounded response. Simultaneously, Martha cried: 'Goodness!', Angie said: 'Oh, it's what he wanted, but . . .' and Evie said, flatly: 'They'll send him far away! He'll be miserable, so he will.'

Seraphina looked from face to face. Their

astonishment was evident, but it was not as great as her own. Last time he had written, he had talked of joining the army but he had seemed to intimate that he would only do so if war broke out. Now he had changed his mind and, irrationally, she felt fury against him rising up within her. Why did he have to spoil everything? It was just like Toby to do something stupid, to bring the war all the way into their kitchen, because now she was sure they would cancel her teacher training course, and whilst the Trueloves might welcome a teacher as a daughter-in-law she was sure they would not feel the same about a nippy from Lyon's Corner House.

She looked at the faces around her once more; their astonishment was not mixed with annoyance, as hers was. She had been so excited at the thought of her very first country house weekend and now Toby had been and gone and spoiled it. If Roger really did ask her to marry him then a wonderful life lay before her. She could have a beautiful modern flat in the city centre, a home in the country in which to spend weekends, wardrobes full of beautiful clothes, and servants to do her housework and ironing. But if war came, none of that would happen. She would probably be forced to do some horrible, uncongenial work, and there would be bombs and danger, and perhaps the horrors of invasion. Why oh why should Toby go and voluntarily join the army when he had said he would only do so if hostilities broke out? She felt, illogically, that by clearly believing in the war he had deliberately ruined her weekend. She threw the letter down on the table without even attempting to read past the first three lines.

Her mother looked at her uncomprehendingly; Angela stared, round-eyed, but Evie snatched up the letter and glared at Seraphina. 'I don't think you're a very nice girl, Seraphina Todd,' she said wrathfully. 'You don't like Toby a bit, not really. The only reason you wanted to read the letter was so you could make sure nothing interfered with your plans.'

Seraphina began to tick her small sister off, then stopped short, realising that Evie had a point. She had made it clear enough in the past that any mention of war was hateful to her and Evie, bright little wretch that she was, had not forgotten. So instead of reprimanding the younger girl, Seraphina smiled, protesting that she still liked Toby, though only as a friend, and tried to take the letter, saying: 'I'm sorry, Evie. It's just that a war, if it does come, will ruin all my plans. Let me read the letter aloud, as Ma wanted.'

Evie looked rebellious, but a glance from her mother convinced her that she should do as she was told. She handed the letter to her sister and Seraphina began to read.

'*Dear All, Many thanks for your last letter; see how good I am, replying only eight days after I received it! And for once I do have some news, for I have just joined the army! If you remember, I did say I was going to do so, last spring, but I had meant to wait until war was declared. However, a friend told me there was a shortage of drivers in the army and that we should both apply at once. Would you believe it, we were told to report to Liverpool to join up! As you can see from the address at the top of the page, though, I'm in Catterick Camp now so you won't be seeing me for a while.*

I live in a thing called a Nissen hut with a great many other chaps and we mess (that means eat) in the cookhouse. The food's all right and the work's really interesting – I hope, Seraphina, that you'll remember I always liked learning new things – but I'll be glad when I get a uniform. There aren't enough to go round, though they've given me overalls. I dare say you'll remember that old motor bike my brother Sid got hold of when I was a kid. I never thought taking the engine to bits and putting it back together a hundred times would be useful, but it set me on the right path and I know more than I thought I did. If you wanted to be a mechanic, Seraphina, they'd probably take you like a shot 'cos I remember you sitting on the garden wall, watching everything we did.

I'm writing this sitting on my bed but it's time I joined my mates for a meal in the cookhouse, so I'll say cheerio for now. I don't know when I'll get leave – someone said in six months – but when I do, Liverpool will be my first port of call. Toodle-oo for now. Your friend, Toby.'

Evie glanced at her sister and Seraphina saw that her lip was trembling. 'I'm going to reply at once . . . well, as soon as I get back from school,' Evie said defiantly. 'And I think you might write to him, Seraphina. You are the only one he mentions by name and he does it in every letter. And now he's in the army, he'll get sent to France, I'm sure he will. I remember Pa saying everyone got sent to France last time there was a war.'

'I would write, only I'm afraid it might give Toby the wrong idea,' Seraphina said hesitantly. 'You see, Evie, when Toby and I were friends before, we were just a couple of kids. We never thought about marriage, certainly never talked about it, but now . . . now there's Roger – and I think of him . . . well, quite differently from the way I used to think of Toby.'

Evie began to protest, but Martha put a stop to all that. She pointed dramatically to the clock above the mantel. 'Look at the time,' she said. 'And in this instance, Fee is quite right; the last thing she should do is raise false hopes. No, Evie, don't start to argue, there's no time. If I'm not down in that shop in five minutes, Mr Wilmslow will be in a bad mood for the rest of the day.' Martha picked up the letter and tucked it into the pocket of her pink checked overall, shooing her daughters towards the door as she did so. 'Off with you!'

Seraphina had bought her evening dress. She thought it was the most beautiful garment she had ever possessed with its low décolletage and long, sweeping skirt. It was made of leaf green taffeta and had cost her every penny of her savings, but she knew she looked good in it and wanted to impress the Trueloves. However, when she and Roger arrived by taxi at the front door of Dussendale House, she felt her stomach churn with an apprehension she had thought foreign to her nature. It was a very large and imposing building, she thought, built of grey stone, with arched windows, a slate roof and an enormous oak front door. They had approached it up a long drive, lined with what Seraphina recognised as rhododendron bushes, though of course the flowers were long over. She had remarked that the lane, as she had called it, must be glorious in May, when the blossoms were out, and Roger had smiled and said yes indeed, though it was somewhat gloomy at this time of year. After a moment's hesitation, he had added that the lane was in fact the drive, and Seraphina was still puzzling over this remark when the car drew up, with a crunch of gravel, before Roger's home.

She had seen big houses before, of course, but had never visited one, and as she climbed out of the car she felt the first glimmerings of fear. She had guessed that Roger's house would be large, possibly even imposing, but this was more like a stately home. It was shaped like an E with the central stroke missing, and just one quick glance at the perfection of the gravelled driveway, the riot of late roses in the beds which surrounded the huge curved lawn, and the view of distant parkland, dotted with ancient trees, made her realise the differences between the Trueloves and the Todds. She had always believed that her bright intelligence and pretty looks put her on an equal footing with anyone, but now, for the first time, she began to doubt this. Her parents had brought her up to be polite, truthful and self-confident, but as Roger took her arm and steered her up the curve of the stone steps towards that mighty front door, her self-confidence began to ooze away. For a moment, a picture of Toby rose, unbidden, in her mind's eye. She saw his rough hair, his kind brown eyes, his lopsided smile. In the past, she had rather despised his parents, but now Mrs Duffy seemed simply a kindly soul who admired Seraphina's looks and gasped over her cleverness. Even Mr Duffy, with his loud and raucous laugh, his broad Yorkshire accent and his habit of gripping an empty pipe between his teeth and talking round it, seemed comfortingly familiar rather than common and crude.

They reached the top of the steps and Roger rang a bell set into the stonework by the door. Seraphina blinked. Even in Liverpool, the girls never had to ring a bell to gain admittance to the flat; they either pulled the key through the letterbox on its dangling string, or simply walked straight in. But presently she heard hurrying feet and the door was flung open by an elderly man in a dark suit. He had a fine head of white hair, a large and rather beaky nose, pink-tipped and shiny, and small, very bright eyes. Seraphina was rather surprised that Roger's father should not immediately smile and welcome her, but she held out her hand, beginning to say how nice it was to meet him, when something stopped her in mid-sentence.

'Evening, Edwards; will you see that someone takes Miss Todd's case up to her room,' Roger said briskly, stepping into the hall and handing over the suitcase which he had been carrying. 'Where are my parents – and Kay, of course?'

Mr Edwards took the proffered case and suddenly smiled at Seraphina, though she noticed he did not do so until Roger began to move across the hallway. It made her feel better, though she realised it probably meant he was amused by the mistake she had almost made, and smiled back.

'Your parents are in the drawing room, Mr Roger,' the man said, indicating the white-painted door nearest them. 'Your mama told Cook to serve dinner at eight since you and Miss would be late.'

'Righty-ho, Edwards. Oh, by the way, Seraphina, this is Mr Edwards; he's been in our employ all my life so he's a very old friend. Edwards, this is Miss Seraphina Todd.'

Seraphina's hand itched to offer itself, but the butler – she supposed he was the butler – merely gave her a little nod and a tiny half-smile, so she followed suit and, almost immediately, was ushered into the drawing room. It was a large and very beautiful room, with full-length windows, a wood fire burning in the grate and a wonderful cream-coloured carpet, covered with pink roses, upon the floor. There were three people in the room: a woman in her late forties, in a beautiful dark dress, with what looked like a diamond necklace round her neck, and a man, who appeared to be in his sixties, sitting opposite her, who got stiffly to his feet at their entrance. There was also a girl, very tall, very thin, with hair as fair as Angela's. She was smoking a cigarette in a long, amber holder, and the glance that she flicked at Seraphina seemed to be both critical and curious. But the old man was coming forward, a hand held out. 'How do you do, Miss Todd?' he said in a deep and cultured voice. 'Let me introduce you to my wife, Mrs Truelove, and my daughter, Kay.'

Both women murmured some sort of greeting and stepped forward to shake hands, and Seraphina smiled and murmured back. Presently, Kay was instructed to take Miss Todd to her room, make sure that she had everything she wanted, and then go to her own room to change for dinner.

'You'd better collect her when you are both ready,' Mrs Truelove suggested, and actually gave Seraphina what in anyone less imposing might have been called a conspiratorial glance. 'This is a big, old-fashioned house and we don't want our guest getting lost and wandering around the passages until she dies of hunger.'

Kay laughed and actually tucked her hand into Seraphina's arm. 'No, and you might meet our family ghost, trotting along the corridor with his head under one arm and a monkey on his shoulder,' she said. 'But you may rely on me, Miss Todd. I'll be back to escort you to the dining room, never fear.'

At noon on Sunday, Mr Chamberlain announced that Britain was now at war with Germany and, suddenly, everything changed.

The Truelove family had assembled in the living room to hear Mr Chamberlain's speech on their wireless set, and Seraphina sat on the long, comfortable couch with Kay on one side of her and Roger on the other. By this time, Seraphina had become quite friendly with Kay, who was only a couple of years older than she, but still felt rather in awe of Roger's parents. When Mr Chamberlain had finished speaking, Mr Truelove got up and switched off the set. 'I suppose it was what we all expected,' he said heavily. 'But it's a nasty moment, nevertheless. However, even Chamberlain has got to live with himself, and how could he do so if we reneged on our promises to defend Poland?' He turned to Roger. 'You'll join up, of course. You've talked about the air force; well, it has to be your choice, but as an army man I'd have thought you would have kept to the family tradition.'

Roger smiled rather bleakly. 'Times change, Father,' he said. 'Most of my friends have put in for the air force.' He stood up and turned to Seraphina, taking her hands and helping her to her feet, though he continued to address his father. 'This is going to be a very different war from the last one, you know. There's bound to be fighting on the ground, of course, but look at the Spanish Civil War and the way that was fought. The outcome might have been very different without air power and the sort of bombing which destroyed Madrid and broke the spirit of the Republicans.'

'I expect you're right, my boy,' Mr Truelove said, sounding suddenly weary. 'You must do as you think best, of course.' He turned to his wife. 'They will have been listening to the wireless in the kitchen as well, but no doubt lunch will be served in an hour, as usual?'

His wife had begun to reply that she would just check with Cook when Kay spoke. 'I mean to join one of the services, Father,' she said quietly. 'We've all been talking about what we would do when war came and I'd really like to join the Women's Auxiliary Air Force, but of course that would be bound to mean living away from home; perhaps even going abroad. I'm told if I join the Land Army I could probably work on a farm within cycling distance of Dussendale . . . would you prefer that I did that?'

Mr Truelove looked undecided but his wife, whose face had been clouded with anxiety, was clearly relieved. 'Oh, Kay, my dear, that would be much better,' she said gratefully. She turned to Seraphina. 'Roger has told us that you are entering teacher training college in a week or so, to complete the course you started before your father died. Will this wretched war mean a change in your plans, too?'

Seraphina shrugged rather helplessly. 'I truly don't know,' she said. 'But I'll get in touch with the college tomorrow morning and find out what will be going on.'

Mrs Truelove left the living room to go down to the kitchen and Roger took Seraphina out to the stables to introduce her to his hunter, a tall, rangy chestnut, with a white blaze on his forehead. 'Tell you something funny,' Roger said, producing sugar lumps from his pocket and handing a couple to Seraphina so that she might feed the horse. 'I found my father down here, a couple of weeks back, and he said he was taking a last look at the horses, since when war came they were bound to be commandeered for the cavalry regiments, as they were in 1914. I didn't say anything, but this isn't going to be a war like the last; no charge of the Light Brigade for the cavalry of thirty-nine. No cavalry, for that matter.'

Seraphina laughed dutifully, though she did not, in fact, think it particularly funny, and when the gong sounded for luncheon she went indoors, meaning to buttonhole Kay and ask the older girl what she should do about her training course. The opportunity did not arise, however, since Roger, clearly restless and uneasy, took her to one side as soon as the meal was over. 'I'm sorry to cut your weekend short – and mine, of course – but I want to get back to the city as soon as possible,' he told her. 'I'm going to return by car – it's a small sports model, a two-seater – which means I can drop you off at your door, if that's all right?'

Seraphina said, rather numbly, that it would be fine. She was still in a state bordering on shock and found that she longed to get home so that she could discuss events with her mother.

Martha was not surprised when Seraphina came into the kitchen early on Sunday afternoon, but she was surprised to see her daughter's companion. He was a tall, blond young man, with a ready smile, dressed in sports jacket and flannels, with a striped scarf tucked into the neck of his white shirt. Seraphina introduced him, for Martha had not been present on the one occasion when Roger had called for her daughter at home. Angela had answered her mother's eager questions in her usual calm and temperate fashion. 'He's charming, good-looking and wears very nice clothes,' she had said. 'But Ma, he's . . . not one of us, if you see what I mean. Pa would have said he's out of the top drawer, and we really aren't, are we?'

'No, we aren't,' Martha had said, laughing. 'But it won't matter a jot, dearest Angie, if they are really fond of one another. I know you think kitchen maids only marry princes in story books, but it can happen in real life, I assure you.'

Angie had looked doubtful. 'But we all thought she was fond of Toby until she said that he was all wrong for her because he was just a railway porter and she was going to be a teacher,' she had pointed out.

Martha had assured her that if Fee had loved Toby, truly loved him, the difference in their social standing would not matter, but now, shaking hands with Roger and welcoming him to her home, she realised that she had not fully understood what Angela had been getting at. This young man was not simply rich, not simply from a good family; he was what, in the old days, would have been called Quality with a capital Q. Hiding her consternation, she bustled over to the stove and put the kettle on, saying as she did so: 'We've heard so much about you, Mr Truelove, that I feel I already know you. How sad that we should meet for the first time on the day that war is declared. I dare say you'll join up, in which case we shan't be seeing much of you, I fear.'

'Well you will, Ma,' Seraphina said, her tone over-bright, over-confident. 'Because Roger is going to join the air force so he's asked me to be his wife. We're getting engaged tomorrow, when the shops are open and he can buy me a ring, though it may be a while before we can actually tie the knot.'

Martha, getting cups and saucers down from the dresser, actually staggered slightly, then recovered herself. 'Isn't – isn't this rather – rather sudden?' she faltered. 'After all, this is a time of great uncertainty. Why, Mr Truelove might be ordered abroad immediately. And Fee, my love, you're only just nineteen. If it hadn't been for the war, I'm sure neither of you would have dreamed of taking such – such an important step.'

Seraphina scowled at her mother, but Roger answered her with his most winning smile. 'You're right, of course, Mrs Todd; if war had not been declared, we could have taken our time . . . that's what you mean, isn't it? But Seraphina and I have known one another for four whole months and, for my own part, I was convinced from day one that she was the only girl for me. I've never been one to wear my heart on my sleeve, but I don't mind telling you that I adore Seraphina and will take the greatest care of her.'

Martha murmured that she had no reason to doubt him and began to pour tea into three cups, whilst Seraphina, pink-cheeked and bright-eyed, hurried across to the pantry and got out a large fruit cake and a tin of biscuits. 'Don't fret yourself, Ma,' she said, giving her mother's hand a warning squeeze. 'We both know what we're doing. Roger drove me back from the country in his little sports car and we talked all the way about what was best to do. I know you think nineteen is too young, but you were only twenty when you married Pa.' She seized her mother's hands impulsively, shaking them as she did so. 'Wish us happy and give us your blessing, Ma,' she said pleadingly. 'We're in love and about to be separated. Make it easier for us.'

Martha sighed, knowing full well that if she forbade the engagement it would simply drive Seraphina into underhand behaviour, and might even make her do something she would later bitterly regret. 'Of course I wish you happy,' she said rather huskily. 'Will you slice and butter some bread, Seraphina? Your sisters will be in from their walk shortly and I'd like to get the meal over and done with by the time the six o'clock news comes on the wireless.'

It was the Saturday before Christmas. Evie and Percy had spent the previous day in the country, cutting holly, all of which they had sold, and they now intended to buy Christmas presents because although, as they were constantly told, 'there's a war on', it did not seem to Evie that it had made much difference. To be sure, Angela had left Bunney's and gone to make uniforms in a big factory, along with her friend Annabel. They got much more money than they had been paid in the shop and though Angela said the work was pretty boring, she enjoyed the company of the other girls and had recently made a couple of shy references to some sort of manager named Bob. He was elderly, a widower with two grown-up daughters, and had taken Angie to the theatre on one occasion and on another to an exhibition at one of the museums. Evie did not think there was anything romantic in such a friendship but her sister had been taking more interest in her appearance for some time and Evie thought this was a good thing.

As for Seraphina, she had been able to start at teacher training college, but was obviously unsettled. Sometimes she talked wildly of joining the WAAF, as friends of hers had done, clearly hoping that this might bring her closer to Roger, but at other times she talked of the schools in which she would most like to teach, even saying that after the war she meant to go to university and get a degree.

Evie could not make her eldest sister out. Toby wrote regularly, telling the Todds all about his life in the army, but so far as she knew, though Seraphina read the letters, she never wrote back, leaving this task to her mother and younger sisters. It was strange because Seraphina still maintained that she liked Toby, though only as a friend. And if I liked someone who had joined the army and been sent off to France I'd write to them, no matter what, Evie told herself. But, of course, there was Roger. He was about to start training to be a pilot and Seraphina had told them that he was almost certain to be sent abroad in order to do this. 'Some of the chaps go to Rhodesia, and others to Texas,' she had informed her family grandly. 'But before they go, the young men are given something called embarkation leave. When Roger gets his, I shall take time off from my course and we'll have a little holiday together.'

Seraphina had said this whilst they were having their evening meal and Evie had glanced anxiously at her mother's face, sure that she would disapprove. She had been right; Martha had said: 'I don't think that's very wise, love. Oh, I know you're engaged to Roger, but you aren't married. I know young men always promise to behave with respect and so on, but you've your reputation to consider. Teaching's a responsible job . . .'

Seraphina had tightened her lips and looked mulish. 'But Ma, he's going hundreds of miles away; we may not meet again till the end of the war,' she had pointed out. 'Besides, you're being most dreadfully old-fashioned. You brought me up to know how to behave. I wouldn't dream of allowing any funny business, if that's what you're afraid of.'

'Yes, but I didn't bring *him* up,' Martha had said, rather repressively. 'What you're suggesting sounds remarkably like honeymoon first and marriage later, which is never a good idea, because once a young man gets what he wants and thinks a girl is easy—'

But Seraphina, her cheeks flying scarlet flags, had interrupted. 'Roger isn't like that and nor am I,' she had said furiously. 'You know what you're doing, don't you, Ma? You're pushing me into marriage, because if that's the only way I can be with Roger, then I'll marry him just as soon as it can be arranged. And if you think he isn't keen on the idea, you couldn't be more wrong. He's pestered and pestered me to set a date, only I wouldn't. But I'm telling you, Ma, I'll do it rather than have to disappoint him over his embarkation leave.'

Evie had felt very uncomfortable and a glance at Angie's face showed her that her sister felt the same. Martha had begun to answer but Angie interrupted. 'I think Evie and I will go out for a little walk,' she had said, her voice unnaturally high. 'You and Fee are trying to have rather – rather an important talk, which is none of our business, so we'll just go for a stroll whilst you get it off your chests.'

Evie had agreed with alacrity, but Seraphina had shaken her head. 'No indeed; you shan't go out on my account. Ma and I have said all we want to say. Evie, if you'll start clearing the table, then I'll begin washing up.'

Right now, however, Evie and Percy were sauntering along Great Homer Street, weaving their way between the fascinating stalls which lined the pavement. They had already purchased small gifts for brothers and sisters and were looking for something for their respective mothers. They each had half a crown left – a great deal of money – and Evie meant to buy Martha a silk scarf to wear tucked inside her grey dress, and a small box of chocolates. She had already bought, and despatched to Toby, five Woodbine cigarettes, and knew that Percy had also bought cigarettes for his father, though she had tactfully pretended to believe his story that 'the fags are for me Uncle Nat'. She would have liked to tell him that he had every right to buy his hateful father a Christmas gift, but the words stuck in her throat. Mr Baldwin had been convicted of manslaughter and sentenced to fifteen years in prison, since it had been impossible to prove that he had deliberately pressed the release on his machine to send the heavy crate crashing on to Henry Todd. He had admitted he had meant to scare the other man, but strongly denied murderous intent. Evie was secretly glad of this, for Percy's sake really. Whilst the trial had been in progress, she had had dreadful nightmares and knew she was not the only member of her family to be relieved that Mr Baldwin had not gone to the gallows for his crime. 'Pa wouldn't have wanted it,' Seraphina had said, white-faced, when they had been told that Mr Baldwin would not hang. 'He never did believe in "an eye for an eye and a tooth for a tooth", even though it's in the Bible.'

'Oh, look, Evie!' Percy clutched her arm and pointed. 'I wonder how much that is? Me mam would love one of them.'

Evie followed the direction of Percy's pointing finger and saw a small statuette of a very beautiful lady wearing a swirling frock, the skirts of which she held away from her body with two hands. She stared at the tiny, perfect features, the delicate fingers and the polished marble of which the little figure was made, and shook her head reprovingly. 'She's probably five or ten bob, but don't forget what we said, Perce. Our mams need useful stuff, and you can't use an ornament, no matter how pretty. Besides, you said if I were getting my mam something to wear, you'd do the same.'

Percy agreed, rather glumly, that he would do as they had decided, and presently they came to a stall selling bright, silky squares with tasselled edges for a price they could afford. Percy bought a vivid scarlet one with white polka dots, and Evie purchased a similar one in blue. Then they went into a nearby sweet shop and bought two quarter-pound boxes of Black Magic. Having completed their purchases, they turned their steps back towards Scotland Road once more.

'What'll we do tomorrer, queen?' Percy said as they dodged along the busy pavement. 'My mam says she hates it when Christmas Eve is on a Sunday, 'cos none of the shops is open and there's nothin' to do but go to church, or sit at home, all miserable like. My mam says she won't lerrus wade into the Christmas grub and she won't cook 'cos she don't want to spoil our

Christmas dinner next day, so it'll be bread 'n' jam an' weak tea for us.'

'So it will for us, only I know very well what I shall be doing tomorrow afternoon, and it'll be a deal nastier than just hanging around,' Evie assured him. 'The government's been and gone and put sugar and meat on ration; it'll start after Christmas. Wilmslows' don't sell fresh meat, of course, but Mr Wilmslow wants to bag up a whole load of sugar so when folk come in with their ration books he won't have to do so much weighing up. Mam said we might as well all go down and give a hand – many hands make light work, she says – but Fee's going off out somewhere and Angie's busy with a lacy jumper which she wants to wear at Christmas, so it'll just be me and Mam.' She did not add that the family would want to visit their father's grave in Burscough after church on Sunday morning, because to make such a remark to Percy would be somewhat tactless, but that was why the sugar-bagging would be done in the afternoon. As for his being buried at Burscough, Martha had been sure it was what Harry would have wanted. 'If he'd been able to live out his time as we'd planned, we would have moved to Burscough, spent the rest of our lives with other canal folk, and died there,' she had told the girls. 'I shall feel he's amongst friends, even though it'll be a tad more difficult to visit than if he were buried in one of the Liverpool cemeteries.'

'I'd offer to give you a hand only I know old Wilmslow would chase me out of the shop and call me names,' Percy said gloomily, interrupting her thoughts. He shot a diffident sideways look at Evie. 'And on Boxing Day we – we're going prison visiting.'

Evie nodded and made a lightning decision. 'We're going visiting Sunday morning; going out to Burscough to put a big wreath of white lilies on our dad's grave,' she said, trying to sound casual but not succeeding very well. 'It's – it's hard for Mam at Christmas. She misses him all the time, of course, we all do, but it's worse at Christmas. When we were aboard the *Mary Jane*, we had such very good times. Even if it was snowing a blizzard or blowing a gale, we'd snug us down in the cabin and have a wonderful roast dinner, and we'd all sing carols . . . oh, Percy, don't look like that!'

Percy wiped his nose on his sleeve, then knuckled his eyes. 'At least you had good times,' he said gruffly. 'When I think of past Christmases, it's always me dad getting drunk and me mam cryin', an' dinner being spoilt 'cos she dared not serve up till he come home. I reckon this Christmas will be better'n that, even though our chicken's so little it's more like a sparrer, and the puddin' will be one of them real plain ones that Samples make an' sell cheap. But I dare say it'll be better grub than them poor devils are give in the forces.'

'I don't believe they do badly; Toby says they have huge cookhouses and some of the food's quite good,' Evie said. 'I'm going to write to him again when I get home . . . I wonder what he's doing now?'

'Hey, Toby, come over here a minute. You've got two letters and a parcel; wharrit is to be popular, eh?'

Toby had been tired, cold and stiff after a long day driving his ten-ton truck back and forth between the front line, which was pretty well against the Belgian frontier, and the rear, where the troops rested when they were off duty. When he had entered the long rickety hut, with its corrugated iron roof and ill-fitting windows, he had felt exhausted and depressed, but at the sight of the small square parcel and the two letters, his tiredness dropped from him like an unwanted cloak, and he hurried forward, grinning at his friend John Boyce, commonly known as Boysie. 'Two letters!' he said, taking them and the parcel from Boysie's outstretched hand. 'Somebody loves me . . . probably me mum.'

He sat down on his bed and slit open the first envelope. It was indeed from his mother and contained several sheets of closely written script. Toby's eyes skimmed briefly over it, checking that all was well with everyone, before he pushed it into his locker drawer; he would read it later when he had time to assimilate all the news without having to rush. The second letter was from Angela, and he slit it open still hoping against hope that Seraphina might have added at least a line, or sent him best wishes for Christmas. It seemed ridiculous that two old friends could completely ignore one another but he supposed that Seraphina, having cast him out, intended to forget all about him as speedily as possible.

Sitting down on his bed, he began to read. Angela was working in a uniform factory and told him that she enjoyed the work and felt she was making some contribution towards the war effort.

I was considering joining the ATS because I'm sure they need women almost as much as they need fighting men, Angela wrote. *We are all doing our best to help our country in our own ways. Evie has been collecting silver paper and clipping stamps off envelopes for ages now and also knitting – mostly blankets, fortunately, since she is shockingly bad at it. She's very impatient and when she drops a stitch, which is often, refuses to go back and pick it up, but simply makes a new one so that, at the end of the day, the object she is making is covered in what looks like moth holes. Of course she can't afford to buy wool in skeins or balls, but goes along to Paddy's market and begs ragged and useless woollen garments from the stallholders. She brings them home and Mother or I unravel them and put them through the wash. Then Evie gets out her needles and begins work.*

I expect Seraphina writes to you herself with all her news, but she is very busy at present with end of term exams so I will just tell you that she is doing very well and though she left her job in Lyon's Corner House, she has taken work on a Saturday in Blackler's, where she sells gloves, scarves and hats to ladies who have need of such things. As you know, she and Mr Truelove – he is a pilot officer in the Royal Air Force – have got engaged. He seems a very nice young man – he has told us we must call him Roger – and I am sure he will be a pleasant addition to the family. If I may speak frankly, Toby, I think we all had hopes for you and Fee, but recently I have begun to see that perhaps it might not have worked out. Fee is still the dearest of sisters but our father's death changed her more than it changed either me or Evie. She has grown a hard shell and it is difficult to know what goes on beneath it.

Toby stared down at the letter. Seraphina had never written him so much as one word since their quarrel, so he had no idea that she was contemplating marriage with horrible Roger Truelove and felt a little sick at the prospect. How could she, he thought wretchedly? Compared to their relationship, which had lasted for years, she and Truelove were strangers. Toby had known that Seraphina had a young man because Evie had mentioned him once or twice, but of course he had refused to let himself believe that the fellow was anything but a casual acquaintance who took Seraphina dancing and to the cinema from time to time. Out here in France, his own chances of any sort of social life were virtually non-existent, but then he had no wish to take out anyone except Seraphina. He had been in love with her for years and though she might be able to turn away from him, he could not follow suit. I'm pathetic, he told himself angrily, but I suppose it's just the way I am. So far as I'm concerned, there's only one woman in the whole world for me. I wish it were the same for Seraphina but it obviously isn't. And the worst of it is, it's all my own stupid fault. *Why, why* didn't I write? It wasn't as if my job was a particularly demanding one because, looking back on it, it was a piece of cake as the RAF fellows say; certainly no harder than what I'm doing at the moment. Yet now I write two or three letters a week and always find something to say. I know it's useless crying over spilt milk but it does seem hard to lose her altogether just because I was never much of a letter-writer.

However, he would have to accept that Seraphina would never be his, he told himself now, turning over the page to finish Angela's letter. There was not much more, just a bit about hoping he would have a good Christmas and saying that they rather dreaded a holiday spent in such different circumstances from those which had attended Christmases aboard the *Mary Jane*.

She had signed off, *From your affectionate friend, Angela Todd,* but had then added a postscript: *I always write as though I am expressing the feelings of my whole family, and so I am I'm sure, but today, because my thoughts are very much with you, so far from us at the festive season, may I tell you that I think of you with deep affection, as though you were, in fact, a member of my own family.* And then there was a shaky little arrow leading to the words: *Happy Christmas, Toby, with love from Angela.*

Toby sat and stared at the postscript; what on earth did Angela mean? In his mind's eye, he conjured up a picture of her fair and gentle face, the soft pale hair, the steady regard of the dark blue eyes. It had never crossed his mind before to consider her beautiful, but now he realised that she was. Oh, she lacked the fire and vivacity of his beloved Seraphina, but she was beautiful, nevertheless, and she had a gentleness of spirit which, he told himself, would be a lot easier to live with than Seraphina's fieriness and unpredictability. And Angela was loyal and steadfast. Now that he thought about it, he realised that she had written to him once or twice a week ever since he had joined the army, and now she had sent him her love. Knowing her as he did, he realised that it could not have been easy for her to put her feelings into words, for he had no doubt that Angela meant what she said. Perhaps it was just because it was Christmas, perhaps it was to ease the pain of the blow she had dealt him when she spoke of her sister's engagement to Roger Truelove, but he knew Angela would never send her love lightly.

He stared down at the letter for some time, wondering what best to do. He could scarcely pretend an affection he did not feel, but he decided that if he ever got leave – if he ever got home again – he would take Angela out, perhaps dancing, perhaps on a long country walk, and see how the two of them got on together. He did not intend to make love to her, but just to get to know her better, and he thought that this would suit Angela too, since she, after all, could not have considered him as anything but her sister's friend until very recently.

Having come to a decision of sorts, Toby folded the letter and tucked it into the top pocket of his battledress. Then, abruptly, he remembered the parcel. His name and details were printed in block capitals and hope blossomed again as he carefully untied the string and began to unwrap the brown paper. You never know, he told himself as he did so, Seraphina may have realised that this Truelove fellow is just a horrible mistake. She may have decided to extend the hand of friendship, if nothing more. If this is a Christmas present from Seraphina . . . oh God, please God, let it be from Seraphina!

He unwrapped the last piece of brown paper and five tiny Woodbine cigarettes rolled on to his lap. They had been encased in a sheet of thin, cheap paper from an exercise book, and with his heart diving into his sturdy army boots, he recognised Evie's handwriting.

Dearest, darling Toby, I doesn't have much money but I know all soldiers smoke cigarettes and you all like to have them. So here are five which I bought you from the shop up the road. I would have sent you some gloves, the sort without fingers which everyone is knitting, though I think it's daft because your fingers are the bits that get coldest, aren't they? The thing is, though, that the ones I knitted for you have come out a bit strange – there's some rather big holes (not just the ones your fingers go through) and Angie says I didn't remember thumbs grow further down your hand than what fingers do, so all my 'meant' holes are in a row, which Angie said were wrong . . . she's so fussy! So I'm knitting you a scarf instead but I'm rather slow; Angie says it will do for next Christmas.

We are all well and are having a nice piece of pork for our Christmas dinner. It is cheaper than beef and besides, my pal Percy and me go scrumping round the stalls every Saturday night and pick up fades which the stallholders don't want. Mam peels all the apples and cooks them up and puts them into jars with airtight lids, so we'll have plenty of apple sauce to go with the pork. It's a piece of leg and Mam rubs salt into the crackling to make it hard and crispy. I wish you could share it with us, Toby; you always said Mam was the best cook in the world and she still is.

Everyone is saying that this is a queer old war; Seraphina's feller calls it a phoney war because nothing much is happening, and no one has tried to invade us yet. Lots of the kids who were evacuated when war started have come back to Liverpool because their mams say they need them here. I didn't go because I had bronchitis and when I got better it just seemed daft, but I wouldn't go now 'cos I'd rather be here than stuck out in the country somewhere by myself.

I must go now as there is a lot to do. Percy and me is going to cut holly an' sell it nearer Christmas. Percy thinks we'll make heaps of money and I want to buy Mam and the girls nice presents. Mr Wilmslow says everything will be rationed before long, which we shan't like. I wish you were home, Toby. We all miss you. Mam says take care of yourself and she'll write soon. Lots and lots of love. Your friend, Evie.

Smiling to himself at her exuberant display of puppy-like affection, he almost missed the postscript, scribbled at the very bottom of the page.

PS Seraphina has just come in so I told her I were writing to you. She said, 'Oh. Tell him to have a good Christmas. Tell him we're thinking of him.' Much love, again, E.

Toby stared, unbelievingly, at the words and then felt a slow smile begin to spread across his face. She was melting, if only a little. He longed to write to her, to apologise all over again for his behaviour, but a new caution warned him that this was not necessarily the sensible thing to do. She might easily resent his getting in touch just when she had got engaged to this Truelove fellow. Truelove! What a ridiculous name. No, he would bide his time. Besides, he and Fee were now on what you might call level pegging. She had written to him, unanswered, for six months, and he had done the same. Now he thought only his personal intervention could affect the issue; letters might merely aggravate it. He picked up the cigarettes and tucked them and Evie's letter carefully into his other breast pocket, smiling as he did so. Evie was a sweet kid and he could rely on her to tell him which way the wind was blowing so far as Seraphina was concerned. Then he remembered that it had been Angela who had broken the news of Seraphina's engagement, and not Evie. But perhaps Evie was trying to spare his feelings; she really did seem to know how he felt about her eldest sister. Sighing, Toby got to his feet and headed for the hut door, glancing once more at Evie's PS which he already knew by heart. Seraphina was thinking of him! It might not be much but it would have to suffice for now. Whistling, he set off for the cookhouse.

Chapter Eight

Dawn comes early in May and so, unfortunately, did the German fighter planes. Light was barely beginning to seep across the land when Toby was awoken as much by the roar of engines as by the pale and creeping grey of morning. He and his friend Boysie were lying in a ditch – fortunately a fairly dry ditch – overhung by a thick hedge, and further along the same ditch the rest of his platoon were spread out in its shelter, but now everyone began struggling to their feet. If they're like me, they're aching in every limb, Toby thought, as his weary muscles screamed a protest. The previous day they had marched forty miles as they had done the day before that, for this was an army in retreat, making its way down to the coast in the hope – probably vain – of being taken off before they were completely overrun by the enemy.

It had all happened so suddenly that none of them had been prepared. The Maginot Line in which the French had placed such total confidence had been a whole war out of date. The Panzer divisions had rolled across it as though it did not exist, though of course it had been the war from the air which had really crushed them. Every day since the Germans had crossed the Belgian frontier into France, the planes had shrieked overhead, machine-gunning, bombing and terrorising as they came. The Stukas emitted a fearsome noise as they dived towards the earth and a pal of Boysie's had said that the planes had sirens on their wings which made that dreadful, unearthly screaming. But most of Toby's platoon neither knew nor cared about the noise; noise rarely kills, but tracer bullets and bombs decimated the fleeing troops and broke their morale. Everyone had expected to make a stand, consolidate, face the enemy. Instead, they had been told at once to retreat so that they could re-form in Britain. It seemed to Toby, now, that this was the most disorganised rabble that had ever called itself an army. They were ill equipped, ill trained and ill informed. They had been making their way towards the coast now for four days and there had been no food provided, though most of them had managed to beg, borrow or, alas, steal from the farms and cottages they passed. They had been told to destroy all heavy equipment, including all vehicles, which was the sort of madness it would take a general to think up, Toby thought vindictively. A man who travelled everywhere by staff car would not consider how thousands of men were meant to make their way across hundreds of miles of unfriendly terrain without so much as a bicycle to speed them on their way. Toby's commander had been furious, had actually dared to load a great many men into a couple of lorries, had commandeered enough jerry cans of petrol to get them to the coast, and had then seen his men forced to disembark to allow a skinny, strutting senior officer, with a walrus moustache and weak eyes, to set fire to the vehicles. When the petrol had exploded, the officer with the walrus moustache had been thrown ten feet, broken both legs, and had all his hair, his moustache and most of his uniform burned off.

They had left him. Thanks to him, there were now no vehicles in which to convey the wounded. When one had to abandon a friend, it was with pain and regret and the hope that the German forces, so close behind, would treat the wounded well, but that officer could have rotted in hell for all the men cared.

'Toby? Ready to move on, old feller?' That was Boysie, stretching and rubbing bleary eyes. 'The rest of 'em's just about coming awake, so if we gerra move on we might forage us up some breakfast.'

Toby nodded. Boysie had been most impressed when Toby had showed him how to milk a cow, crouching in the field and milking it into his tin helmet. And then there had been the eggs. Toby had found a hen's nest deep in an overgrown ditch, and he and Boysie, and several other members of the platoon, had eaten the eggs raw since they were marching, and in any case had no means of cooking them.

As the men abandoned the ditch, a dive bomber came hurtling towards them, its guns spitting. Everyone scattered, and afterwards did not re-form even into the ragged line which had crept along when the sky had been clear of any aircraft. Now, they journeyed in twos and threes, dodging from tree to hedge, diving gladly into a wood when they reached it, hating the flat water meadows upon which a man showed up like a flake of snow in a coalfield.

Toby and Boysie ate a handful of raw turnips, drank some milk from a cow whose udder bulged – she was glad of the relief – and Toby found time to wonder why the farmer had not brought his beasts in for milking. Further along, the reason was clear enough: the farm had been bombed flat to the ground, a thread of smoke still rising from a burned-out barn. God knew who would milk the cows now, Toby thought in some distress. And God knew how this country would ever recover from the hammer blows the Germans were raining on it. Surely one did not conquer a country and then raze it to the ground? But Toby guessed that this was only happening because the British Expeditionary Force was retreating slowly across the land, trying to reach the channel ports; as soon as the army was totally destroyed, then the bombardment would stop and life would return, to some extent at least, to normal.

Another aeroplane roared overhead, the bullets it was pouring down on to the little lane they were traversing kicking up spurts of dust. The two men hurled themselves into the ditch for the dozenth time in an hour and Boysie said uneasily: 'I dunno as we'll ever make it, old pal. Me belly thinks me throat's been cut, I'm that hungry, and me bones is aching from chucking meself into these perishin' ditches. How about finding somewhere to kip down for a few hours? Then we could walk at night – we'd be safer, I reckon. Any idea how much further we've gorrer go?'

Toby had no idea but he did not mean to say so for he knew they must simply keep going whilst they had the strength. 'It can't be far now,' he said cheerfully. 'Haven't you noticed? The nearer we get to the coast, the hotter the bombardment. Oh aye, I reckon we're closer than you think.'

Boysie gave him a weary grin out of his dirt-smeared, exhausted face. 'I reckon you're right,' he said. He was still carrying his rifle though his gas mask had gone long ago. 'C'mon then, best foot forward!'

They reached the coast soon after midnight, having been instructed by an officer that they must head for Dunkirk since it had been arranged that the men would be picked up from there. By now they were bone-weary, stumbling along in the darkness with many other men. They were all white-faced, exhausted and starving hungry, but worst of all they were leaderless. In the dark it was impossible to pick out the badges of rank, but in any event it was every man for himself, because of the constant bombardment and the dreadful conditions.

Toby had been afraid of missing Dunkirk, but as soon as they got within a few miles of it they could see it all right for it was on fire, lighting the sky with a fearful golden glow which at first glance he had thought was the approaching dawn. Boysie, trudging along beside him, remarked that the Jerries had lit a signal flare which would guide the British ships to the troops, though doubtless this had not been their intention. No one laughed, though, when they were near enough to see the damage which had been inflicted on the small town. There was very little left of it and a thick pall of black smoke hung over the ruins.

'The poor people,' Toby muttered. 'I hope to God they were given some warning before the bombs began to fall. Then at least they might have saved themselves, even if their homes and businesses were gone for good.'

Boysie snorted. 'This is war, you fool,' he said roughly. 'What warning did we have that the bleedin' Belgians were going to give in and the French were going to retreat through our lines? It were a complete shambles and we were caught up in the middle of it.'

Someone stumbling along beside them said quietly: 'We might have guessed something of the sort would happen, though. Half of us never got no equipment and what we did have had been used by our dads during the last lot. Them Germans know what they're doing and that bleedin' Führer of theirs knows what they need 'cos they practised during the Spanish Civil War. And they've got the most modern stuff you could wish for.'

Another voice, this one with a Scottish accent, spoke out of the darkness. 'Them poor bloody Belgians though; they fought like tigers, blew up the bridges, did their best to keep the Huns out, unlike the French. If the Frogs hadn't broken and retreated through our ranks, I reckon we could have made a stand.'

'Ah well, fellers, you know what they say: *He who fights and runs away will live to fight another day.*'

It was an older voice and Toby, peering through the darkness, caught a glimpse of greying hair above the man's dirt-smeared face and guessed he must be a regular, aware of a thing or two which the volunteers had yet to learn. He grinned at the man. 'That's what General Brooke's hoping, I imagine – that we can somehow get across the Channel, re-equip ourselves, and fight on,' he said. 'But how they mean to get us back is beyond me.' He gestured to the ruined town ahead of them. 'Look what they've done there! If we reach the beaches, then I reckon as soon as daylight comes the aircraft will be over our heads again, strafing anything that moves. And we can't fight back, 'cos they made us destroy all our weapons.'

'I hung on to my rifle for a bit,' Boysie remarked, 'but it were heavy and I'd no ammunition for it, so there weren't no point.' He turned to Toby. 'At least we can both swim, old feller, and it looks as though it may come to that.'

Someone ahead of them turned. 'Less of that, lad,' he said in a broad Yorkshire accent. 'My brother's in the Royal Navy; the Senior Service won't let us down.'

Toby and Boysie crawled through the sand dunes as dawn was beginning to blanch the sky in the east. They looked down towards the sea and Toby thought that the beach was now no longer a strand but a battleground. There were huge craters where bombs had dropped, and bodies that once had sprawled in the sun now sprawled in the abandonment of death. Yet, as the light strengthened, he could see the lines of patient men snaking down towards and into the sea, until some of them were up to their shoulders in water. Toby realised that the slope of the beach was very long and the water correspondingly shallow, which meant, of course, that the patiently hovering ships could not come in to pick up the men they had been sent to save. Instead, little boats were ferrying the troops out to the larger vessels, working indomitably through the hail of machine-gun bullets, the crash and thunder of falling bombs, and the devilish shriek of the Stukas.

Boysie hoisted himself up on to his knees. 'We'd best be moving down or we'll get left,' he said huskily. 'If only we had an ack-ack battery then we could fight back. Where's the RAF then?'

Toby shrugged. No use complaining, or feeling bitter. And no use joining the long queues until there was at least a chance that you might get to the head of one and be taken off. Hunger gnawed at his belly and fear gnawed at his mind, but he knew he must ignore both, as everyone on these accursed beaches was ignoring them. He heaved a sigh and moved to a more comfortable position, and as he did so something rustled in the breast pocket of his battle dress. A letter? Wearily, he unbuttoned the flap and drew out a piece of paper in which was wrapped . . . good God, it was Evie's Christmas present. He felt a smile begin, then felt tears rise, unbidden. He choked them back and held out the cigarettes to the men nearest him. 'Anyone gorra match?' he enquired rather unsteadily, and ignored the ribald comment, 'Your face and my arse', which immediately came from three separate throats.

Good old Evie. He had tucked the cigarettes away and forgotten all about them and now, when he needed something desperately, there they were.

Evie was sitting at the kitchen table, spreading margarine on slices of bread, when Seraphina burst into the kitchen. It was a warm day and her coat had flown open and the neat cotton frock she had donned to go to her college classes that morning already looked weary, but her face was alight with excitement. 'Evie, they're taking them off,' she said, her voice pitched higher than usual and her eyes bright. 'The BEF, I mean. I met one of my old customers from Lyon's – he's a rating in the Royal Navy now, and he says he's been ordered back to his ship and they're going to set off for France right away. Everyone's going ... why, the good old Mersey ferries are going ... so it looks as though our fellers must have reached the coast. Oh, God, I hope Toby – and all our other friends – will be home in a day or so.'

Evie threw down her knife and jumped to her feet. 'Oh, Fee, if only you're right,' she said, seeing her sister's face through a blur of sudden tears. 'Is there anything we can do to help? I can row a boat, you know, and I'm sure I could help stoke, if they need stokers.'

Seraphina laughed. 'There's nothing we can do up here. It would be different if we lived down south, at one of the channel ports, but the fellers will probably be put on trains once they get back to England and end up all over the place. My customer said he thought they were going to be sent back to where they first volunteered. As for being able to row, what do you think the Channel is – the lake at Prince's Park? No, the boats that go across the Channel will be ships really, like the *Daffodil* and the *Iris*, but I expect they'll want volunteers to man the railway stations because whenever the trains stop the WVS will be handing out sandwiches and hot drinks, or so they say.'

'Who says?' Evie said, almost dancing with impatience. 'I want to help – I want to help! It's all right for you and Angie, you're both doing something towards the war effort, but even my knitting isn't good enough . . . no, don't deny it, I caught Angie unpicking that scarf I were making for Toby and knitting it up again without the holes.'

Seraphina giggled. 'Look, you do as much as any other kid your age,' she said. 'But as for helping in the evacuation of the British Expeditionary Force . . . well, that isn't for children, particularly girls. I don't want to hurt your feelings, queen, but you are only twelve. And come to that, training to be a teacher isn't what I'd call war work.'

Evie heaved an exaggerated sigh. 'But you knit lovely. You must have made at least twenty pairs of mittens for the troops and yards and yards of scarves,' she observed. She ran across the kitchen and reached down her coat from the hook at the back of the door. 'Just tell Mam I'm going down to the Pier Head to find out what's going on and see if I can help,' she said. 'I may be gone ages and ages, so none of you are to worry.' She began to turn the handle, then looked back over her shoulder at her sister, her face alive with mischief. 'I reckon they'll bring your Roger home if they're bringing the BEF back, because France won't be safe for anyone,' she observed. 'Then I suppose you'll get married – more fool you! I'd sooner marry Toby any day, meself.'

Seraphina opened her mouth to protest just as the door slammed behind her sister, so she sat down in the chair Evie had vacated and began spreading margarine on the loaf her mother had thoughtfully sliced before going down to work in the shop. She wondered just what her sister intended to do. She suspected that it would probably include activities of which their mother would disapprove, such as trying to sneak aboard one of the ships bound for the rescue mission, but she had sufficient faith in the seamen to believe that Evie's attempts to board would be thwarted. And if she wants to help the WVS, then why not, Seraphina thought, spreading furiously. In half an hour, Angie and her mother would come in from their respective jobs and be glad to have a meal already prepared for them. Not that bread and marge was a meal, exactly, but there was the good smell of stew coming from the big black pan on the stove and another pot, which she guessed held potatoes, was just waiting to be pulled over the flame. Evie says she does nothing for the war effort, but enabling Mam and Angie to get on with their work and come home to a decent meal is more than I do, Seraphina told herself. And I wonder if she's right and Roger really will come home from France? That would be wonderful.

Roger was piloting a Spitfire now, and eight weeks ago had been sent to France – before that he had been really far away, in Rhodesia, learning his trade – where she supposed he would now be attacking the Luftwaffe and defending the retreat of the BEF. Seraphina smiled down at the beautiful sapphire ring, with its encircling diamonds, which graced the third finger of her left hand. Dear Roger! He had wanted to marry her before he left for Rhodesia, but her mother had said firmly that if one married in haste one repented at leisure, and had begged her not to do anything so rash. Seraphina had been tempted to ignore her mother's words but had finally complied, mainly because her teacher training course was an intensive one and allowed her little or no time to plan the sort of wedding she would have liked. However, if he really did come home now, she thought that they would marry after she'd taken her final exams in June, only a matter of two weeks away.

She got up from her seat to pull the potato saucepan over the heat and move the stew off it and heard foot-falls on the iron stair. Good; it would be Angie returning from her work at the uniform factory. Seraphina smiled to herself. Angie had changed a lot since starting at the factory, for she had speedily risen, from being an ordinary machinist, to the post of super-visor and hand-finisher. Seraphina had thought Angie would let the girls in her charge ride roughshod over her, but she had been wrong. Other girls at the factory told Seraphina that Angie never shouted or lost her temper and was always willing to spend time explaining how to get the best out of the machines if one of the girls was falling behind with her work. She joined them in the canteen and sometimes went to the pictures with them, yet somehow managed to keep both their respect and their liking and this, Seraphina knew, was no mean feat. Seraphina had done a good deal of practical class work and now knew the narrow path one had to tread between being liked and losing the respect of her pupils. Seraphina loved to be popular but recognised that popularity can sometimes only be bought by losing control, and she admired Angie greatly, for her sister could not send a rowdy machinist to the headmaster for punishment, or give her six hard wallops on the palm of her hand with the classroom ruler as a teacher could.

Seraphina pulled the pan of potatoes over the heat

and turned to smile as the kitchen door opened. Angie smiled back and came right into the room but did not remove her coat. 'Have you heard the news, Fee?' she asked, before Seraphina could so much as open her mouth. 'They're bringing the BEF back from France, which means that Toby will be coming home. A member of the WVS came to the factory asking for volunteers to go down to the station. They say our boys are arriving in a pretty bad state so they want women to hand out sandwiches and hot drinks. The Salvation Army will be there, you may be sure, helping in any way they can, but we all agreed we'd go down to Lime Street as soon as our shift finished, and do anything we could to help.' She looked questioningly at her sister. 'What about you, Fee? Are you going to come too? I popped into the shop on my way past and told Ma what I was doing. She said she'd like to help but she would do so later in the evening.' She glanced around the kitchen. 'Where's Evie? I made sure she'd have been indoors by now, helping to get the meal.'

Seraphina laughed shortly. 'Evie has pipped you at the post,' she said drily. 'She's gone off down to the Pier Head, hoping to sneak aboard one of the ships bound for France. As if they'd let a kid of her age do anything so crazy! But look, you'd best get something to eat before you go. Will stew and bread and marge do? Only the spuds won't be cooked for twenty minutes or so.'

Angie, however, shook her head, though she reached for the jar of jam and two rounds of bread, and made herself a thick sandwich. 'I'll eat this on my way to the station,' she said. 'I'll have the stew when I get in tonight. TTFN, Fee.'

*   *   *

224

Toby and Boysie spent two days and nights in the sand dunes, dug in against the marram grass with their eyes fixed on the beach below, and their ears resounding with the fearful din of enemy aircraft overhead, and several times with horrendous explosions as one of the ships waiting to take the troops off was hit.

Toby thought that he would never forget the scenes of carnage on the beach below, or the bravery of the men awaiting their turn to be picked up. The little boats took aboard as many men as they could safely hold, heaving them over the gunwales and into the relative safety of their small craft, and then helping them to climb aboard the big ships. There was no panic, no sign that the men were aware of the fearful danger in which they stood. They queued across the sand, then walked stoically into the water, only stopping when it reached their necks. Fortunately, the sea was calm with scarcely a wave disturbing the surface which was just as well, Toby reflected. Had any sort of sea been running, he doubted whether a tenth of the men would have reached the patiently waiting ships.

They decided to move at dusk on the third day and discovered for themselves the sheer awfulness of being completely exposed to enemy fire. Useless to duck or dodge when the bullets rained down, you just had to pray that this one did not have your name on it. But the queue of men moved steadily forward until Toby's ankles, then his knees, and then his waist were in the water. His battledress was ripped and filthy and he saw men around him shedding theirs since it was possible that they might have to swim to reach the rescue craft. As the sky gradually lightened the Luftwaffe returned, and behind him Boysie said bitterly: 'Where's the Brylcreem boys then? We've been here days and norra sign of them.'

By now, they were up to their chests in water. A small man with red hair scowled at Boysie. 'My brother's in the air force, flying one of the old Stringbags,' he said aggressively, in a strong Scottish accent. 'He'll be up there somewhere. The trouble is we've not got the numbers, else our fellers wouldnae sit back and see us taking it like this.'

'Sorry, mate,' Boysie said apologetically. But Toby realised his friend was speaking to empty air; the red-headed soldier had disappeared. Hastily, he took a deep breath and ducked under the surface. The small soldier had stepped into one of the many underwater shell holes and might have drowned had Toby and Boysie not heaved him out and supported him between them. The little Scot, coughing and gasping, and spouting water like a whale, thanked them hoarsely, and whilst they were still supporting him a boat drew alongside them and a peremptory voice ordered: 'Chuck him aboard and get yourselves aboard too. It's dangerous work coming in close to the shore; the sooner we're off again, the sooner we can be back to pick up more of your mates.'

Toby tumbled on to the bottom boards and simply lay there, suddenly realising that he was too tired even to worry about the hail of bullets or the concussion of bombs. He had not eaten for three days and had been awake day and night. He was filthy, soaking and defeated. Now, he slept.

Evie had gone to the Pier Head but had immediately realised she had no chance of sneaking aboard a vessel so had made for Lime Street station. She saw a train come in, saw the soldiers streaming off it, and knew why the grown-up ladies handing out hot tea and sand-wiches wept. Every man was filthy, worn out and dressed in a uniform which was little better than rags. Many were no more than boys, many were wounded, and all had despair written large on their pale countenances. She saw young men she had known and scarcely recognised them, but she did not see Toby.

'But this is only the first batch,' she heard one WVS say to another. 'From what I've heard, they'll be coming for days yet. Don't worry, Esther, your Jack will be here. Why, the British army can't afford to lose fellers like Jack. But it may be a day or two, possibly more, before he arrives. You can't stay on the station all that time, but I'm sure you could share the task of waiting for him with some other member of the family if you think it's important for him to be greeted by someone he knows.'

'I think it's very important, judging by the state of most of the fellers we've seen,' the other woman said seriously. 'I don't see why I shouldn't stay myself . . . I can snooze in the corner of the refreshment room, between trains.'

Evie thought about Toby. She knew he was fond of his large family, knew they were fond of him, but Toby had always been a bit of a loner, escaping from the crowded, tumbledown cottage whenever he could, spending more time with the Todds than he had with them. Now, the thought of him returning to England to find no one waiting on the platform was horrible to her. Seraphina had spurned him, made it plain she preferred Roger, and though Evie was sure that this was just a phase her sister was going through, she still hated to think of Toby's disappointment if he should find no one waiting.

Evie had always been resourceful. She borrowed a piece of paper and a pencil from a passing porter, wrote a note to her mother explaining that she meant to stay on the station to welcome Toby and would bring him back to the flat when he appeared, and then gave it to a very small dirty boy, telling him to deliver it to Wilmslow's on the Scotland Road where her mam would reward him with a few coppers or possibly – eyeing his skinny frame – a sandwich or a buttered scone. The child's eyes brightened at the mention of food and he snatched the note and made off. Evie settled down to wait.

It was three days and two nights before her vigil was rewarded. In that time, both her mother and sisters had visited the station, stayed there for as long as they could, and then left. Of course, they had urged her to return home with them, but by this time Evie was very much the pet of both the station staff and the WVS ladies. She had her own corner in the Ladies' Waiting Room, her own blanket and a cushion someone had found up, and reliable friends who made sure she was woken whenever a train came in. Everyone thought her devotion to duty touching; most thought it was a brother for whom she waited, but they were all happy to have her with them, handing out sandwiches, cakes and cups of tea, laughing and joking with the exhausted and filthy troops, whilst her eyes scanned every weary, stubbly face in a vain search for her old friend.

She had almost stopped believing that he would ever appear when, in the late afternoon of the third day, an arm went round her shoulders and a bristly cheek was pressed to hers. 'If it isn't little Evie Todd,' said Toby's voice. 'What the devil are you doing here, luv? And does your mam know you're out?'

Evie dropped her basket, flung both arms round Toby's neck and burst into tears. 'Oh, Toby, Toby, I'm so glad you're alive,' she sobbed. 'I wanted to help, of course I did, but I wanted to find you most of all. I meant to try to get aboard one of the ships so I could help to bring you fellers off, but they wouldn't let me, so I've waited here instead. Mam and the girls say I'm to take you back to the flat. Then you can have a proper meal and a good night's sleep before going on to Micklethwaite.'

'But how the devil did you know I'd come here first?' Toby asked, wonderingly. 'I didn't even know myself until we were being marshalled on to the train.'

'Seraphina said that everyone was going to be sent back to where they first joined up. I – I didn't think she were thinking of you, exactly, but I remembered you'd told us, right after you joined, that you'd been sent to Liverpool to sign up. So I just knew you'd be coming back here.'

Toby put a weary arm round her shoulders and rumpled her hair. 'And when they told us we were headed for Liverpool, there was me thinking it seemed as though fate wanted me to come to Seraphina's home town, even though I knew she had . . . other interests.' He sighed, then gave Evie a brief hug. 'Oh, well – it doesn't really matter. What matters is that I'm back and that you came down to meet me. Shall we go?'

'Yes; we'll catch a tram and be home in no time,' Evie said. 'Isn't it *awful* that we had to let France and Belgium and everybody down? But at least you've got home safely. Will you have to go on being a soldier? Well, I suppose you will, but I expect you'll stay in England, because everyone says the Germans are bound to try to invade us, so we'll need heaps of soldiers to fight them off.'

'They told us to go home and await further instructions,' Toby said gruffly.

'Oh . . . hang on a moment, Toby. I've just spotted Mr Johnson – he's a member of the railway staff – and

I ought to tell him I've found you, because he – and everyone else – has been ever so kind. I've even got my own seat in the corner of the Ladies' Waiting Room, where I've had a snooze when there have been no trains due.'

She broke away from him but Toby caught her arm. 'Hang on a minute! Just how long have you been on this station, young lady?'

Evie twinkled at him. 'Three days and two nights,' she admitted. 'I've been handing out sandwiches and cups of tea, telling people which platform they needed for which train, cleaning the waiting rooms . . . oh, I've been doing my bit, honest I have, Toby.'

Toby grinned, then rubbed his hands across his tired, travel-stained face. 'You're incredible, Evie Todd,' he said. 'C'mon then, let's go and tell this Mr Johnson that you won't be around for a bit.'

The queue for the tram was a long one and tired though he was, Toby had done a good deal of sitting on the train, so when Evie suggested walking home he was glad to agree. As they strolled along the pavement, he looked sideways at his companion, thinking to himself that she was a grand kid, full of courage and good humour. It was a pity she was so plain, with her straight light brown hair, small twinkling eyes and mischievous monkey face. She would never be a beauty like her sisters. He remembered her father lamenting that Evie had taken after himself and not after his wife, as the two older girls had. But Toby thought that this was no bad thing; Harry was the finest man he had ever known and right now, to Toby's prejudiced eye, it seemed that Evie was going to be just like him. Kind, generous, always thinking of others, never considering himself, Harry had been head and shoulders above all the other barge masters. Evie was only a kid but she was shaping up to be just like her dad, not only in looks but in character too.

Then Toby thought of Martha, of the constant struggle she had shared with Harry whilst aboard the *Mary Jane*, and of the worse struggle she had had since his death. So to be like her was a pretty good way to be as well. But though Seraphina and Angie were like Martha in looks, he did not think that either of them had inherited her nature. He thought, bitterly, that Seraphina seemed to want a career and a rich husband more than anything else, and Angie was too meek and biddable; he could not imagine her standing up for herself or coping with a lively family and a difficult job.

'Nearly there,' Evie said cheerfully. 'The shop's closed which means Mam will be in the flat getting the tea; I can't wait to see her face when you walk in. And I reckon Seraphina will be home, too.'

Martha was at the stove, withdrawing a large meat and potato pie from the oven, when someone banged on the back door. Seraphina was sitting at the table finishing off some of her college work and did not even look up, and Martha thought, rather crossly, that examinations were all very well but even the most dedicated student could answer the door when she could see her mother was busy; had, in fact, got her hands all too full. But Seraphina wasn't a bad girl, only a bit thoughtless, Martha told herself. She said, crisply: 'Door, Seraphina,' and her daughter immediately got to her feet. She would have gone to the door, but suddenly it was hurled open and Evie bounced into the room, dragging a tattered figure behind her. Martha stared, gasped and dropped the meat and potato pie on to the table. Then she was in Toby's arms, hardly knowing how she had got there, hugging him, tears running down her cheeks. The last time she had seen him had been just before he left for France. He had been cheerful, bronzed by the summer sun and by living an outdoor life, and he had looked smart in his uniform, his forage cap at a jaunty angle on his dark, close-cropped hair. Now, he looked terrible: his face was drawn and pale, his eyes were hopeless and his uniform hung in rags. Martha held him back from her, trying to brush off her tears until she saw that he, too, was weeping. But it would not do to notice, she realised that. Instead, she ushered him to the table and sat him down, sweeping Seraphina's books and papers aside as she did so.

Her eldest daughter came forward a trifle timidly. 'I'm glad you're back, Toby,' she said, rather stiffly. 'You must have been through a terrible time. Angie and I, and Ma, too, have been down at the station helping the WVS whenever we could, and we heard some dreadful stories. But I'll clear my stuff out of your way and go and make up the bed in the small room with clean sheets, so you can get your head down as soon as tea's over.'

She bustled out of the room before Toby could reply and Martha was just considering following her daughter and telling her to be a little more gracious when the back door opened again and Angie came into the room. She uttered a squawk of pleasure upon seeing Toby, who struggled to his feet just in time to give her a hug as she cast herself at him. Martha stared; this was meek, shy Angela! But then, Martha remembered, her daughters had known Toby most of their lives and probably considered him the brother they had never had.

'Oh, Toby, it's wonderful that you're home and safe,'

Angela was saying, gently pushing him back into the chair once more. 'I can see you've had a horrible time . . . oh, your arm! I think, before you eat, you should be cleaned up a bit. Ma, where's the First Aid box?'

Martha crossed the kitchen and, without ceremony, unbuttoned Toby's ragged shirt. On his left arm, a cut ran from wrist to elbow, still sluggishly bleeding, and there were scratches, abrasions and bruises all over his torso. Martha winced, then glanced approvingly at her middle daughter. 'Good girl, Angie; I'm ashamed to say I hadn't thought . . . didn't realise . . . but you're quite right. Evie, go and run the bath. Angie, go downstairs and borrow a pair of trousers and a shirt from Mr Wilmslow . . . and some shoes. Tell him he'll have them back within a few days. I'll just pop the pie back into the oven and fetch the First Aid box.' She smiled encouragingly at Toby. 'Take your time in the bath, lad; my old dressing gown is hung on the back of the bathroom door so you can slip into that when you're clean, and I'll see to your wounds after we've had supper.'

Evie, returning from the bathroom to announce that the bath was ready, said curiously: 'Did they shoot at you, Toby? Ugh, that cut on your arm is horrible.' She looked doubtfully at Martha. 'Ought he to go to the Stanley, Mam? Only you can't have had much experience with bullet wounds.'

Martha laughed as Toby shook his head, assuring them both that the wound on his arm had been caused by flying shrapnel and that everything else was just scratches and bruises, and nothing to worry about. 'And I'm not going to any hospital, young Evie,' he assured her. 'Your mam's been binding up my knees and putting sticking plaster on my cuts and scratches all my life, pretty well, so I dare say she'll cope with this little lot, no trouble. And I'll be quick as quick in the bath, because that pie smells like heaven and I can't wait to get outside it,' he ended, grinning at Martha.

After supper, Martha cleaned up Toby's various hurts, as she had promised, and then the whole family sat round the table with mugs of cocoa whilst Toby told them a little of what it had been like, waiting on the beaches. When he had finished his brief description, Seraphina remarked that she was glad he and his comrades were home, and hoped that her fiancé would soon follow them. 'Because the air force won't be allowed to leave until all the land forces are safely away, I don't suppose,' she said. 'I read in the papers that the air force were protecting our troops as best they could by keeping the Luftwaffe at bay.'

Martha thought her daughter spoke somewhat defensively, and noted the flush which crept up from her neck and invaded her face. She had been ashamed of the coolness of Seraphina's greeting earlier, but now she realised that, at the tender age of almost twenty, Seraphina did not know how to handle the situation. That she was still fond of Toby, Martha never doubted, but she thought it was a sisterly fondness and told her herself that, in all probability, the sooner Toby realised this the better it would be for everyone concerned.

But Toby was staring across the table at Seraphina, his eyes glittering dangerously. 'Keeping the Luftwaffe at bay?' he said incredulously. 'Why, we didn't see hide nor hair of the RAF whilst we were on that beach, being bombed and strafed day and night by the Luftwaffe. I don't know where the Brylcreem boys were, but it certainly wasn't in the skies above Dunkirk.'

Seraphina stiffened and deeper colour flamed in her cheeks, but before she could speak, Evie cut in. 'I dare say you were unlucky, Toby, and it were just your bit of beach that they didn't patrol,' she said quickly. 'Gosh, I'm tired, Mam. Don't wake me too early tomorrow, will you, only of course I don't want to miss my breakfast.'

Martha watched as the hot colour slowly ebbed from Seraphina's cheeks and was glad when her eldest daughter leaned across the table and took one of Toby's hands in hers. 'Toby, I'm really sorry I've been such a pig to you,' she said, speaking if anything a little more loudly than usual. 'We've all been worried about you, me as much as anyone, but I suppose I felt I was being a bit disloyal to Roger because he's still in France, so far as I know – and possibly in a good deal of danger. But you're my oldest friend and – and I'm really fond of you. In fact, you're like a brother to me.'

Toby grinned, but gently disengaged his hand. 'It wasn't as a brother I saw myself, but I dare say I'll come to terms with it,' he said mildly, and Martha thought, rather sadly, that he was still hoping, whatever he might say.

Seraphina got to her feet and went round the table. She gave Toby's shoulder a small, reassuring pat, then cleared her throat and spoke. 'I'm dead tired, Mam; I think Evie's right and it's time we were all in bed. Goodnight, everyone.'

As she spoke, she turned and left the room. Martha looked at Toby and saw that his lids were drooping. Poor lad, he had gone through enough for one day, she told herself, guiding him through the doorway and into Evie's tiny slip of a room. She had laid out a pair of Harry's pyjamas on the bed and just hoped that Toby had enough strength left to get into them, since she did not think that Mr Wilmslow would want the clothing he had lent to be slept in. 'I can see you're worn out, Toby,' she said gently, standing in the doorway. 'Do you want any help into those pyjamas?'

The young man shook his head and swayed, sitting down hastily on the bed and beginning to unbutton Mr Wilmslow's Sunday shirt. 'I'll be all right,' he said huskily. 'And I reckon I'll sleep like a perishin' top; it's been quite a day.'

Martha glanced around the room and saw that Seraphina had put a glass of water and two aspirin tablets on the tiny bedside table, and had lowered the blackout blind and pulled the curtains across. She drew Toby's attention to the aspirins, then bade him goodnight and left him, closing the bedroom door softly behind her.

Evie had dropped into a deep sleep the moment her head touched the pillow but now she found herself suddenly awake, though she had no idea what had roused her. She wondered at first if it had been simply Angie, moving in her sleep, that had disturbed her, but then she heard a most peculiar sound; the sort of sound made by an animal in agony. A long, drawn out wail ending in a hoarse shout brought the tiny hairs on her arm and on the back of her neck prickling erect. For a moment, still dazed with sleep, she could not think where the sound had come from; then she remembered the reason why she was sharing a bed with her sister. Toby had come home from France and was in her little boxroom, sleeping in the small bed, and it was he who had made the terrible noise.

She waited for a moment, but then the noise began again and she slid out of bed and padded across the floor towards the door which led on to the communal landing. She had reached it and was twisting the handle when she heard bedsprings creak behind her. She turned and could just discern Angie, halfway across

236

the floor, and Seraphina sitting up in bed. 'What is it? It must be an animal, caught in a trap,' Angie said in a husky whisper.

Evie realised that her sister thought herself back on the canal where such things could and did happen. 'Get back to bed, Evie; I'll rouse Dad and he'll . . . oh, my God!'

'It's Toby; I think he's having a nightmare,' Evie said. 'Is it dangerous to wake someone when they're having a nightmare, Angie?'

As she spoke, she had tiptoed across the landing, and soon all three sisters were ranged beside Toby's bed, looking down at him. Because it was a warm night, their mother must have returned, once she knew Toby slept, released the blackout blind and opened the window. Cool air blew into the room and in the dim light, Evie could see the sweat standing out on Toby's pale face and the way his fingers writhed at the sheets, as though he thought himself tied down by them.

'I don't know . . .' Angie murmured. 'What do you think, Fee? Should we wake him?'

'I don't know, either,' Seraphina said tremulously. 'I think we ought to fetch Ma.'

Evie, however, had no time for such scruples. She ripped the covers off Toby, knelt down by the bed and put both her skinny arms round his neck, pressing her cheek to his. 'It's all right, it's all right,' she crooned, as though comforting a very young child. 'Evie's here, Evie's got you safe, Evie won't let you fall.'

'I don't see why you say that; he's never been in an aeroplane in his life, so why should he be afraid of falling?' Seraphina said, a little sharply. 'I thought you were going to wake him up.'

Evie turned a fierce look on both her sisters. 'I don't know why he's upset but I read in a book once that years and years ago, when we were all monkeys, we knew that falling out of tall trees was the main cause of death and it stills frightens us today . . . the thought of falling, I mean.'

'Oh,' Seraphina said, rather blankly. 'Do you want me to get Ma?'

But Evie shook her head and continued to cradle Toby, and presently his arm shot out and he clutched her convulsively, murmuring something about the beach and the bombs and the great might of the enemy close behind them. He seemed calmer, however, and snuggled his face into the pillow whilst his breathing, which had been rapid and noisy, quieted, though he still continued to clutch at Evie's skinny little body.

After a few moments, Angie said rather tremulously: 'I – I think you'll be all right to leave him now, dearest. You've got school in the morning and I think you ought to get what sleep you can.'

Evie gave a tiny, breathless giggle. 'I'll come as soon as he lets go of me,' she murmured. 'But no sense in all of us standing about. You go back to bed; I don't suppose I'll be long.'

After some hesitation, Seraphina and Angela returned to their own room, but Evie remained, getting stiffer and stiffer. Kneeling on the cold floor was painful enough, but because her arms were up round Toby's neck all her muscles began to protest, and she soon realised she could not remain in her present position for much longer. Accordingly, she began to try to wriggle clear of Toby's grip, but every time she did so he began to show signs of returning to his nightmare. In the end, Evie hitched herself half on to the bed and curled up on the very edge, murmuring soothingly every time he moved until at last his grip relaxed and she was able to return to her sisters' room, though she left the door open in case the nightmares returned.

Angie had gone to sleep in her absence but Seraphina had not. She was sitting up, looking white and worried and had pulled back the curtains so Evie was able to see her face quite clearly. 'Evie, listen to me,' Seraphina said. 'If Toby has another nightmare, you are not to get out of bed, do you understand me? I shall go to him. I've treated him badly but he does understand now that I'm in love with somebody else, so there can be no harm in my restoring our old friendship. I – I mean to write to him when he leaves here, and – and if he doesn't reply, it will serve me right.'

Evie climbed back into bed, trying to prevent her cold feet and icy knees from jabbing into Angela and waking her up. 'Okay, Fee, and if you don't hear him, I'll wake you,' she said wearily. 'What's the time? Is it nearly morning?'

'I heard the church clock chime three a while ago,' Seraphina said, lying down. 'Provided nothing else happens, we've got three or four hours before we need to get up. Good night, Evie, and – thank you. You're a grand girl, really you are. You don't just look like our Pa, you're kind, like he was.'

'That's the nicest thing anyone ever said to me,' Evie mumbled sleepily. 'Good night; you're not so bad yourself.'

Chapter Nine

Toby awoke. For a moment, he could not remember where he was or how he had come there. Then he felt the cool breeze coming through the open window, heard the subdued hum of traffic and remembered. He was safe! He had crossed the Channel and had found Evie – or been found by her – on the station platform and she had brought him back to the flat above the shop where the Todds lived.

Toby sat up on his elbow and looked carefully around the room. This must be Seraphina's bed he was sleeping in. As the eldest, she was bound to merit a room of her own, even though it was so small that it lacked any other furniture except an old kitchen chair and a tiny, home-made bedside table. He saw there was a glass of water on it and two white tablets and realised he was extremely thirsty. He picked up the glass and drained it, noticing as he did so that he was wearing a pair of faded, striped pyjamas which were not his own.

He could hear no sound from the flat itself and had no idea of the time, so perhaps he ought to get up. Even as the thought crossed his mind, there was a gentle knock on the bedroom door, which creaked open very slowly, revealing Seraphina's beautiful face. She smiled shyly at him, then came fully into the room, carrying a mug of tea. 'Everyone's left the house except me, but this is examination week so I don't have to be in till eleven o'clock,' she said, matter-of-factly. 'You'll want to wash but there's nowhere in this room to put a washstand. However, I've taken a can of hot water to the room opposite and you can wash in there and then get yourself dressed. The stuff you were wearing isn't good for anything but chucking out and Mr Wilmslow says you can let him have his decent clothes back next time you come calling. When you're ready, you can come through to the kitchen. I'll make you porridge and toast and then I expect you'll want to get in touch with your mam and dad.'

Toby agreed that he would do as she said and she disappeared. Hastily, he drank the tea and went through into the room opposite to wash, but even as he scrubbed something niggled at the back of his mind, something which had happened during the night. He had been having a horrible dream, a nightmare really, and someone had come to him, someone with soft hands and a soothing voice. Someone who had held him in her arms and told him not to be afraid, told him he was safe. He had half opened his eyes, had seen a fair, much beloved face. Surely it had been Seraphina? But then there was also Angie, and though the girls were so different in many ways he knew they were superficially alike; knew, too, that Angie rather liked him – and not as a brother, either, he thought with sudden grim humour. Had it been Angie who had cuddled him the previous night? Yet somehow it did not seem like Angie, who was so timid and shy.

The thought nagged at him, and as he dressed himself in the borrowed clothing – the trousers were a trifle on the long side and the shirt sleeves reached his knuckles and had to be rolled back – he finally decided there could be no harm in mentioning the matter to Seraphina. Accordingly, when the two of them were seated at opposite sides of the kitchen table, eating porridge, he asked her outright. 'I'm afraid I may have disturbed you last night,' he said rather diffidently. 'I had some fearful nightmares and I suppose I must have shouted out. At any rate, someone came and told me I was all right, and it was only a dream. Did you come into my room, Fee?'

Seraphina nodded. 'Yes, I did, but you soon quieted, so don't worry about it.'

Toby felt enormous elation and gratitude. Despite the coolness that had come between them for so many months, she had come to him in his hour of need, had comforted and stayed with him. He knew very well that it had been an act of sisterly affection and not that of a lover, but he could not quite suppress the hope, now that he had gained her friendship once more, that love might follow. After all, he was sure she had loved him once; why should she not love him again? He smiled at her and took her hand in both of his, pressing it tightly. 'Thanks, Fee,' he said huskily. 'You don't have to tell me you're going to marry someone else, because I know it. But it's grand that we're friends again. We really are friends, aren't we? Will you – will you write to me? I swear I'll write back, I swear it on my mother's life.'

Seraphina smiled at him, her beautiful, brilliant smile, and stood up. Then she leaned across the table and kissed him. 'Of course I'll write, Toby,' she said. 'You were always my bezzie, as they say in these parts, and you are still. But I think we ought to walk down to the Telegraph Office and send your parents a telegram – and your unit, I suppose – letting them know you're safe. Then you can come back here for a bite to eat. Mam usually makes a snack for herself and anyone else who's around.'

Toby agreed to this, and presently the two of them

set out into the fine June morning. Toby felt as elated as though the return of the BEF had been a victory and not a defeat; he and Seraphina were friends again, and when she tucked her hand into the crook of his arm as they walked along the Scotland Road, he could have sung with happiness.

There was a long queue at the Telegraph Office, and as soon as his telegrams were despatched Toby walked Seraphina to her college and then returned to the flat. He had told his parents he would be home some time that very day, because he did not think it fair to remain with the Todds, not whilst he was in danger of waking the whole family with his horrible nightmares.

But he was still with them when Churchill's speech was relayed to the nation on the six o'clock news and was stirred and strengthened by the Prime Minister's words: '. . .*we shall fight on the beaches, we shall fight on the landing grounds, we shall fight in the fields and in the streets, we shall fight in the hills; we shall never surrender.*'

When it was over, Toby saw that he was not the only person in the Todds' small kitchen with tears in his eyes. He chose that moment to say goodbye and to promise them that he would return if he possibly could, before he was posted to whatever theatre of war might seem appropriate. 'We'll come with you to the station,' Evie said eagerly, rushing across the kitchen to fetch her jacket. 'You'll come too, won't you, Fee? Angie? Mam?'

They all went in the end and Toby, climbing aboard the train, felt that his cup of happiness was full. He waved until the station was out of sight, but though he told himself he was waving to the whole family, in his heart he knew that his eyes were fixed only on Seraphina.

★　　　★　　　★

'I know a wedding's awfully important, but what's the point of being a bridesmaid when you don't have a special dress?' Evie grumbled. She was standing in front of the mirror in the girls' bedroom, trying to adjust a circlet of small white roses on her slippery brown hair and glaring at herself in the spotted mirror which Angie had bought on Paddy's market before the war had started. 'Look at me! I'm all arms and legs. I grew out of this dress last summer, so why Mam should think it's suitable I just don't know.'

Angie laughed. 'You look very sweet and that pale primrose colour is just right for a bridesmaid,' she said. 'Anyway, I offered you my last year's dress and you didn't care for it, and I've let the hem on that one down as far as it will go, so stop grumbling. Think of poor Seraphina; she's always longed to be a proper bride, all in white, and she's had to settle for a grey suit and a pair of court shoes she bought in 1938. As for Ma, she's wearing a dress I remember she's owned for at least six years, and maybe longer.'

'Oh, all right, I know it's the same for everyone,' Evie said, turning away from the mirror. 'Now if Seraphina had been sensible and joined the WAAF as she said she would, she could have borrowed the WAAF wedding dress and looked really glamorous.'

'Ye-es, but you know very well that if she had joined the WAAF, she would have been posted as far away from Roger as they could get her,' Angie pointed out. 'And she is doing war work at the ROF in Long Lane, making guns.'

'And she's an Air Raid Warden,' Evie reminded her sister. 'But she and Roger have got it all planned; when he's on leave, he'll come to Liverpool, and when she's free, she'll go across to him.'

'Yes; she told me yesterday life would be lots of little

honeymoons,' Angie said, giving an appreciative chuckle. 'Aren't we lucky it's such a beautiful sunny day, though? October can be tricky, but the sun hasn't stopped shining since it rose, so I reckon the photograph should be a good one; something to remember if . . .'

'What do you mean by "if"?' Evie enquired. They had been about to leave the room, but now the younger girl turned wide, reproachful eyes upon her sister. 'The Battle of Britain's been won, Mr Churchill says so: *Never has so much been owed by so many to so few,*' she quoted. 'Oh, I know the war isn't over, but surely it won't be long now? Mam said that Hitler's invasion fleet had been bashed to bits by the good old RAF, and no one seems to be talking about fellers dressed as nuns hiding their parachutes in ditches any more.'

As she spoke, the two girls were hurrying down the stairs which led to the kitchen, where they found Seraphina and Martha putting the finishing touches to the buffet lunch which would be served when the ceremony was over. Because this was the first proper spell of leave Roger had had since before Dunkirk, the wedding had been arranged at short notice, so there would be few guests. Roger's father was working at the War Office in London and his sister was up in Scotland, serving with the WRNS, but his mother had promised to attend and would meet them at the church. Roger's friend Dick was to be his best man, and a couple of other pals from his squadron would attend the wedding breakfast. On the Todd side, there was just the family themselves, Mr Wilmslow, and Seraphina's friend Daphne. Martha would have liked to invite old friends from the canal, but there was really no time, so they had contented themselves with a small wedding reception. Mrs Bunwell had also been invited since she and

Martha were friends and colleagues these days. Because of the mounds of paperwork caused by rationing, Mrs Bunwell now worked for the Wilmslows at least three days a week, releasing Mr Wilmslow to count coupons, check supplies and fill in vast numbers of forms. She had been much gratified by the wedding invitation and had offered to leave the church before the bride did, in order to hurry home and get the kettle on the stove and the sausage rolls warming in the oven. Martha had accepted gratefully and now smiled a welcome as her daughters entered the room. 'You look very pretty, my dears,' she said, and Evie beamed back at her, eager to return the compliment.

'You look very pretty yourself, Mam,' she said, and meant every word, for Angie, the best dressmaker amongst them, had given her mother's dark green cotton dress a pretty lace collar and cuffs and had pinned a small bunch of pink rosebuds on the lapel of her coat. Seraphina, delicately placing sprigs of parsley on plates of sandwiches, smiled approvingly at her younger sisters. 'You do us great credit, girls,' she said brightly. 'Roger already thinks you're positively gorgeous and I'm sure his mother will be most impressed.' She glanced up at the clock above the mantel. 'But it's time we were off; I refuse to be late for my own wedding.'

Later that afternoon, Seraphina and Roger sat side by side in a train which was rumbling its way to Betws-y-Coed, in North Wales. Seraphina glanced sideways and felt a little thrill of pride; Roger was so handsome in the uniform of a pilot officer, and when he smiled at her and squeezed her hand, she thought herself the luckiest girl in the world.

She had never been to Betws-y-Coed before, but

Roger had fired her with his own enthusiasm for the little village set deep in Snowdonia. 'I came to Betws for the first time when I was fifteen, on a mountain climbing course,' he had told her. 'After that, climbing got into my blood and whenever I had a spare weekend, I'd get on the train and book myself into any of the little guesthouses with a vacant room. As I grew older, I drove myself down and got into the habit of staying at the Plas Coch. Mrs Eirwen Evans could always find me a bed and I reckon she's the best cook in the whole of Snowdonia.' He had smiled lovingly down at Seraphina. 'I don't intend to do any climbing on our honeymoon, but it's ideal country for rambling, so I hope to introduce you to your first walking holiday.'

Seraphina had agreed that she would love a holiday spent mostly in the open air in surroundings of such astonishing beauty, but now she began to wonder whether she would be able to keep up with Roger. There was also the fear that he might find such a pastime tame, for he had told her many stories of his exploits whilst climbing. She knew about the importance of wearing the right boots and carrying the correct equipment. She had heard of ropes and the special knots used to secure them, of crampons for icy weather and how to ascend a 'chimney'. Abseiling, she now knew, was a fast way of descending a mountain and she also knew that every route had its own name, from the easy, beginners' slopes to the sort of climb which men off to the Himalayas used for practice.

Seraphina glanced around the carriage. Every seat was taken and many of the occupants were probably as familiar with the mountainous scenery passing the windows as was Roger. Several of them were speaking in Welsh and, for a moment, Seraphina felt she was in an alien land, but then she chided herself. She was with Roger, her handsome husband, and she was sure she would speedily feel as at home in the mountains as he did. She leaned back in her seat. Mrs Evans had promised to have a meal ready for when the train got in, and tomorrow Roger meant to take her for a gentle stroll out of the village to see the Swallow Falls, one of the Seven Wonders of Wales. When in full spate, he told her, the falls were a wonderful sight, though he feared that after such a fine summer they would not now be at their best. Nevertheless, he was sure she would be impressed, and, in any event, would enjoy having lunch at the hotel opposite the falls.

The train slowed down and Roger stood up and began to get their bags down from the luggage rack. Seraphina got to her feet, feeling a flutter of anticipation in the pit of her stomach. She had tried not to think about her wedding night, but now that they were about to descend from the train it was impossible to completely dismiss it from her mind. Roger was always kind and gentle, but suddenly she found herself wishing that it was Toby who was taking her arm, helping her down from the train. She knew Toby so much better than she knew Roger. His company would have held no fears for her; she would not have felt awkward, or ill at ease, with a young man she had known all her life.

She picked up her own small bag and Roger put an arm about her shoulders and gave her a comforting squeeze. 'Nervous, my love?' he asked. 'Don't you worry; Mrs Evans is a charming woman and will make you as welcome as she has always made me. We're going to have a wonderful time, I promise you.' As he spoke, he was guiding her along a narrow path which led towards the main road. They crossed it, turned right and very soon were outside the Plas Coch Guest House.

They climbed a short flight of stone steps but Roger had barely raised his hand to the knocker when the door shot open. A small, skinny woman stood there, beaming at them.

'Welcome, welcome; did you have a good journey?' she said, in a soft sing-song voice. 'I heard the train come in so I stood in the bay window watching for you, and your dinner's ready when you are, though I thought you'd like to go to your room first.' She turned to Seraphina, holding out a hand. 'How do you do, Mrs Truelove? Nice to meet you, it is.'

Seraphina shook her hand and then the three of them climbed the steep flight of stairs and were shown into a large room, described by the landlady as 'the best front'. There Mrs Evans left them, after informing Seraphina that the bathroom was the door opposite and that the water would be nice and hot.

'This is very grand,' Roger said approvingly, surveying the room. 'I've been staying here on and off for years, but I've always had one of the single rooms which overlook the mountain at the back.' He sat down on the large double bed, which was covered with a pink satin counterpane, and gave an experimental bounce. 'I say, this is a good deal more comfortable than the ones in the back rooms, I can tell you.'

Seraphina felt the heat rise in her cheeks and, to hide her confusion, gave Roger's shoulder a small push. 'Don't sit on top of the counterpane; you'll crease it horribly,' she admonished. 'Let's take it off and fold it very carefully and lay it across the back of that chair . . .' she indicated one of the two, very pink upholstered chairs which stood in the bay window, 'and then we can take turns in the bathroom.'

'Or we could both go in the bathroom together,' Roger said. He laughed at her expression. 'We're married, darling Fee; there's nothing wrong with washing our hands in the same basin. Why, later on we're going to share this wonderfully comfortable bed, and . . .'

But Seraphina had slipped out of her coat, thrown her hat down on top of it and made for the bathroom. 'No nonsense; I'm starving hungry so I mean to hurry,' she said firmly. 'Oh, Roger, isn't it nice to wonder what is for dinner and not to know exactly what's in store because you've cooked it?'

'Well? I don't suppose you've ever seen anything like that in your life before!'

Seraphina shook her head, gazing in awe at the tumbling water of the Swallow Falls as it cascaded down on to the rocky bed below. 'It is wonderful,' she breathed, and then had to repeat the remark since the sound of the falls had drowned her voice. 'Can we get any nearer?'

Roger nodded and put an arm round her waist, drawing her close. 'I knew you'd love it here, as I do,' he said contentedly. 'When the war's over, I'd like to live in the mountains, but whenever I've mentioned it to my parents they always say: *What would you do?* And of course there's no answer to that, or not one I've discovered as yet, at any rate. Father suggests that I buy a weekend cottage down here and I suppose that's the sensible thing to do, but one day . . . oh, one day I mean to try my hand at teaching others to climb and to enjoy the mountains. Still, that's for later.' He took his hand from her waist and indicated a narrow pathway through the scrub which surrounded the falls at this point. 'It's a bit of a scramble so I'll go first, then if you fall you won't go far.'

Seraphina followed him. She decided that being

married to Roger was even more wonderful than she had dreamed it would be. He was so careful, so considerate, so eager for her happiness and peace of mind. How foolish she had been to wish – just for a moment – that she had married Toby instead of her wonderful, wonderful Roger. Together, they began the difficult descent.

It was November and Evie and her mother were in the kitchen, waiting for Angie and Seraphina to return home after their day's work. Evie was sitting at the table, finishing off her homework, and had just put her pencil down when Martha gave an exasperated sigh. 'I've run out of pepper! How ridiculous, and just when I'm trying to do that French cabbage Seraphina raved about when she came home from North Wales. Could you run down and ask Mr Wilmslow to let you have some, do you think? Black pepper, not white, mind . . . I've plenty of white.'

Evie twisted round in her chair, pulling a dubious face. 'I could, but the shop's shut and Mr Wilmslow hates it when you bang on the door and he has to come through from his living room,' she observed. 'And if I go to the back door, then he'll moan about having to go through to the shop. If you've got plenty of white pepper, can't you use that instead?'

Martha sighed. 'Well, I could, but I've used a hefty lump of margarine already so I don't want to spoil the cabbage by using the wrong pepper,' she said, rather reproachfully. 'Seraphina said her landlady told her to grate a drumhead cabbage and fry it in a big knob of margarine, then add salt and black pepper to taste. She never said a word about white pepper.'

Evie got to her feet. 'All right; I'll go to the back door, and then if there's a drum of black pepper in his kitchen perhaps he'll let me borrow it for a few shakes,' she said, giggling at her own pun. She looked across at her mother, busily stirring the grated cabbage with a large wooden spoon. 'Mam, what's wrong with Seraphina? Ever since she got back from her honeymoon, she's been . . . oh, different. And now she says she's going to join the WAAF, and she was dead set against doing that before she married because she said they'd be sure to send her miles away from Roger.'

Martha continued to stir the cabbage. You could trust Evie to be sensitive to the slightest change of atmosphere, she thought ruefully. She herself had noticed that Seraphina seemed to have something on her mind, but she had hoped that her daughter was simply missing Roger and would settle down again once she had been to visit him. She still hoped that there was nothing wrong, but now that Evie had mentioned it she wondered whether she ought to have a word with her eldest daughter. The trouble was, there was nothing you could put your finger on; in fact, if Evie had said nothing, the little niggling worry in the back of Martha's mind might simply have disappeared, because she did not think Seraphina was unhappy, exactly. Perhaps she and Roger had had some little disagreement which they had not managed to resolve during the course of their week away. She knew that Roger had said he would like to live in the mountains after the war and she supposed that Seraphina might have been dismayed at such a prospect. After all, her daughter was a trained teacher and she did not speak Welsh, and Martha supposed that a teaching job in Snowdonia for a non-Welsh speaker would be difficult to find.

'Mam? Did you hear what I said?'

Martha smiled at her small daughter and nodded.

'Yes, I heard. I'm sorry, love, I went off into a bit of a dream. Marriage changes people, and since Roger has been posted to Lincolnshire, I think she's realised that they're going to be apart no matter what, so she might as well join the WAAF and feel she's doing her bit for her country.'

'Oh,' Evie said rather doubtfully. 'Then you think everything's all right between her and Roger, Mam? Only when I asked her if she was going over to Lincoln next time her shifts means she gets three days off on the run, she said she'd think about it. And then she said she might go and see Toby.'

'Well, Toby's an old friend, and in his last letter he said he'd got embarkation leave, which means he's going abroad,' Martha explained. 'The trouble is, if Roger is flying, Fee won't be able to see him anyway, so it would be a waste of her leave as well as all the expense of a cross-country journey.'

Evie nodded wisely. 'I know. *Is your journey really necessary?*' she quoted. 'But Seraphina was horrid to Toby for ages and ages, yet now she writes to him almost every week – more than she does to Roger, in fact.'

Martha laughed and pulled the cabbage away from the heat. 'Your sister telephones her husband whenever she gets the chance, and I'm very sure she writes to him almost every day, only she does so during the breaks at work,' she said. 'Don't you go imagining things, young Evie! And having wasted five minutes of my precious time, you can jolly well go and fetch that black pepper or I'll give you a clack with this wooden spoon.'

Evie laughed but set off, clattering down the metal stairs, and Martha returned to her task of making the meal. She had not been worried, nor even particularly surprised, when Seraphina had announced her intention of joining the WAAF; she had simply thought that her daughter had realised she was unlikely to see a great deal of her husband whilst she was in Liverpool and he was in Lincoln, and she had always been keen to join one of the services. But that she might go to visit Toby had been news to Martha; Seraphina had never even hinted at such a thing to her mother, and now that she had heard it from Evie's lips Martha felt extremely uneasy. Seraphina and Toby had always been close, but when Roger had appeared on the scene it had been clear to Martha that the relationship between Toby and Seraphina had been more like that of brother and sister than that of young lovers. In fact, Seraphina had said as much, yet now, when she was a newly married woman, she was talking of spending her precious leave with Toby Duffy instead of with her husband.

Martha examined the cabbage and decided that it was cooked. She pushed it to the back of the stove and pulled the large kettle over the heat, deciding as she did so that she would have a word with Seraphina. After all, her daughter's decision to join the WAAF would affect the whole family and she could use that as an excuse for a private chat. At the same time, she could mention that Evie had told her of Seraphina's intention to visit Toby and see what sort of a response she got. She supposed, uneasily, that Seraphina might have realised she had made a dreadful mistake in marrying Roger, but if that were so, the worst thing she could do would be to try to rekindle her friendship with Toby. It would not be fair either to Roger or to Toby himself and besides, Seraphina had been brought up to regard marriage as a commitment for life. Harry had always made it plain that so far as he was concerned, divorce was seldom, if ever, acceptable. A couple married in church, exchanged vows, made promises. Harry had taught his daughters that holy matrimony was a lifelong bond and divorce was a secular business, never acknowledged in the eyes of God.

The sound of footsteps on the metal stairs brought Martha back to the present with a jolt. How idiotic she was being! Seraphina had talked about Roger with real affection, had admired his ability both as a walker and as a climber, for he had scaled a couple of peaks, just to show her how it was done. For all I know, Martha told herself, she could have decided to join the WAAF to be nearer Roger; there were a great many airfields on the eastern side of the country and the chances were that Seraphina would be sent to one of them. What was more, Seraphina was not above teasing her youngest sister. The older girl knew that Evie had had a crush on Toby for years, might even have been saying she meant to visit him simply to get a rise out of her sister. For Evie had asked Martha, when Toby's last letter arrived, whether her mother would accompany her to the Duffys' crowded little house so that they could wish Toby luck and work out a secret code which would enable him to tell them precisely where he was posted without the censor's chopping out any word which might give the enemy a clue as to where British troops were stationed.

Martha had been doubtful, because now that the work in the shop was complicated by rationing she had very little spare time, but Evie had set her lips in a way which Martha knew well, so she had suggested Evie ask one of her sisters to accompany her instead. Evie had pulled a face but agreed that she would do so, and there the matter had rested.

The back door burst open and Evie shot into the room, a pepper pot in her hand. 'He's in a good mood,' she said breathlessly. 'He said you could have three shakes free, the next three for a penny a shake and the final three for tuppence each. And he said he fancied a taste of that cabbage 'cos you was a grand cook.'

Martha laughed, took the pepper pot and shook it over the cabbage, then gave the mixture a brisk stir before spooning a helping into a pottery mug and handing it, and the pepper pot, to her daughter. 'You might as well take it back straight away and tell the old miser that the cabbage is payment for the extra shakes,' she said. 'But don't be all night . . . ah, I can hear the girls on the stairs. Best wait till they're indoors before you go back down; there's no room to pass if you meet them halfway.'

The two older girls came into the kitchen and Martha looked searchingly at Seraphina. She was laughing at something Angie had said and appeared to be in a good mood. As soon as the older girls were in the kitchen, Evie hurried out, and Angie announced that she would have to shoot straight through to the lavatory since she had had no chance to go before leaving work. As Seraphina moved past her mother to hang up her hat and coat, Martha put out a hand to check her. Seraphina looked enquiring. 'What is it, Ma? And where was Evie off to in such a hurry?'

'I borrowed some pepper from Mr Wilmslow and she's returning the pepper pot,' Martha said briefly. 'Fee, my love, is everything all right between you and Roger? Only Evie mentioned that you were thinking of visiting Toby while he's on embarkation leave.'

Seraphina stared at Martha. 'Wrong? Whatever should be wrong?' she said, in a brittle voice. 'We had a wonderful honeymoon and of course I'm missing him dreadfully. As for visiting Toby . . . well, Evie suggested I might take her over to the Duffys' place, and – and I thought, if she really wanted to go, we might put up at the local pub for a couple of nights and make a bit of a holiday of it.'

Martha raised her eyebrows. 'Why didn't you tell her that?' she said bluntly. 'According to Evie, you simply said you'd thought of visiting him instead of going over to see Roger. And I know you're talking about joining the WAAF yet you were dead against it before your marriage because you thought you might be posted to Scotland, or Cornwall – somewhere where you wouldn't be able to visit Roger regularly, at any rate.'

She was watching Seraphina as she spoke and saw the colour rise in her cheeks, but her daughter answered readily enough. 'I've already applied to join the WAAF and I'm pretty sure they'll accept me. I'll hear by post in the next week or so. That's why I didn't actually tell Evie that I meant to take her with me to see Toby – because I could get my posting any day now and that would put a stop to a trip to Micklethwaite. The same applies to Roger, of course; I can't arrange to spend time with him and then discover the WAAF want me at one of their training centres just when I'd planned to visit him. See?'

'I see,' Martha said slowly, telling herself that she should be reassured but not really believing in the somewhat glib explanation her daughter had given. Seraphina had always been able to think on her feet and Martha had a shrewd suspicion that her daughter had been doing just that. 'Well, I think you'd better tell Evie when she comes back that you won't be going to see Toby at all. I know she's only twelve but she does worry about you, as indeed I do myself.'

'Well, I worry about you,' Seraphina said. 'When the war started, you talked about getting war work, something with a decent wage, yet here you are still slaving away for that horrible old miser downstairs and never complaining when he expects you to work all the hours God sends. So you can just stop worrying about me and Roger and start worrying about yourself. I dare say you think I've not noticed that old Wilmslow is growing attached to you, but I have, and I don't like it one bit. Pa would tell you . . .'

'That's quite enough of that,' Martha said swiftly, but with heightened colour. 'You know very well we can only keep the flat whilst I continue to work in the shop, and as for Mr Wilmslow's *attachment*, that is pure – or rather impure – imagination, Fee. He has grown very much easier to work with because he needs me so much – he and I are the only ones who truly understand coupons and points, allocations and prices, and all the forms we have to fill in now. And though I know he's a stingy old blighter, he doesn't have an easy life. Mrs Wilmslow nags him constantly. She offers to help count coupons but always seems to lose interest halfway and she will keep talking to him when he's trying to do the books. As for what your pa would say, I think I knew him rather better than you did. If you think he would object because I do my best to see that the Wilmslows – *both* of them, Fee – have a hot meal once a day and someone to keep them company of an evening now and then, then you're wrong.'

Seraphina sniffed. 'All right, Ma; I'd forgotten that the flat went with the job, so to speak, but if you're going to criticise what I do, now I'm a married woman myself, then I don't see why I shouldn't criticise you.'

Martha felt anger surge up within her but banished

it, carefully counting to ten before she replied. 'I was not criticising you, I was just asking if everything was all right,' she said quietly. 'You are quite at liberty to criticise my behaviour if you think I deserve it, but—'

Seraphina had been standing on the opposite side of the room, facing the small kitchen window and tossing remarks over her shoulder, but now she whipped round and enveloped Martha in a fierce hug. 'I'm sorry, I'm sorry,' she babbled. 'It's all my fault. I'm hitting out before I'm hurt, being beastly to you because I'm worried about Roger and our marriage and the way I feel. I *do* love Roger, but I don't think I know him terribly well, and he's so handsome . . . and there are WAAFs on his station, lots of them . . . oh, Ma, I'm in such a muddle! I didn't know being married was like this and I want to go and see Roger but I don't know how to behave any more. I don't know what's right and what's wrong – not for married people, I mean.'

Martha returned her daughter's hug with one of equal fierceness, feeling a great weight roll off her shoulders. She chided herself for never attempting to explain the facts of life to her bright, intelligent daughter, but she had assumed that Seraphina would be as knowing as most modern girls appeared to be. 'Darling Fee, between a man and his wife, nothing can be wrong,' she said firmly. 'Well, nothing which is loving and gentle and kind, at any rate. He – he isn't violent, or anything like that, is he?'

'No, no,' Seraphina said. She was weeping openly now, and pulled back from her mother's embrace to dry her eyes with the backs of her hands. 'No, he's kind and good, honestly, Ma. It's just that I miss him terribly and worry that he'll find someone else . . . but now I've told you, I don't feel so bad. And I will go and visit him just as soon as I can. Oh, Ma, I feel so much better now I've told you.'

At this point, Evie came back into the kitchen. Presently Angie joined them and they took their places round the kitchen table to eat their meal. Martha noticed Evie eyeing her eldest sister shrewdly, but the child said nothing, and when Seraphina told her sisters that she had applied to join the WAAF and expected to be posted in a very short time, Evie and Angie were loud in their envy and Seraphina was soon laughing and joking, and explaining to Evie that this was the reason why she could not accompany her to visit the Duffys.

By bedtime that evening, Martha thought that her daughters were happier than they had been for some while. She went off to her room feeling that she had accomplished a good deal by talking frankly to Seraphina. She found herself hoping, however, that her eldest daughter would not be posted before Christmas. They had always been together over the festive season in the past, and she knew that Christmas would not be the same if her eldest were far away.

But if she had married in peacetime, she would have gone to her new home weeks ago, she reminded herself, snuggling her face into her pillow. So I suppose that is something I have to thank Hitler for. Smiling to herself at the thought of thanking the Führer for anything, she slept at last.

Evie was doing the marketing, accompanied by Percy who was getting excited at the thought of the festivities to come, for Christmas was only a few days away. Because of the shortages, Martha and Mrs Baldwin had given the children a list and told them to plug away until they had got as much as possible. Only then would the families know what sort of Christmas they would have.

Rationed goods, of course, would be available to everyone, albeit in tiny quantities; it was unrationed goods for which the two children were scouring the shops and the stalls on Great Homer Street and Paddy's market. Clothing was not rationed but was becoming more difficult to find and more expensive, so Martha had commissioned Evie to try to buy stockings for her sisters as well as anything such as scented soap, talcum powder or lipsticks so that she and Evie would have something to send Seraphina and Angela for Christmas Day. For Angela, fired by her sister's example, had joined the ATS, and since both girls were still in the early stages of training, they would not be home for Christmas.

'Look, Evie! There's handkerchiefs for sale. Do you think our mams would like a couple? From us, I mean – you and me? Or have you already buyed something for your mam?'

'I bought her a nutmeg and a bottle of rennet so she could make us a junket, but I did that 'cos I love junket,' Evie admitted. 'And I got her five balls of pink wool off the woman in the market who buys up old jumpers and unpicks 'em. But a hanky would be nice; how much are they?'

'Dunno; can't see,' Percy said briefly, then lowered his bullet head and charged at the people between himself and his objective. Evie clutched his belt and got dragged in his wake so that they ended up hard against the stall with the hankies barely six inches from them.

Percy shot out a hand to pick one up and the stall-holder promptly leaned across and hit his knuckles with a handy coat hanger. She was a fat, hard-faced woman, wearing a black coat buttoned up to the neck, and a purple felt hat pulled well down over her narrow brow. 'No thievin', you nasty little slummy,' she said hoarsely, and her breath clouded around her mouth in the cold air. 'Them handkerchiefs is best cotton, not for the likes of you.'

Percy stiffened indignantly. He was wearing decent clothes in honour of the school holidays and rightly objected to being referred to as a slummy. But Evie, wriggling past him, glared up at the woman in righteous indignation. 'Best cotton? They ain't even new; you've given 'em a good boil in your copper and then ironed 'em into squares,' she said scornfully. 'And they's only plain white, norra border nor a bit of embroidery on any one of 'em. What's you charging?'

The woman's hard, mean little eyes flickered from Evie to Percy, then down to the handkerchiefs. 'They're sixpence each and they certainly is new, brand new, so they're cheap at the price,' she said truculently. '*And*, I'm rationing 'em, only one to a customer.'

'Oh aye? And I can see you've been havin' to fight buyers off,' Evie said sarcastically. 'As for sixpence each, that's bloody highway robbery. Why, you'll be lucky to get tuppence. It ain't as if they're big; I reckon one good blow and you'd have to put it down for washing.' She turned to her companion. 'C'mon, Perce; let's find a stallholder who ain't charging fancy prices for second-hand goods what's probably full of holes anyway.'

The woman swelled with indignation but both children, used to the ways of such women, stood their ground, and the stallholder, realising that these kids might really be customers, let her breath out in a great cloud of steam and rubbed her mittened hands together. 'Well, I ain't denyin' they're a trifle second-hand,' she admitted cautiously. 'If you was to buy two each, I dare say I could let you have 'em for tenpence a pair.'

Percy gave a crow of triumph. 'You said they were rationed to one per customer,' he jeered. 'Now you're sayin' we can have two. Make up your mind, missus.'

'I can give a discount if you buys in quantity,' the woman said loftily. 'But lower'n tenpence a pair I will not go, so you can make your mind up on that one. Now come on, you either want 'em or you don't, an' if you don't, clear orf, or I'll send someone to fetch a scuffer, 'cos you're makin' a bleedin' nuisance of yourselves.'

Evie gave Percy a delighted nudge. Whatever the woman might say, the bargaining had now begun, and since no other customers had shown the slightest interest in the handkerchiefs – indeed, there were no other customers – she thought they might well end up with the handkerchiefs they wanted at the price they meant to pay. 'We only want 'em if the price is right,' she said grandly. 'They ain't bad, but as I said, they's plain white.' She turned to Percy. 'I think we ought to take a look at the rest of the goods afore we goes spendin' our dosh.'

The woman began to protest, actually bending down and spreading out the handkerchiefs for their closer inspection, and after ten minutes of brisk bargaining Evie and Percy left the stall with eight white handkerchiefs between them, which had cost them a shilling each.

'Fruit and vegetables next,' Evie said cheerfully, heading for the area of the market which sold such things. 'If you see a queue, we'll join it 'cos it might be for oranges. One of the girls at school – her father works on the docks – said they've unloaded a ship full of oranges. And you never know, someone might have some onions. Are there onions on your mam's list?'

Percy consulted his list, then nodded resignedly. 'Yeah, an' carrots. Someone told me mam that if you grate carrots into cake mixture, instead of currants and sultanas and that, it tastes just as good. I don't believe it meself but she'll try anything will me mam.'

'Yeah, so will mine,' Evie agreed. 'An' Mam says to try to get hazelnuts or walnuts, 'cos you can crush them up an' stick 'em in the cake mix, an' at least they grows in England. But of course, we shan't be able to ice the cake even if our mams do manage to find enough stuff to make one. Oh look, there's a queue! C'mon, Percy!'

By four in the afternoon, the children's shopping was complete and they were making their way home, discussing the sort of Christmas that could be enjoyed in wartime. 'Mam says if there are no more raids, she'll take us both to the pantomime at the Empire after Christmas. Mind you, I reckon there's afternoon performances . . . matinees they call them . . . so even if there are raids, she could take us to one of them,' Evie said, standing down her large canvas marketing bag for a moment, to ease the ache in her arms. 'That 'ud be a treat, eh, Perce?'

'I don't see what difference raids make,' Percy said, standing his own bag down. 'After all, if a bomb's got your name on it . . .'

'Yes, I know what you mean, but ever since the end of November, when all them folk were killed in the shelter out Wavertree way, Mrs Wilmslow has refused to leave the house when there's a raid on. It's awful awkward for Mr Wilmslow because he's a warden and Mam doesn't like to leave the old girl by herself, so she rushes me to the shelter and then rushes back to the Wilmslows'. Sometimes she persuades Mrs Wilmslow to get into that sort of cage thing . . . what's it called . . . but sometimes the old girl refuses to move from her bed. Then Mam has to run back to me in the shelter so's I'm not all on me own, but she worries that Mrs Wilmslow might need something. So you see, she wouldn't like to be away from home when a raid was on.'

'You mean the Morrison shelter when you say that cage thing,' Percy observed, heaving his bag up once more and setting off along the crowded pavement. 'Well, a mat'nee would be just grand.'

'Yes it would; I love the pantomime,' Evie said, as they drew level with the end of Lawrence Street. 'See you tomorrow?'

''Spect so,' Percy said. 'I've still got to buy spuds so I reckon Mam will send me out again.' He chuckled. 'She's that glad to have me back, you wouldn't credit it.'

'So am I,' Evie said generously, though the return of the Baldwin young from the country, where they had been evacuated seven months ago, had put quite a strain on Mrs Baldwin and Evie's own mother had felt obliged to give the other woman what help she could. Mrs Baldwin had never got the knack of baking bread and cakes and such, and frequently turned up at the flat with some of her rations in a string bag so that Martha might show her, for the umpteenth time, how to do it.

The Baldwin children had come home because Mrs Baldwin had realised that Percy was old enough to get a job, and because Ron was so unhappy that he had started bedwetting. The children had been separated, as were many large families, and the woman who had the care of Ron and Emmy was a mean and spiteful spinster who disliked all children, and beat Ron almost as a matter of course at the slightest excuse. Percy's foster mother had been very different: a kindly, generous woman who fed him well and pleaded with Mrs Baldwin that her charge be allowed to stay, but Percy's mother had insisted that he return to Liverpool. Not only could he get a job, but he was a great help about the house. In Percy's absence, Evie had made other friends, girls of her own age, and though she would never have dreamed of admitting it to Percy, she frequently longed for the days when she and her school friends had shopped and gossiped together, gone round to each other's houses, and shared secrets. None of this was possible with Percy in tow, but Evie knew that her old friend needed her and did her best to explain to her girlfriends why she had to spend so much time in his company.

'Evie! Evie Todd! Where's you been? Where's you goin', come to that? I hope you ain't too high 'n' mighty to walk along of an old friend!'

Evie stopped in her tracks and turned towards the speaker. Because she had been thinking of her school friends, she was doubly surprised to find herself confronting Lizzie Duffy, the eldest of Toby's sisters. The girl was in ATS uniform and had pushed her cap to the back of her head. She looked very different, but Evie knew her at once. 'Lizzie! What on earth are you doing in Liverpool, queen? I knew you were in the ATS because Angie and me went up to your place last month to say cheerio to Toby, but I didn't know you were stationed near Liverpool.'

'I'm not . . . well, not so's you'd notice,' Lizzie said cheerfully, putting up a hand to smooth her pompadour of light brown hair back into place. She was a pretty girl with hazel eyes, a great many freckles, and a wide unselfconscious smile. 'I'm stationed just outside Blackpool – my, it's grand up there – and the ATS has taught me ever such a lot. I can type now, you know, and do bookkeeping and all sorts. I reckon that when the war's over I'll get meself a decent job . . . unless I'm married, of course, which I'm telling you is on the cards. I've got a real nice feller – he's a Tommy – but he was sent abroad when Toby went, so now it's just letters.'

'Is he going to India, like Toby?' Evie said, then clapped her hand guiltily to her mouth. 'Oh, goodness, I'm not supposed to say that, am I? But I expect you and your feller have some sort of code so he can tell you where he's going.'

Evie had put her bag down again as they spoke and now bent to pick it up once more, and Lizzie seized one of the handles. 'I'll give you a hand with your marketing, love,' she said. 'I'm on me way home for a forty-eight but my train doesn't go for another two hours, so I thought I'd pop in and say hello to your mam. It were a bit of luck meeting you, though, because I've no idea where your mam's shop is and they say the Scotland Road is a real long one.'

'Well, we're here, 'cos the next shop is Wilmslow's, where me mam works,' Evie said joyfully. 'Our flat's over the shop, but I expect Toby told you that. And you'll be just in time for a cup of tea and whatever we're having for supper. You know Seraphina's in the air force, same as her husband?'

'Aye, and Angie's in my little lot. We were real astonished when Toby told us Seraphina were married,' Lizzie admitted. 'We always thought them two would make a go of it – Toby and Fee, I mean – but I dare say it wouldn't have worked out.'

'You're probably right,' Evie agreed. She swerved round the corner and began to ascend the staircase. 'Oh, it's grand to see you again, Lizzie. We've only had one letter from Toby and that took weeks and weeks to reach us. But Mam says things like that happen in wartime and we just have to make the best of it. C'mon; Mam's in the kitchen, I hear her clattering pans. She'll be that pleased to see you!'

Chapter Ten
Christmas 1940

Martha and Evie went to the station to see Lizzie off after they had fed her with a home-made vegetable pie, a pile of mashed potatoes, and stewed apple and custard to follow. They were back in the flat and settling down for a cosy evening at their own fireside when they heard the familiar sound of the air raid siren. Evie sighed and began, hurriedly, to finish her row, for she was still knitting squares for blankets, though she was doing so a good deal more efficiently than she had done at the beginning of the war. Martha was knitting too, making a pretty bedjacket for her employer's wife. 'I wish I could knit like you, Mam,' Evie said wistfully. 'Your needles go so fast they almost disappear, yet you never lose a stitch, or mess up that pretty pattern. Will you finish it by Christmas Day, do you think? Mr Wilmslow will be awfully disappointed if you don't because it's his Christmas present to Mrs Wilmslow, isn't it?'

Martha nodded, her needles flying even faster as she, in her turn, finished the row she had started. 'Yes, that's right, and I'll finish it easily; I might even do so tonight if we're stuck in that perishing shelter for hours and hours,' she observed, tucking her work into her knitting bag.

Evie got to her feet, sticking her needles through her ball of khaki wool, and dropping it into her mother's bag. 'What'll we do now, Mam? Is Mr Wilmslow on duty already, or will he wait for you to arrive before he goes off?'

'He'll wait for me to arrive, so I think we'd best go down to the shop first,' Martha decided. 'I'll make sure Mrs Wilmslow is comfortable – or as comfortable as can be expected – and then I'll come with you to the shelter. After all, it would be perfectly possible for Mrs Wilmslow to join us if she wished. Her husband went to a lot of trouble to get her a wheelchair and the shelter isn't that far away, but she's made up her mind she's safer in her own place, and if that's how she feels, there's nothing anyone can do about it.'

'Well, why don't we stay here too?' Evie asked hopefully.

Martha knew her daughter hated the dank mustiness of the big public air raid shelter, and though bunks and blankets were provided she always took extra bedding and made sure that Evie was well wrapped up before they set out. Nevertheless, by the time the raid ended everyone was always cold, stiff and eager to get back to their own beds, if only for an hour or two. Despite the discomforts, however, Martha was in no doubt that the shelter was the safest place to be, and she gave Evie's suggestion short shrift. 'We'll go to the shelter,' she said at once. 'It's made of reinforced concrete and is mostly underground anyway, which means it's a good deal more secure than either the flat or the premises behind the shop.' As she spoke, she had been collecting what she called her air raid bag, tipping boiling water from the kettle into the big flask, and supervising Evie into her thick outdoor coat, scarf, woolly hat and gloves. 'Be a pet and fetch me that half-loaf from the bread bin, the pot of rhubarb and ginger jam, and the bread knife,' she said, bustling about.

'Honestly, a few days' freedom from raids and I forget how important it is to be prepared.'

'You sound like a boy scout, Mam,' Evie said with a giggle, shoving the loaf, the pot of jam and the bread knife into the canvas bag. She cocked her head, listening intently. 'Oh, do hurry, Mam. I can hear that thrum thrum which the bombers make as they cross the Irish Sea!'

Martha listened but could hear nothing. However, she was well aware that Evie's acute hearing could pick out such sounds long before she herself was aware of them, so she snatched her coat off the hook, ran over to shut down the front of the stove, and then hustled her daughter out of the flat, being careful to switch off the light before opening the door.

Mr Wilmslow was crossing the back yard as they descended, obviously waiting for them and eager to be off. 'She won't let me take her down to the shelter,' he said wearily, 'but mebbe she's right. She's terrified of being buried alive. She says even if it weren't hit, being stuck in there, breathing the same air as half Liverpool, would likely give her pneumonia, so I've given up trying to persuade her to see sense.' He smiled rather ruefully at Martha, raising one sandy brow. 'Imagine what me life 'ud be like if I shovelled her into the wheelchair, then slipped on them damned slithery steps while I were carrying her into the shelter and broke her leg or her arm or something. Imagine if she did catch a cold . . . only it 'ud be influenza . . . the mind boggles, don't it? No, we'll leave her in her own home since that's what she truly wants. I've done me best to make her comfortable and I've promised her I'll nip back if there's a lull, but if you can just pop in for a moment and make sure she's got everything she'll need . . .'

Martha could hear the planes herself now and glanced round rather wildly, then handed the canvas bag to Evie. 'You go down to the shelter, love; I'll follow as soon as I've seen to Mrs Wilmslow,' she said briskly. 'Go along now, and hurry.' She jerked her head towards the sea. 'It sounds to me as if this is going to be a big raid, so the sooner you get inside that shelter, the better I'll be pleased.'

Evie looked rebellious, but Mr Wilmslow took the canvas bag from her and put a heavy hand on her shoulder. 'I'll walk you down there, see you safe inside,' he promised. 'Your mam will be following you in no time at all. Come along now, gerra move on, young lady; us wardens like to be on duty before the raid starts.'

Martha watched the pair disappear round the corner of the house, then ran towards the back door. She let herself in, closed the door behind her and went through the small kitchen into the living area, where Mrs Wilmslow lay in her large bed, propped up by pillows and with her wireless set, a flask, a cup and a packet of sandwiches neatly arranged on the small side table. She was reading a woman's magazine but put it down as soon as she saw Martha. 'Well, I'm glad you've got here at last,' she said peevishly. 'You needn't tell me there's a raid on because my dear husband lit out as soon as the siren went, ages ago. He has no time for me when he can go off and take care of other folk, I'm telling you. There was me, desperate for the toilet, but would he give me a hand? No, he was too busy making himself a cup of tea and naggin' me to put me coat on and let him push me through the streets like a perishin' freak show. I've told him over 'n' over that I won't go making an exhibition of meself, but does he listen? No, he don't . . .'

Although Mr Wilmslow had many faults, he always treated his wife with gentleness and consideration, but Martha knew the uselessness of trying to make Mrs Wilmslow appreciate her husband's attentions. Instead, she went swiftly towards her, snatching the other woman's pink dressing gown off the foot of the bed. 'Mr Wilmslow couldn't have realised you needed the toilet,' she said gently. 'I'll just help you into this . . . where are your slippers?'

'They're under the bed,' Mrs Wilmslow said grudgingly. She pushed back the covers and began to struggle towards the edge of the mattress. She was pitifully thin, her limbs so twisted with arthritis that Martha always handled her with great care, realising every time she saw her out of bed that the constant pain she suffered must be the reason for her ill temper and continual nagging. With great care, therefore, she inserted the thin, twisted feet into the brown felt slippers, then put an arm round the older woman and almost carried her across the room and through the narrow doorway into the tiny WC. Once, it had been outside, but Mr Wilmslow had blocked up the outer door and knocked out a part of the wall so that his wife could enter it without having to brave the elements.

Martha saw Mrs Wilmslow settled, then went back into the kitchen to check that everything was as it should be. The fire was banked down and Mr Wilmslow had laid a breakfast tray for his wife so that he would be able to make her porridge, tea and toast next morning before starting his day's work. Martha nodded to herself, satisfied, then remembered the commode. If it was placed directly against the bed, Mrs Wilmslow could, in an emergency, get on to it and then return to her pillows without help. It was not easy for her, but it was infinitely better than an attempt to reach the WC would have been. Martha carried the chair across the room and stood it on the far side of the bed. She did not think Mrs Wilmslow would need it again that night but she told herself it was better to be safe than sorry. She had just completed the task when Mrs Wilmslow's thin and quavering voice called her name, and she hurried over to the WC to attend to her.

By the time the old lady was back in her bed – and grumbling that Mr Wilmslow had left her sardine sandwiches, which she hated – bombs were beginning to fall, the tremendous crashes and bangs causing both women to jump. 'They're attacking the docks,' Mrs Wilmslow said, sounding almost pleased, though God knew, Martha thought, the docks were a deal too close for comfort. 'I wonder if I should gerrin that Morrison thing; what do you think, Mrs Todd?'

Martha hesitated. She thought it would be a good deal safer for the old woman since the Morrison shelter had been erected under the big old dining-room table, but it took a great deal of time to get Mrs Wilmslow – and all her bedding – into the rather cramped quarters and she knew that by now Evie would be dreadfully distressed by her mother's non-appearance, might even be worried enough to come searching. However, she was here now and did not much fancy making a dash for the shelter under such horrendous conditions, for even through the blackout blinds she could see the brilliant flashes as bombs and incendiaries rained down upon the city.

'Well? What d'you think?' Mrs Wilmslow repeated rather plaintively. 'I can't say there's much comfort in lyin' on the floor but I suppose it's safer.' Sighing internally, Martha agreed that that was so and began, once again, to help Mrs Wilmslow out of bed and back into her warm dressing gown. Before she had even got her on to her feet, however, Mrs Wilmslow had changed her mind. 'No, I shall stay in my bed,' she announced, kicking off her slippers and beginning to unbutton her dressing gown with her poor twisted fingers. 'You might make me a cup of tea, Mrs Todd, before you go off. Then I can save the flask for later, when I'm all by meself.' As Martha swung Mrs Wilmslow's legs into bed, the old woman added hopefully: 'Only mebbe you'll stay till the raid's over, seein' as anyone going out there will be takin' his life in his hands.'

Martha cocked her head, listening to the crashes and enormous explosions which were making the night hideous, but when she spoke, it was firmly. 'I'll make you a cup of tea, Mrs Wilmslow, but then I really must go, raid or no raid. Your husband took Evie to the shelter for me and I must join her as soon as I possibly can. Besides, you know what these raids are like; the aircraft come over in waves, so the next time there's a lull I'm afraid I'll have to go.'

'It's too bad; Mr Wilmslow's got no right to leave a sick woman alone,' Mrs Wilmslow grumbled. 'I've a good mind to come to the shelter with you, Mrs Todd.' She chuckled. 'That 'ud serve 'im right. He'd have a good scare if he came back to find me gone.'

'That isn't very kind, Mrs Wilmslow,' Martha said briskly, handing the older woman a cup of well-sweetened tea with a digestive biscuit in the saucer. She was well used to Mrs Wilmslow's delaying tactics, having suffered from them frequently in the past. If she gave her the slightest encouragement, Mrs Wilmslow would insist that Martha help her to dress and get her into the wheelchair with most of her worldly possessions in a bag on her lap, and would let herself be pushed as far as the outer door before suddenly changing her mind and making Martha put her back to bed. 'Now just you drink your cup of tea and eat your biscuit, and before you know it Mr Wilmslow will be popping in to make sure you've got everything you need and very likely you'll go off to sleep and wake to find the raid is over.'

'Aye, mebbe you're in the right of it. Get me a couple of them aspirin tablets out of the medicine cupboard in the kitchen; they'll help me to go off,' Mrs Wilmslow said.

Martha could have screamed. As she had expected, the lull had arrived, though already she could hear the next wave of bombers approaching. She shot into the kitchen, grabbed the small bottle and tipped two aspirin into the palm of her hand, then ran back and put them on the bedside table. 'There you are,' she said briskly. 'Good night, Mrs Wilmslow; see you in the morning.'

Mrs Wilmslow sniffed, but picked up the tablets and popped them into her mouth, then took a swig of tea. 'If I'm spared,' she said bitterly. 'Likely I'll be dead as a doornail. It ain't right to leave a sick woman . . .'

But Martha heard no more; she was across the kitchen and out of the back door and running down the street, heading for the shelter.

It was a long night, and several times the blasts were so close and the noise so tremendous that Martha, clutching Evie tightly in her arms, could not begin to imagine what sort of carnage was being wrought in the streets above their heads. Usually, the people in the shelter kept their spirits up by singing carols, playing guessing games, or something of that nature, but the tremendous noise made such diversions impossible.

Several times during the course of the night Martha went to the end of the shelter, pushed aside the curtain and went up the steps to take a look around. But she always descended again before she had caught anything but a glimpse of the fires raging in the docks, for there was no point in lingering when the danger was so great.

When the all clear went, there had been comparative quiet for some time. Martha and Evie wearily gathered up their belongings and made for the steps with everyone else. The sky was beginning to lighten in the east, but a quick glance around showed that the fires still burned in the docks, and the familiar outlines of warehouses were familiar no longer, for in the place of a good many of them were jagged gaps, black against the flames.

As they turned their footsteps towards home, Mr Wilmslow came up, pushing his tin hat to the back of his head. He was blackened by smoke, his eyes red-rimmed, and he looked exhausted, but he spoke cheerfully enough. 'What a night, eh, Mrs Todd? I thought I were a goner over and over, but it seems the bomb with my name on it didn't fall last night. I passed the shop as I were comin' along; the right-hand window's been blowed out, so I'll come in wi' you now and nail cardboard over it, just till I can get hold of a bit of wood to do the job properly.' He gestured towards the warehouses. 'All that food gone up in flames, Mrs Todd! And the ships what were sunk, you wouldn't believe. Oh aye, the docks took a right pasting, so they did.'

'I never thought . . . do you mean to say the government are still storing food in warehouses close to the docks?' Martha demanded. 'What arrant stupidity! Why, they've known for months that Hitler meant to send his bombers to Liverpool, so why store the food in such a danger spot? I'm telling you, Mr Wilmslow, they ought to have a woman in charge at the Ministry of Food.'

'Aye, I dare say you're right. I reckon them oranges'll be marmalade by now,' Mr Wilmslow said wistfully.

Martha knew he was fond of an orange and, as he took her heavy bag from her, patted his arm consolingly. 'Well, since you've had such a dreadful night, I'll let you into a secret. Young Evie here queued for nearly two hours yesterday, but she managed to get two grand big oranges and we mean to give them to you as a Christmas box. So you see, all the oranges didn't get burned up.'

They reached the shop as she spoke, and Mr Wilmslow took a bunch of keys out of his pocket, unlocked the door, and ushered them inside, locking it firmly behind them. 'I don't want no early customers poppin' in before I've had me breakfast,' he said gruffly. He glanced hopefully at Martha. 'I s'pose you wouldn't be willing to feed all of us, down here, while I get meself cleaned up and out of me uniform? Then I can start blocking the window up.'

Martha agreed that she would do so and the three of them went into the back room. Mrs Wilmslow was not in her bed, so Martha assumed she had somehow managed to get herself to the WC, but Mr Wilmslow stopped dead in the doorway. 'What's goin' on?' he asked, his voice higher than usual. 'Where's Mrs Wilmslow? My God, where's the bleedin' wheel-chair?'

All three of them stared, unable to believe their eyes, and Martha saw that it was not only the wheelchair that was missing, but also the older woman's dressing gown and slippers, and the big Gladstone bag which she always kept by the side of her bed. Another glance showed her that the packet of sandwiches, and the flask of tea, were no longer on the bedside table.

For a moment, she thought wildly of the Morrison shelter, but when she looked it was empty, and besides, Mrs Wilmslow would not have needed the wheelchair in order to reach the dining table. And even as this thought occurred to her, she glanced across at the back door and saw that it was not properly closed. Dumbly, she jerked Mr Wilmslow's arm and pointed. 'She's gone out through the back door,' she whispered. 'Do you think someone came for her? Only I can't imagine who would do so.'

Evie ran over to the back door and pulled it open and Martha, following her, saw that the yard was empty. Mr Wilmslow gave a deep, martyred sigh. 'God alone knows where she's bobbied off to,' he said resignedly. 'But she can't have gone far because she wouldn't have left until the all clear sounded. Look, Mrs Todd, if you get on with making the breakfast, young Evie and meself can search around, question folk. Right?'

'All right,' Martha said wearily. 'As you say, she can't have gone far.'

Evie trotted along beside Mr Wilmslow, scanning the streets. Despite the earliness of the hour, there were quite a few people about; most, she imagined, having emerged from the shelters. The air was dusty and smelled of burning, though it was very cold. Evie thought wistfully of the warm kitchen, the porridge that her mother would be making, and the nice hot cup of tea which would accompany it. Mr Wilmslow stared ahead. She could read the worry in his face, but thought there was little reason for it. After all, Mrs Wilmslow was grown up and sensible and could not be far away.

As they progressed along the road, Mr Wilmslow began to mutter. 'She might have gone along to see Mrs Bunwell . . . only I wouldn't have thought she could have got that far. But we'd better – Oh my God, what's that?'

They were passing a narrow alley, and as he spoke Evie saw the wheelchair; it was lying on its side, and the Gladstone bag in which Mrs Wilmslow kept all her most precious possessions lay beside it, gaping open. The man and the girl ran forward together. Mr Wilmslow righted the wheelchair and looked round wildly, but it was Evie who saw the small, crumpled figure lying twenty yards further up the alley, close up against a sooty brick wall.

It was Mrs Wilmslow, and she was dead.

They pieced together what must have happened later in the week, when the formalities of funeral arrangements and so on had been dealt with. The obvious explanation, that she had left the house after the all clear had sounded, could not have been the case, since Mr Wilmslow had passed the shop on his way to the shelter and had seen no sign of his wife or the wheelchair. In order to get so far, she must have left the house during a lull in the raid, and the doctor who examined her body said she had almost certainly died as a result of a blast.

Martha felt terribly guilty and knew that Mr Wilmslow felt the same but, as she told him, there was little that either of them could have done. 'In wartime, everyone has to do their duty; mine was to my daughter and yours was the work of an ARP warden,' she told him. 'You tried to persuade her to come down to the shelter, and I stayed with her as long as I could; it's useless reproaching yourself, Mr Wilmslow, because it's happened, and we can't undo it.'

'I know, but if I'd been with her it wouldn't have happened . . . couldn't have happened,' Mr Wilmslow said heavily. 'She must have been terrified . . . think how she hated the wheelchair, was determined never to be seen using it. Yet she got into it herself, dragged the bag on to her lap, and somehow managed to wheel herself all the way to where we found her. I suppose terror must have lent her strength, but oh, if I'd stayed . . .'

Martha told herself that briskness was her only course. She too wished now that she had stayed with the older woman. But if she had done so, it might easily have been Evie lying in the hospital mortuary, and Evie had her life before her.

But it made up Martha's mind that she should get her child out of the city. Evie had refused to be evacuated when the war had started, and Martha had agreed that the child might stay in Liverpool. But somehow Mrs Wilmslow's death had brought home to Martha as nothing else could the dangers which lay in wait for all of them. The second night of bombing had been even worse than the first, and Christmas had been a subdued and miserable time for them all. Evie wanted to stay but Martha decided she would simply have to put her foot down. Evie must be evacuated, for if anything happened to her, Martha knew she would never forgive herself.

Martha was sitting before the fire, knitting a new school jumper for Evie, who was in bed, for it was past ten o'clock. Outside, the wind howled, and occasionally sleet spattered against the window pane. It was almost the end of January 1941, and Evie had been despatched to a small village on the Wirral on the 5th of the month and returned home on the 7th.

She was very pink-cheeked and bright-eyed and refused, totally, to return to the village though she had admitted, airily, that her foster mother had been a kind and generous woman.

'But I won't leave you here all by yourself, with that horrible old man coming up every night, like as not, to get you to work overtime on his wretched books,' she had said roundly. 'I've written to Seraphina and Angie, and I'm sure they'll both say I've done the right thing. If you'd like to come and stay with me in the country, that would be grand, but I won't leave you alone here, and so I'm telling you.'

'But Mrs Baldwin's sent the younger children off again, though admittedly not to the same foster parents,' Martha had pointed out. 'Look, darling, what do you think your pa would have done if he'd been alive? He'd have sent you to safety, that's what, and he would expect me to do the same.'

Evie, however, was adamant, repeating constantly that her place was with her mother, that she did not trust Mr Wilmslow to take care of her, and that if sent away she would simply run home every time. She saved her strongest argument till last. 'I should always have to run away at night,' she had explained, 'and get lifts with anyone who would stop for me – lorry drivers, van drivers, soldiers, anyone. You say you'd never forgive yourself if we got bombed . . . well, how would you feel if I was murdered by someone giving me a lift?'

Martha had been forced to laugh but had given in and now, she thought, glancing around the kitchen, she was glad of it. Despite her fears, there was still a school to which Evie could go every day, and though, no doubt, the bombers would not give up so easily, they were having a bad winter, with clouds, sleet and snow making bombing raids difficult, if not impossible. Furthermore, she really appreciated Evie's company and the child had been quite right: when Mr Wilmslow was not on ARP duty, he came up to the flat, as of right. Admittedly, he usually carried loads of paperwork, but even so, she knew there would have been talk had not Evie always been present at these sessions. Martha supposed she could have hinted Mr Wilmslow away but thought it would have been a cruel thing to do, for he was missing his wife abominably and talked of her often, though Martha secretly thought that he was seeing her through rose-coloured spectacles. He had told Martha, half shyly and half defiantly, that she should have known Mrs Wilmslow in the days before her crippling illness had struck. 'She were only in her early forties and a prettier, sprightlier woman you couldn't hope to meet,' he had said reminiscently, a smile tugging at the corners of his narrow mouth. 'She was into everything in them days: worked in the shop, ran a Brownie group, organised the ladies' sewing circle. She were full of fun, were my little Ruby, and a great one for helping others.'

Martha had murmured encouragingly, but found it difficult to believe that the spiteful, crabby sixty-year-old she had known had ever been the 'little Ruby' whom her husband remembered so fondly. But it clearly helped Mr Wilmslow to regard his dead wife as a saint and Martha was glad that he should do so. After all, she knew that Harry had been the best husband in the world and she found it a great comfort.

A coal shifted in the grate, bringing Martha abruptly back to the present. She glanced at the clock and decided that she might as well damp the fire down and go to bed herself. Then she remembered that she had meant to write letters this evening and felt a stab of guilt. The girls loved to get her letters so she tried to write once a week, but it had been ten days since she had last had an evening to herself. However, it would not matter if the letters were almost identical – indeed, they would have to be, if she were to finish both before her eyes closed of their own accord – particularly since Seraphina was in Norfolk and Angela in Devon, so they never met.

Martha got out her pad of notepaper, her pen and a bottle of ink, and began to write. *Dear Seraphina*, she began, and even as she did so her daughter's lovely fair face appeared in her mind's eye, so that the letter became almost like a chat between the two of them. Martha wrote on.

Seraphina was hurrying past the bulletin board when ACW Betts hailed her. 'Hey, Fee, there's a couple of letters for you; want them?'

Seraphina turned back at once, a smile spreading across her face. Everyone wanted letters because it was your one contact with the outside world, or at least the world of home. 'Thanks, Betty,' she said, taking the proffered envelopes and seeing at once that the first was from Toby and the second was from her mother; nothing from Roger, but then they telephoned one another two or three times a week. They had had only one brief meeting since she had joined the WAAF, when she had gone into Norwich in the gharry and Roger had begged a lift from a friend, and they had spent a delightful weekend exploring the ancient city.

Seraphina pushed the envelopes into her pocket and grinned at her friend. 'As if anyone would ever say no to a letter,' she remarked. 'I'm on my way to the cookhouse, so I'll read them while I have my brekker; are you coming?'

'Naturally,' the other girl said laconically. She was small and dark with a round, rosy face and very striking pale grey eyes. She and Seraphina had been at training camp together, had been moved to Norfolk at the same time, and had bagged two beds next to each other in one of the long Nissen huts in which the WAAFs were quartered. ACW Betts was married to a lanky aircraftman stationed up in Scotland, and since she and Seraphina were the only married girls in their hut, this was another bond between them. They also worked together in the offices, though both hoped to do something more interesting than clerical work once their first six months in the WAAF was up. Seraphina wanted to work as a driver whereas Betty thought that R/T operating would be more interesting. 'Any fool can drive a lorry or a truck,' she had said, rather contemptuously. 'Think of the brash young idiots in delivery vans who careered round the streets before the war!'

'Some of my best friends were van drivers,' Seraphina had said loftily. 'Anyway, I like the outdoor life, and you must admit, it 'ud be fun to drive a squadron leader or an air commodore to important meetings.'

'And you a teacher!' Betty had marvelled. 'It's your duty, Aircraftwoman, to use your brains for the good of the air force, so don't you go letting me down and saying you want to train as a driver when you could do a much more important job standing on your head.'

'Oh? I didn't know you had to talk on the R/T standing on your head,' Seraphina had said innocently, and then had to flee the hut when Betty, hairbrush in hand, had endeavoured, she had said, to knock some sense into her pal.

The disagreement had still not been resolved, though privately Seraphina had accepted her friend's argument and meant to apply for a better job than driving, but right now the two girls walked briskly towards the cookhouse, their feet crunching on the frozen snow, whilst the letters rustled comfortably in the pocket of Seraphina's battledress.

There was a queue in the cookhouse, but it was moving quite fast. Seraphina checked that her irons were in her pocket – one carried one's eating utensils everywhere – then took a battered tray from the pile on the counter. A fat man, with a greasy apron hung low on his hips, sloshed porridge into a dish, slammed it on Seraphina's tray and banged two rounds of toast beside it. Seraphina thought, regretfully, that the toast would be cold and leathery and the porridge lumpy, unlike the lovely smooth porridge and hot toast which her mother had made every day for her family. She put a splash of milk into her mug and then filled it with tea from the urn: a very different brew from the cup of strong, sweet tea she would have had at home. At the end of the counter, another cookhouse worker smeared a tiny amount of margarine on to her plate. Then Seraphina turned away, found a table and sat down. Betty joined her. 'What's up with you, Fee?' she asked in an aggrieved voice. 'Didn't you notice the feller with the porridge was handing out a couple o' bits of streaky?'

'Bacon? Oh lor, I was so busy thinking about my letters that I never noticed,' Seraphina said wistfully, but she knew better than to return to the queue. The man in the greasy apron would remember that she had been round once but would 'forget' that he had not given her any bacon; no doubt he had already earmarked her share either for himself or for a friend. Oh well, it just went to show that you had to be on the alert all the time or someone would make sure you missed out.

Seraphina propped her letters against her mug of tea and began to spoon porridge. Actually, it wasn't too bad and it was good to have something hot and filling, for the weather was icy and had been so for weeks.

'Here, Fee, you can have my second rasher of bacon. Go on, fold it in that bit of toast and gobble it down,' Betty said generously. 'Your pa's a grocer, isn't he? Next time your parents send you a parcel we can go shares.'

'My mother works in a grocer's shop; my father died before the war,' Seraphina reminded her friend. 'And he was a barge master on the canal, not a perishin' grocer. I sometimes wonder if you listen to a word I say!'

'Sorry, sorry. I do remember, of course I do,' Betty said apologetically. 'It's just that my mind runs on food, rather. But your mum's a widow and the chap she works for is a widower, so naturally I thought they'd mebbe make a go of it.'

'Oh did you?' Seraphina said frostily. 'Well you can forget that, because Ma's got more sense than to marry an old skinflint, even if he is a grocer. Thanks for the bacon, though. Next time it turns up in the cookhouse, I'll pay you back, honest I will. But now just shut up and eat your leathery toast while I read my letters.'

It was the work of a moment to read Toby's letter since the censor had been busy. Seraphina was sure that most of the censors grew bored with reading other people's mail and so removed more than was necessary. What was more, Toby's letters were usually brief. She knew he was in India and had enjoyed his descriptions of the bazaars, the strange, twisted little streets of the nearest town, and the countryside, but having described his surroundings once he could scarcely do so every time he wrote. Still, it was grand to hear from him. Seraphina pushed the letter into her pocket and picked up the one from her mother. Martha had penned three closely written sheets and her letters were always fascinating since they spoke of people Seraphina knew well. She chuckled to herself as she read of Evie's latest exploits. Her sister and various pals had got up very early one morning in order to make an enormous snowball by rolling it along the centre of the quiet snow-covered roads. They had reached Northumberland Terrace and were thinking of turning home when they had lost control of it as they crossed the end of Havelock Street. The snowball had charged down the steep hill, gathering momentum as it went, and, naturally, increasing in size every moment. Fortunately, Netherfield Road was not as busy as it would become later in the day, but even so, the huge snowball had burst against the side of a tram, causing that vehicle to shudder and at least one angry passenger, and the conductor, to alight and come seeking vengeance. However, the steepness of Havelock Street had defeated their pursuers and Evie and her pals, giggling wildly, had made good their escape.

But you know your sister and her horrid little friends, Martha had written, *they disappeared like frost in June, but I believe it taught them a lesson. Evie actually said that had the snowball hit a horse and cart, or someone on a bicycle, it could have caused a dreadful accident, or even a death. So you see, it made her realise how easily she could have been in real trouble. In future, I believe she'll think before she acts and not after.*

Seraphina, still giggling, handed the letter to her friend. 'That's my sister Evie all over,' she said. 'Oh, I do miss her – and my mother, of course – but we're due a week's leave in a couple of months, so I'll go home then.'

Her companion looked at her rather oddly. 'What about Roger?' she said bluntly. 'Why not go up to Lincoln?'

'Oh! Well, I suppose it depends if he's free,' Seraphina said, rather vaguely. 'If he's got leave, we might both go home.' She glanced at the clock above the long counter. 'Hurry up with that tea, Betty, or we'll be late for work and that would never do.'

Angela loved the ATS, even though she had never imagined that she would do so. The camp at which she was stationed was on the outskirts of Dartmoor and today, despite the cold and the snow which covered the ground, they were on map-reading exercise. Warmly wrapped up in every item of clothing she possessed, she led her small group up on to the wildness of the moors, carefully following the planned route and constantly referring to the large scale map of the area with which each group had been supplied.

She had read her mother's letter before she set out and had thoroughly enjoyed the tale of Evie and the gigantic snowball and of her sister's constant search for 'something off the ration'. Now, regarding the snowy landscape around her and seeing the glint of a stream to her left, Angela remembered an earlier letter from Martha which had described how Evie had gone off for a weekend on the canal when the *Mary Jane* had docked in the city and had returned on Sunday night with what her mother described as *a guilty grin, a dozen very large potatoes, and two sticks of sprouts*. It was odd, Angela thought, how one's way of life changed one's outlook. Reading that letter, she had felt rather shocked. What had been fair enough on the canal seemed remarkably like theft when one no longer spent one's life travelling through fields of tempting produce.

Still, since Ma had accepted the vegetables and wrote about their acquisition without a qualm, Angela supposed that it was she who had changed. She wondered if Seraphina, who would have received a letter very similar to her own, would feel that Evie had stolen them, then dismissed the matter from her mind.

I'll tell Albert about Evie and the snowball, if he's in the mess this evening, she decided. He's such a nice fellow; I know it will make him laugh. Albert Reid was the chaplain attached to Angela's camp. He had wanted to join the RAF but his sight was poor – he wore small, steel-rimmed spectacles – so the air force had turned him down, and though he had subsequently applied for both the navy and the army they too had rejected him; poor eyesight had ruled out the navy, and flat feet had caused him to be spurned by the army as well. However, when he had applied for a chaplaincy with the army he had been accepted, and he was energetic in protecting his new flock.

Angela, who was rather shy and very diffident with members of the opposite sex, enjoyed Albert's unde-manding company and discovered that he had hidden depths. Although a bachelor in his early thirties, he loved children and had organised the local evacuees not only into Sunday school classes, but also into more amusing activities. The rector of the small local church was in his seventies and appreciated Albert's help to such an extent that he let him use the hall attached to his church for various functions. Angela had speedily become involved, and had found herself much more at ease with Albert than with any of the other young men in the camp. In fact, she had twice attended the cinema in his company and had enjoyed both expeditions.

But right now she should be concentrating on leading her group to their destination and not thinking, wistfully, of the warmth of the mess, and Albert, tall and rangy, giving her his shy, delightful grin as soon as she appeared in the doorway.

At this point, Angela's thoughts broke off in confusion; whatever was the matter with her? Albert was just a friend, nothing more, yet when she thought of him a warm glow suffused her – she, who had never taken any man seriously, never, she realised now, been in love.

Her thoughts might have continued in this vein, but at that moment Private Wilkins tugged at her elbow. 'I reckon we're almost home and dry, Todd,' the other girl said excitedly. 'See that buildin' over there, with the thatched roof? I reckon that's what we're bein' led to . . . there's blue smoke in a sorta smudge an' all, and the sergeant said there'd be a hot meal waitin' when we arrived. Cor, I'm bloody freezin' an' bloody starvin' as well; let's hurry!'

Toby sat in the mess tent, occasionally taking a bite out of the slice of flat and rather tasteless bread before him and brushing sweat – and flies – from his forehead as he did so. Spread out before him was his latest letter from home. It was from Evie; her ill-spelt, lively missives arrived pretty frequently and gave him a good deal of pleasure. She kept him up to date with all the news, though he had realised quite early on that she never reported bad tidings if she could help it. She had written of the Christmas raids on Liverpool but had contrived to pick out the lighter side of happenings which must, he guessed, have been terrifying. She had said that old Mrs Wilmslow had died but it had been Seraphina's letter that had enlarged on the old woman's death; Evie had not admitted that she had died as a result of the raid. Thinking it over, Toby decided it was affection for him which kept Evie's letters light and was glad of it, for not only could he do nothing to help but the letters took such ages to reach him that even sympathy, so long after the event, seemed almost super-fluous.

Now, sweltering in the Indian heat, he read her description of the biggest snowball in the world and its dramatic descent down Havelock Street into Netherfield Road with amusement and more than a touch of envy. He could see the scene in his mind's eye, clear as clear: Evie warmly wrapped up, but with her woolly gloves soaked and her fingers frozen from pushing the snowball along, the wind whipping her nose and cheeks to scarlet, whisking her long, straight hair out from under the shelter of her little cap. She would be laughing, bossing the other kids, enjoying every moment . . . until the snowball made its bid for freedom and crashed into the tram. He sighed and got to his feet, feeling the sweat begin to trickle down his back. It was no use repining and he guessed that a good many people back home would envy him the heat which he was cursing. He could be a good deal worse off, he knew that, because he had not been involved in any sort of fighting since Dunkirk. His regiment was here to train new Indian recruits in the ways of the

British army and then to be trained themselves in the art of jungle warfare, for it was commonly supposed that the Japanese would try to take India, believing that the Indian people would welcome them as a means of freeing themselves from the yoke of the British Empire.

Toby thrust the letter into the pocket of his khaki drill shorts. Better get a move on or his troops would wander off, for raw recruits knew nothing of discipline and had to be treated very like ignorant young children, until they began to realise what was expected of them. Toby went out of the tent and the sun hit him like a blow on the head, instantly banishing all thoughts of Liverpool and snow. It was impossible to believe that such conditions existed at that very moment, even three thousand miles away.

'*Mary Jane*! Ahoy there, *Mary Jane*!'

Evie leaned over the parapet of the Houghton Bridge and waved excitedly as the long shape of the canal boat eased over towards the bank and Hetty looked up from where she stood at the tiller. 'You coming down for a bit, Evie?' she shouted. 'Jimmy ain't with me; he's gone to talk to someone at the Ministry of Ag. and Fish. I dunno why, but I could do wi' a bit of extra help when it comes to loadin'.' She grinned up at Evie. 'I see your ma hasn't managed to get rid of you yet then, despite the raids and the landmines and the firebombs an' all.'

Evie belted to the end of the bridge and slithered down on to the canal path, giving the horse's enormous rump a friendly slap as she passed. 'You're looking well, Gemma. I suppose hay isn't rationed,' she remarked, and smiled as the horse's ears flicked back and her head turned to glance at Evie over her shoulder, though her steady pace never faltered. Evie jumped aboard the boat, answering Hetty's question as she did so. 'No, though she tried pretty hard at first to make me go and live in the country,' she said cheerfully. 'I love the country, but this is my war just as much as it is me mam's, and I wouldn't leave her, not for a million pounds. It's not that I don't trust Mr Wilmslow, 'cos he's nowhere near as bad as he used to be, but I'm thirteen now and really useful. Mam works like a slave in the shop and goes out with the WVS when there's a raid on, handing out tea and butties to anyone who's been bombed, or to the workers – firefighters an' that. I make her a hot meal when she gets home tired, do the housework, get the messages . . . oh, all sorts. So there's no way she's packing me off to live in the country, no fear!'

It was a fine, sunny day in early April and the feel of the deck beneath her feet – and the smell of dinner cooking in the small cabin – brought a rush of remembered happiness to Evie's mind. Oh, how she had loved living and working on the canal, and how she missed it! If only Pa hadn't decided to move into the city it would have been he who was at the tiller now, and Martha who had set the pot of what smelt like rabbit and mixed vegetables on the stove in the tiny cabin. And she would sleep at nights with her two sisters in the cabin of the butty boat, and listen when she woke to the old horse cropping the grass, to a lark rising up and up in the clean country air, to the soft lap of the water and the murmur of the wind.

But the war had changed everything for everyone. Jim and Hetty had told her of their narrow escape when the canal had been bombed last December; the bombs had burst the bank so that the poor old *Mary Jane* had been cast ashore, high and dry. It had taken Jim and Hetty a good deal of time, and money, to get her whole and back to the canal, and they had lost over fifty per cent of their cargo, which had been sugar. Fortunately, they had not had to recompense anyone for the loss, but they had had to manage with almost no personal possessions for weeks and weeks, until they had the money to replace what had been destroyed.

'Well, chuck?' Hetty said genially, steering the boat away from the bank again. 'It's been a while since you and me met. We've had no more damage, though one of them bleedin' incendiaries landed on the deck when we was moored up Wigan way. But Jim just kicked it into the water – I were in bed but he were still on deck – so that were all right.'

'We're still all okay too,' Evie said. 'There have been raids, a few, and a fair number of false alarms. I hate them worse than the raids because you have to get up and go down to the shelter and lose a night's sleep, and it's all for nothing.' She glanced around the boat. 'Is it sugar again? That you are going to take aboard, I mean?'

'Dunno,' Hetty said vaguely. 'Probably. But we heard on the grapevine that the last raid destroyed tons and tons of food in the warehouses along the docks. I know the flour mills in Birkenhead were hit, for a start. So we just goes down to the quayside and gets our orders there.'

'Oh, I see; yes, Mr Wilmslow said he didn't know what the country were going to do for food 'cos most of it had gone up in flames,' Evie said, remembering. 'How do you manage to get your groceries and so on, Hetty? Surely you can't go to the same shop, like everyone else. There must be other rules for folks like you.'

Hetty laughed. 'Since when has anyone ever give a moment's thought to *folks like us*?' she asked derisively. 'We're just like the rest of you, only we have to think ahead and make sure we're in the right place at the right time. And of course, there are some perks that country folk get which we pick up on, like vegetables in season, or a few spuds from out the clamp. Folks in the villages what've known us for years are good, too. I had as nice a piece o' pork from old Mr Tomlinson's pig as I've ever tasted, a couple o' weeks back. Oh aye, some folks is real good to us. But you never said as how the girls is gettin' along. I know you'll have had letters, but have you seen 'em lately?'

'No, but they're coming home in a couple of weeks,' Evie said exultantly. 'It'll be grand to see them again, just grand. And they'll be back for a whole week. Mam thought that if the weather stayed beautiful, we might have a day or two out in the country. You can't go to the seaside any more, not round here, at any rate. It's not allowed, but the country's okay.'

'Did you say they were both coming back?' Hetty asked, rather incredulously. 'Even Fee? Don't she want to see that new young husband of hers? He's still in England, ain't he?'

'Oh aye, but he's on a course,' Evie said quickly. 'Fee's going across to Lincoln to see him the last weekend, though. I say, that rabbit stew smells good!'

'You can have a plateful as soon as we dock,' Hetty said at once. 'And tell your mam she and the girls is welcome to join us aboard the old *Mary Jane* for a trip on the canal, if they fancy a change of scene. I know we've often talked of it but we'd be real glad to see you all, would Jim and me.'

Evie said she would pass on Hetty's invitation to her mother and then began to tell her friend all about school and how she helped Mr Wilmslow to make up people's rations, but the mention of Seraphina and Roger had brought a nagging worry back into her mind.

Something was the matter with Fee, she was sure, though no one else seemed to have noticed anything. She had not liked to question Seraphina and had tried to accept her mother's explanation, but she still thought that something was not right with her eldest sister. Never mind; this time I'll ask Seraphina outright, whilst she's on leave, she decided. After all, if I don't know what's the matter I can't help, and I honestly think Fee really does want help, even if she won't ask for it.

Chapter Eleven
May 1941

The girls returned to Liverpool on a Saturday, at the beginning of May and, by a happy coincidence, met on Crewe station coming from opposite directions, and so were able to travel together for the last part of their journey. They managed to get two seats together on the crowded Liverpool train so that they were able to converse in low tones, despite the proximity of other passengers.

They both knew that the city had been bombed the previous night and hoped to encourage their mother to take herself and Evie out of danger, for it was pretty clear that the port would be a constant challenge to the Luftwaffe and Scotland Road was too close to the docks for comfort, they thought.

'Someone told me that a bomb had landed on Lime Street station so we may find ourselves having to get a bus in for the last few stops,' Angela said, but was immediately reassured.

'No, it's all right. A fellow who'd come from Liverpool and was waiting for his connection on Crewe station started chatting to me.' Seraphina grinned at her sister. 'He was trying to pick me up – one of the disadvantages of being a blonde, as I'm sure you've found – but when I told him I was going to Liverpool and wondered whether I'd get there without being diverted, he said I'd be okay. There was a bomb, but since his train had got out he was pretty sure mine would get in.'

'Good,' Angela said. 'That's one worry less. Mam rang my camp, by the way, and actually got through to me to reassure me that she and Evie were all right. She said it might be sensible if we spent our leave somewhere else, but when I suggested that she and Evie should meet us somewhere, like Chester, and we'd have a week together in lodgings, she said that was impossible. Saturday is the busiest day in the shop and she's determined not to leave Mr Wilmslow in the lurch. I take it she rang you as well?'

'She did, but she had to leave a message because I was working,' Seraphina explained. 'I wonder what sort of a week's leave it's going to be, though, if the Luftwaffe are going to concentrate on the docks.'

'From the sound of it, there won't be much left for them to concentrate on,' Angela said gloomily. 'Still, Ma is really sensible. Of course, when she's on duty with the WVS she has to go to whichever distribution point she's given, but she always makes sure that Evie's as safe as can be before she does so.'

'The worst part of it is that you and I are comparatively safe, you in your camp on Dartmoor, and me in my airfield,' Seraphina said. 'But when I pointed that out to Ma, she reminded me that WAAFs crossing from one side of the airfield to another, or just walking along country lanes, have been strafed and dive-bombed, and I'm sure your camp has been attacked once or twice. Anyway, there's no arguing with her; she just lets such remarks roll off her back like water off a duck.'

After that, the girls' conversation turned to the lives they were living in the forces, which in some ways were very alike, and in others totally different. Angela shyly admitted that she had a boyfriend who had talked of marriage, and Seraphina, discovering that he was a chaplain, said that she supposed he was a very sober and proper young man: a fitting partner for her sober and proper sister.

Angela laughed but assured Seraphina that, chaplain or no, Albert was great fun, amusing and very intelligent. 'As for me, I might have been sober and proper once, but I'm not any longer; the war has changed all that,' she said. 'Once, all I wanted was my own little business, my own little home and a friend – Annabel for choice – to share it with me. Now I don't care whether I never have that little business; I'd rather have Albert and a crowd of noisy, happy, dirty children. So there!' she ended defiantly. She did not add that she had wanted Toby, too; that dream, like the others, had faded as her feelings for Albert had ripened into love.

The train was about to draw into Lime Street station, and Seraphina got to her feet. She felt, obscurely, that her sister had somehow overtaken her, though she could not have said precisely why. 'I'm sure Albert is a grand bloke,' she said, heaving her kit bag from the overhead rack. 'I don't suppose anyone will meet us because I couldn't even guess at what time I'd arrive, but I've been sitting down most of the day, so I wouldn't mind a walk.'

Angela agreed that a walk in the fresh air would be pleasant after being stuck in stuffy trains for hours at a time, and presently they got down and looked around them. There were signs of damage if you looked hard enough, Seraphina decided, but the station was so crowed that it was difficult to pinpoint exactly where bombs had fallen. She turned to Angela to remark on the fact just as a small figure came wriggling through the crowds towards them and flung both arms round Seraphina's neck.

'Fee, oh, Fee, it's wonderful to see you! I've been hanging around this perishin' station since midday. Mam reckoned you couldn't possibly arrive before then – unless you flew – and now here are the pair of you together!' Evie stopped hugging Seraphina and transferred herself, like a small limpet, to Angela. 'Oh, Angie, we've missed you so much. It's grand to have you home! I just hope those bloody Jerries will go somewhere else tonight because I'm that fed up with crouching in a shelter for hours at a time. Mam won't let me join her in the WVS canteen, not until I'm fourteen, which isn't fair, because if I were a boy I could be a messenger for the Air Raid Wardens, and firewatchers, and them . . .'

'It's lovely to see you, Evie,' Angela said gently, as her small sister stood back, beaming at them. 'And it's most awfully good of you to meet the train, but I think we ought to get back to the flat as soon as we can. We're both starving hungry and dying for a cup of tea, so let's hurry.'

Evie took a hand of each girl and towed them through the crowd towards Lime Street itself. 'I came here on a tram. I suppose you could try for a taxi, which could be quicker,' she said, rather doubtfully, 'only the queue's a mile long already.'

'We thought we'd walk,' Seraphina said. 'It's not that far and we could do with some fresh air. Good thing it doesn't get dark until late, now that summer's nearly here.'

They emerged on to the pavement and one glance at the taxi queue was sufficient to make all three girls turn decisively in the direction of Scotland Road, though Evie said: 'I'm afraid you won't get much fresh air; the bombs make everything dusty and the fires along the docks are still burning. Last night was awful . . . noisy, I mean . . . but maybe they'll let us alone tonight.' She glanced up at the clear blue sky ahead. 'I just wish thick black clouds would come over,' she added wistfully. 'If the clouds are really dark and low, it's not so easy to find us, though last time that happened poor old Birkenhead bought it.'

By the time they reached home, Seraphina felt she could have murdered for a cup of tea and it was the first thing her mother thrust into her hand as they entered the flat. Seraphina laughed and hugged her mother, holding the mug perilously out to one side, and then found that she was crying. Sniffing, sobbing and hugging, the four of them spent an emotional few moments before Martha dragged herself free of their clutching hands and bustled over to the stove. 'Thanks to young Evie here, it's liver and onions,' she said triumphantly. 'And thanks to Hetty, it's liver and onions and mashed potato and, of course, lots of lovely gravy and spotted dick and custard for afters.' She turned to look at her daughters with a considering eye. 'Not that either of you look as though you've lacked a square meal since I saw you last,' she added, almost accusingly. 'I can see the WAAF and the ATS manage to feed you pretty adequately.'

Both girls laughed, though Seraphina pointed out that Evie looked half starved if ever anyone did. 'And I know you, Ma – you'd have made sure she was fed, even if you had to half starve yourself,' she said jokingly. 'Only, as it happens, Angie and me know that Evie's got hollow legs. You can feed her like a prince and she'd still look more like a string bean than a human person.'

Evie bounced across the kitchen and punched Seraphina lightly on the shoulder. 'You're calling me skinny and I'm not, I'm slim, or slender, or whatever it is the magazines call their heroines,' she said indignantly. 'And I don't see that either of you look fat at all, you look just right.'

'So do you, queen,' Seraphina said remorsefully. 'And Ma's right, the forces do feed us pretty well, even if it is lumpy porridge, overcooked potatoes and Spam.' She sniffed, raising her nose in the air, in a parody of the Bisto Kids advertisement. 'My goodness, liver and onions; how good they smell! But I thought onions were in short supply? Folk are always complaining they can't get 'em.'

'Evie went down to the canal a couple of weeks back and gave a hand, and Hetty magicked up a whole string of onions and a sack of potatoes,' Martha said proudly, jiggling the frying pan. She jerked a thumb at the table, already laid for the meal. 'Sit down, girls, and get outside this little lot, and then with luck we might get a couple of hours' sleep in our own beds before the siren goes.'

'Oh?' Angela said, taking her place at the table. 'But you were bombed last night, Ma, and the night before that; surely it won't happen three nights in a row?'

'It's a clear night,' Martha said quietly. She slid liver and onions on to each plate, then indicated the tureen full of fluffy mashed potato, and the big blue jug of gravy. 'Eat first and talk later,' she commanded. 'Another mug of tea, anyone?'

Much later that night, entombed in the stuffy depths of the nearest shelter, Seraphina, Angela and Evie cuddled on to one of the hard little bunks. The noise from outside was unbelievable, worse than anything any of them had experienced before. The shelter shook every time a bomb landed near them, which was every few moments, or so it seemed. Seraphina thought that presently the brick walls of the shelter and the great steel and concrete reinforced roof would simply give up the unequal struggle to remain intact and fall in upon them, but it did not happen.

In the early hours of the morning, Martha joined her daughters. She was white-faced and filthy but she, and the two women who accompanied her, smiled brightly and said that they had been told, now that their supply of both tea and butties had run out, to get themselves into a shelter.

'Whass it like out there?' an old man, with a draggly grey beard and a stained mackintosh, enquired hoarsely. 'Me head's ringin' from the crashes an' I can't think straight no more, but I does know me daughter, livin' out at Bootle, don't always go to the shelter. Are they bombin' out Bootle way, missus?'

The three women exchanged glances, and the eldest of them replied. She was a plump woman with a great many freckles and curly ginger hair touched with grey at the temples. 'It's impossible to say for certain, of course,' she said quietly, 'but I'm sure the wardens wouldn't let your daughter stay in her own home on a night like this. Anyway, the bombs might not have fallen so far out of the city; they seem to have concentrated their best efforts – or rather their worst efforts – on the docks and the city centre.' She patted the old man on the shoulder. 'I'm sorry I can't be more definite, but it's pretty bad out there.'

The old man sat down once more. Seraphina saw that he was trembling but knew they could do nothing more to reassure him. Downright lies would not help, for the old man would find out they were lies soon enough.

Evie was curled up in the corner of the bunk and Seraphina had thought that her little sister slept, but now she saw that Evie's dark eyes were wide open and even as she glanced towards her Evie sat up. 'Anyone got any tea left?' she shouted, above the tumult of the raid. 'Mr Benjamin ain't feeling so good.'

Why didn't I think of that, Seraphina asked herself as a hugely untidy woman, whom she recognised as a stallholder from Paddy's market, surged across the shelter, a large flask in one hand. She unscrewed the top and poured what remained in the flask into it, then handed it to the old man, putting her arm round his shoulders as she did so and giving him a reassuring squeeze. 'Here y'are, Benjy, me old mate,' she said huskily. 'Drink that up an' you'll feel better in no time. Me lad's in the navy so I added a spoonful of rum to the tea when I were makin' it.' She chuckled hoarsely. 'That'll put hairs on your chest, as me lad always says.'

Evie giggled. 'Has it put hairs on your chest, Mrs O'Mara?' she asked cheekily. 'And if it puts hairs on your chest, how about your chin, eh? Why, if you drank enough of it, you could make a tidy penny joinin' a circus as the bearded lady!'

Seraphina opened her mouth to tell Evie not to be so cheeky, then closed it again. The fat old stallholder was laughing, the old man in the stained raincoat was laughing, Martha and her two WVS friends were laughing, and now other people began to tease the stallholder, to laugh and crack jokes. Seraphina looked at her sister's small, crumpled face and thought, wonderingly, that Evie could teach them all a thing or two. The entire atmosphere in the shelter had changed. People began to sit up and take notice of what was going on around them instead of crouching miserably on the bunks and benches, pretending to be asleep, each one shut up in their own little circle of fear.

Martha and her friends came and perched on the bunk beside Seraphina, for the shelter was packed. 'You have to hand it to Evie,' Seraphina whispered in her mother's ear. 'She must be scared stiff – well, we all are – but you'd never think it, would you?'

Martha put her arm round Seraphina and gave her a squeeze. 'I don't know what I would have done without her, since you and Angie joined up,' she admitted. 'Nothing seems to faze her except the thought of being sent away, and no matter how bad the raids get, I shan't suggest it again.'

Angie, who had been writing a letter in the dim bluish light, which was all the shelter afforded, leaned across Seraphina and spoke directly to Martha. 'She's thirteen now; in another year she'll be working, so there's really no point in sending her away, unless you go with her, of course.'

Martha snorted. 'You know I won't . . .' she began, just as another enormous explosion rocked the dugout. When the noise began to die down, she spoke once more. 'This is the worst night we've had; easily the worst. If the flat survives, I'll be astonished. And if it goes . . . well, Evie and I will just have to think again, that's all.'

When the all clear sounded, everyone stumbled out of the shelter, clutching their personal possessions. The steps were covered in grit – brick dust from the bombed buildings, Seraphina assumed – and when they reached the top and were standing on the pavement in the brightening daylight, she gasped at the devastation around them. The warehouses surrounding the docks were ablaze still, and against the fires she saw the silhouettes of the troops who had been drafted in to try to keep the warehouses safe, scuttling backwards and forwards in their completely vain attempts to douse the flames. Where had stood buildings which she had always known as a part of the scene were just gaping, blackened holes. The roadway itself must surely be impassable, because of the rubble, the jetting water mains and the twisted tram rails which had resulted from the bombing. Yet when they reached the shop, both it and the surrounding buildings were still intact and just as they went down the side passage towards the flat Mr Wilmslow appeared, looking drawn and tired, though he grinned at them cheerfully enough, pushing his tin hat to the back of his head, and rumpling Evie's long hair. 'I'm that glad to see you, ladies,' he said. 'There were a moment when I were down by the docks and that bleedin' barrage balloon landed on the *Malakand* when I thought I were bound to be a goner. And there were another moment, when I could ha' sworn one of the landmines came down almost on top of the shelter. Me and a few other chaps raced over there, but either the wind or the heat from the burning buildings had caught the parachute, so instead of falling straight like, it were carried away across the dock and disappeared into the water. Aye, it's been a bad night; the worst so far, I'm thinkin'.' He made as if for the front door of the shop, digging in his pocket for a key.

'You come up to the flat with us, Mr Wilmslow, and I'll get everyone some breakfast,' Martha said, and Seraphina heard the gentle note in her voice and thought that Evie's kindness came directly from Martha. She knew her mother disliked her employer, thought him a mean old skinflint, had once told

Seraphina, privately, that he sometimes cheated his customers if he could get away with it. Yet now, when he was doing his best for the war effort, when he had no one to make his breakfast or wash his filthy clothes, Martha would help him, despite her personal feelings.

Together, the Todd family and Mr Wilmslow ascended the iron staircase and entered the familiar kitchen.

By Wednesday morning, Seraphina felt positively punch drunk and longed for nothing so much as a proper rest, for the air raids had continued with equal ferocity every single night since they arrived home. Sitting in the kitchen, listlessly eating her breakfast porridge, she looked round at her mother and sisters, and Mr Wilmslow, and felt ashamed that she dreaded the nights ahead and longed for the comparative peace of her airfield. Martha and Mr Wilmslow were both far worse off than she, for they worked in the shop all day and could not even come down to the shelter at night. Since their arrival home, though, she and Angie had managed to help a bit and Evie, as usual, took on getting the messages and a good deal of the housework and cooking. Angela and herself worked in the shop from opening time until one o'clock, which meant that Mr Wilmslow and Martha got four hours' sleep at least. The trouble was, both she and Angie found it impossible to sleep in the air raid shelter so they usually tried to go to bed around three in the afternoon, sometimes actually sleeping until eight or nine at night, though the strain of listening for the air raid siren made sleep difficult.

'More tea, queen?' Martha looked lovingly across the table at her eldest daughter. 'I'm that sorry your leaves have coincided with the worst of the bombing, and I wish you'd go off into the country for the few days that are left. But to tell you the truth, I'm too tired to argue with you . . . too tired to do anything much, apart from keeping on going.'

'We're all tired,' Mr Wilmslow said, scraping his spoon around the porridge bowl. 'I keep telling myself that the bloody Huns will soon realise there's nothing left in Liverpool worth bombing, but it doesn't seem to happen. So I've come to a decision.' He pointed a finger at Martha. 'I shan't be needing you in the shop until next Monday, do you understand me? Mrs Bunwell and meself will manage as best we can, and you and your girls will go into the country and have some time together. Don't worry about the money – I'll pay. I spoke to an old friend of mine, by telephone, last evening – she's a farmer's wife out on the Wirral. Her sons are all in the forces so she's got several spare bedrooms and she's agreeable to having the Todd family stay from today till Saturday, so it's all arranged.' He saw Martha begin to open her mouth and cut her short. 'No, I won't hear a word against it. You're not being fair to the girls, Mrs Todd, because they're given leave from their jobs to ease the stress of forces' life, and these here raids don't do that, do they? You'll have to take your ration books, of course, but knowing Mrs Noakes she'll feed you well and you'll have a proper rest each night and time together during the day.'

Across the table, Martha smiled at him and Seraphina saw that her mother's eyes were bright with tears. 'It's awfully good of you, Mr Wilmslow, and I will go, though I shall feel dreadful leaving you with all the work and no one to cook, or clean, or shop for you,' she said. 'But I know you're right, really, about the girls being given time off for a good reason, and I know they won't go without me. Tell you what – when Evie and I come back, you must promise to visit Mrs Noakes for a few days yourself; then we'll both be in a better state to face whatever is to come.'

'Mebbe I will at that,' Mr Wilmslow said. 'I don't deny I'm weary to the bone; it's been a great help having the girls take over the shop in the mornings, but I'm often so perishin' tired I can't sleep. Now, you want to make your way down to the Pier Head, get a ferry to Woodside and catch a bus from there . . .' He frowned with mock ferocity at Martha 'You'd best be on your way or I'll want to know the reason why.'

Seraphina could have wept with relief at the thought of leaving the devastated city. She could also have hugged Mr Wilmslow for his generosity of spirit, though she was determined that he should not pay for her holiday. She could well afford to do so but knew her mother was probably quite hard pressed, and thought she would leave the matter of payment until she had talked to Martha and Angela. She glanced at Evie, who was beaming. The girl rushed round the table and gave Mr Wilmslow a hearty hug and a kiss on the cheek, which he pretended to wipe off disgustedly, though Seraphina could see he was secretly delighted.

'Thank you, thank you, Mr Wilmslow; anyone who calls you an old skinflint when I'm around will gerra knuckle sarnie,' Evie said joyfully. 'Oh, it'll be grand to have a few nights' proper sleep and to be on a farm, with pigs and ducks and that. I wonder if there's a pony? Mebbe I could learn to ride.'

'Gerron wi' you,' Mr Wilmslow said gruffly, getting

to his feet and shooing Evie and the others towards the kitchen door. 'Go and start your packing.'

Seraphina and Angie went to their room and began slinging their small possessions into their kit bags, but as soon as this was done Angela turned to her sister. 'Fee, would you think it absolutely awful of me if I went straight back to camp instead of going to the Wirral with you and Mam? You see, Albert had been told that his regiment will almost certainly be sent abroad and – and I'd like to spend some time with him before he goes. I suppose it's awfully selfish, but . . .'

'You'd better ask Ma rather than me,' Seraphina said, rather stiffly. She thought that, if Angela did go back to camp to be with her chaplain, it would show her, Seraphina, in rather a bad light. She had made Roger's course an excuse to come home instead of going to stay in Lincoln, but the course was now over. However, she knew that if she too said she was not going with them, her mother and Evie would refuse to go to the Wirral, so perhaps it was more selfish to go to Roger than to stay with them.

As though she had spoken the words instead of thinking them, Angie turned to her. 'I *am* being selfish, aren't I?' she said remorsefully. 'I'm sure you'd much rather be with Roger than with Ma, no matter how much you love her, but you're not going to let her down. Oh, I won't either. It was mean of me to suggest it. Only – only Albert will be going so far away and – and Roger isn't likely to be stationed abroad, is he?'

Seraphina bit back the sharp retort that Roger was in deadly danger every time he flew a sortie over enemy territory, and said that Angela had every right to want to be with her young man. Then she despatched her to see how Martha took the suggested change of plan and was not surprised when Angela came back, beaming, to say that Martha had completely understood; indeed, had insisted that Angela should go.

So it was only three Todds who arrived at the Noakes's farmhouse, late that afternoon, and settled down to enjoy tea, chunky ham sandwiches, a bowl of hard boiled eggs and several plates of scones and cakes served by a beaming Mrs Noakes, who clucked and fussed over them as she took them to their rooms. 'You poor dears, you look worn to the bone; what you want is a real good night's sleep,' she said warmly. 'Why not go for a nice walk along the lanes to give you an appetite for supper? And after that I'll warrant you'll all sleep like newborn babes.'

She was a tall, big-bosomed lady, with abundant white hair, rosy cheeks, and a wide, generous mouth. Seraphina liked her on sight and wished, devoutly, that she could persuade her mother and sister to remain with Mrs Noakes whilst the bombing raids continued. She knew it would be useless to try, however; Martha would never fail in what she thought of as her duty and Evie would never leave Martha.

Still, this was an interlude of peace in wartime and as such they must all make the best of it.

Martha had encouraged Angela to return to Devonshire not only because she was delighted to see how her daughter had blossomed once she was away from home, but also because she knew she must talk to Seraphina and find out what, if anything, was wrong with her beautiful and talented daughter. Ever since Evie had mentioned the matter to her, Martha had been uneasily aware that all was not well with her eldest. The explanation she had given Evie had been as much for her own benefit as for her small daughter's, but, like Evie, she had nourished a secret, nagging worry ever since. Seraphina was very happy as a WAAF and had begun training as an R/T operator, which was responsible and important work, but she did not make time to go and see her husband, and had actually come home to Liverpool for her week's leave when Martha was sure she could have arranged her time off to coincide with her husband's if she had wished to do so. She had told Martha, airily, that Roger, who had been piloting Wellington bombers, was at Church Broughton, along with his crew, doing a course. But Martha guessed that this was just a fortunate coincidence and had nothing to do with the real reason why Seraphina had come home for her week's leave.

Now, however, with Angie off at her camp and Evie so eager to help with the farm work that she would probably spend every day feeding baby lambs, or perched on the back of the fat old pony, Martha thought that at long last she might be able to find out what ailed Seraphina. Of course, she might be wrong; there might be nothing the matter at all. Certainly, it was odd that Seraphina had only met her husband once since their honeymoon, but the exigencies of service life could, Martha supposed, account for that.

'Have you finished, Mam?' Evie's bright voice, from across the breakfast table, broke into Martha's thoughts. 'Only I promised Joyce that I'd give a hand with the milking and that I'd collect the eggs, too. I meant to get up real early only it was so quiet and peaceful that I didn't wake at all until I heard the clatter of milk pails out in the yard. So I guess I've missed the milking, but I might still be in time to get the eggs. Joyce is ever so nice – she's fifteen, not all that much older'n me – and she says we can drive into the village in the pony and trap later, to get her mam's messages . . . only she called them errands. So can I get down, Mam?'

Martha laughed at the childish phrase which she had not heard on Evie's lips for some years, but nodded her agreement and saw Evie fly from the room before turning to smile, ruefully, at Seraphina. 'This is the sort of life Evie should be living,' she observed. 'Now, what would you like to do this morning, my love? I'm ashamed to admit that, though I slept like a log, I'm still dreadfully tired, but it's a wonderful warm day and I think a nice country walk would be good for both of us.' She patted her stomach. 'Egg, bacon, fried bread and black pudding is a good deal nicer than a bowl of watery porridge and a slice of leathery toast, but I can't afford to burst out of my grey working skirt, so I think we should try and exercise or we'll go home on Saturday looking like a couple of porkers.'

Seraphina agreed readily and suggested that they should walk to the village. 'I've got some of my sweet ration left; it would be a nice gesture to buy Mrs Noakes something in the sweetie line for when we leave her on Saturday,' she suggested. 'I expect Mr Wilmslow told you that I tried to make him let me pay Mrs Noakes for our bed and board, but he wouldn't allow it, so I'd like to buy him something as well – just to show him that we're truly grateful.'

'That's a lovely idea,' Martha observed. 'Although I didn't much care for him at first, I've grown accustomed, I suppose, and now I can see his good points. He's not nearly as mean as he was – he pays Mrs

Bunwell generously when she works in the shop – and though I won't take money for working in the evenings on all the government bumph that has to be filled in, he tries to make sure I don't lose by it; a bottle of Camp coffee or a couple of tins of baked beans appear on the kitchen table whenever I've nipped out for a few minutes. I wonder what you could buy him? Cigarettes are the obvious thing, I suppose – he never smoked at all before the war, you know, but now he usually buys ten Woodbines a week. I tell you what, if we can't find anything in the village, we'll take a bus to Chester. I don't suppose Evie will want to come, but it would be a nice change to see Chester again.'

Seraphina agreed with this plan and presently the two of them set off, walking slowly along the leafy lane in the direction of the village. After some desultory conversation about the farm and the surrounding countryside, Martha took her courage in both hands and voiced what was on her mind. 'Fee, my love, I hope you won't be offended, but have you and Roger had some sort of tiff? Only I know you don't see much of him and I'm sure you could have deferred your leave until Roger could have had some time off as well. He's such a delightful young man, I – I can't imagine him deliberately distressing you.'

There was a long silence during which Martha wondered, apprehensively, whether she had overstepped the mark or had simply imagined that there was anything wrong between Roger and her daughter. She glanced at Seraphina's face but the girl looked thoughtful, neither angry nor offended. Martha opened her mouth to apologise, to say that she had not meant to interfere, but before she could say anything Seraphina, who had been staring abstractedly ahead, turned to face her, giving her a small, almost shame-faced smile.

'Yes, there is something wrong, though I dare say you'll not think it very important,' she said quietly. 'Roger – Roger doesn't want children.'

Martha gazed at her, perplexed. 'But isn't that understandable in wartime?' she ventured. 'You're both in the services, with no home of your own in which to bring up a child. Don't you think that perhaps Roger is just being sensible?'

'I don't know,' Seraphina said slowly. 'I did think that at first but now I'm not so sure that Roger will ever want children. There are men like that, Ma; they think of children as a burden, an added responsibility.'

'And you think Roger's one of those men? I think you're being rather hard on him, my love,' Martha said. 'When Harry and I first married, we decided we would defer having a family until we could afford to look after them properly, and we were so happy aboard the dear old *Mary Jane* that we didn't miss children for those two years. I think you'll find, Fee, that the majority of women want children and the majority of men go along with the idea without any real enthusiasm. When the children arrive, of course, it's completely different; my goodness, your father worshipped you, thought you were the most marvellous creatures alive, would have done anything for you. So I think you'll find, when the war's over, that Roger will agree to having a family and will love the babies when they arrive as much as Harry loved his little ones.'

There was another long silence, then Seraphina stopped short and gave her mother a hug. 'You're much wiser than me so I'm sure you're right,' she said humbly. 'The truth is, Ma, that Roger and I don't know each other very well yet. A simple disagreement gets exaggerated into a quarrel and when you part on a sour note it's – it's impossible to forget the things the other one has said, impossible not to dwell on it when you're lying alone in your bed at night. But I won't do that any more, I promise you, and I'll go and see Roger the very next time I get a chance. I'm sure, when we're together, we'll work it out – because I really do love him, you know.'

'Yes, and you're used to having your own way,' Martha said, giving her daughter's hand a squeeze. 'And now let's forget our troubles and enjoy our walk.'

Seraphina returned to her airfield and was in her hut by six o'clock on Saturday evening despite the difficulties of cross-country travel in wartime. Most of the WAAFs were in the hut, tidying up after their day's work, and Seraphina plonked herself down on her bed to unpack her kitbag, stowing her belongings with more haste than care in the locker which separated her bed from Betty's. Betty, combing out her short dark hair so that it framed her rosy face, turned and beamed at her friend. 'Gosh, it's been a long week,' she observed. 'We've been really worried because the news coming out of Liverpool has been dreadful. Someone said a hundred and fifty thousand people had been killed and practically every house in the city had been razed to the ground, but rumours spring up like that in wartime. It can't be true – can it? You look fine.'

'I left the city last Wednesday, but the raids were horrendous, worse than anything I'd ever imagined,' Seraphina admitted. 'And judging from the local papers, the bombing went on after we left; is probably going on still, for that matter. I wish Ma and Evie would listen to reason . . . but hopefully the worst is over now and they can begin to pick up the remainder of their lives.'

'Poor them. But how did you enjoy your leave?' Betty asked. 'Did you go to relatives? Oh – you didn't go to the canal, did you? I believe bombs hit it at some stage.'

'No, we went to a farm; Ma's employer treated us to three days' bed and board. It was grand,' Seraphina assured her friend. She ran a comb through her thick golden hair, pinned it into a neat coil at the nape of her neck, then checked her appearance in the long mirror which hung beside the door. 'Mrs Noakes fed us like royalty; a bit different from the cookhouse,' she observed, going through the doorway into the sunshine of early evening. 'Oh well, all good things come to an end, and anyway I love my work here, so I mustn't complain.'

Later that evening, when most of the girls were in the mess, Seraphina and Betty went for a walk along the perimeter track, enjoying the last sloping rays of the sun and the sweet scents of the long meadow grass which, in two or three weeks, would be cut for hay. They walked in silence for a while, then Betty turned to her friend. 'Well? You haven't said much about your leave; I bet it was wonderful seeing your family again. Angela was on leave at the same time, wasn't she? Did anyone wonder why you'd not gone to see Roger?' She chuckled. 'If I'd passed up a chance to be with my old man, my mum would have a thing or two to say, I can tell you.'

Seraphina sighed. 'Yes, I suppose any mother would want to know what was going on,' she admitted, 'and my mother is no exception; she asked all right.'

'And what did you tell her?' Betty asked curiously. 'It's not an easy thing to discuss with your mum, is it?'

'I told her the truth,' Seraphina said. 'I told her that Roger didn't want children.'

'And that was *all* you told her?' Betty asked incredulously. 'It wasn't exactly the truth, the whole truth and nothing but the truth, was it? But I'm sure you and Roger will work it out once you're seeing a bit more of each other, and maybe knowing what had happened – or rather, what had *not* happened – would only upset your mum, and embarrass her, of course.'

'You're right there,' Seraphina agreed. 'My mother's a marvellous person but you know my father was a lay preacher, and my mother runs her life on what you might call Christian principles. I think she'd be quite shocked to know that – that ours isn't a real marriage; that it isn't just children he doesn't want, it's – it's me.'

Betty slipped her hand into the crook of Seraphina's arm. 'Of course he wants you,' she said, in a scolding voice. 'He's probably terrified of doing it wrong and making a fool of himself. A man doesn't marry a woman he doesn't want. It's – it's just that some men find the sex business embarrassing, difficult to cope with. I bet your Roger thinks he'll make a mess of it so he keeps hanging back.'

Seraphina sighed. 'He said, during our honeymoon, that he was afraid of hurting me and even more afraid that I might get pregnant. I understood, or thought I did, and apart from not . . . well, you know . . . he was very sweet to me. But when we had that weekend in Norwich, and I plucked up my courage and said I'd been to the MO and got some . . . *things* for him to use, he seemed to take offence.' She sighed. 'I expect I handled it all wrong. I called him into the bathroom when I was in the tub and tried to persuade him to come into the water with me. He went bright red in the face and did a sort of flounce, and when I climbed out of the water and went towards him, he said "*Keep*

319

off", in a really cross, hissing whisper, and slammed out of the room. It – it was really humiliating, Bett; I felt how a tart must feel when a feller rejects her advances. That night I slept by myself in that big, comfortable double bed and I don't think Roger went to bed at all. We met at breakfast – it was jolly awkward, I can tell you – but afterwards he tried to pretend there was nothing wrong and I got angry and said if he was going to walk out on me again, I'd go back to my airfield. He begged me not to, begged me not to ruin his leave, agreed that we should talk about it and not pretend nothing had happened. The odd thing is, we had a grand day together, and when we got back to the room he made a long speech about the wickedness of bringing children into a world at war. He – he said the things the MO gave me were seldom completely reliable which was why he hadn't . . . oh, damn it, Bett, nothing had changed. I went to bed – we both did – but it was after two o'clock before I fell asleep. I got up at six, went down and had an early breakfast all by myself and left without saying goodbye.'

'Very understandable,' her friend said. 'I'd have done the same. To tell you the truth, Fee, I don't think I can advise you except to say keep seeing him whenever you get the chance. And if you decide it's never going to be any different, then remember, this is the 1940s; divorce is perfectly possible, though they don't make it easy for you.'

'Divorce! I'm very sure no one in our family has ever been involved in a divorce, and I bet the Trueloves are just the same,' Seraphina said. 'But I will try to make a go of it; last time we spoke on the phone, he suggested he might come to Norfolk again the next time he has a few days free. The trouble is, Bett, that every time we meet and . . . and nothing happens, the rift widens, if you see what I mean.'

Betty nodded. 'And now let's change the subject,' she said. 'I wonder how your mum and your little sister are getting on? I expect you'll get a phone call later this evening to let you know they're okay.'

Scotland Road, when Martha and Evie reached it on the Saturday evening, was almost unrecognisable. Although they knew, from listening to the wireless, that the last raid had been a couple of days before, devastation was everywhere. Masonry from bombed houses had fallen across the roads, which were pocked with craters, and a thick pall of dust hung over the stricken city. The smell of burning hung horribly in the air and it was hard to recognise where they were as they made their way towards the flat.

When they reached it, a worse shock was in store. The shop front was there, but it looked as though it might fall down at any moment and there was no glass in either of the large windows; of the flat above it, there was no sign. Martha and Evie stood in the road, clutching each other's hands and gazing at the destruction of everything they had possessed. After a few moments, however, Martha pulled herself together and went towards the shop. She peered through the window frame and saw a movement inside. It was Mr Wilmslow. 'Don't try and come in through the door. Come round the back,' he said. 'This lot happened a couple of days ago. God knows where I'll put the stuff I'm salvaging, but it can't stay here. There's been looting already, and you can't blame folk. When you've lost everything . . .'

Martha interrupted. 'Mr Wilmslow, you should know better than to be doing that,' she said, glancing nervously at the precarious state of the walls and ceiling. 'And you a warden as well. What's the point of picking up what are probably damaged goods anyway, when it's not safe to be in there at all? Why, you've spent the last couple of years telling folk to keep clear of bomb damage, yet here you are, risking your life for a few tins of sardines! Come out of there at once or I'll report you to the authorities.'

'What authorities?' he asked derisively. 'They're run off their feet right now 'cos the telephone exchange was hit so no one can't ring relatives. The Bryant and May factory has gone, with a loss of God knows how many jobs. Lewis's is gutted, the water mains is ruptured; the tram lines are twisted and useless . . .' He chuckled grimly. 'The authorities have got their hands full without poking their noses into my affairs. Why, almost every shop in the city is like this one and I reckon it's my duty to save any food I can because all that stuff they stashed away in the warehouses along the docks has gone up in flames, and I heared on the wireless that London's the same. Besides, the rooms at the back of the shop are not too bad. Come and give a hand, Mrs Todd, 'cos the quicker we move the stuff the better.'

Martha sighed, then glanced at Evie. 'I dare not let you come inside, love, in case the whole place falls on us,' she said gently. 'Will you stay out here while I help Mr Wilmslow to salvage what we can?'

She said it hopefully but was not at all surprised when Evie shook her head. 'No I won't,' her daughter said baldly. 'Old Wilmslow's no fool; if it's safe enough for him – and you – then I reckon I'll be okay. And he's quite right, you know; the stuff which is usable ought to be got out just in case the place does cave in.'

Martha nodded reluctantly. 'I suppose you're right. Come along, then. But God knows where we'll lay our heads tonight.'

'There's always the shelter – if it hasn't been bombed, that is,' Evie said. 'C'mon, Mam, the sooner we can get the shop cleared, the better.'

Incredible though it seemed, by the following Monday Mr Wilmslow was in business once more and the Todds had found somewhere to lay their heads. Just down the road was a small tobacconist's shop with a flat above it. By some miracle, both shop and flat were intact, but the old man who owned and ran it had had enough. He and his wife were both over seventy and had decided to go and stay with their daughter, who lived in the small village of Higher Kinnerton in Cheshire. When Mr Wilmslow approached him he was very willing to rent both shop and flat to the younger man, since the money would come in useful. His stock, depleted anyway by the war, would be sold gradually by Mr Wilmslow and the money the latter received would be sent to old Mr Butler in instalments.

Martha, taken to view the flat by her employer, agreed that she would be happy to take it, especially since the rent was no higher than that charged by Mr Wilmslow for her previous home. The flat was smaller – it only had one bedroom and no bathroom – but there was a reasonable living room, where the older girls could sleep when they came home on leave, and she and Evie would share the double bed in the small bedroom. Martha would inherit all the Butlers' furniture and linen, as well as their crockery and cutlery, since their daughter's small cottage was fully furnished, so the flat had been rented as it stood. 'Warts and all,' Mr Butler had said genially, when the arrangement had been made. 'And if the place is still intact when peace comes, I reckon Mr Wilmslow will buy it off of me instead of renting it, so that's all right.'

Mr Wilmslow himself would have to sleep in the stockroom, on a makeshift bed of some sort, but Martha would continue to provide his meals, since the stockroom was just that, and had no facilities for cooking, though there was a sink with a cold water tap in one corner.

On her first evening in the new flat, sitting at the Butlers' kitchen table, trying to sort out the paperwork so that they could claim for either lost or irretrievably damaged goods, Martha was not surprised when the kitchen door opened and Mr Wilmslow came in. What did surprise her was the fact that he was carrying a bunch of flowers: purple and white lilac, and a couple of scarlet peonies. However, she smiled at him as he laid the flowers down upon the table.

'What's all this then? My, doesn't that lilac smell wonderful? It reminds me of the *Mary Jane* – many a cottage garden has a lilac tree on the back fence and the scent from them wafts across the canal . . . lovely. Where did you get them, Mr Wilmslow?'

'Oh . . . here and there,' Mr Wilmslow said airily. 'Mrs Todd, I want to – to regularise this here situation. I know it ain't long since my wife died, but I guess you've realised I couldn't go on wi'out you. You're a grand worker, a grand cook and a grand mother to them kids of yours.' He chuckled. 'That young Evie's a real caution but she's more help than many a lass twice her age.'

He stopped speaking and looked expectantly at Martha, who looked back with an uncertain smile. What on earth was he getting at? 'I'm not sure quite what you mean, Mr Wilmslow,' she said slowly. 'I'm not thinking of leaving your employ, you know. Oh, I wanted Evie to go into the country but she won't do it and I'm the same; I'm here for the duration.'

'Aye, I know that,' Mr Wilmslow said. He sounded cross, Martha thought. 'You must know what I mean, Mrs Todd. Why d'you think I waited until young Evie was in bed before I come up this evening? Dammit, why d'you think I brung you flowers?'

Martha was beginning to have an inkling of what was to come. She said hastily: 'It – it doesn't matter, Mr Wilmslow, I'm sure everything is as regular as regular, if you see what I mean. You don't have to – to say any more. I can only assure you that I don't mean to leave you in the lurch, and . . .'

'That ain't the point, Mrs Todd – Martha, I mean,' Mr Wilmslow said. His voice had risen and so had his colour, Martha noted with trepidation. 'I'm – I'm rare fond o' you, Martha. I've been screwing up me courage to pop the question for a couple of months now. I know there's only one bedroom in the flat but I could box off a bit of a room down here so's Evie had somewhere to sleep . . . and . . .'

'You could box off a bit of the room so that *you* had somewhere to sleep,' Martha said, rather crossly. 'Whatever would people think, Mr Wilmslow, with your wife so recently passed on?'

'They'd think I were doin' the right thing by you, makin' an honest woman of you . . .' The look on Martha's face must have warned him that this was the wrong approach for he said hastily: 'What does it matter what people think? Circumstances alter cases, they say, and our circumstances are bleedin' difficult, what with the shop and the flat being destroyed, and more'n half the stock gone with 'em. Besides, that makeshift bed is perishin' uncomfortable . . . for a full-grown man, I mean. It 'ud suit a young slip of a thing like Evie down to the ground.'

'I dare say, but I'm not hanging out for a husband,' Martha said firmly. 'Why, Mr Wilmslow, I don't even know your first name and you've never called me by mine until this moment. We rub along very well as employer and employee, but marriage . . . well, that's a different kettle of fish.'

Mr Wilmslow snatched up the bouquet and for an awful moment Martha thought he was going to throw it on the fire or chuck it through the window, but instead he carried it through to the sink, filled a jug with water, and jammed the flowers untidily into it. He stood the jug on the sideboard and then sat down opposite Martha. 'I reckon I said it all wrong and I'm real sorry if I offended you,' he said, and there was a humble note in his voice which Martha had never heard before. 'To tell you the truth, Mrs T— I mean Martha, I've always had a fondness for you. I knew it even when me wife was alive, but I knew it were wrong, too, so I told meself over and over that you were just a nice woman, a friend. But now it's different; you're a widow and I'm a widower, and we're working cheek by jowl and living cheek by jowl an' all. Can't you, won't you, think again? I'm not good wi' words but if you'd agree to be my wife, I'd – I'd do right by you; can't you see I mean it?'

'I'm sure you do,' Martha said, though in fact she thought Mr Wilmslow's main concern was for his comfort, which gave her an idea. She did not want her employer pestering her with suggestions that they should marry whenever they were alone together; best stamp on it here and now, she decided. 'Look, Mr Wilmslow . . .'

'Arthur; call me Arthur,' Mr Wilmslow said eagerly.

'I reckon Arthur and Martha sound well together, don't you?'

Martha, who thought they sounded like a not very good nursery rhyme, merely smiled. 'That's as maybe, but names aren't really important,' she observed. 'What is important is that I loved Harry with all my heart and couldn't possibly consider marrying again. What's more, my daughters would be very upset. So if you mention the matter again, deeply though it would distress me, I shall have to start looking round for a new job and somewhere else to live. It might be best, in fact, if Evie and I left the area altogether . . .'

Mr Wilmslow gave a howl of protest and Martha was sure his pale face actually whitened. He leaned across the table and grabbed both her hands, holding on so tightly that his fingers dug into her flesh. 'No, you mustn't go, you mustn't leave me,' he said wildly. 'It's all right, Martha – Mrs Todd, I mean – we'll leave things as they are, if that's your final word. I only thought things should be regularised . . . I mean, you've got my ration book . . .'

Martha laughed; she couldn't help herself. 'It's all right, Mr Wilmslow. If I did leave, and I hope I shan't have to do so, then I'd give you back your ration book,' she assured him. 'But I think that we should forget this entire episode, pretend it never happened, then we can go on comfortably as friends and colleagues. I assure you, no one will think the worse of either of us.'

For a few moments, Mr Wilmslow stared at her. His mouth worked but no words came out and Martha saw, with some distress, that his eyes were bright and shiny with what might possibly have been tears. To save him embarrassment, she went over to the stove and pulled the kettle over the flame. 'I'll make us a nice cup of tea and then I think we'd best both go to bed,' she said, over her shoulder. 'We've got a hard day's work ahead of us tomorrow and you never know when those perishin' Germans will decide to give us another bashing.' She filled the teapot, poured two cups of tea and added conny-onny, then handed Mr Wilmslow his cup. 'All right, Mr Wilmslow?'

Her employer nodded. 'Perhaps it's for the best, Mrs Todd. But it would have been nice to have a wife again, especially one who could do her share in the business,' he said wistfully, and began to drink his tea.

Chapter Twelve
June 1942

'Letter for you, Toby.' Toby's friend Miles grabbed his arm and shoved the letter into the top pocket of his pal's shirt since both Toby's hands were engaged in carrying the rather frail bowl, made of banana leaves roughly sewn together, which contained his booty. Miles looked hopefully at the bowl. 'What have you got there? Gosh, is it curry and rice? Going to give me some?'

'I'll give you half for handing over my letter,' Toby said. Extra food was difficult to come by in Changi, but letters were even rarer. God knew what the Japs did with the POW mail – probably used it to light their fires – but his mother and Evie, who were his most regular correspondents, numbered their letters so that he might read them in order. Unfortunately, Letter 2 was often followed by Letter 22, proving that few of the missives from home ever reached their destination. POWs were supposed to be allowed to send and receive mail, amongst other things, but here in Changi men were only allowed to despatch standardised cards with preprinted comments which they could tick. Sometimes, however, the Japs did hand on letters which arrived for their prisoners and today was clearly one of those occasions.

The two of them crossed the compound and went into the hut. Once, Changi had been a British army barracks, but not with probably three thousand men confined in it. Now, it was just a collection of tumbledown buildings and a good deal of wire fencing, though this was regularly breached by the prisoners when they sallied forth in search of food.

Toby and Miles squatted on the ground near their sleeping mats and Toby produced the curry and rice. It had seemed well worth the price which Toby had paid – his trusty fountain pen – but now it looked rather small to be divided between two ravenously hungry men. Still, friends were precious and Toby knew that Miles would have shared every last grain of rice with him had their positions been reversed. He held the improvised bowl out. 'Dig in,' he said brusquely, and watched as Miles transferred the first handful to his mouth. Then he followed suit, and they ate, turn and turn about, until the delicious curry was only a memory.

'Did you have any trouble getting through the wire?' Miles asked presently, sitting back with a satisfied sigh. Because rations were so inadequate in the camp, their guards turned a blind eye to the practice the men had adopted of sneaking out into the surrounding countryside, when things got desperate, in order to barter their possessions for food. Of course, if you were caught coming back in, the guard who had seen you would insist on a half share, but the men had grown cautious and Toby had managed to get out and back without being spotted.

He said as much and Miles grimaced. 'If only Singapore wasn't on an island, then we'd stand a chance of getting out of here and living on the country,' he observed. 'But after what happened to those sailors . . .' He shuddered, remembering something which no man who had been forced to watch it could ever forget. 'Well, you could call it a disincentive to any sort of bid for freedom,' he finished.

'I know. The worst thing was, the bloody Japs enjoyed it. They laughed and joked whilst . . .' Toby pulled a face. 'I try to forget it, but it's always there in the back of my mind.'

'I'm the same,' Miles said. He peered at the envelope which Toby was just pulling from his pocket. 'Who's it from?'

Toby glanced at the handwriting and felt a tiny flutter. It was from Evie. He still longed for a letter from Seraphina, but he had not heard from her for months, though he told himself, stoutly, that she would still be writing to him; it was simply that the letters never arrived. Evie's letters were always good value because she talked – or wrote, rather – of her family in the most natural and amusing way. She often included snippets about Seraphina, and had mentioned that her husband had been posted to North Africa. He had also got the feeling that Seraphina's marriage was not all it should be. Evie had hinted that her sister's relationship with Roger had been less than satisfactory, even before he was sent abroad. She had told him that the couple had not shared Seraphina's very first leave and this, more than anything else, had given him hope. Had he been in a similar position, he would have moved heaven and earth to spend that week with his golden girl, but it appeared that Roger had not made the attempt.

'Well, I'll go and see what everyone else is up to,' Miles said, getting to his feet. 'What did you barter for that curry and rice, anyway? You did pretty damn well. Last time I went over the wire, I took four six-inch nails and a khaki handkerchief, and all I got was . . .'

'. . . some very suspicious-looking fish and sweet potatoes,' Toby finished for him, grinning. 'It was very nutritious, I'm sure, though of course we do get some sweet potatoes from the gardens, when they're in season. I bartered my fountain pen this time. Since we can't write letters home, I thought we might as well eat it, so to speak.'

Miles grunted and wandered out, heading in the direction of the gardens which the POWs had started to cultivate. These were a great source of food when the vegetables ripened, but they had to be guarded night and day or the produce would have been stolen by the guards, who were fed no better than the prisoners themselves. Being more used to the diet, however, the Japs remained healthier than their charges, whose weakened state caused them to fall prey to any illness or infection around.

But right now, Toby felt comfortably full of curry and rice, so he sat back and ripped open his letter. Dear little Evie! He could see her monkey face as clearly as though she stood in front of him, see the sparkling dark eyes and the straight, lank hair which fell down past her shoulders. Incredibly, this was letter 31; poor kid, he could imagine her disappointment and rage had she known that almost all the letters she so lovingly penned never reached him.

It was not until he was on the third paragraph of the letter that something she said made him sit back and think. *Mam met me out of work yesterday,* she had said. *I'm sure I told you that the Rotunda disappeared in the May blitz last year but not all the picture houses were hit. We went to the Forum on Lime Street. I've not been there before but it's lovely. It's not terribly big but very rich, with beautiful paintings and comfortable plush seats. The film was George Formby in* Turned Out Nice Again, *with Peggy Bryan. It was very funny and a little bit rude – well, you know what George Formby's like – but Mam and I laughed at all the jokes and now we keep singing 'Auntie*

*Maggie's Remedy', only of course we can't remember all
the words. Afterwards, we went to a nearby café for our
supper. It was great. Mr Wilmslow would have liked to come
as well – he dearly loves a laugh, though you wouldn't
think it – but Mam said it was a girls only outing. It was
as well because GF was working in an underwear factory
in the film and some of the jokes were a bit near the knuckle.
So we had our outing, just Mam and me, which was wizard.*

Toby sat back on his heels. He had not seen Evie
for two years; he still thought of her as the pale and
rather dirty child who had greeted him on the station
platform after Dunkirk, but now that he thought about
it she must have turned fourteen, and be working, of
course. Not realising that he had received almost none
of her letters, she would assume that he had heard all
about her leaving school and about her new job.
Maddening not to be able to explain, but he had given
up, long ago, any attempt to get in touch with anyone.
The Japanese had been signatories to the Geneva
Convention, or so he believed, but they took no more
notice of it than they did of any normal rules of human
behaviour. He let his eyes flicker down the rest of the
closely written sheet but the only thing he picked up
on was that her friend Percy intended to join the Royal
Air Force just as soon as he was old enough.

I shan't miss him as much as I would have done once,
she observed, *since he's hardly ever at home and we don't
go about together any more because he's got a girlfriend!
Her name's Sandra and I told him she must be mad as a
hatter to go out with a spiv like him, but he only laughed.
Did I tell you he was a spiv? During working hours, he's
mate on a delivery van, taking supplies from the docks to
places as far away as Manchester and Bradford, but in the
evenings he hangs about street corners, wearing a suit so
sharp it's a miracle he don't cut himself and hissing out of*

the corner of his mouth: 'Fancy a nice lean piece of beef for the weekend, missus? Or a pair o' nice silk stockings?' I reckon he nicks stuff off of the delivery van . . . well I know he does . . . but when I charged him with it, he said it were perks of the job and everyone does it. Then he had the cheek to offer me a tin of peach slices . . . oh, Toby, I know you're a POW, and I guess the food is pretty boring, though I know all about Red Cross parcels – we send you one whenever we can afford it, and I'm sure your mam does too – but we've been told what they contain and it's the sort of stuff we get with our ration books. But at the thought of peach slices – in syrup, Toby – I nearly fished out my wages and bought them then and there. It took all my courage and resolution to tell him where to put his peach slices. But I did it and I'm proud.

Toby put the letter down for a moment whilst he laughed and mopped his streaming eyes. Peach slices! They had all heard about the delights of Red Cross parcels, but not a single one had ever arrived in Changi, or, at any rate, had ever been given to any POW. He had heard that such parcels contained wonderful luxuries like dried milk and powdered egg, tinned sardines and corned beef, but he did not think anyone had ever mentioned peaches. Still smiling, he returned to Evie's letter. From her remark about the Rotunda, he guessed that there had been no serious raids since the May of the previous year, for if she was going to the cinema with her mother it sounded as though life had returned to normal, or at least as normal as it could be in wartime.

He was nearly at the end of the second page now and here was news, at last, of Seraphina. Toby felt his heartbeats quicken as he read her name.

Seraphina got a forty-eight last week and came home with a friend of hers who is also an R/T operator. She's married and her husband is in the air force, so she and Fee have a lot in common. I heard them talking one night when they thought I was asleep, only I couldn't drop off. Mam had a bad cold and was snoring like anything, so I sneaked out and went into the kitchen for a drink of water. They were in the living room with their bedrolls laid out on the floor – this flat is tiny compared with our old one – but it was a hot night and they weren't asleep, either. It's wrong to listen, but I didn't, Toby, honest to God, I didn't. I heard, which is quite different from listening. They were talking about divorce and the Betty girl said you could get one if you could prove non-consummation . . . well, something like that at any rate. It isn't a word I know but I guess it means unfaithfulness, wouldn't you say? Anyway, Seraphina said it wasn't the sort of thing one wanted to say out loud, let alone in court, and the other girl said better a bit of honesty than being trapped for life. So I reckon, when the war's over, either Seraphina or Betty will be giving her husband the go-by. What do you think? Mam says I shouldn't ask you questions because she's heard that Japanese POWs aren't allowed pencils or writing materials, which would account for neither your mam nor me getting any letters from you. I still look every day for the postman, hoping for a letter from you, but if you can't reply it doesn't matter. I shall still go on writing once or twice a week because I always did like you best and I guess I always will. I know you're Seraphina's pal really, but you were awful kind to me. Even if you only use my letters to light your fire, or worse, I guess you won't mind reading our news, so I'm going to keep on.

Must close now, but one more thing; I cadged a lift off Percy the other day and went and visited your mam and she and your dad are fine. So are your brothers and sisters. I know she writes regular, but not as often as me because two of your brothers are in the forces, Fanny is in the

335

Wrens and Lizzie in the ATS, and she has to write to them all.

So take care, darling Toby, we all send loads and load of love, even Fee, because she's still your pal. Yours faithfully, Evie.

Toby laughed again at the formal ending to the chatty and loving letter, but had to wink away a tear at the thought of Evie running to meet the postman every day in the hope of getting a letter from him. If only he could have got in touch by some means! If only he could ask questions as well as answer them, come to that. Until Evie mentioned it, he had completely forgotten that they were in a new flat, one he had never seen. And just what had the girls meant about getting a divorce? He knew what non-consummation meant all right, but he could not imagine that any man would be fool enough not to consummate a marriage with someone as beautiful and desirable as Seraphina. It must be the Betty girl, who might be as ugly as a pan of worms for all he knew, though, in his experience, pretty girls usually went around together; hunting in pairs, they called it.

However, with two young married women, this rule would most definitely not apply. Sighing, Toby folded the letter and pushed it into the pocket of his ragged drill shorts, then ducked out of the hut and made for the gardens tended by the British prisoners. There were many nationalities in Changi: Dutch, British, one or two Americans, Australians, all sorts, and at first they had disagreed over everything, such disagreements sometimes ending in violence. It was not until the prisoners themselves noticed how the Japanese enjoyed the spectacle of such behaviour that they mended their ways, and began to respect each other's points of view.

Toby approached a group of men, talking excitedly.

Miles was amongst them and turned to punch Toby lightly on the shoulder. 'Guess what? They're selecting groups of men to help them build some bridge or other, out in the sticks. Captain Deveril says they're only choosing fit men; chaps who haven't been reduced to skin and bone by dysentery, or some other disease. If we get chosen, we might have a chance to escape, because I think they said the bridge was in Burma, and the Burmese hate the Japs.'

Someone standing nearby turned at Miles's words. 'It's not just a bridge, it's a railway,' he told them. 'The feller in charge of Changi is going to give a talk in about ten minutes, explaining things. That's why we're all here.'

'A railway!' Toby exclaimed, unable to keep the interest out of his voice. 'I wonder what sort of railway it is. Well, neither you nor I have had dysentery, Miles. I'd say we were in quite good shape, so we're likely to find out.'

Toby was right. The chief officer in charge of the camp addressed the prisoners, telling them that if they obeyed orders and worked hard they would be well treated, but if they disobeyed orders, tried to escape or failed to complete the work given them, then they could expect no mercy from their captors. He also told them that, as they got further north, 'rest camps' would be provided, where they could spend their free time.

Many of the men, Toby and Miles included, had little faith in such 'rest camps' but were desperate for more freedom – and more food – than they were allowed in Changi. Rations for working men must surely be better than the meagre portion allotted to men idling away their lives in a POW camp, and they thought their chances of escaping and getting back to British India would be far higher as they went north.

So they volunteered, along with many others. Next day they were loaded on to army vehicles which drove them out of the prison and over to the railway platform, where a great many cattle trucks awaited them. The guards herded them into the trucks, kicking, beating and shoving until each truck was crammed to capacity, then the doors were slammed shut and very soon the nightmare journey began.

The trucks were made of steel, with sliding doors which did not shut properly. Being cattle trucks they had no windows but, in any event, for the first day or two of the journey the train mainly passed through enormous rubber plantations so that there was no scenery worth a second glance. Because they were made of steel, the trucks were horribly hot during daylight hours as the relentless sun beat down, but at night they were freezing cold. Draughts whistled in through every crack and crevice – and there were many – and Toby thought that they might have frozen stiff had not the body warmth of so many men, crammed into so tiny a space, provided some relief from the icy cold.

The train did stop occasionally. At least once a day, the men were supplied with a bucket full of rice, one to each truck, and with a bucket of drinking water, though since this last was filled at any passing ditch or stream it was sometimes decidedly murky. Perhaps it was the water which gave most of the prisoners dysentery, or perhaps it was the rice which had sometimes gone sour in the heat before it reached them, but whatever the cause, there was a good deal of sickness.

They reached an area of paddy fields and when the

train stopped the men were glad enough to get out for short periods, to stretch their cramped limbs. Then they discovered that the paddy fields, and the ditches surrounding them, were full of small fish which they could catch. They gave them to their Japanese guards to cook with the rice and, for the first time, there was a little variety in their diet.

Toby lost count of time, though he was fortunate in not contracting dysentery – or not as badly as some, at any rate. Miles, who had been a medical student before the war, had told him, from the first moment they entered Changi, that hygiene was all-important. He and Toby were careful to go without the rice when it was sour and to examine any food or drink offered them to make sure it did not contain either maggots or eggs, and their caution paid off to an extent, for neither young man was seriously ill on that terrible journey.

The train drew in to their destination at last, after five dreadful days, and the men were pushed and harried out of the trucks as they had been pushed and harried into them. They were counted, which took several hours, and then marched through a small and very dirty village into the camp whence they would go, daily, to whichever part of the railway needed their labour.

Toby and Miles had thought the journey horrendous, but when they saw the new camp they realised that worse was to come. The whole place was ankle deep in thick and oozing mud; the Atap huts in which they were to sleep were constructed of flattened bamboo canes and inside the men slept on bamboo platforms. Mud was everywhere and the prisoners who had been there for some time were in dreadful physical condition; more like walking skeletons than living men. They told the newcomers that rations were meagre; mostly just water to drink and boiled rice to eat, and not very much of that. The old hands told them that the Japanese guards here were very different from those in Changi. Here, they had a definite task to perform, which was to force the men to work, regardless of sickness, disease or injury, and the methods they employed could be as harsh as they wished.

When they prepared for sleep that night, having been told that they would move on next morning, Miles whispered that if they survived this lot, he reckoned they could survive anything. Inside, Toby trembled at what was to come but he put a brave face on it.

Next morning, when they were herded out of the hut, he tried to look around him, to interest himself in his surroundings. Miles, who was fair-haired and fair-skinned, kept his own face impassive as they slogged along, even when one of the guards, a Korean as it happened, hit out at him viciously with a short cane he carried, raising a scarlet bleeding weal across his back. So far as Toby knew, his friend had done nothing which could be considered offensive, save possibly to glance at the man as they passed him. He heard Miles mutter 'Little yellow bastard' beneath his breath and glanced apprehensively around, but the man had disappeared. Praying that they would somehow manage to steer clear of him, Toby marched on.

Autumn came and Evie set off for work with a rare piece of exciting news to pass on to her friends. That morning, as she and Martha and Mr Wilmslow ate their breakfast porridge, the post had come rattling through the door. Evie had jumped up; she was always first to get the post if it were possible since she still hoped, desperately, for a letter from Toby, but when she clattered back up the stairs again she handed two letters to her mother and one to Mr Wilmslow. 'Nothing for me,' she had said resignedly, sitting down and beginning to eat once more. 'I bet yours is another of those wretched things from the government, Mr Wilmslow.'

'Course it is,' Mr Wilmslow had said, glaring at the official brown envelope. 'I've forgotten what it's like to receive ordinary mail.' He had peered, inquisitively, at Martha across the table. 'Are yours from the girls?'

'That's right,' Martha had said. She slit open both envelopes, then spread the contents before her on the table. 'Seraphina's fine, but in a dreadful rush, so only a few lines. There's much more from Angela ... oh, goodness gracious!'

'What is it? Nothing horrid, I hope,' Evie had said anxiously. 'Or is it something nice? Is she coming home on leave?'

'Yes she is, in a manner of speaking,' Martha had said, in a rather hollow voice. 'And she's bringing her friend Albert Reid back with her so that we can meet him. They – they're going to be married on 21st November, so they're coming home to get the banns read and so on. Oh, dear me, my daughter's going to be a vicar's wife!'

'What's wrong with that?' Mr Wilmslow had said, rather belligerently. 'At least he's not likely to go round the city floggin' black market cheese and illicit silk stockings.'

Evie had glared at him. She had known he was having a dig at Percy and though she disapproved of her old pal's new employment, she did not want Mr Wilmslow rubbing it in, so she had said: 'Just because someone's a vicar, that doesn't make them a saint, though I'm sure Mr Reid is a very nice vicar, of course, otherwise Angie wouldn't be thinking of marrying him.'

She had turned to her mother. 'You ought to be delighted, what with Dad being a lay preacher an' all.'

'I am delighted,' Martha had said, rather defensively. 'It's – it's just rather daunting having a son-in-law who's a vicar. Still, I'm sure you're right, pet, and he's a lovely young man.' When Evie would have spoken again, her mother shushed her. 'Let me read the rest of my letter,' she had commanded. 'Oh, Lord!'

'What *is* it?' Evie had cried. 'Oh, don't say she wants me to be a bridesmaid because I won't do it. It was bad enough being Seraphina's bridesmaid in that awful tight dress and I won't be made to look such a guy again.'

'No, it's all right; it's just that Albert's parents – his father's a vicar too – want us to book them into a quiet guesthouse for the weekend of the wedding. Oh, Lord, that'll mean entertaining them . . . feeding them as well, I suppose.' She had turned to Mr Wilmslow. 'What'll we do, Arthur? I'm sure Angie's friends will want to see her married. And then there's canal folk who knew us before the war . . .'

'Don't worry, Martha; we'll manage something and no doubt they'll bring their ration books,' Mr Wilmslow had said grandly. He had finished his porridge, pushed back his chair and had stood up. 'I'd better go down and open up or Mrs Bunwell will start banging on the door and shouting.' He had turned to Evie. 'Come along, young woman, you don't want to be late for clocking in.'

Evie had agreed that this would never do, had snatched her coat off the back of the kitchen door and headed downstairs. Unlike their former home, this flat had no separate entrance and could only be accessed through the stockroom, so she had followed Mr Wilmslow down, picked up the A board, which proclaimed that Wilmslow's was open for the sale of groceries, sweets and tobacco, and erected it on the pavement, and then had hurried on her way. She was working in Litherland in a very large clothing factory and had to catch a bus each day, though she was thinking of buying a bicycle – if she could get hold of one, that was. She had been saving up ever since starting work and had quite a nice little nest egg, so could afford to purchase a second-hand model if anybody was willing to sell.

She was actually on board the bus, rattling through the damaged streets, when it occurred to her that her mother, in extremis, had addressed Mr Wilmslow as Arthur, and in reply he had used her mother's given name of Martha. Hello-ello-ello, I wonder what that means, Evie thought to herself. She had noticed, of course, that Mr Wilmslow and her mother had grown easier and friendlier ever since starting work in the new shop, but had given the matter no thought at all. Now she was forced to consider it, for not only had Martha called Mr Wilmslow Arthur, she had also appealed to him over a matter which was strictly family. *What'll we do?* she had said, not *What'll I do?* which was what Evie would have expected her to say.

The bus rattled on whilst Evie considered, for the first time, whether she might, one day, end up with Mr Wilmslow as a stepfather. Once she would have hated the idea, would have fought, energetically, to prevent it, but war, or her mother's influence, had changed Mr Wilmslow for the better. He was far less mean and far more generous, both with his money and with his time, she realised. Because he came to them for all his meals, and spent most evenings in the flat, he had shown a different side of himself, she supposed. He treated her with rather awkward jocularity and was still extremely shy with the older girls, but he had a quirky sense of humour and was fond of the wireless, insisting that they should have Music While You Work playing softly in the background whilst he and Martha served their customers. He never missed ITMA or Workers' Playtime and often repeated the jokes to customers who had not managed to listen in.

Well, if Martha was growing fond of him, Evie supposed it was no bad thing. No one could deny that he took care of her mother, did his best to see that she did not work too hard, though Martha often pooh-poohed his suggestion that she should do less. 'I don't have to tell you there's a war on,' she had said reproachfully, only the previous week, when Mr Wilmslow had tried to take a pile of paperwork away from her. 'If we both slog away at it, it'll be done in half the time and then we can both have a bit of a rest.'

The bus drew in to the pavement and Evie roused herself from her abstraction; this was her stop, and a couple of her friends were hopping down from the platform and joining the stream of girls heading for the factory. 'Wait for me! Jeannie, Phyllis, wait for me!' Evie shrieked, leaping off the bus and clouting another passenger with her handbag as she did so. 'Sorry, missus, but I'm trying to catch up with me mates . . . oh, Miss Pinner, I'm ever so sorry. I didn't realise it were you.'

Miss Pinner tightened her lips then opened her mouth as if to speak, but Evie did not wait for the telling-off she knew would be coming. Hefty Miss Pinner was a supervisor, and not a popular one either. But we aren't in work now, Evie thought defiantly, panting up to a group of her friends. She addressed them a trifle breathlessly. 'Girls, you'll never guess what's going to happen on 21st November! My sister

Angie is getting married . . . that'll only leave me, in my whole family, still unwed.'

Phyllis and Jeannie turned and Phyllis smiled down at her. 'Oh, poor little Evie,' she said mockingly. 'Past fourteen an' norra feller in sight. Well, I always did say you was a born spinster. Though there is a feller, isn't there? Someone in the army what you write letters to? I've seen you, scribbling away in your dinner hour.'

'I don't know nothing about that feller, but I do know she were thick as thieves wi' Percy Baldwin when they were kids,' Jeannie said. She lived in the next court along from Cavendish and had known both the Baldwins and Evie herself for some time. 'You'll have to ask young Percy to make an honest woman of you, queen.'

Evie snorted. 'Some chance,' she said scornfully. 'Why, he's a perishin' spiv, sellin' stuff on street corners, talkin' out of the corner of his mouth . . . you wouldn't get me goin' steady with him if he were the richest, handsomest feller in the world. And as for Toby – he's a POW in Malaya, or at least I think he is, because they can't write back, you know, the horrible Japs won't let them. We had a couple of cards, just letting us know that he was in Changi, but we've had nothing since. And anyway, he's Seraphina's feller really.'

They had entered the factory and were queuing up to clock on. Phyllis turned to stare at her. 'Seraphina's feller? But you said he was in North Africa flying with the RAF.'

Evie giggled. 'Sorry, sorry. I mean Toby *was* Seraphina's feller, before she married Roger. But sometimes I get the feeling that she still likes Toby very much and I wonder if – if perhaps she wishes she'd married him and not Roger.'

'She's probably just sorry for him, because from

what I've heard, being a POW can't be much fun,'
Phyllis said wisely. 'But it's hard on a wife, being separated from her husband, perhaps for years.' She looked
seriously across at Evie as they reached the head of the
queue. 'You don't want to say things like that, you
know, kid. I'm not married and perhaps I won't ever
be, norrif my Reggie gets killed, but I wouldn't like to
think that just writin' to an old flame might make folk
think I didn't care about Reggie no more.'

Evie moved up, clocked in, then trotted along behind
her friends, saying remorsefully, 'Yes, you're right,
Phyllis. I'm sorry – I spoke without thinking. I expect
poor Fee misses Roger like crazy but can't talk about
him to us, because we don't really know him. So she
talks about Toby, because I can't remember a time
when he wasn't in and out of our lives. But oh, how I
wish he – I mean Toby – could get in touch with us,
just so we knew that he was still all right.'

Jeannie and Phyllis were both older than Evie; Jeannie
was seventeen and Phyllis nineteen, and now they
exchanged speaking looks. Evie, glancing from one face
to the other as they approached their workbench, saw
Phyllis's eyebrows rise and Jeannie give a tiny nod. Then
Phyllis spoke. 'Evie, we weren't going to say anything
to you, but what you said just now – about getting in
touch, I mean – has changed our minds. After work
today, Jeannie and I are going to see a Mrs Amelia
Smith. She's a sort of gypsy . . . well, no, p'raps that's
not quite the right word. She calls herself a psychic and
she claims to be able to get in touch both with people
who have passed over, as she calls it, and with folk who
are far away. Jeannie wants to know how her brother
Alf is getting along – he's in North Africa, like your
sister's hubby – and I want to know about Reggie. Oh,
I know I do get letters from Italy, but they're pretty

rare – few and far between I should say – so we thought we'd go along and see if there's anything this woman can tell us. Would you like to come?'

Evie took the cover off her big commercial sewing machine, then looked up at her friends. 'I'll come, but you'd better know straight off that I'm not sure I should,' she said frankly. 'I remember, when Dad was killed, that someone suggested Mam should try to get in touch with him through a . . . medium, I think she called herself. Mam was absolutely furious. She said that Dad was in heaven and the woman was nothing but a nasty impostor. Still, this is a bit different, I suppose. Yes, I'll come.'

When work had finished for the day, the three girls set off for the address Phyllis had been given. Evie had half expected to be ushered into a witch's hovel, complete with black cat, a cauldron over the fire and a woman in a pointy hat. Instead, the door of a neat, terraced house was opened by a fat, grey-haired woman with a face seamed with wrinkles and bright, dark eyes. The woman led them into a pleasant parlour, then took them, one by one, into a dimly lit kitchen. Phyllis went first, then Jeannie, and Evie went last. As she entered the kitchen, her heart began to bump violently and she considered saying that she had changed her mind, wanted no part of it. But that would have been cowardly, and besides, she was curious, so she followed Mrs Smith into the room and sat down on the chair indicated. Mrs Smith sat down opposite her and pulled into place between them a small stout table, upon which rested a crystal ball. She dusted the ball tenderly, then leaned forward and peered into its depths. 'What is your young man's name? And where is he at present?' she asked, in a surprisingly matter-of-fact voice, but Evie immediately took exception to the question.

'He's *not* my young man,' she said firmly. 'He's just a friend, though a very good one. His name is Toby, and he's in Changi POW camp in Singapore.'

Mrs Smith leaned closer to her crystal ball, so close that Evie thought if it had been an ice cream cone, she could easily have licked it. 'Changi, Changi, Changi,' the elderly woman said in a hoarse whisper. 'Show me Toby, who is in Changi.'

Fifteen minutes later, the three girls left the small house, first dropping a donation in the small wooden box just inside the front door. Evie pushed her money through the slot with a certain reluctance, for she had not believed one word Mrs Smith had said. She had made Toby's life in Changi sound almost idyllic, with thick jungle surrounding the camp, and the men making pets of small monkeys and brightly coloured parrots which came within the wire fence. She had said the men were well fed, that they had a theatre and regular cinema shows and that the people of Singapore had taken them to their hearts and frequently passed them gifts. Evie remembered the card she had received from Toby when he had first entered Changi, upon the bottom of which he had written very faintly, in pencil: *Food scarce, conditions harsh.* After that, Evie had gone to visit Mrs Duffy and had read her card, the bottom line of which read, in equally faint pencil: *Everything poor but we'll survive.*

So Evie emerged on to Bostock Street certain that she had not heard a word of truth from Mrs Smith, and just as certain that Phyllis and Jeannie, so much older and wiser than she, would regard what had been said to them with equal scepticism. Instead, they had been tickled pink, and Evie speedily realised that this was because Mrs Smith had told them what they wanted to hear. According to her, Alfie had had a bad cold but was recovering well and would soon write to his family again. And Reggie was enjoying Italy, helping the peasants as they worked amongst the vines and keeping well clear of those German troops who still remained in the country.

They asked Evie what she had been told but Evie simply said, flatly, that Mrs Smith had not been able to get in touch with Toby. She knew that if she said she had not believed a word her friends would first try to persuade her that she was making a mistake, and then begin to grow annoyed.

Presently, the three girls parted and Evie hurried home to the flat over the shop, determined not to tell her mother where she had been. In fact, Martha did not question her. She looked up as Evie entered the kitchen and smiled, then swung open the oven door to reveal three empty plates within. 'Poor old Evie, I guess you missed the bus and had to walk,' she said gaily. 'You chose a good night to be late, actually, because we had a consignment from the Ministry of Food, which all had to be unpacked and sorted out, so we were late ourselves. I meant to make a pile of sandwiches but Mr Wilmslow said we had all worked hard and needed a hot meal of an evening, so he's gone down the road for some fish and chips.'

'Fish and chips!' Evie said, joyfully, slinging her coat on to the peg. 'Oh, I love fish and chips. Had a good day, Ma? I bet you told every soul who came into the shop that Angie's getting married, didn't you?'

'I did,' Martha said, smiling.

Later that evening, when the fish and chips were no more than a memory, Evie decided that she would confide in her mother after all. It had occurred to her that if anyone could get in touch with Toby, it would be someone who knew him and loved him, not a total stranger, and she decided that if she emphasised her scepticism there would be no harm in telling Martha she had visited Mrs Smith. She had to wait until Mr Wilmslow had gone down to his bed in the stockroom, because she did not want to upset him by reminding him of his own loss, but fortunately he was tired and went to bed early.

Martha listened to her story seriously and without interruption, and she also seemed to think quite hard before making up her mind what to say. 'You know I don't believe in trying to get in touch with the dead; it seems to me a wicked intrusion, even if it were possible, which I am sure it is not. But it's understandable, in time of war, that folks should want to get in touch with family or friends whose fate is uncertain. Of course it would be nice to believe what the old woman told you, but I agree with you: if Toby was going to get in touch with anyone by means of some sort of thought transference, then he wouldn't need an intermediary, he'd do it straight off with someone he loved and trusted.

'Seraphina,' Evie breathed. 'He'd get in touch with Seraphina, of course! I wonder if he's tried? If I wrote and told her, do you suppose that Seraphina would try to get in touch with him?'

'No I don't,' Martha said, emphatically. 'Seraphina's a married woman and knows her duty. Besides, though she and Toby were good friends when they were a great deal younger, they've grown apart; why else would she have married Roger?' She leaned over and stroked her daughter's cheek. 'You're very fond of Toby and I'm sure he thinks of you as a younger sister. You've been so good, writing him letters, never letting him down, so if he gets in touch with anyone it ought to be you.

When you go to bed tonight, say your prayers and explain to God that you are anxious about your friend and would like news of him. Then think about him, relive some happy time in your life and his, and perhaps, even if he can't get through to you, your pleasant memories will get through to him.'

Evie jumped to her feet, flew across to where Martha sat by the fire, and gave her a smacking kiss on the cheek. 'Thank you, Ma, thank you, thank you,' she gabbled. 'I'll do just as you say, and who knows? It might work!'

They were building a bridge, a railway bridge, of course, to cross a mighty river. Fortunately, it was not in flood, but even so, it was pretty deep in the middle. Toby was up to his waist in water, arms above his head, bearing the weight of one of the huge tree trunks which would presently be pulled into position on the piles which had been driven deep into the river bed during the previous days. On the bank, a great elephant trudged along, pulling a sort of trolley containing more tree trunks; a small Burmese perched up on the animal's neck shouted orders. Toby's arms ached unendurably and his body ached too, especially the half of him immersed in water, for though the day was hot and the humidity high, the water itself was cold. He glanced sideways at Miles, then at the sun, thanking heaven that it was at last beginning to descend towards the horizon. The ache in his arms was becoming unbearable; if he did not get some relief soon, he would be unable to sleep tonight, and sleep was essential, for when the next day dawned they would be back here, repeating the terrible task, until the bridge was complete.

The Japanese guard on the bank shouted an order

as the last trunk was swung into position, and Toby lowered his arms, groaning at the pain which followed, but hurrying out of the water as fast as he could. The guard on duty was much hated for his sadistic practices – his nickname was Nero – and Toby tried to give him a wide berth, but he slipped on the muddy bank and felt the crack of a rifle butt on his shoulder before he was able to scramble to his feet and head back towards the Atap huts. The men had to constantly rebuild these flimsy edifices as they moved further along the route the railway was to follow.

They reached the hut and Toby collapsed on to his bamboo shelf, too tired to think about the rice which would presently be distributed. When it came, though, he ate his share eagerly, then asked Miles to take a look at his shoulder. Wounds could go septic easily out here, but the blow had not broken the skin, Miles reported, though there would be a magnificent black bruise there by morning. Satisfied on that score, Toby rolled on to his sleeping platform and immediately began to suffer from the cramps which always attacked him as soon as he relaxed.

Groaning, he leaned down and pulled the thin and filthy blanket over himself because, as night drew on, the temperature would drop and the hut would become freezing cold. Sleep, sleep, sleep, you fool, he urged himself. You've got to sleep or you won't be able to work tomorrow. If you don't work, you won't eat and if you don't eat, you'll die. Sleep, damn you, Toby Duffy.

He slept, and for the first time since leaving Changi, he dreamed of home. There was a girl, very beautiful, very loving. They were down by the canal, wandering along in autumn sunshine. There was a wood; they gathered hazelnuts, filling their pockets, laughing at one another's attempts to reach the higher branches. There were blackberries, rich and glossy. The girl scratched her fingers, trying to reach the best and biggest, but they continued to pick until the basket she held was full. Then they were on the canal boat, the good old *Mary Jane*, and a wonderful smell of rabbit stew came drifting up to where they sat on deck. Presently, they went below and ate the stew, accompanied by big, floury potatoes and followed by an apple pie. Then, as the sun sank in the west, he and the beautiful girl wandered along the towpath beside the great black horse, and they talked of school, and recited poetry to one another, and laughed a lot.

When he awoke, Toby could not believe his surroundings: the bamboo hut, the muddy floor, his own arms and legs, skeletally thin, looking totally unlike the self that he remembered. But he had slept, and slept well, and all through the terrible and exhausting day which followed there was a quiet pool in his mind. He had escaped from this hell on earth for the entire night, and now he remembered again that he had a great deal to live for.

When they stopped for a brief break in the work, he told Miles about the dream and Miles looked at him curiously. 'Was it the girl who married someone else?' he asked bluntly. 'Serena, isn't that her name?'

'No, she's Seraphina,' Toby said. 'I can't swear to who it was because I never saw her face clearly, but I think it must have been her. After all, we shared so much. Fee and I went blackberry picking, nutting, digging for potatoes, trapping rabbits . . . oh, we were up to all sorts when we were young. The second sister, Angela, hardly ever came with us, but the kid did. Evie, that is.'

'Evie? I've heard you mention that name before,'

Miles said thoughtfully. 'She wrote to you when you were in Changi, didn't she?'

Toby felt a stirring of affection inside him at the thought of those bright and breezy letters, coming so regularly. 'That's right, and I bet she writes every week, still,' he said, getting to his feet at the sound of a screamed order from outside. 'She's a broth of a girl is Evie; she's not pretty, got a face like a monkey, but you can't help liking her.' He turned to the doorway. 'Coming, coming, you little yellow bastard,' he said.

The sisters assembled in the flat above the grocer's shop on 21 November. Seraphina and Evie had spent the night on the living-room floor in order that Angela could share her mother's bed, and had been glad of all the extra blankets Martha could provide, because it was extremely cold and at floor level it was impossible to escape from the draughts. Angela was more excited than either her mother or her sisters had ever seen her before, and Seraphina, who had very nearly decided to give the wedding a miss, was glad that she had not done so. Her sister was alight with happiness, deeply in love with a tall, thin, rather serious young man, and ecstatically happy at the thought of becoming a wife and, in the fullness of time, a mother.

Seraphina envied Angela because she was about to marry a man she truly loved, and who truly loved her, but the reason Seraphina had considered missing the wedding had nothing to do with envy. The fact was, she herself had fallen in love without even realising what was happening, and though Pilot Officer Eddie Harding had begged her to think about applying for a divorce, she still could not bring herself to do anything so definite. She knew that she had mistaken her feelings for Roger when she had agreed to marry him;

these had not been love but a sort of crazy infatuation and, she now admitted, a desire to punish Toby for not appreciating her. Yet marriage to Toby would have been another enormous mistake, for looking back she could see that their friendship had been just that: friendship and nothing warmer. If she had continued to live on the *Mary Jane*, they would have drifted apart, but because she had moved away he had somehow glamorised his picture of her and decided they meant more to each other than they actually had done.

Seraphina, getting dressed slowly and carefully in her Number Ones, thought that human relationships were a lot more complicated than she had ever dreamed. Once she had believed she could only love an outstandingly handsome man – Toby was very handsome, though in a quieter and less obvious way than Roger – but Eddie was not handsome at all. He was of medium height, stockily built – she had always liked tall men, six footers – and he had curly, bright ginger hair, white eyebrows and eyelashes, eyes as green as gooseberries, and a broken nose, sustained during a game of rugger before the war. No one, not even Seraphina herself, could have called him even passably good-looking, let alone handsome, yet she knew that he was everything she had ever wanted. He made her laugh, taught her more than she had dreamed there was to know about aeroplanes, took her out in the unreliable old sports car which he shared with three other young officers, teased her, cuddled her and made her feel both loved and desired, which was more than Roger had even attempted to do.

And now that she was loved, she felt truly sorry for Roger and wished there were some way that their marriage could be ended without hurting him. After all, he had been as deluded as she over their relationship, for she was still convinced that, had he truly loved her, he would have been able to cope with the physical side of their union without effort. For some reason, though, he had found that part of marriage distasteful, and now he was as trapped as she, and probably as desperate to escape.

Once, the thought of all the pitfalls that lay ahead would have terrified Seraphina, made her edgy and cross, difficult to live with. But because she had Eddie, she found she could contemplate what faced her with equanimity. She had never slept with the young pilot officer, nor did she intend to do so, but as soon as the war was over she would apply for a divorce and then she and Eddie meant to go far away, to Australia or Canada perhaps, and start their lives anew, leaving Roger to tell whatever story suited him best, without fear of contradiction.

Seraphina's thoughts were interrupted when the living-room door burst open and Evie's head poked round it. 'Are you ready?' her sister said, but did not wait for a reply. 'Can I have a word, Fee? Only there's something that's been worrying me . . . and brekker isn't ready yet. Mr Wilmslow got some bacon – don't ask where from – so it's bacon and scrambled eggs in ten minutes.'

'Come in, then, if you want to talk,' Seraphina said, drawing back the curtains and rolling up her bedding, pushing it out of sight behind the sofa. She looked searchingly at the younger girl. 'Are you all right, Evie? You looked strained and pale yesterday, when I arrived home, but I thought you just needed a good night's rest. Only you still don't look like your cheery self.'

'I'm fine,' Evie said hurriedly. 'Well, I've – I've had some rather nasty dreams . . . oh, Fee, if you'd just let me explain . . .'

356

'Fire ahead,' Seraphina said. She hoped very much that Evie was not going to question her about Roger. Her youngest sister was extremely sensitive to the thoughts and feelings of others. If anyone had picked up on the fact that something was seriously wrong with the Trueloves' marriage, it would be Evie, Seraphina knew.

However, it was neither Seraphina nor Roger of whom Evie wanted to speak. 'It's . . . it's Toby,' Evie said, rather hesitantly. 'You know I've been writing to him for ages, don't you? Well, some time last month, two of the girls I work with took me to see this woman, Mrs Smith, who said she was a psychic . . .'

Seraphina listened while her sister outlined the story, then raised her eyebrows enquiringly. 'Well, if you didn't believe her, why have you told me all this?' she said, rather plaintively. 'Toby hasn't written to me any more than he has to the rest of you. Indeed, I'm sure . . .'

'No, no, that isn't what's worrying me,' Evie said hastily. 'You see, I told Mam, and she agreed with me, that Toby would likelier get in touch with someone he knew and loved, rather than with a complete stranger. She said to try thinking about him and sending him good thoughts – happy ones, you know, of better times – so I did that . . . well, I still do it, to tell you the truth. Every night, after I've said my prayers, I think about happy times on the canal and scrumping trips into farmers' orchards, and fishing for tiddlers with a flour bag on a split cane . . . all sorts. *You* know, Seraphina.'

'You are a kind little soul, Evie,' Seraphina said gently. 'I'm sure if anyone can get in touch with Toby, you can. But you mustn't do it if it worries you and makes you ill, though why it should I'm not sure,' she finished candidly.

Evie took a deep breath, then exhaled slowly. 'It didn't upset me, not at first,' she said slowly. 'But lately, it's a bit as though I was getting little flashes of where Toby is and what he's doing, and – and it's awful, Fee, really awful. There's jungle, and horrible insects, and a trench with nasty things in, crawling with maggots. Tiny, flimsy huts and snakes which wriggle out from under your foot, and beastly things like crabs or lobsters, only smaller, with curled over tails. If they sting you, you die. And there's other things, worse things. Small, squat men, with yellowish skin, hitting out with sticks and rifle butts and bayonets, anything.'

Seraphina stared at her sister, appalled. If Evie was having dreams like that, no wonder she looked pale and ill. It was all imagination, of course, but even so, she could see Evie was truly worried by the dreams, as indeed anyone would have been. But how to stop them? And now she came to think of it, it was downright weird that Evie should go off to sleep whilst thinking of the happy times they had enjoyed in the past, and then have ghastly nightmares. Evie was staring at her, clearly hoping for some sort of resolution of her problem. Seraphina sighed. 'You do know they're only dreams, don't you? In other words, your imagination is running away with you. If I thought the dreams would go away if you stopped – well, stopped trying to get in touch with Toby, then I'd advise you not to send him happy thoughts, but it can't possibly be that.' She stared rather helplessly at her sister. 'Have you been reading up about Singapore?'

Evie nodded. 'Yes; and not just Singapore. I've been reading up about all those countries, the ones between Singapore and India, I mean, because I always listen to any programme on the wireless about the war in the Far East, and an awful lot of people who know the area think the Japs will try to reach India, conquering as they go. You see, Toby might have escaped and then been recaptured, up country somewhere . . . there's a railway, you know . . .'

Seraphina's face cleared. 'Well, there's your answer, queen. You've read so much about it that it's become real to you, and because it's such extremely unpleasant terrain, it's somehow got into your dreams. Perhaps you ought to get something really light and cheerful out of the library – Dornford Yates writes awfully funny books, you'd like them – and try to steer clear of the more frightening programmes on the wireless. There's a lot of entertainment specially provided to take one's mind off the war; stick with that.'

'All right,' Evie said, rather doubtfully. 'And – and thanks, Seraphina.'

Soon after that, it was time for the family to make their way to the church where they watched an ecstatically happy Angela exchanging vows with an equally happy Albert. Then they went on to the church hall where Mrs Bunwell and Mrs Baldwin had been hard at work for hours, setting out food on trestle tables. Martha had not wanted to buy on the black market, and she and Mr Wilmslow had done their best, but in the end she had been approached by Percy, who had offered tinned fruit for the trifles, a quantity of sausage meat to be transformed into sausage rolls, lard for the pastry and three pounds of dried fruit for the concoction of the cake. Martha had opened her mouth to say that she could manage without illegal goods, but had felt ashamed when she saw the pleading look in Percy's eyes. 'It's me wedding present to your Angie,' he had said humbly. 'It's a gift, Mrs T. You were real good to me when I were a kid and

I ain't never forgot the wrong me dad did to Mr Todd. I wanted to give your Angie something and I reckoned this might be more useful to the whole family than half a dozen pairs of silk stockings or a hundred Woodbines.'

Martha had laughed but had accepted his generosity and now, looking at the number of people crowding into the church hall, she was devoutly glad she had done so. For the past three weeks, she had been cooking and contriving, and it seemed that her hard work had paid off, judging by the appreciative murmurs as her guests saw the spread set out before them.

Martha hurried over to where Mrs Baldwin and Mrs Bunwell were pouring tea into the thick white cups provided by the hall. 'You've done a wonderful job and I'm really grateful,' she told them. 'But now you must let Seraphina, Evie and myself take over whilst you join the other guests. Where's Percy, Mrs Baldwin?'

'He's in the kitchen refilling the kettles and putting them on the gas,' Mrs Baldwin said. 'If you're sure, Mrs Todd, me and Mrs Bunwell here would like to have a word with the bride. What a shame she couldn't wear white – she would have looked a real picture – but most brides wear uniform these days and she's in such a glow . . . well, I've never seen her look lovelier.'

Soon the assembled company were seated at the trestle tables enjoying a meal of almost pre-war proportions. Martha had sat down between her two elder daughters but had to keep jumping up to refill plates and pass food, so she was grateful when Mr Wilmslow put both hands on her shoulders, just as she was about to get up again, and said gently: 'You are mother of the bride, my dear, and you shouldn't have to keep acting as waitress. Evie is being very good indeed and young Percy is making sure that cups are kept filled, so just you sit back and enjoy yourself and let the three of us cope, for a little while at least.'

Martha looked up at him, smiling. 'I don't know what I'd do without you, Arthur,' she said, keeping her voice low. 'You're a tower of strength. I know you didn't really approve when I accepted Percy's gift but you never said so.' He was still holding her shoulders and she put a hand up to gently squeeze his fingers. 'Thank you for everything.'

Chapter Thirteen
May 1945

Evie ran along the pavement and swerved into Mr Wilmslow's grocer's shop, her face alight with excitement. 'It's over!' she shouted, twirling around like a dancing dervish, to the astonishment of a couple of elderly women waiting at the counter while Martha and Mr Wilmslow made up their orders. 'It's over, it's over, it's over. Will rationing end tomorrow? Oh, but I feel so cheated. Fee and Angie both joined up and did their bit for their country, but just because we were making uniforms they called it "essential work" and wouldn't let me join, and now it's too late; there isn't a war to fight any more.'

'Dismissed you early, did they?' Mr Wilmslow said. 'Well, so far as I know nothing's changed, not regarding rations, I mean. We had the wireless on, of course, and heard Mr Churchill's announcement, but so far as we're concerned folk have still got to eat so we can't just close up, not like the perishin' clothing factory can.'

Martha smiled at these embittered words and came out from behind the counter and gave her daughter a hug. 'We're all glad it's over because Roger and Albert will be coming home . . . and Percy, of course . . . but we mustn't forget that the war in the Far East is still on,' she reminded her daughter. 'Not that the Japs will stand out for long, not with the whole world against them.'

'I haven't forgotten; I couldn't,' Evie said humbly.

'But – but don't you think we'll get news of Toby now? I'm sure he's still alive and the minute he's able to do so, he'll get in touch.'

'Course he will,' Mr Wilmslow said gruffly, clearly repenting of his earlier remarks. He turned to Martha. 'Shall we close, my dear? Only I reckon if we make our way to St George's Plateau, there'll be all sorts of celebrations goin' on, which I wouldn't want you to miss, nor Evie either, because victory don't happen every day.'

'That's a good idea,' Martha said. 'Coming, Evie?'

Evie beamed at her but shook her head. She went behind the counter as she spoke and began to put the first customer's rations into a brown paper bag. 'No thanks, Ma; I've arranged to meet Jeannie and Phil just as soon as we've changed out of our mucky old work clothes, so I'll finish off here for you, while you do whatever you have to do. We'll probably see you later, I expect.'

Once the customers had left the premises, Evie hung the 'Closed' sign on the door and locked up, then went upstairs and changed into a thin cotton dress, for it was a warm afternoon. She unpinned her hair, ran a comb through it and considered pinning it up again, then changed her mind. It was nice to feel the silky pageboy bob swinging against her skin. Besides, she only wore her hair loose on special occasions; if this wasn't a special occasion, what was?

As she got ready, Evie remembered something else. Her mother had promised Mr Wilmslow that, when peace arrived, she would marry him and Evie was still not sure that her sisters would altogether approve. She thought Angela would be quite pleased for her mother simply because Albert and Mr Wilmslow had got on well from the start, but Seraphina's feelings about marriage – any marriage – were still somewhat equivocal. There was no doubt in Evie's mind, and nor, she thought, in her mother's, that Seraphina's marriage was not a happy one and was unlikely to survive for long once the couple were constantly in one another's company. Martha, Evie knew, did not approve of divorce and thought that Seraphina and Roger should at least try to resolve their differences and make a go of their marriage, but Evie did not believe for one moment that this hopeful plan would work. She thought that Seraphina and Roger were two very different people from the hopeful young couple who had gone so joyously off to honeymoon in Snowdonia. Of course, the same must apply to a great many married couples, kept apart for five or six years by the exigencies of war, but there had been something wrong between Seraphina and Roger right from the start. Evie walked over to the looking glass on the washstand and surveyed herself critically. She was seventeen years old and just beginning to realise that, plain or no, she was attractive to young men. In fact, she often went to the cinema, or to a dance, or sometimes just for a walk, with the young men home on leave from the forces. She enjoyed their company, made them laugh, sometimes even allowed an old friend such as Percy Baldwin to kiss her good night, but she always made it perfectly plain that they meant nothing to her save as friends.

Percy, she knew, would have liked to be serious, wanted to be able to call her 'his girl', but she knew instinctively that she would never feel for Percy the way a woman feels for the only man in her life.

Sometimes, she thought she would never marry; after all, if Seraphina could make a mistake, little Evie could make a worse one. I'll be an aunt, she told herself, a fun-loving, popular aunt to Angie's kids and to Fee's as well, of course, because once she's free of Roger she'll wed Toby and live somewhere beautiful and quiet in the country, and have a great many children who can come to stay with me at holiday times, so that I can take them to the pantomime in winter and for trips on the Mersey in summer.

After a careful scrutiny in the mirror, she took a faded blue cardigan out of her drawer and tied it round her waist by its sleeves. She guessed that the celebrations would continue into the night, but did not intend to cover her blue gingham dress with her one and only coat, which was navy, serviceable and also threadbare. The cardigan would be fine for such an occasion.

Presently, she descended the stairs, walked through the stockroom where Mr Wilmslow slept, and through the shop into Scotland Road, which was crammed with people waving flags, blowing whistles and singing songs, all hurrying towards the city centre. She fished out the key which she wore on a ribbon round her neck and locked the door behind her, then set out for the meeting place that she and the girls had agreed on.

Halfway there, she suddenly realised that she was not sharing the excitement and optimism of the crowds on the pavements; in fact, she felt increasingly miserable and knew it was because of Toby. How could he marry Seraphina and produce a number of nephews and nieces for her to spoil if the war with Japan went on and on? She tried to push out of her mind the thought that he could be killed, but it was always there; a grinning spectre waiting to pounce on her when she was down.

Evie shook herself. She was being really stupid, because when it came down to it Toby was just her dear friend who would, she hoped, become her sister's lover and husband. It was right and proper that she should be concerned for him but not that she should allow her worry for him to ruin tonight, victory night.

Startled at her own thoughts, she stopped short, and was cannoned into by a young man in air force uniform who seized her by the shoulder, whirled her round and gave her a smacking kiss. 'Well of all the luck, and in this crowd, too,' he exclaimed. 'I only got back an hour ago but as soon as I'd seen me mam and got rid of me kit bag and that, I come searchin' for you. Only the shop were all locked up and the woman next door said as how she thought you'd gone off wi' your mam and old Wilmslow to lerroff a few fireworks of your own. I thought I'd go to the Plateau, and who's the first person I see, hurrying along the pavement? Oh, Evie, ain't it just great? Victory, I mean.'

'Yes, wonderful,' Evie agreed. 'Fancy you getting leave just at this moment – you always fall on your feet, don't you, Perce? But to tell you the truth, I'm not feeling that cheerful. You remember Toby, don't you?'

Percy slid an arm round her waist and gave her an affectionate squeeze. 'Course I remember him; tall, good-looking chap wi' yellow hair an' blue eyes. Married your sister,' he said confidently. 'He's out in Africa, somewhere, ain't he? Don't say he's bought it!'

Evie glared at him. 'That's Roger, not Toby, and he's not been killed, if that's what you mean,' she said coldly. 'Toby was Seraphina's boyfriend when we lived on the canal, but they fell out and she went and married Roger by mistake – well, I think it was a mistake,' she amended hastily. 'Toby's in the army, not the air force, and he was sent to relieve Singapore when the Japs attacked, and got taken prisoner. We've hardly had a word from him since then, which is over three years, and somehow victory doesn't seem so wonderful when you've a pal like Toby still in the thick of it.'

Percy whistled thoughtfully. 'I know what you mean,' he said. 'There have been stories . . . there was that business of all the fake letter cards, back in '44. Yes, I quite see that having a pal in the power of those little yellow bastards might well spoil the celebrations for anyone. Only, surely it's your sister who should be anxious, more than you?'

'Oh she is, I'm sure – anxious, I mean,' Evie said hastily. 'And of course I can't help Toby by making myself miserable so I'll do my best to be bright and cheerful.' She twisted within the circle of his arms to look up at him, reflecting that the gangling, spotty youth she had met before the war had turned into a husky, nice-looking young man. 'But I've arranged to meet a couple of pals outside Lime Street station, so I can't stay with you, much though I'd like to.'

Percy agreed, reluctantly, that they would part outside the station, but in the event the crowds defeated them and they were unable to get further than the Forum, so Evie spent the celebrations with Percy. The church bells which had been silent for almost six years added their clangour to the hooting of shipping and the shrill whistles of railway engines and presently, as it grew dusk, lights blazed out from every window. The two young people watched the fire-works ascending into the starlit sky, hugged one another and wept, but Evie knew that she was weeping for the poor lost souls in the Far East, whilst Percy was weeping for joy.

When at last the two of them turned towards

home, pushing their way through the singing, swaying crowds, Percy made a remark which cheered Evie considerably. 'They're saying, in the officers' mess, that the war in the Far East ain't likely to last long,' he told her. 'They're going to attack Japan with everything they've got . . . some new secret weapon, somebody said . . . because the Japs are said to fight to the death, you know, so they've got to be totally crushed.'

'As long as they don't crush the POWs along with the Japs,' Evie said, rather apprehensively. 'Oh, Percy, I pray for Toby every night and now I'm praying that the whole war will end soon, not just half of it.'

Percy gave a queer look which Evie found hard to interpret, but he said nothing until they stood outside the shop whilst Evie fished her key out and fumbled it into the lock. She turned to him to say good night and to thank him for his company, and would have slipped inside, but Percy stopped her with a hand on her arm. 'Hang on a minute, Evie. I've asked you, in the past, to be my girl. I've said I want to marry you when the war's over, but you've always pushed me back. I know you've been out with several other fellers but they've always assumed you was going to be serious wi' me. Tell me, queen, are you hoping that this Toby . . . I mean, is it him . . . ?'

Evie interrupted, feeling her face begin to grow hot. 'I just *told* you, he's Seraphina's feller,' she said furiously. 'Would I try to take my sister's feller, Percy? No, I would *not*, even if I could, which just isn't possible. Seraphina's the most beautiful girl I've ever seen in my whole life; she could have any man she wanted and I'm sure she wants Toby, so if you want to stay friends with me, Percy Baldwin, don't even think such a thing.'

★　　　★　　　★

When she had gone, Percy stuck his hands in his pockets and whistled, thoughtfully, beneath his breath. Poor little Evie! She could say what she liked; it was plain as a pikestaff to Percy that Evie had had a crush on her sister's boyfriend and he suspected that this had turned into something much warmer, simply because of the old adage, 'Absence makes the heart grow fonder.' But if Seraphina's marriage really was going to break up, then it was highly likely that the girl would go back to her first love. And then, Percy told himself, I must seize my opportunity. After all, I've loved Evie for ages, and though of course I've been out with a dozen or so girls in the last two or three years, none of them has ever meant as much to me as Evie has.

He remembered her as a skinny little kid with a crumpled Pekinese face and a quantity of lank brown hair. When that face had changed to near beauty, he had no idea, for it had been a gradual process; he just knew it had happened. Her large brown eyes, thickly fringed with black lashes, her small, straight nose and V-shaped mouth, and the smooth oval of her face had enchanted others beside himself. Oh, there were more obviously pretty girls; both Seraphina and Angela with their golden curls, bright blue eyes and rose petal complexions were probably considered better looking, but to Percy – and a good few others – there was something about Evie which transcended mere prettiness. He thought perhaps it was a certain sweetness of expression, a mischievous twinkle, plus a good deal of liveliness, that attracted him so much.

Percy turned into Lawrence Street. He had no idea what Toby looked like, but knew himself to be a handsome fellow, who had a way with girls. He thought his slightly raffish air attracted the opposite sex, though so far it did not seem to have worked with Evie. But that's because she's in love with a dream, he told himself, crossing the road and heading for Cavendish Court. Once this Toby's home, and Evie can see him with her own eyes, then my chance will come. That is, if he comes home. He had not told Evie what else they had been saying in the officers' mess: that the Japanese POWs were shockingly treated and that the vast majority of them would never come home at all. One reason for hitting Japan with everything they'd got was, the officers were saying freely, that the Japs would avenge their defeat by killing every European they could lay their hands on.

Percy was not a callous young man, but he had very little imagination. He felt vaguely sorry for this Toby chap but intended to do everything in his power to cut him out with Evie – if cutting out was necessary, that was.

Whistling, 'This is the Army, Mr Brown', he headed for his own front door.

The railway had been finished for a considerable time but Toby, Miles and a good many others were still constantly at work, at first maintaining the track and rebuilding a number of bridges, and then pressing on into Burma for what the Japs described as 'essential war work'.

The rebuilding of the bridges had seemed particularly hard, since the men were sure the Japs must have realised that untreated wood, driven into deep water, would be attacked by all sorts of pests. Beetles soon made such structures highly unsafe, and concrete piles and cross sections had to be erected in place of the crumbling wood.

It was in the course of repairing the bridges that

Toby fell foul of a vicious Korean guard, nicknamed Genghis, partly because the men said he had a face like a camel, but mostly because of his vicious behaviour towards the prisoners. Toby had pointed out that the man was only violent toward those taller than himself, but since Genghis was barely five foot high, this included every other man in the camp. One of Genghis's favourite tricks was at roll call time, when the men had to make their way out of their huts and get their orders for the day. Upon approaching Genghis, the men had to place their palms together and bow profoundly, and it was Genghis's habit to hide in a nearby bamboo thicket so that there was no one to whom the men could bow. If they simply bowed to the empty space where he should have been, Genghis counted this as insolence as punishable as not bowing at all, whereupon he would leap out from his hiding place and strike the offenders with any implement to hand – rifle butt, bayonet, or his malacca cane – before giving them their orders for the day, as though nothing untoward had occurred.

Mostly these blows, though painful, were aimed at backs, legs or shoulders, but on this occasion the night had been rainy and Toby had slipped as Genghis charged at him. The subsequent blow had opened up his face from his left temple to the left-hand corner of his mouth. Fortunately, Miles had dealt with the cut swiftly and efficiently, finally stitching it so that it would not flap open and become infected. It had taken two men to hold Toby down whilst Miles worked implacably, assuring Toby as he did so that his friend would thank him for it one day.

For two or three days, Toby's face was agony, but Miles insisted that it be kept clean, covering it with a piece of torn off shirt tail, and within a week Toby was able to push his injury to the back of his mind; within a fortnight, Miles removed the cotton stitches and assured his patient that, though he would always bear a scar, it had not ruined his beauty completely.

By the time the wound no longer troubled Toby, the men had moved on from maintaining the line and repairing bridges. Now, they were marched into the Burmese jungle where they performed two tasks. They dug out huge caves in the hillside which were to be used as ammunition dumps, and then they were ordered to dig tank traps, though what sort of tanks would be employed in jungle this dense, no one had any idea. Miles, looking down on one of these 'tank traps', remarked that, from the air, it would resemble nothing so much as a huge communal grave, waiting to be filled with the dead, and Toby, eyeing the depth and size of it, could only agree, as a chill ran down his spine.

That night, as they slumped, exhausted, on to their bamboo beds in the little Atap hut they had constructed, Toby sat up on one elbow and addressed his friend in a low whisper. 'Miles? What you said about the tank traps – you meant it, didn't you? You think we're digging our own graves. But why? After all, we've been pretty bloody useful, all these years; why kill us now?'

'Because we've not only dug these so-called tank traps, we've also dug the ammunition dumps, carried the ammo to them and helped to camouflage them. In other words, we know too much,' Miles said grimly. 'But we're well into Burma now, and I don't intend to face a firing squad if I can help it. Let's make a break for it in a couple of days . . . no, why not tomorrow? We'll get some things together and make for the nearest

Burmese village, get the head man on our side, promise him . . . oh, anything, if only he'll hide us from the Japs.'

'I dunno,' Toby said doubtfully. 'Remember that fellow who lit out a week back? The Japs paid the Burmese to hand him over, and they did. You can't blame them; the only Europeans they've seen are nothing but slaves. The Japs are in the ascendant all right, so far as the Burmese are concerned, and the villagers have got wives and kids to consider. Still, we'll think about it.'

The Japs usually woke them as soon as first light began to steal across the makeshift camp, but next morning Toby opened his eyes to find it was broad daylight. He sat up, puzzled, just as Miles stirred too. Miles rubbed his hands through his hair, knuckled his eyes, and then looked up at Toby. 'What's up? Why haven't the guards started screaming and shouting and using their rifle butts on anyone still lying down?' He cocked his head, listening intently. 'I don't like the look of this at all; I reckon when we go out, that bloody firing squad I mentioned will be hidden in the trees, ready to mow us down. Can we get out at the back, sneak off into the jungle?'

Toby was beginning to say that that might be the most dangerous move of all when they heard a subdued hum of chatter and Nick Barnes, their orderly, appeared in the entrance to the hut. He was grinning. 'You won't believe it, fellers, but they've all gone. Every single guard – Japs, Koreans, the lot. If you ask me, they've been recalled for some reason, but whatever it is, I reckon we'd better start making for Ban Pong. There's no point in staying here. Get your stuff together and we'll leave as soon as everyone's ready.'

Still nervous in case this was a trap, the men did

not walk along the railway track but kept to the shelter of the jungle, though they never moved far from the gleaming rails which led back, eventually, to civilisation. On the second day, they came to a Burmese village where they were told that the war was over; Germany had surrendered months earlier and Japan had surrendered a couple of days before. The Burmese talked of a big bomb and much panic and many deaths but the prisoners could not make head or tail of it; the only thing that mattered to them was that the war was over. The villagers gave them rice, but they would need a good deal more than that if they were to walk the hundreds of miles back to Singapore.

Toby and Miles grinned at one another as they trudged along, but then Toby stopped short, staring at the rails. They were vibrating, ever so slightly, and he grabbed Miles's arm and shouted ahead to where Nick Barnes slogged solidly onwards. 'Nick! There's a train coming. Better get deeper into the jungle. Miles and I will hang about here and watch to see what's happening.'

The men disappeared into the jungle and Miles and Toby watched through a fringe of leaves until the train came into sight. Then, with a shriek which echoed the whistle of the engine, they climbed the bank and began to dance with joy. The train was flying Red Cross flags on the front and was manned by British soldiers . . . rescue had come at last!

The letter came towards the end of August and it was addressed to Evie Todd and family. Even though Evie had not seen the writing for years, she recognised it at once and beamed across at her mother. 'Oh, Mam – it's to the whole family, but my name's been put first. It's from Toby; I'd know his writing anywhere!'

'And mine's from Angie,' Martha said, looking up from her own letter, her face rosy with pleasure. 'She's given in her notice . . . oh well, whatever you call it . . . and she's going to leave the ATS because she's going to have a dear little baby. Oh, Evie, I'm going to be a granny!'

Mr Wilmslow, solemnly eating porridge, looked up sharply. 'That's it, that's me mind made up,' he said decisively. 'I will not marry a grandmother so you'd better get a move on, young Martha. I've not reminded you, more than once every day, that you promised we'd wed as soon as the war were over, but now we've got to bustle about a bit. When's this baby due?'

'Honestly, Arthur, what a thing to say,' Martha protested. 'But I suppose it's fair enough; I did promise, after all. The baby's due towards the end of January so I suppose we could tie the knot in about six weeks, in mid-October. How would that suit you?'

Evie, staring from one face to the other, actually saw shy pleasure flit across Mr Wilmslow's somewhat lugubrious countenance and thought, suddenly, that her mam could do a lot worse. It was plain that Mr Wilmslow adored Martha, and Evie realised now that her mother was truly fond of the old fellow. She watched Martha smile across the table at Mr Wilmslow. 'There you are then, that's settled,' she said briskly. 'And now, young Evie, you can open that letter and tell us where Toby is right now.'

Evie opened the letter slowly and with great care, and took out two thin, closely written sheets. She scanned them quickly then said: 'He's in hospital in Singapore, but says everyone is having a sort of check-up, so it doesn't mean he's ill. He says the Japs kept them very short of food, which was mostly rice anyway, so they are all horribly thin; the hospital authorities don't want to let them go until they're fatter – they're calling them "bonebags" – and of course they've got no clothes to speak of. Tatty shorts and a bit of blanket, but nothing much else. Oh, I'd better read you the next bit.' She cleared her throat, then began to read carefully: '*The RAF are flying us out in great big transport planes – the Brits, I mean – so a good few of us will be home quite quickly. I've a pal called Miles, who was a medical student before the war – he had passed all his exams and just had to do his finals when war broke out. He's put in to go back home as soon as possible so he can start being a doctor properly, and they've said he'll be repatriated just as soon as he's fit enough; I don't think they'll make any special plans for railway porters, though! Not that I intend to go on being a railway porter when I get back to Civvy Street. After what I've been doing these past few years, I reckon I'll go for something a bit more interesting.*

How are you all? We've received no mail for years – not since Changi, in fact – but I think about you all the time. I wonder about working the canal – we had some good times then, you and I, Seraphina. Remember when we went blackberrying along the cut and you tried to squeeze past me and fell in the canal? Evie was so keen to get you out that she kicked over my basket of black-berries and I boxed her ears. Dear little Evie, forgive me for reminding you of my horrid actions that day, but that's a dream I dream quite often, I don't know why. I'll come and see you just as soon as I get back to Blighty. All the best, Toby.'

'Well, isn't that lovely – that he's going to come and see us, I mean, and is fit and well, even if he is thin,' Martha said as Evie finished reading. 'He was like a son to me and like a brother to you three girls.' She saw Evie open her mouth and went on hastily: 'I know Seraphina was fond of him, dear, but that was long ago. Now come along, let's get breakfast cleared away and then we must all be off to work.'

'There's a PS,' Evie said, rather hesitantly, as her mother gathered up the crocks and carried them over to the sink. 'He says he's afraid we may not recognise him because of some wound or other ... as if we wouldn't. Why, I'd know Toby amongst ten thousand – I'm sure we all would.'

'I'm going down to open up,' Mr Wilmslow said. 'Get a move on, Evie, or you'll be late. Martha, my love, I'll leave you to finish up here, if you don't mind, and then you might as well go shopping because I've no doubt you'll want a new dress, or a suit or something, for our wedding.'

Martha gave a snort. 'Where will I get the coupons?' she asked. 'And don't say I can buy some off Percy, because he's a changed feller since his time in the air force. Besides, I don't believe in it – the black market, I mean.'

'I happen to have some clothing coupons by me and you're welcome to them, my dear,' Mr Wilmslow said, with dignity. 'What do I want with new clothes? I haven't got no fatter nor thinner, and me black pinstripe will do as well for a wedding as for a funeral. Besides, I reckon young Evie could do with a new skirt and jumper ... I trust you aren't thinking of bridesmaids, are you?' he finished, with obvious dismay.

'Of course I shall have bridesmaids, half a dozen of them, and I plan to be married in white, with a big bouquet of cream-coloured roses and a lace veil with a train twenty feet long,' Martha said gaily. 'What a fool I'd look; the vicar would probably refuse to marry us and have me committed to the nearest asylum.'

Mr Wilmslow permitted himself a wintry smile. 'You'll look grand in whatever you wear,' he observed. 'I'll be that proud . . . now just you choose something pretty for yourself and Evie and remember, I'm not only providing the coupons, I'll also part with me money.'

Martha looked up sharply. 'You will not,' she said roundly. 'When we're married, it'll be different, but Evie and I will buy our wedding clothes. Though we're very grateful for the offer – and for the coupons, of course.'

Mr Wilmslow gave a deep sigh, held the door open for Evie and then followed her down the stairs and into the stockroom. Here they parted, Evie making her way through the shop and out of the front door, erecting her umbrella as soon as she stepped out on to the pavement, for it was raining steadily. Sloshing through the puddles on the way to her bus stop, she went over Toby's letter in her mind. Although it had been addressed to her and to the family, she felt that it had really been intended for Seraphina and decided, after a short inward struggle, that she would put the pages into another envelope and send them on to Seraphina at her airfield.

Evie's bus came along and she jumped aboard. Her job at the clothing factory was changing, for the staff were beginning to make ordinary garments, and she had decided that as soon as she could find alternative work she would leave. She had been going to evening classes, doing a business course, and both her short-hand and her typing were now sufficiently good to mean that an office job was on the cards. However, she had been well paid for making uniforms, and if the money remained the same she would happily make demob suits until the right job turned up.

The conductor tinkled the bell and the bus began to move forward once more. Evie saw a friend in front of her and squeezed past a couple of fat old shawlies, apologising as her dripping umbrella snagged in someone's basket. She was longing to tell everyone that the war really was over for her because very soon now Toby would be returning home. 'Hey, Lily!' she squeaked, as soon as she was near enough. 'You'll never guess what I got this morning!'

It was 22 December and Seraphina was preparing for a week's leave, which she would spend at home in Liverpool. Fate had decreed that she would not be spending Christmas, as she had planned, with Eddie, but then neither would she be spending it with Roger. She had written to him, asking for a divorce, as soon as the war ended, but he had responded by first ignoring her letter, and then turning up at her airfield full of righteous indignation and tears. She had felt sorry for him at first, but such feelings had speedily evaporated when he told her, bluntly, that he did not intend to give her grounds, and nor would he ever admit that he had not consummated the marriage. 'If you want to make our private lives public property, then I suppose you might be able to prove something, but I imagine you've probably been carrying on with someone else whilst I've been abroad, so that horse won't run,' he had said, and there was a sneer in his voice and a look in his eye which had made Seraphina shudder and turn away.

After that, she had gone to a solicitor, but he had not been at all helpful. For a start, he had kept glancing out of the window as she spoke, tapping his wristwatch and holding it to his ear, rudely interrupting her by answering the telephone whenever it rang, and finally telling her that she would find it difficult to persuade a judge that non-consummation of the marriage was sufficient grounds for divorce in her case. 'These things happen in wartime,' he had said loftily. 'Young men are under a good deal of stress; they're away for long periods – perhaps even for years – as you say your husband has been. I'm sure, now that he's home, he will speedily put things right. Good morning, Mrs Truelove.'

Seraphina had wanted to scream, to pick up the large ruler on the desk and hit him over the head with it, to throw his wretched telephone straight through the glass of his office window. She had paid for this interview and he had not even listened to her, even though, deeply embarrassing though it had been, she had assured him that she had not been with anyone else since her marriage, and certainly not before that. Unfortunately, her knowledge of the law was not sufficient to tell her whether she would have to allow Roger back into her bed if he wanted to force the issue, but, law or no law, she had no intention of returning to him. She had made a colossal mistake in marrying him, and now that she had met a man she could both respect and love she did not mean to allow Roger to ruin the rest of her life.

Having realised that it would not be possible to spend her week's leave with Eddie, she had decided to go home to Liverpool. It was high time she told Martha what a farce her marriage was, because until she understood she feared that Martha would be aghast at the idea of a divorce. Once she knew, however, that the marriage had not been consummated – never would be – then Seraphina was certain not only of her understanding but also of her sympathy and support.

So, at ten o'clock on the following day, Seraphina set off for Liverpool. Sitting in the train she made her plans. Roger knew where she lived and might come searching for her. So, having thought the matter over, she had decided that when she was demobbed she would go down to the little village in Devon where Angie and her Albert already occupied a thatched, pink-washed cottage opposite the war memorial and close by the church of St Lawrence. Seraphina had visited her sister six months earlier and had fallen in love with the peaceful little hamlet, perched on its rounded hill, the narrow, sunken lanes, the beautiful countryside and the tumbling River Torridge which meandered round the foot of the hill in summer, and roared noisily seawards in winter. Seraphina knew she would be welcomed, even though the cottage only had one spare room, for, naturally, she would pay her sister a fair rent and curates and their wives, she knew, were always short of money. She hoped that she might get work somewhere in the area, to tide her over until she was free to marry Eddie. She had put the idea to Angela, who had received it with great enthusiasm and said that her sister would be bound to find work in the nearby town of Okehampton.

Seraphina had not told Angela why she meant to move away from Liverpool but had a shrewd suspicion that her sister realised there was something wrong between herself and Roger. Once she got to Devon, she would tell her the truth, of course, and thought that Angela would understand completely, enter into her feelings and encourage her to end the marriage, for Angela was looking forward to the birth of her baby

381

and had told Seraphina she meant to have a large family. The thought of a marriage in which the husband refused to allow the wife to have children would, Seraphina knew, be repugnant to her sister.

The passenger beside her, a young woman in ATS uniform, suddenly dived a hand into the breast pocket of her tunic and produced a letter, much read and travel stained. She began to read it and abruptly Seraphina remembered that she had received a letter herself that morning. Now she took it from her pocket and glancing down at it recognised Evie's handwriting. She tore open the envelope – it was a long letter, for there were a couple of sheets of thin, utility paper within – and began to read.

Dear Fee, Wonderful, wonderful news! We had a short letter from Toby yesterday saying that the hospital will discharge him at the end of December. He's sorry to miss Christmas, of course, but thrilled to be coming back to Blighty once more. He says the thing that had worried him most was called a tropical ulcer; it took ages to get well and could have gone even deeper than it did, but he says now there is just a hole in his leg, quite clean and pink, and it doesn't hurt at all. I know you're coming back for Christmas, which is lovely, but couldn't you explain things to your wing officer and ask if you could delay your leave for a week? Seraphina glanced at the date at the top of the letter. As she had guessed, it had been written ten days ago, for the Christmas post always delayed mail. There would have been no chance of her changing her leave even if she had wanted to. She returned to the letter.

If you come home later when Toby gets here you could spend some time with him and you're such old friends. I'm sure he'd like see you, though of course he'll be pleased to see us, too. Well, I say 'us', but really it will be just me,

Mam and Uncle Arthur. I call him Uncle Arthur now because saying Mr Wilmslow to someone who is related to you by marriage sounds a bit unfriendly. However, if you can't, you can't. From what I've heard from other POWs, Toby will get a couple of months' salary – maybe more – so that he can have a proper break before starting work again. He might like to take a train down to Devon and visit Angie for a few days; if he does that, and if you're demobbed by then, of course, why don't you go along? It would be awfully nice for Toby to have someone to explore the countryside with . . . but it's up to you, of course. Dear Fee, can I speak honestly of what is on my mind? Things haven't been right between you and Roger and I'm so sorry for it. If there's ever anything you'd like to tell me, remember, I'm not a child any more. I'm going to be eighteen in March, and I know an awful lot about things, even things like marriage, so if you want to talk, you know I wouldn't tell anyone.

Must go now; I'm starting a new job after Christmas, as a junior shorthand/typist, with a firm of solicitors. I shall be working mostly with the junior partner – he's the one who does most of their divorce cases. Much love, Evie.

Seraphina sat back and smiled to herself. How sweet and ingenuous Evie was! She could not, of course, have the faintest idea that Seraphina's marriage was a marriage in name only, but she had clearly realised that all was not well. I shall explain things to Ma but I don't believe I'll have to tell Evie very much, she thought, carefully drying her eyes on her hankie and cramming the letter into her pocket. I'm really lucky in my family. Some girls dread having to tell their mother and sisters that they intend to divorce, but I know Ma, Angie and Evie will understand.

*   *   *

Toby was flown home in January and found the freezing temperatures, when he stepped out of the huge plane, a daunting experience. But the nights in the jungle had often been cold and he felt, in his new warm clothes, that he could face most of what his country had to offer. He arrived in Liverpool as the early winter dusk was coming down and looked, almost unbelievingly, at the devastation illumined by the many street lamps and the glow from shop windows. He had known the city had been hard hit but, irrationally, had expected it to have been rebuilt. Now he saw grimly that this was not so. He knew he was still gaunt and pale, but had expected to be surrounded by rosy smiling faces and well-dressed people, for surely such should have been the signs of victory? But the folk hurrying along the pavements looked weary and worn and Toby, standing undecided outside Lime Street station, wondered what he should best do.

Now that he had actually arrived in the city, Toby found he was hesitating. Everything was so strange! Perhaps it would be better if he went home to Micklethwaite first, took things slowly, did not rush into anything. He had half turned back towards the station when another thought occurred to him. If Seraphina had spent her Christmas leave with her family, then there was just a faint hope that she might be there still. And he acknowledged, now, that he wanted to see her; they had so much to talk about. He told himself he would never forget how the memories of their past happiness had kept him going during the most terrible of his days as a POW. Then there was her selfless devotion to him after Dunkirk, when she had knelt by his bed all night, holding his hand and fending off the fearful nightmares from which he had suffered.

Telling himself that he owed Seraphina a good deal, he set off along the pavement. He paused for a moment by a tram stop, but he had already discovered that he was miserably ill at ease in cramped and confined spaces; that crowds filled him with apprehension, though he had no idea why. So instead of waiting for the tram, he decided he would walk and set off at a brisk pace, keeping to the outer edge of the pavement since this made him feel less hemmed in. These feelings won't last, he told himself; it's simply a matter of growing accustomed. I must get in touch with Miles because I'm sure he'll be suffering from very similar feelings, and he is a good deal better equipped to cope with them than I am.

He drew in a deep breath of the chilly night air, then coughed as the cold caught at the back of his throat and grinned to himself. Yes, it would take some getting used to, this new freedom; he would definitely contact Miles.

Evie ran across the wide pavement outside her office and took a flying leap aboard the tram which was just starting to move. The conductor shouted at her but she gave him a wicked grin, shrieked that she was sorry and charged up the stairs and on to the upper deck, knowing that he was unlikely to pursue her up here in order to throw her off for daring to board the tram as it was moving.

There was a seat, too, since the young man who had been occupying it had got to his feet and was making his way down the stairs in order to be first off when they reached his stop. Evie sank into it and looked about her. All day she had had a trembly, excited feeling in the pit of her stomach; all day she had felt as though today was special, though she could not have said why.

Seraphina had gone back to her airfield a couple of weeks before and had telephoned the shop – Mr Wilmslow had had a telephone installed and the whole family competed to answer it whenever the bell rang – to say that her demob papers had arrived and she hoped to be going down to Devon in a couple of weeks.

Evie knew that her sister had confided in Martha regarding her marriage – in fact, she had even spoken to Evie about it, asking Evie about her boss, Mr Blewitt. Evie had been able to give her a reassuring report; Mr Blewitt was young, attractive and go-ahead, and dealt with his many clients – mostly women – with considerable sympathy and understanding. Encouraged by Evie's words, Seraphina had made an appointment to see him and had come away from his office looking happier than she had done for some time.

Evie had longed to ask her sister what had transpired – she knew better than to ask Mr Blewitt – but Seraphina had not been terribly forthcoming. 'It'll be all right,' she had said when Evie had questioned her. 'I liked your Mr Blewitt very much indeed and he said he saw no reason for me not to be granted a divorce within the next six months or so, which suits me because . . . well, you can't marry someone who isn't even in the same country, can you?'

Evie had longed to remind her that Toby would be in the same country as Seraphina pretty soon, but had kept quiet. Time enough when Seraphina was divorced to bring her and Toby together again. The tram drew up at a stop and suddenly she was on her feet and pushing her way towards the top of the stairs, tumbling down them, leaping off the platform with such force that she almost knocked over a stout, bespectacled man carrying a briefcase and wearing a thick, navy blue coat. He protested sharply, grabbed at her arm, told her she should be a bit more careful, if he had gone down on this icy pavement . . . but Evie was not listening. She tore off up the road and grabbed at the stiff, new-looking overcoat of a young man walking along on the outside edge of the pavement. 'Toby! Toby! Toby!' she shrieked. 'Oh, Toby, you're back, you're back!'

Chapter Fourteen

It was a wonderful moment. Toby – for it was he – stared down at her incredulously and then, with an exultant laugh, picked her up in his arms and hugged her tightly, and she could feel the tremble running through him. 'Evie,' he said huskily. 'Oh, Evie . . . where have you sprung from, and how did you know it was me?'

Evie felt the warmth of his breath on her hair, the pressure of his arms about her, and for a moment was so happy that she scarcely heeded his question. Then, reluctantly, she pulled back from him. 'I was on top of the tram and saw you walking along. As for recognising you, how could I do anything else? You're a bit thin, but otherwise you're just the same. But how did you recognise *me*? There's a huge difference between twelve and eighteen. Indeed, if you're going to tell me I haven't changed, I shall be very insulted!'

Toby put his arm about her shoulders and kissed the side of her face. 'Well, you're taller,' he admitted. 'But it isn't just that. I thought about you an awful lot while I was in Burma and somehow, knowing you were getting older each year, I suppose the picture of you in my mind got older too.' He turned her to face him, smiling down at her with real affection. 'How pretty you've grown! You're a bit like Seraphina. Oh, I know you've not got her colouring, and once I'd have said there was no resemblance, but now I really do think you're a little bit like her.'

'Gosh!' Evie said, wide-eyed. 'That's a compliment and a half, that is.' She slipped her arm through his and smiled up at him, seeing the changes which the war had wrought but thinking them unimportant. 'Were you on your way to our flat, Toby? I do hope so, though I'm afraid there's one disappointment in store for you. Seraphina has gone back to her airfield, but of course if you want to see her you can go over to Norfolk . . . oh, no you can't, because she's being demobbed and then she'll go straight down to Devon to stay with Angie and her husband. I suppose you could go down there . . .'

'No I couldn't,' Toby said, as they began to walk along the pavement in the direction of the shop. 'I wrote to my old boss from Singapore and in a couple of days' time I'm going to start to learn to be a signalman. I was looking for a job in a signal box when war broke out and I'd started to try to learn the book, only by now I've probably forgotten most of it.'

'Oh, I see,' Evie said, rather doubtfully. 'But – but do you really want to work for the railways? I mean, won't it remind you of – of the Burma railway and all the dreadful things that happened there?'

Toby chuckled. 'I wouldn't let that put me off,' he said. 'I've always been keen on the railways – the English ones, I mean – and besides, being a signalman is the sort of life I've always wanted. It's an enormous responsibility, you know, but it's work I thoroughly enjoy, and that's what matters to me now.'

'Oh, Toby, will you put in for one of the really big signal stations, like Lime Street?' Evie asked eagerly. 'It would be lovely to have you near, especially when—' She broke off short, biting back the words *when you and Seraphina are married*, remembering that Seraphina had not yet said anything to Toby about her forthcoming divorce.

She waited for Toby to ask her what she had been about to say, but he did not do so. Instead, he put his right hand over hers, and tucked it into the crook of his left arm. 'No, I'm afraid I haven't changed that much. I'm still not ambitious and I don't suppose I ever will be. I'm hoping to get a signal box on my own stretch of line – the Settle to Carlisle road. I know it's a long way from Liverpool and Micklethwaite, but when I have time off I'll hop aboard a train and go to see my family or you Todds.'

Evie laughed. 'I've only just realised it myself, but the only Todd left is me,' she reminded him. 'Seraphina's a Truelove, Angie's a Reid and Mam's a Wilmslow.'

Toby laughed with her. 'And you've grown so pretty that it won't be long before you change your name too,' he remarked. 'What's it to be? I guess you've had a score of fellers since I was last here, but I seem to remember you had a pal called Percy Baldwin who was rather keen on you. Evie Baldwin has a nice ring to it.'

Evie shook her head. 'Marriage is for other people,' she said decidedly. 'I'm going to have a career and I shall be an aunt to my sisters' kids, which will suit me just fine. Do you like children, Toby?'

Toby shrugged. 'I hadn't really thought about it,' he said honestly. 'In Burma, all any of us could think of was simply survival.' He grinned suddenly, and Evie thought that he looked young again. 'I don't know whether you know it, but when I left home us older ones had two younger brothers and a little sister. Now, I've got five younger brothers and two little sisters, and our poor little cottage is stretched to bursting point. That's why I only spent a couple of days at home and then came on here, because it really isn't fair on my mum having to cope with a grown man as well as all those kids. And anyway, I want to get some uniform before I start work.'

'I did know about the new babies as they came along,' Evie told him. 'It's a long way from here to your village but whenever I went aboard the *Mary Jane* for a bit of a holiday on the canal – not that it was a holiday because I only did it when they needed me – I popped in and saw your mam and got up to date with her news. So you aren't planning to live at home again, then?'

Toby shook his head. 'No. I left home when I got my first job with the railway and I've never lived at home since. They may want me to go on relief first of all – that means turning up at any signal box where a man is ill, or on holiday, all along the line – and that would mean lodging wherever I was sent. But once I get a box of my own, of course, I'll mebbe rent a place.' He looked dreamily ahead of him. 'I'd keep a few hens and a pig or two, and make a proper garden, with flowers and fruit as well as vegetables. I'd like that.'

Evie secretly doubted whether Seraphina would share his enthusiasm, but was saved from having to comment because they had reached the shop and she was pushing open the door. Martha was behind the counter whilst Mr Wilmslow, halfway up a stepladder, was stacking cereal boxes on an upper shelf. 'Hello, Mam,' Evie said cheerfully. 'You'll never guess . . .'

Her mother smiled at her but turned towards Toby. 'Can I help you, sir?' she asked.

Toby stared at her and Evie saw a slow flush creep across his face so that the scar flamed more lividly than ever. 'Oh, Mam, don't pretend you haven't recognised

Toby,' she said quickly. 'He hasn't changed at all, not really.'

Martha gave a squeak, lifted the flap in the counter, and emerged to take both Toby's hands in a warm clasp and stand on tiptoe to kiss his cheek. 'Dear Toby, it's wonderful to see you again, and Evie's right, you've hardly changed at all. But I wasn't expecting to see you, of course, and you were against the light . . .' She turned to where her husband was ponderously descending the steps. 'Arthur, come and say hello to Toby.'

The two men shook hands and Mr Wilmslow said that they might as well shut the shop because he was sure Toby would have a lot to tell them. He reached up and took some tins off one of the shelves. 'Mrs Wilmslow is making minced beef and carrots for our supper,' he said genially. 'If we pop in a tin of baked beans it'll stretch to four instead of three, and we can finish off with tinned rhubarb and custard, one of me favourites.' He looked thoughtfully round the shop. 'When Evie told me you'd be coming to see us I put a bottle of South African sherry away so's we could all have a drink; now where the blazes has that gone?'

Martha, who had returned to the other side of the counter, dived beneath it and produced a dusty bottle. 'Here it is!' she said, triumphantly. 'Evie, put up the "Closed" sign; we've got a great deal of talking to do.'

By the end of April Toby was deemed fit, both in his own estimation and in that of his teachers, to apply for a job as relief signalman on the Settle to Carlisle line. He had been assured that there would be a permanent job there before winter set in, but in the meantime he would be gaining the very best sort of practical experience.

His first digs were with a plate layer and his wife, who had a tiny cottage amongst the fells. He lodged with two other men, Billy and Sam, and the three of them would work eight-hour shifts over a seven-day period, and would then have three days off. The job was to last a fortnight, whilst the man Toby was covering for was visiting his married daughter in Scotland. 'You'd best do a couple of day shifts to start off with,' Sam told him, 'and I'll take you to the box meself and show you the ropes. You're in luck; both meself and Billy own bicycles and you're welcome to borrow one or t'other to get you to and from the box. It's a six-mile ride, so you'll need to leave yourself plenty of time to do the journey. You'd best get Mrs Smith to put you up sandwiches and a flask. Can you cook?'

Toby replied, rather cautiously, that he was a dab hand at cups of tea and bacon and eggs, but wouldn't claim to be much good with pastry or cakes. Sam chuckled. 'There's a Russell stove with a bit of an oven on the top,' he explained. 'If you get stuck in the box for a double shift, which can happen, then you'll be right glad of that old stove. Many a rabbit stew I cooked on it during the war, and one of me pals used to make blackberry and apple jam and sell it to passengers at the nearest station.' He grinned at Toby. 'But since you're relief, and we'll be moving on at the end of two weeks, you won't be wantin' to start no cottage industries, I dare say.'

Toby agreed, but very soon realised why so many signalmen started small sidelines of their own. Some roads were very busy, and at certain times the Settle to Carlisle was one of them, but there were other times when the signalman had nothing much to do for hours together. Toby was conscientious, and took care to plan his shift so that he was on the alert when a train was due. He enjoyed the challenge of being in complete control but found that sometimes the empty hours, when there was no train in his vicinity, dragged. He had always been a keen reader but had not thought to provide himself with books and determined to do so in future.

After a fortnight, he said a regretful goodbye to Mr and Mrs Smith; she was a grand cook and considering the small sum he had paid her weekly – a half-crown – had provided him with excellent meals. The spring was a chilly one, especially high in these fells, and once he had begun to grow accustomed to the life, he had preferred to take food which could be cooked on his stove to the sandwiches Mrs Smith had at first made for him. Accordingly, before he set off for each shift, he had gone to the village shop and bought a couple of eggs and a loaf of bread, some milk and anything else the shop could provide which did not need coupons or points, for naturally he had handed his ration book over to Mrs Smith as soon as he had arrived.

Forewarned being forearmed, when he was given his next assignment he bought a quantity of second-hand books, a large pad of writing paper, a bottle of ink and several envelopes before he set off for his new digs, hoping that they would be as good as his previous lodgings. He had only written one letter from his first signal box, and that had been addressed to Evie with a request that she might pass it around the rest of the family, but at the second box he was more organised and enlarged his correspondence to include his mother, Seraphina and Miles, who was now a fully fledged doctor, working in a large hospital in Leeds. It was grand to receive replies, though these

394

took some while to reach him since they had to be sent to Settle, where the stationmaster would forward them on to whichever signal box Toby was occupying at the time. Toby, enjoying every moment of his new life, had few opportunities of visiting either Liverpool or his home village, but he had learned his lesson and wrote regularly to Evie, asking her, as before, to pass his letters on. This was, he admitted to himself, a bit of a cheat since he frequently received three or four replies to one letter. Angie was full of the antics of her tiny new son, and Seraphina, working as a teacher of lively seven-year-olds in a small village school, was equally full of news. She had stayed with her sister until the little boy was three months old, but then she had moved into lodgings which meant she could walk to her school each day and seemed content with her lot.

Then, in September, Toby got a permanent job. He was to work in one of the highest signal boxes in England, in wild and rugged country miles from anywhere, with the Pennine hills rising all about him and the line cutting through deep embankments and tunnelling its way through the highest of the fells. The only snag to his new appointment was that there was no nearby village in which he could lodge and he would have a long walk to get to work each day. However, his new job did not start until a week after the present one finished, which would, he was told, give him plenty of time to sort out digs for himself and to negotiate the buying of a second-hand bicycle.

Jubilantly, Toby sent a telegram to the Wilmslow shop both admitting his need and warning them of his imminent arrival. *Week off stop Need bike stop In Liverpool Wednesday*, it read, *Regards Toby*. He hoped that Mr Wilmslow, who knew all his customers and most of his neighbours, might manage to find him a suitable bicycle, for Toby did not fancy walking five miles to work each day and five miles back. He finished his last relief job on Friday night and caught a bus to the village nearest his new signal box, where he went into the tiny local shop and explained his predicament. The man he was replacing had not lodged in this particular village, but one even further away, and it looked as if Toby might have to follow his example. However, the lady who ran the shop, fat Mrs Wetherspoon, was a kindly soul and saw Toby's look of disappointment when he asked the time of the bus to the next village. 'There ain't one, lad, not till Monday, so that means tha'll 'ave to use Shanks's pony,' she told him. 'And thou's no bike, either, I'll warrant, 'cos they've been like gold dust ever since war. But look on, lad, you're a slender one. I've got a slip of a room upstairs which I scarce use. It's too small for owt but a camp bed. As you can see, I'm busy int shop so I can't feed thee except for breakfast, but if tha'd like use of room and provide thy own grub, then it's thine for half a crown a week.'

Toby was bowled over by this offer and accepted at once. 'Happen I'll be getting a bike,' he told her. 'I've a pal in Liverpool – a local shop owner actually – who's keeping an eye out for one. But it's most awfully good of you, Mrs Wetherspoon, to let me have the room and I promise I won't get in your way or cause any sort of bother.' He hesitated. 'Would – would it be all right if I borrowed your kitchen for half an hour or so each day, though? I'll eat cold food as much as I can, but with winter coming on . . .'

'Tha's welcome to have the use of me kitchen, though I don't have electric or gas, just a coal stove. Water comes from a pump int yard and lavvy is an earth closet down by woodshed.' She looked at him hard. 'If you want truth, young man, it's all round village that you were a prisoner of them wicked Japs so I reckon it's duty of every decent Englishman to give thee a bit of a leg-up, like.'

Toby grinned at her. 'I never thought I'd live to be thankful to a perishin' Jap,' he said cheerfully. 'God knows, they did their best to make our lives hell, but it seems they've brought me one bit of luck, because lodging with you . . . well, it couldn't be better.'

Encouraged by this, Mrs Wetherspoon led him up an extremely steep flight of tiny wooden stairs to the room she had mentioned. It was indeed tiny, with no space for a washstand or even a chair, just the bed. In addition, the ceiling sloped so sharply that he could only stand upright against the door and the window started below knee level and ended at his ankles. However, there were three stout hooks on the back of the door where he could hang what little clothing he would need, and the view from the window, when Toby knelt down and peered out, was superlative: rolling fells, bosky woodland – red-gold with autumn at this time of year – a tumultuous river glittering in the sunshine and, in the far distance, the outline of a mighty viaduct, standing clear cut against the misty fells.

'Well?' Mrs Wetherspoon's voice was a little doubtful. 'I don't deny it's small and there's no room for any sort o' heating, but I've plenty blankets and curtains are thick and will keep out worst of cold. I know window's low, but . . .'

Toby straightened up as much as he could and beamed. 'It's grand, just grand,' he assured her, ducking out of the room and following her down the narrow stairs. 'You can't imagine the sort of huts we had in Burma, Mrs Wetherspoon, but . . .'

'Don't tell me,' the woman said quietly. 'I had a son, Bobby, who were killed on that bloody railway. If I'd a better room, tha should have it, but my Bobby managed fine in there until he went to war.'

'I'm sorry,' Toby said inadequately. 'If I'd known, I wouldn't have said what I did about the Japs, because they did the worst they could and if you ask me they richly deserved those atom bombs.'

'When will tha be wantin' to move in?'

'Next Friday, if that will suit you,' Toby said. 'I shall be going to Liverpool for a few days to see if I can track down a second-hand bike, but I actually start work in the box first shift on Saturday so if I can move in the night before, that'll be grand.'

Evie burst into the shop, which was empty of customers, a triumphant smile on her face, and handed her mother a bulging brown paper bag. 'I passed Mr Grimshaw's shop on Great Homer and he called me in for a moment. He's a lovely man, he is, and of course he's registered with us for groceries. When I got into the shop, he asked me if I'd like three oranges and a lemon. One of the oranges is split, but only a tiny bit – oh, and there's three apples as well, big cookers. Has Toby arrived yet?'

'No, not yet,' Martha said placidly, 'but I dare say he'll be along soon.'

'He'll be hoping we'll have found him a bicycle. Any news on that front, Uncle Arthur?' Evie asked.

'Aye, there's an old boneshaker for sale down Horatio Street. It belonged to Mrs Kray's eldest boy, but he's gorra job in London and she don't think he'll want it there. She's askin' thirty bob so I said when the lad came this way he could tek a look and she's promised not to sell it to anyone else until she's had the yea or nay from Toby himself. I give her an ounce of tea,' he added, half apologetically. 'You don't get anything for nothing these days, norreven a rusty old pedal pusher.'

'Oh, that's great,' Evie said joyfully. 'I'm sure Toby will be able to make it good as new. I seem to remember Dad saying he was pretty good with engines and that.'

'Aye, and he'll likely persuade her to knock off a bob or two,' Mr Wilmslow said wisely. He turned to the stockroom. 'Put the "Closed" sign up, Evie, there's a good gal, and then we can have our suppers.'

Toby would have been a welcome visitor in any circumstances, but the fact that he arrived bearing a pair of rabbits, a stout bag full of windfall apples, a large bottle of home-brewed cider and a bag containing a dozen eggs made his welcome assured. 'Mum thought you'd be glad of a few extras seeing as I'm going to be staying over with you for a couple of nights,' he said, piling his gifts up on the kitchen table almost as soon as he reached the flat. They had moved Evie's camp bed from the stockroom to the living room and borrowed another one for Toby to sleep on. This was now erected in the stockroom and he had laid his bed roll out on it on his way upstairs.

'Is there anything you'd like to do, after we've had supper?' Evie asked, as she and Martha began to stow away the food he had brought. 'Would you like to go to the flicks? It's a bit late to book for the theatre but we could try, because it gets dark early so there's not much point in going to one of the parks. Or would you prefer a quiet evening in?'

'I'd like to take a look at that bike,' Toby said at once. 'It's the devil of a long walk from my lodgings to the signal box, and would take me well over an hour without transport. So you see, it's quite important that I get myself some wheels.'

'Aye, you're right; the quicker you see the bike, the sooner you'll know whether it'll fit the bill,' Mr Wilmslow said approvingly. 'And I wouldn't like to think of that ounce of tea being wasted.'

'Oh, you. You aren't the skinflint you'd like us to believe,' Martha said teasingly. 'Though you're right, of course; the sooner Toby sees it the better. And now let's have our food. It's only Woolton pie followed by stewed apple and custard, but I dare say it'll keep you going until breakfast tomorrow.'

As they ate, Evie eyed Toby covertly. She had not seen him for a good many months and thought he looked immensely better. His skin had taken on the rosy tan which she remembered of old, his hair seemed thicker and curlier, and there was a sort of easy strength in his movements which had been lacking upon his arrival from the Far East. She thought he looked lovely and guessed that, when Seraphina and he eventually met again, the years would roll back and her sister would be truly in love with him once more. She had said as much to Martha but her mother had scoffed at the idea that Seraphina and Toby had ever been in love. 'They were just a couple of kids when we lived on the canal,' she had reminded her daughter. 'Why, they were only seventeen when your pa decided to change his lifestyle; Seraphina hadn't met any young men apart from Toby, and if you ask me, she thought of him as a brother, and still does.'

But this conversation had taken place a couple of weeks before and now Evie tucked her arm into Toby's as the two of them set off to examine the bicycle. 'Are you thinking of visiting Devon, to see Seraphina?' she asked innocently. 'I told you, didn't I, that she's hoping to get a divorce? It – it would be a real thrill for her to see you again, Toby. I mean, I know you write to one another, but it's not the same as meeting, is it?'

'No, and it would be grand to see her, but I'm not planning a visit. It's too far to go on my time off and I shan't be due for any holiday until I've worked my first year,' Toby pointed out.

'Well, she's a teacher and has all the school holidays; she could come up north then,' Evie said.

'If she comes home for Christmas, I might manage to have a day with you then. I realise you wouldn't be able to put me up,' he added hastily, 'but there's plenty of lodging houses where I could get a bed. Still, that's for the future and it's up to Seraphina, really. I don't know much about divorce, but I believe a woman who wants such a thing has to be extremely careful who she meets and how she behaves until what they call the decree nisi is granted. And now let's change the subject, if you don't mind. How well do you know this Mrs Kray? Your stepdad seemed to think I might bargain her down a bit, but there's them as will bargain and them as won't. Which sort is she?'

'I dunno,' Evie admitted honestly, unabashed by what some might have seen as a snub. She guessed that Toby's feelings for her sister were still locked in his heart, which must mean he did not fancy discussing them. 'I know the boys quite well, but I've only met their mam once or twice. Still, no harm in asking.'

An hour later, they made their way back along the Scotland Road, but this time Toby was pushing an elderly bicycle for which he had paid the princely sum of 18/6d. Mrs Kray might not have reduced the price by so much as a penny, but by a great piece of good fortune her son, Jimmy, had come home whilst they

401

were examining the bicycle and had whistled expressively when he had heard the sum of thirty bob mentioned. 'Dammit, Mam, I only paid ten bob for it meself, and that were back in 1940,' he told her. 'Mind you, it's bleedin' difficult to lay hands on so much as a kiddy's tricycle these days. So I reckon eighteen and a tanner would be fair to both parties.'

Toby had paid over his money at once and Evie could see he was well pleased with his bargain. They walked home planning how Toby would strip the bike down, in the Wilmslows' back yard, next day, and put right all the things that were wrong with it. 'I'll need new brake locks, a new front tyre, front and rear lights, and one of those leather bags that you strap on to the back of the seat to keep a puncture outfit, a couple of spanners and my dinner in,' Toby planned. 'I wonder what it'll cost me to take it all the way back to my station? I only paid a quarter fare to get here and back, though I believe it should have been more, but railway chaps are good to each other. We're not exactly overpaid, and a friendly guard might look the other way when I put my bicycle into his van, which will save me a bob or two.'

When Evie returned from work next day, she told Toby that she would scarcely have known the bicycle. It had been rusty and dirty, the front tyre completely flat, the saddle worn down to the springs, but Toby had changed all that. He had bought a new saddle and a new front tyre and had worked away at the rust until the frame was as clean as a whistle. In fact, when he rode it round the yard, she told him it looked as good as a new machine and would doubtless repay his care with years of trouble-free cycling.

Toby laughed and dismounted and pushed the bicycle into the stockroom, through the narrow back door. 'Yes, it does look pretty good,' he admitted. 'In fact, I bought myself a chain and padlock, just in case someone else took a fancy to it. Now, Evie, the business part of my stay is over and we can have some fun. What would you like to do this evening?'

In the end, they decided to stay in and play cards, and Toby talked about his new job, the countryside in which it was situated, and his digs. He was unable to describe, fully, the wild beauty of the scenery and told Evie that she really must come up and visit him, though such a visit would have to be made in summer since she could only be accommodated in one of the neighbouring houses when their lodger was taking his annual holiday.

'But – won't I see you until then?' Evie said, rather helplessly. 'And what will you do if – if you get married, Toby? You can't have a wife living in one place whilst you live in another, you know.'

Toby grinned affectionately at her. 'Look, I'm going to be very frank with you, Evie. You think that Fee has fallen out of love with that handsome yeller-headed feller she married and will get a divorce, but myself, I don't see it. If she were free . . . well, I suppose that would be different . . . but she isn't. And even if she were free, that doesn't mean she'd want to dive straight into marriage with someone else. Come to that, it's been years since Fee and I were close and I'm not at all sure that I want to marry anyone, so give it a break, will you?'

'Well, no, I won't,' Evie said, rather aggressively. 'Just what *does* a signalman do when he wants to get married?'

Toby laughed. They were sitting side by side on the couch, with a small table before them upon which the cards were spread out. He put his arm round her shoulders and gave her a quick hug and then, to her astonishment, gave her a kiss on the cheek. 'They look for a cottage to rent, because a wife needs her own home, I suppose,' he said. 'And I expect they put in for a signal box in a less lonely part of the line where it's possible to get such accommodation. But why are you so interested, little Evie?'

'I'm interested in you because you're one of our oldest friends,' Evie said thoughtfully, aware that her cheeks were warming and might give her away. 'And I'm interested in the railway because I suppose it's a bit like the canal. Oh, I know a canal is far less complicated – no points, or signals, or anything of that nature, just bridges and locks and tunnels to be negotiated – but they are alike in a way, you know; they're both means of transporting goods from one place to another.'

Toby laughed again and rumpled her hair. 'Yes, I suppose you've got a point,' he said. 'Do you plan to go back on the canal one of these days, Evie? Not that it's much of a career for a clever kid like you.'

'Toby, I am not a kid,' Evie said, trying for dignity. 'I know I'm not as tall as either of my sisters, but I am eighteen, you know. A young lady, in fact, so don't go calling me a kid again or I'll give you a knuckle sandwich.'

Toby laughed, and squeezed her again before releasing her. 'Young lady or no, you're a right caution, Evie Todd,' he told her. 'And since I'm to be off early in the morning, we'd best get to bed.'

'Right,' Evie said. 'I'll be coming to the station with you tomorrow so I'll get up early and bring you a nice cup of tea to start your day off right.'

*　　　*　　　*

It was still dark when Toby and Evie reached Lime Street station, but there were quite a number of people about. The two of them went to the refreshment room and had tea and toast, and chatted until Toby's train pulled alongside the platform. The bicycle was chained up outside, so Toby unlocked it and the two of them made for the guard's van. They got the bicycle aboard and then Toby found himself a seat. It was a corridor train and he accompanied Evie back to the platform, glancing at the station clock. 'If your offices aren't open yet, you'd best go back to the refreshment room after you've seen me off and have another cup of tea and some more toast,' he advised. 'And don't forget to write often, because I love getting your letters, I really do. And there's a telephone box in the village, so I'll try and give you a ring a couple of times a month. And just you take care of yourself,' he added.

Evie was touched by his reference to her letters and agreed to go back to the refreshment room. She descended on to the platform since the guard was coming along slamming doors, and when he had passed Toby let the window down and leaned out. Then he caught her in his arms and kissed her soundly on the mouth. 'Thanks for a wonderful two days,' he said huskily. 'Oh, Evie, you're the nicest kid . . . I mean young lady . . . I've ever met. Take care of yourself, and remember, I'll be thinking of you. I really . . .'

But at this moment the guard blew his whistle and called to Evie to stand back, and the train began to move. Toby was shouting something but she couldn't hear what it was. Sighing, she stood on the platform and watched the train – and Toby's waving figure – until it dwindled from sight.

It was not until she was seated in the refreshment

room, telling herself that his kiss had meant nothing, had been merely that of a friend who had enjoyed a little holiday with her, that she guiltily acknowledged that her own feelings for Toby were no longer merely friendship. She had hero-worshipped him when she was a little girl, and now that she was older she had been and gone and fallen in love with him. Of course, he was Seraphina's young man and her sister was so beautiful that she, Evie, stood no chance, but that no longer mattered. She would love Toby until her dying day, whether he married her sister or someone else, and she found a certain relief in acknowledging it.

'Your order, miss.' The plump lady in the crisp white overall, standing beside the table with a plate of hot buttered toast, beamed at Evie as she stared blankly up at her. 'Seein' your sweetheart off, was you? Ah well, the war's over now, so I dare say you'll be seeing him again quite soon.'

Evie took the toast but shook her head. 'He's not my sweetheart,' she said, her voice very low. 'He's – he's just a friend.'

The woman smiled knowingly. 'The way he hung on to you and kissed you when the train was starting to draw out looked more like a sweetheart than a pal,' she observed. 'Enjoy your toast.'

Toby continued to lean out of the window and wave until the little figure was out of sight. He realised he had nearly made a great fool of himself, nearly told her how important she had become to him. He had kissed her on impulse and for a moment had imagined that her lips had clung to his, that she had begun to melt in his arms, but that had been wishful thinking, of course. Every morning, he looked into his shaving mirror and saw the great livid scar which disfigured

406

his thin, hollow-eyed face, and knew that no woman, not even loving little Evie Todd, could want to wake up each morning to find such a face on the pillow beside her.

When he had first returned to England, he had realised, with astonishment, that the love which he had imagined he felt for Seraphina had simply disappeared. He should have known it ages before, of course, during his years of captivity, when he had found himself unable to envisage her face, unable to see in his imagination the beauty which he knew existed. He had tried hard enough, goodness knows. He had conjured up rich corn-coloured hair, milky skin, eyes blue as sapphires and a rosy, kissable mouth, yet when he had tried to put them all together . . . well, he just couldn't, that was all.

On the other hand, Evie's small, brown, unremarkable face had never been far from his mind and he had dreamed of her often. Of course, he had thought of her as a child, but now, home again once more and meeting her on equal terms, he knew that she was a young woman, and a delightful, desirable one at that. But not for him. No, not for him. He was years older than her, scarred, disillusioned, and still without any real ambition. No, he wasn't a good subject for marriage, not with anyone. He knew, now, that Seraphina had never had any strong feelings for him, save those of friendship, and that he had never truly loved her, either. If he had done so, they would not have fallen out in the first place, for what sort of man did not write letters to the girl he was supposed to love?

Sitting there in the stuffy railway carriage, he thought about the sisters. They were grand girls, all three of them, and he was sure that Evie would marry, as Angela and Seraphina had done. He knew, of course, that Seraphina was awaiting a divorce, but he knew, too, that she would marry again. As for Evie, he supposed she would give in to the blandishments of Percy Baldwin, and even as the thought entered his head he found himself wanting to punch Percy on the nose, grab him by the collar and chuck him into the Mersey, do anything but let him marry Evie.

Startled at the violence of his own feelings, he reminded himself that he had no chance in that direction, no chance at all. She was too young, too lively, too sought after. He leaned back in his seat and turned his thoughts to the work he was about to start. Marriage was for other men; men not scarred either physically or mentally by a long and brutal war. Determinedly, Toby began to think about signals, points, semaphore and similar matters.

When Seraphina had written to say she would be coming home for Christmas and would be bringing a pal, Martha had concluded, understandably she felt, that the pal would be a fellow teacher, someone at the same school as her daughter. She had written back immediately, of course, reminding Seraphina that they had no spare room and that she, her friend and Evie would have to have camp beds in the stockroom because at Christmas it would be far too complicated to have them sleeping in the living room.

That had been earlier in December and Seraphina had rung the very next day to assure her mother that her pal would not expect to be put up in the Wilmslows' flat but had already booked a room in a small guesthouse not far from the Scottie.

Martha had been relieved, and grateful, but then the pips had gone and somehow she had never got round to any further discussion of Seraphina's friend.

So when, on 23 December, the door had opened and Seraphina had entered the shop Martha had not, at first, realised that the extraordinarily plain young man who had followed Seraphina inside was the 'pal' her daughter had mentioned. The shop was crowded with women getting their rations in before Christmas, and Seraphina had to push her way between them, apologising as she did so. She reached the counter and she and her mother hugged briefly across its width. Then Seraphina turned and grabbed the sleeve of the plain young man in air force uniform. 'Ma, this is Eddie Harding, the friend I told you about,' she said, rather breathlessly. 'We stopped off at the guesthouse and left his case there and I thought we'd buy fish and chips for everyone's supper tonight, unless you've got something planned? But right now we're gasping for a cup of tea; is it all right if I go up and make one for us and bring a couple of cups down for you and Uncle Arthur?'

Martha was so busy staring at Eddie Harding that there was an appreciable pause before she answered. 'Yes, of course it's all right . . . and Arthur and I could just do with a cuppa,' she gabbled. 'How d'you do, Mr Harding? Oh, I'm so sorry, you'll think I'm most dreadfully rude, but Seraphina never told us . . . I mean, I thought you'd be arriving much later . . . and I didn't realise you were – you were such an old friend . . . I mean, she didn't say she'd known you during the war . . .'

The young man was grinning and blushing, holding out his hand and then dropping it back to his side as he realised Martha could not possibly reach him from where she stood. 'It's all right, Mrs Wilmslow,' he said, in a deep and pleasant voice. 'I guess there are quite a lot of things Fee hasn't liked to mention, which is why I'm here now. But I can see you're extremely busy so we'd best leave explanations until the shop is closed.' He had taken his cap off when he had entered the shop but now he stuck it on the back of his head in order to pick up Seraphina's suitcase and have a hand free to put into the crook of her arm. 'Is it all right if we go up to your flat now?'

'Of course, of course,' Martha said quickly. She glanced across to where Arthur was diligently taking down an order and putting the required items into a box as he did so. 'I'd introduce you to my husband, but as you can see we're rushed off our feet at present. Mrs Bunwell, who helps out as a rule, has gone off to do some Christmas shopping of her own, so we're rather short-handed.'

'Oh, it's all right, Ma, we understand,' Seraphina said, rather impatiently. 'Can we go through this way? Only it's so much quicker than traipsing right down the Scottie until we reach the jigger and then having to come all the way back again just to reach the rear door.'

'Yes, of course you can,' Martha said, and watched her daughter's back disappear with something very like relief. She glanced across at Arthur and saw he was looking as surprised as she felt, then chided herself for her foolishness. She should have guessed that her beautiful, lively daughter would have men buzzing round her like bees round a honeypot. A happy and successful marriage would have put a stop to that sort of thing, but she had known for a long time that Seraphina's marriage was neither happy nor successful. In the circumstances, it was not surprising that Seraphina had acquired a boyfriend. Now, with her divorce looming, she must be considering remarriage and, being a dutiful daughter, wanted her mother, and the rest of the family, to meet the young man concerned.

'Thank you, Mrs Buxton, and if you don't come in before, have a lovely Christmas,' Martha said as her customer picked up her stout American cloth bag and turned to leave the shop. 'Yes, Mrs Higgins, what can I do for you?'

Christmas had been a success, Martha decided, as she saw her daughter and Eddie off at the end of their week's stay. Everyone liked Eddie and it had been nice to see Seraphina happy and relaxed. The couple had made no secret of their affection for one another, though Seraphina had explained to Martha that she and Eddie did not mean their friendship to stand in the way of her obtaining her divorce. 'But it won't be long now, it's just a matter of formalities really,' she had said jubilantly. 'Then I shall give my school a term's notice, which is only fair, and after that we mean to have a quiet wedding.'

'It's a wicked shame that it can't be solemnized in church,' Martha had said, rather wistfully. 'But of course that's impossible.' She smiled at her daughter. 'Poor Fee, the war ruined your chance of a white wedding the first time round, and your previous marriage has spoiled your chance this time.'

Seraphina had beamed at her mother. 'I don't care if we marry in sackcloth and ashes, so long as we can be together,' she admitted. 'I'd love little Evie to be a bridesmaid, but so long as she comes to the wedding . . .'

Martha's eyebrows had risen almost into her hair. 'Of course she'll come to the wedding, as will anyone else from round here that you invite,' she said. 'What made you sound so doubtful?'

Seraphina had smiled. 'My little sister thinks I ought to marry Toby; can't imagine anyone not being in love with him,' she explained. 'It's odd, because she really likes Eddie, she told me so, yet when I said that we were getting married she muttered something about not making up my mind too quickly and it's being unfair not to give Toby a chance. Still, she'll grow up one of these days and realise there's more to love than long acquaintance.'

Now, having watched the young couple out of sight, Martha turned back into the shop. It was always quiet after Christmas. Arthur was restocking the shelves and Mrs Bunwell was mopping the floor, wielding the mop with great vigour in order, Martha suspected, to keep herself warm, for it was bitterly cold and the tiny paraffin stove, which was the only form of heating in the shop, could not combat the chill.

Arthur looked up as Martha came behind the counter. 'We'll close and go up and have a decent hot meal since there's few customers around,' he remarked. 'It'll be a bit warmer up there, though not a lot. Everyone's complainin' that there's norrenough coal to go round but we can huddle over the fire and hot up some soup.' He smiled lovingly at his wife. 'You make the best vegetable soup in Liverpool, Mrs Wilmslow.'

'And the best potato pie,' Martha said, grinning at Mrs Bunwell. 'And if I could get my hands on some decent ingredients . . .'

Mrs Bunwell hurried across the shop and put up the 'Closed' sign, shooting the top bolt across as she did so. 'Do you want me this afternoon?' she asked. 'Only it's that quiet and I could do wi' an afternoon in me own home.'

Martha went into the stockroom and fetched Mrs Bunwell's hat, coat and thick woollen muffler, carrying them across to the old woman as Arthur said: 'You're right, Mrs B., there's no work for two of us, lerralone three. You go off now and we'll see you Sat'day.'

Martha helped Mrs Bunwell into her coat, then unbolted the door for the other woman to slip through. After that, she rebolted it and she and Arthur made their way up to the flat. It had been some time since they had been able to keep the stove burning all day and the kitchen seemed cold and unwelcoming, but Martha balanced the pan of soup on the Primus stove, pumped it up and lit it, and very soon the delicious smell of the vegetables and the flickering of the flame gave the room at least the illusion of warmth and cheerfulness.

Martha cut each of them a thick slice off the loaf and when the soup was simmering, poured it into two bowls. She turned down the Primus but left it on for a little warmth. Then she sat down, opposite her husband, and began to eat.

'This is grand,' Arthur said contentedly, spooning his portion. He cocked an eyebrow at her. 'I always make meself scarce when you and Seraphina are having a heart to heart, but I reckon you won't think I'm poking me nose in if I says I like young Eddie and I'm glad they're intendin' to get wed.'

Martha leaned across the table and gave the hand not engaged with the soup spoon a squeeze. 'You are a dear, Arthur Wilmslow. I agree that they're doing the right thing,' she said. 'As soon as Seraphina's divorce comes through, they'll name the day. And if they're half as happy as you and I, they'll be very happy indeed,' she ended.

Opposite her, Mr Wilmslow ducked his head and

she saw that his eyes had filled with tears. 'That's the nicest thing you could have said to me, old lady,' he said huskily. 'You mean all the world to me, Martha Wilmslow . . . and your cooking ain't bad, either. Here, you make the tea while I wash the crocks.'

Chapter Fifteen
February 1947

Toby woke when his alarm went off and reached out a groping hand, hastily, to turn it off, then cuddled even further down the bed for five delicious minutes. He always tried to turn the alarm off promptly since the fragile walls of his tiny bedroom meant that Mrs Wetherspoon could easily be woken when she had no need to rouse herself. At present, he and his mate were doing twelve-hour shifts, seven days a week, because the weather was so severe that their relief had not managed to get through. Toby leaned up on one elbow and peered out through the darkened pane. It was snowing again; the flakes whirled thickly and Toby, sighing, swung his legs out of bed, wincing as his warm feet met the cold boards. He knew he ought to have a thorough wash but, predictably, the water in his ewer was frozen solid, so he just scrambled into his uniform, adding an enormous thick jersey which Martha and Evie between them had knitted him for Christmas, and made for the stairs. Stumbling down, he fished out his heavy gunmetal watch and checked the time. In this sort of weather, a bicycle was not much use. Instead, this morning he intended to walk, carrying a big coal shovel with him in case he had to fight his way through drifts, and that meant that in order to reach the signal box to relieve Tom at eight o'clock, he needed to leave the house at six. Since it was now half-past five, he would have time to boil the kettle, cut himself a thick slice of bread and marge, and maybe even do a carry-out. This task was usually performed by Mrs Wetherspoon, but because he was leaving home an hour earlier he imagined he would have to do for himself this morning. Halfway down the stairs, he knew he was mistaken. Warmth crept towards him and the good smell of cooking, and when he reached the kitchen Mrs Wetherspoon greeted him with a beaming smile, a large plateful of scrambled eggs on toast and an enamel mug of steaming tea.

'Gosh,' Toby said inadequately. 'You are good, Mrs Wetherspoon, but you needn't have got up. I'd have managed.'

His landlady shook her head wisely. 'Thy stomach'll need a good lining on a day like this,' she observed. 'An' what's more, I've packed up all the food I can spare 'cos I reckon if thou reaches that box, tha'll be stuck there until the blizzard eases. I've lived here all me life but I've never known a winter like this one, an' I'm sure the wind's set in for a day or two. Now stop argufying and get outside o' this little lot.'

Toby sat down, only too glad to obey, though his eyes opened a little when he saw the box of provisions she expected him to take. 'I can't deprive you, Mrs Wetherspoon,' he said reproachfully. 'If you really think it's going to snow me in, then it'll likely do the same to you. Just put a loaf, a tin of corned beef, some baked beans and a screw of tea and sugar in a bag and that'll do me fine.'

Mrs Wetherspoon, however, shook her head firmly. 'Nay, lad, there's nowt in that box that I can't manage very well wi'out. We're not like the rest of the country; up here int fells we're used to this sort of weather most winters, but, like I said, not normally this bad. They've rationed spuds to two pounds a head in some cities, cut the meat ration to a bob, and they say they'll likely cut bread ration an' all. An' there's no fish 'cos o' the weather, an' precious few vegetables, I guess. But here in the country we grow our own spuds – I've a hundredweight sack in the shed, to say nothing of a big pile of carrots, swedes and turnips. I gleaned a sack of grain when harvest was over, so me hens are still laying, though not as good as in the summertime, and though the Ministry would have me shot at dawn if they knew, I've still the best part of a haunch of salt pork stowed away in me cellar, so I'll not be short of meat for a few weeks yet.'

'Well, if you're sure . . .' Toby mumbled, finishing his breakfast and standing down his empty mug. He got to his feet, and taking down his coat began to struggle into it. His peaked cap would soon have been whirled away by the wind, but the woolly hat Evie had knitted – which looked remarkably like a tea cosy to him – could be pulled right down over his ears and could not possibly blow away. Then he wrapped his big muffler twice round his neck and put on his marvellously warm sheepskin mittens. He was already wearing two pairs of thick socks and stepped into his wellingtons, hating the chill of them but knowing they were a deal more suitable in this sort of weather than his regulation boots.

'I guess I'm ready now, Mrs Wetherspoon,' he said cheerfully, pulling open the back door and gasping as icy wind and snow swept into the room.

The shovel was almost three feet deep in snow, but he pulled it out of the drift, tucked it under his arm, and pulled the door to whilst he reached for the box of food. Mrs Wetherspoon lifted it, then eyed him doubtfully. 'I don't know . . .' she was beginning, and then her face cleared. 'Hold still a moment,' she said, and presently reappeared with an old canvas rucksack. She tipped the contents of the box unceremoniously into the pack, then helped Toby to loop it over his shoulders. 'Happen that'll be easier for thee,' she said, as Toby opened the kitchen door once more. 'Go careful now,' she urged him, 'and God speed.'

Despite his best efforts, it took Toby almost three hours to reach the signal box. Half the time he was walking along ways he had once known well which now were only marked out by the tops of the high hedges. He had to dig his way through half a dozen drifts but at least the digging warmed him up for a short while, though he thought, dismally, that his feet might have belonged to someone else altogether, and his fingertips and the end of his nose ached with the cold.

As he got within sight of the signal box, which was perched on an embankment, the blizzard eased and he saw the small figure of Tom, booted and coated, coming to meet him. Tom was a man in his early forties, friendly and easy-going, but now his face was creased in a worried frown. 'I saw you coming like a little black beetle in the snow,' he said, as soon as greetings had been exchanged. 'There's no trains come through since yesterday evening, and I'm keen to be off 'cos when I left home last night Susan – she's me youngest – had croup and my Mary were fair worried out of her life. Whether I'll get home or not, I can't say, but you got through, so why not me?'

'You live further off,' Toby reminded him. He stuck his shovel into the snow and slid the rucksack off his back. Delving around in it he found a Mars bar which Mrs Wetherspoon had popped in at the last moment and handed it to the other man. 'Here, take this. Mrs Wetherspoon gave me enough food for a week, I should think, so I shan't miss it. See you tonight, Tom!'

The two men went their separate ways and Toby, climbing the steps to the signal box, saw that the line was deep in snow and wondered how long it would be before a snow plough came through. One thing was certain: he need not worry about the signals, or anything of that nature. No engine could possibly get through in either direction until the line had been cleared.

He opened the door and let himself into the box and was immediately surrounded by delicious warmth, for the ubiquitous Russell stove burned brightly, keeping the windows clear of snow, and enabling him to see a good way down the line in either direction. Not that it would do him much good, not whilst the road remained snowbound.

Toby stood down the rucksack and began to take off his outer garments. He and Tom had rigged up a line so that they might dry wet clothing and he pegged out his clothes, then turned his attention to the big water container, checking that there was enough water left to make a journey to the nearby stream unnecessary. To his relief, the container was nearly full and he was pleased to see that Tom must have spent a good while fetching in coal from the nearby dump, for there was fuel enough to last several days, if they were careful.

Toby glanced around him. The signal lamps stood on their bench, filled and cleaned, ready for action when the snow cleared and night came. Everything else was as it should be, and when he lifted the small tin kettle that, too, had been filled, so he only had to perch it on the stove to start preparations for a cup of tea.

As the warmth gradually seeped through him, Toby's fingers began to ache and the chilblains on his wrists to itch and burn, but this was a pain he knew would pass. He fished out the bottle of milk Mrs Wetherspoon had provided, poured some into his enamel mug, and then stood the bottle outside, in a box they kept for that purpose. Who needed a refrigerator when the snow would do the job for nothing?

Presently, sipping a mug of tea, he got out the big exercise book in which they wrote down anything of moment which happened. Later, when he had nothing much to do, he would consult this book when writing his letters. He filled in the date and the fact that it had taken him three hours to reach the box through the blizzard, then decided he would write to Evie. She had enjoyed his letters and he had told her he loved getting hers, which were always full of news and gossip, though God knew when this one would get through in these conditions. Still, he would ask his landlady to post it when he returned to the village tonight. He supposed, glumly, that Tom would not make it back before nine o'clock at the earliest, so if you added another three hours for Toby's own homeward journey, that would make it . . . gracious, well after midnight before he reached his lodgings. He had a key, of course, so would not have to wake Mrs Wetherspoon, but the whole idea was daft because he would have to be up again and on his way only four or five hours later. Tom would realise this, of course, so Toby decided he might as well make up his mind he would be working a double shift. Not that it was work, exactly, for no one had appeared to clear the line, but you never knew. By morning, a freak wind might have carried the blizzard elsewhere, enabling a train with a snow plough before it to come chugging up from Settle or Carlisle.

At two o'clock, Toby made himself a jam sandwich and ate an apple. At seven o'clock, he had mashed potato and corned beef with HP Sauce sprinkled all over it and at midnight, having waited in vain for a sign of Tom's approach, he pulled his chair up close to the stove, rolled his muffler into a small pillow, draped himself in his heavy overcoat, and went off to sleep, tired as much by boredom as by the small activities in which he had engaged.

Martha, Arthur and Evie were sitting round the table, eating potato pie and cabbage by candlelight, when somebody rattled the back door. They were all in their overcoats, hats and gloves, because they had so little coal left that they dared not light the stove, and the electricity cuts, which seemed to come at the most inconvenient times, meant that one was reliant upon candles indoors and an electric torch without – if you could get hold of the batteries, that was.

Evie got to her feet, but before she could reach the door it burst open and a tall figure, muffled to the eyebrows in coat, scarf and woolly hat, came running up the stairs talking all the while. 'Ma, Evie, Uncle Arthur! My divorce is through and they've closed my school because the boiler burst, so I've got a week off . . . well, probably more than a week because the plumber said he couldn't do anything about mending the boiler until the thaw sets in, and that could be a month or more away. And wouldn't you know it? My darling Ed has been told to stay in Egypt because he wouldn't be able to land back on his airfield anyway. So I thought I'd come and see you all, and give you the good news.' Seraphina had been smiling, but suddenly the smile disappeared to be replaced by a look of puzzlement. 'Oh, I'm awfully sorry. Are you just off out somewhere? And why the candles? Gosh, it's cold in here.'

Martha got to her feet, shaking her head indulgently as she hugged her eldest daughter. 'Darling Fee, it's lovely to see you and I'm so glad you've got your divorce. But you must know that the electricity situation is desperate, so the government keeps cutting off supplies. And don't tell me you've got tons and tons of coal down in Devon because we've got none at all, so we can't have a fire.'

'We're not on mains electricity, remember,' Seraphina said, rather smugly. 'We have oil lamps all the time and my landlady has got woodburning stoves, one in the kitchen and one in the living room. All the lodgers – there are four of us – spend a good while at weekends collecting wood. The men saw up fallen trees and us girls forage for branches and twigs, so we're not too badly off. You poor things!'

'Oh, we do all right, by and large,' Evie said defensively. 'And anyway, the winter can't last for ever, can it? The thing is, they've cut everyone's hours at the office – we're all working a four-day week – and a lot of our schools are closed, too. So there's a good deal of chaos about.'

'Yes, it has been awful; I do read the papers,' Seraphina said. 'In a way, I'm glad Eddie's out of it, lucky beggar, only I get lonely, knowing he's so far away. And though I know he'll be warmer than we are, he might be in awful danger. But I write to him every week and he writes back, so at least we're in regular touch.'

'What about Toby? Don't you ever write to him?' Evie said, rather reproachfully. 'He's stuck up in a signal box, somewhere in the fells, and I heard on the wireless that the snow's so deep there, whole villages are cut off. Why, they're having to send supplies in by aeroplane . . . even hay for the horses and the sheep, because of course they can't get at the grass, not through all that snow.'

'Oh? I didn't know Toby ate grass,' Seraphina said flippantly. 'He'll be all right. What's a bit of snow when you're snug inside a signal box? It isn't as though he were actually working on the line, like a plate layer, and besides, he came out of Burma all right, didn't he? I shouldn't worry myself about him, if I were you.'

Evie took a deep breath, feeling fury well up inside her. 'You don't know anything about him, Seraphina Todd,' she said furiously. 'You've never even seen him since he's come home, because you couldn't be bothered to change your leave that first Christmas. And that's why you don't know that his face was cut open by one of the Jap guards, or how horribly thin he was—'

'What have I said?' Seraphina cut in, looking injured. 'Toby was my friend when we were both kids. The only reason he was friendlier with me than with the rest of you is because we were the same age. Now, so far as I'm concerned, he's a part of my past like Bertie from the *April Lady*, or Clem Gilligan from the *Liverpool Rose*.' She turned and glared at Evie. 'Do you write to Clem and Lizzie? Do you exchange postcards with Bertie? I bet you don't, so how dare you criticise me for not running round after Toby?'

'You know very well that Toby was in love with you and still is, despite your horrid ways,' Evie shouted. 'You and your Eddie had a pretty soft sort of war but Toby had an appalling time, worse than you could possibly imagine. He was starved, tortured, made to work like a slave, even when he was ill. Just think about that, Seraphina Todd, before you make up your mind to marry that Eddie!'

'I am *not* Seraphina Todd, I'm Seraphina Truelove, and if Toby is fool enough to be in love with someone he's not seen for years, then that's his business.' Seraphina's cheeks were scarlet. 'And if he told you how he was treated by the Japs, then he had no right to do so. If you ask me, you take up the cudgels too quickly on his behalf.' She grabbed Evie by the shoulders and stared very hard into her sister's flushed and furious face. 'Why, I do believe you're in love with him yourself!'

'I'm not, and he never told me anything. I heard it from other people,' Evie screamed wildly. 'As for being a Truelove . . . don't make me laugh! The only person you truly love, Seraphina, is yourself!'

'Girls, girls . . .' Arthur Wilmslow said, rising to his feet. He turned to his wife. 'Whatever brought this on? Do stop them, my dear, before—'

'Evie! Seraphina! Behave yourselves . . .' Martha began, but it was already too late. Seraphina had slapped Evie hard across the face and was endeavouring to shake her, holding tight to both shoulders again, whilst Evie's small, booted feet clunked relentlessly into her sister's shins. Martha ran round the table just as Arthur did, and seized Evie whilst Arthur grabbed hold of Seraphina. They managed to separate the two, though not before each had inflicted damage on the other. Seraphina's golden hair, which had been caught up in a shining bun on the back of her head, had come loose and Evie's right cheek was scarlet, whilst her left was paper white.

'You're a horrible, horrible girl, Fee, and it will serve you right if beastly Eddie treats you the way your first husband did,' Evie raged. 'I hate you, I hate you!' She was still furious and, but for Martha's grip on her, would have returned to the attack once more, but it seemed that her elder sister was beginning to calm down. She had shaken herself free from Arthur's grip and now approached Evie, albeit cautiously.

'I don't know what started all this, but I'm truly sorry I slapped your face. It was a horrid, unladylike thing to do,' she said remorsefully. 'And I'm sorry if anything I said hurt your feelings, because I'm sure I didn't mean to. But it's not wrong to love someone, you know. You were always fond of Toby; you were the one who stayed with him all night when he came back from Dunkirk. And you were the one who wrote and wrote and went on writing, even when he couldn't send so much as a line in reply because he was a POW of those wicked Japs.' She leaned over and very gently kissed the cheek upon which her finger marks showed in long scarlet weals. 'Please forgive me, darling little Evie.'

There was a long, doubtful silence, then Evie carefully disengaged herself from Martha's grip and patted her sister's hand. 'It's all right; I think we were both a bit mad,' she said gruffly. 'But . . . do you truly mean that Toby has no chance with you? Not even if he were to come here, some time in the next week, and tell you he loves you and wants to marry you? Because I'm sure he does,' she ended, with more than a trace of defiance.

Seraphina sat down on one of the kitchen chairs and shook her head. 'No, I'm afraid there's no one for me but Eddie,' she assured her sister. 'And the chances of Toby getting back here are pretty slight, you know. The railways are in complete chaos because of the terrible weather; it's taken me twenty-six hours to get here from Devon, so I can't see Toby, who is even further north, making it in under a week. But never mind that, darling Evie. Let's talk about weddings. I'd love you to be my bridesmaid, and Eddie's managed to get hold of a length of parachute silk which we'll have made up for you, just as soon as you give me the word. It's white, of course, but it can be dyed cream, or blue, or pink, if you would prefer that. Do say you will.'

Evie had gone over to the teapot which stood on the draining board and was pouring her sister a cup of tea; now she looked across at her and smiled a trifle tremulously. 'If anyone wears parachute silk, it should be the bride,' she pointed out. 'But don't let's discuss it now; after all, you can't marry anyone just yet.'

Next morning, Evie was up bright and early, when it was still dark. She had had a restless night for her mind kept worrying at the necessity to get a message to Toby, to reach him somehow. Yet if Seraphina was speaking the truth – and she had never known her sister to lie – there was no point in telling Toby that Seraphina was now free. It would be like offering a child a bar of chocolate and then snatching it away. In her own mind, however, it was important that Toby should know how things stood, perhaps even important that he should know Seraphina was now beyond his reach.

When she heard her mother stealing towards the kitchen, she slid out of bed, grabbed her clothes from the chair upon which she had tossed them the previous night, and hastened in the same direction. Martha looked round, surprised to find that anyone was up beside herself. 'Evie! Do you know what the time is? You don't need to get up for another half hour at least . . . I was going to make a pot of tea and take everyone a cup. Is Fee still asleep?'

'Yes, and snoring,' Evie said. To her own surprise, she found that all her doubts had somehow resolved themselves in the brief period of sleep she had enjoyed before being awoken by her mother's stirring. 'I told you last night that I wasn't needed in the office for the next couple of days, didn't I? Well, I hope you don't mind, Ma, but I'm going to try to reach that Gawdale place where Toby lodges. I need to speak to him, to tell him that Fee and Eddie are going to get married.'

Martha, setting out cups on the table, turned round, astonished eyes on her daughter. 'But Evie, love, you heard what Fee said last night; the railways are in chaos and you must know from listening to the news on the wireless that the roads are the same. You could try sending a telegram but you can't possibly go yourself. Truly, love, I simply can't allow it. It won't help anyone if your body is found frozen stiff and dead as a door-nail by the side of some country road.'

'I'll try sending a telegram first,' Evie said. 'But if there's no chance of a telegram getting through then I must at least try. But I promise you, I won't take unnecessary risks, and I'll keep in touch. I know a lot of telephone wires are down but there are bound to be some still working, so if I can I'll ring you each evening.'

'Evie, you're eighteen years old, which is still a child in the eyes of the law,' Martha said, with what firmness she could muster. 'I forbid you to risk your life on a wild goose chase. Go to the telegraph office by all means; go down to Lime Street and ask the station-master if he can get a message through to a signal box on the LMS line. And then come home. Is that clear?'

'Yes, Ma; I'll do as you say,' Evie said humbly. And presently, well wrapped up in every warm garment she possessed, she slid out of the house. Following instructions, she went to the telegraph office first but to no avail, so she trudged to the station. There were some trains still running but the station staff offered little hope of her reaching such a wild and desolate desti-nation as Gawdale. By now, however, Evie was grimly determined. She went to the Post Office and drew out all her savings, then returned to the station where she bought sandwiches and some suspicious-looking rock cakes from the refreshment room. Then she boarded a train heading north. It was crowded with worried people, all discussing the fearful weather, all anxious to reach their destinations yet doubtful of doing so. Evie, always at ease with her fellow men, was soon on good terms with everyone else in the carriage. She settled back in her corner seat and wondered how many hours would pass before she had to leave the train and take to the road, in the hope of a lift of some description. She knew that the army had been mobilised to try to get supplies through to stricken villages and decided that, if the worst came to the worst, she would act like the page in Good King Wenceslas and dog the army's footsteps. Of course, this would only work if they were heading for Gawdale, but there was no point in meeting trouble halfway. Evie closed her eyes and presently drifted into an uneasy sleep.

Toby had not been surprised when Tom had not turned up that first night, and when he looked out of the signal box at the conditions raging outside he was not surprised when no one appeared on the second day, either, nor had he been particularly worried. He had plenty of coal to keep the Russell stove alight, enough food for the time being, if he was careful, and a pile of books to keep him amused, as well as the letter he was writing to Evie, adding a little bit each day.

On the morning of the third day, he decided that he would try to fight his way through to the nearest stream because he needed water. Melting snow was a slow and tedious business, but he would take an axe and cut himself a big square of ice since the stream was bound to be frozen. Accordingly, he set off, the axe under one arm and the rucksack slung over his shoulder, for he did not intend to touch the ice more than he had to, but would put it straight into the rucksack. During the night, the blizzard had eased and finally stopped, and the morning was brilliant. To be sure, the wind still gusted, whirling snow off the heavily laden trees to make miniature blizzards of its own, but the pale sun cheered him and gave great beauty to the vast white snowscape of the fells and valleys. The sunshine was golden, the shadows blue, and once he climbed down from the signal box Toby spent a moment or two just staring. Then he began to struggle towards the stream. He reached it after an hour's hard clambering, hacked out a big block of ice, then had to split it into three pieces to get it into the rucksack before turning for home. He was halfway back to the box when he had a piece of luck. He saw something half buried in the snow beside the tracks he had made on the way out and was now following back, and on digging it out found it was a rabbit, dead and frozen stiff, but still in reasonably good condition. Toby jammed it into the pocket of his heavy coat; rabbit stew would make a delicious change from his diet of corned beef and baked beans.

As he climbed the steps which led into his signal box he realised that the trip down to the stream had done him a great deal of good. To be sure, he had been very snug inside the box, but he had not realised how lethargic he had become. Now he felt awake and tinglingly alive and his limbs rejoiced in the work he was giving them; quite reluctant, it seemed, to return to the sedentary life they had enjoyed for the past few days. However, there was work to be done in the box. Toby cast one last regretful look at the beauty of the scenery around him, noticing that the cutting was completely filled in so that the land looked flat, then heaved his bag of ice into the warmth, hastily tipping it into the big tin jug and setting this close to the stove. Presently, he would decant some into a pan, put the pan on the stove and when the water was good and hot have a strip-down wash. But he must skin and joint the rabbit for the pot first, since that was mucky work.

Mucky work it certainly was, but it got easier as the rabbit thawed out and soon he was able to pour off some hot water to wash in and slip the rabbit joints into the remainder. He had already prepared carrots, turnips and potatoes, thinking to make a vegetable stew – or blind scouse as Liverpudlians called it – so he tipped the vegetables in with the meat, replaced the pan lid and pulled it over the flame once more. Then he turned back to the tin bowl, got out the soap and a towel, and began to remove his clothing. Clad only in underpants and vest, he washed briskly, his eyes still on the scene outside the windows, though he had to rub himself a little porthole in the steamy pane in order to see out.

It had been bitterly cold outside, but it was almost too warm within so he padded around the box in his underwear, setting things in order, and thinking how grand it would be if rescue came soon so that they might share the rabbit stew. A solitary life was all very well, but he realised he was beginning to feel lonely. However, he knew that whilst the permanent way was impassable the LMS would be losing money, so the bosses would attach a snow plough to a locomotive and get the gangs out on the road just as soon as they thought it safe to do so.

On the stove, the stew began to bubble and Toby pulled the pan to one side, since he knew rabbit stew should simmer and not boil briskly. Then he opened the door and tossed his washing water out into the snow. As he did so, he realised that the wind had changed direction. It was no longer the dreaded 'helm', as the locals called it, but a warmer wind out of the west, bringing the promise that spring – and a thaw – was on its way.

But it was still cold, so Toby closed the door once more. Though the snow now had a glistening crust, he knew it would take more than a bit of sunshine and a change of wind direction to thaw this lot out. Snow ploughs and gangs of plate layers, plus any casual labour the bosses could get their hands on, would be needed, for Toby knew from what others had told him that not even the strongest snow plough could get through a blocked tunnel; that needed a gang of determined men to get it clear. A snow plough, after all, pushes the snow to left and right, and in a tunnel this is simply not possible.

Toby glanced towards where he knew the tunnel lay, then up the track whence help would come. He was about to turn back to his stew when a movement caught his eye. Someone was coming! In the far distance, trudging along the snow-covered permanent way, was a tiny black figure. Tom? No, he would not come from that direction. One of the inspectors then? But that did not seem likely. Another hard stare convinced Toby that it was not the ganger, being nowhere near big enough. But it might be one of his men, trekking ahead of the gang, sent forward to tell Toby to put the kettle on, since the plate layers would need a mug of something hot when they stopped for a breather.

Toby looked, consideringly, at his stew, then filled the large blackened kettle and stood it beside the pan on the stove. After all, the man walking along the line might or might not be the precursor of a larger group; if he was not, then he was welcome to share the rabbit stew, but such a stew needed a couple of hours' cooking at least, and his visitor would probably appreciate a cup of tea while he waited.

Toby went back to the window; the small figure was nearer and he suddenly remembered his state of undress and went cold all over. Some chance he would have of promotion if an inspector found him in vest and pants, more intent upon his forthcoming dinner than upon his work. Hastily, he scrambled into his uniform, got out the old tea towel he used as a cleaning cloth, and began to wipe the steam off the windows. Then he opened the little side lights, knowing that this would keep the panes at least partly clear, and checked, for the hundredth time, that the lamps were filled and ready for evening, that his timesheet was completed correctly, and that the steps leading up to the door of the box were clear of snow and ice. Then he returned to his vantage point. The figure was closer now, but still completely unrecognisable. It could, Toby told himself, be almost anyone: man, woman or child, or even a visitor from another planet. It also occurred to him, rather belatedly, that the figure might not be heading for the signal box at all but might merely be using the permanent way as a means of getting between the villages on either side.

Toby decided that he would call out to the chap as soon as he got within hailing distance. He went to the door, opened it, and leaned out, then realised there was no need; the figure had changed direction and was heading straight for the signal box. Toby held the door a little open, eyeing the muffled figure with consider-able puzzlement. If this was a railwayman, it was the smallest one Toby had ever met. He opened the door a little wider, began to speak, and then stopped short as the figure pulled a muffling scarf away from its face and grinned up at him.

Toby gasped; he would have known that grin anywhere, and those big brown eyes. 'Evie!' he said, and heard his own voice rough with surprise and emotion. 'Oh, Evie, you little devil! How in God's name have you got here? There've been no trains for days, nor buses, not even a tractor. How . . . ?'

But then his arms were round her and he was pulling her into the box, slamming the door shut behind him, unravelling scarves, removing her soft woollen hat, and in an excess of love and relief kissing her wide brow, her small straight nose, her pointed chin.

Her reaction was surprising. 'Stop it, Toby,' she said pleadingly. 'I've come a long way to give you . . . oh, dear . . . to give you bad news. It's all been my fault; I let you believe what I believed, only it wasn't true. And what does it matter how I got here?' she added. 'I'm here, and you've got to listen to me.'

Toby stepped back, feeling as though she had slapped his face. He had known all along that she could not love him, but even so, her rejection hurt. To cover his emotion, he began to help her out of her coat and to push her gently towards the stove. 'I'm sorry, Evie,' he said humbly. 'I didn't mean – I know you couldn't possibly . . . but what's this bad news you have for me?'

Evie held out her hands towards the stove, then began to rub her fingers briskly, giving an involuntary little moan as she did so. 'I thought it was bad enough when my hands went freezing cold, and then stopped being anything at all, but it's worse when the feeling starts to come back. Oooh, it's perishing agony.' Then she took a deep breath and turned to face him. 'I let you think Seraphina was really in love with you and that was why her marriage wasn't working. It was all my fault, because Fee wasn't very nice to you, was she, so I should have guessed . . . but I didn't, I'm afraid. And – and then she came home at Christmas and brought a fellow called Eddie with her. We all liked him but I couldn't believe anyone, not even Seraphina, could prefer him to you, Toby. I thought that as soon as she was free – properly divorced from Roger Truelove, I mean – that she'd realise where her heart lay and want to marry you.'

Toby snorted and began to speak, but Evie hushed him with a small, icy cold hand across his mouth. 'No, let me finish,' she commanded. 'And then, three or four days ago, Fee came home. She told us her decree nisi had been finally granted and she and Eddie meant to marry as soon as he came home from Egypt. And instead of smiling to myself and thinking she would soon come to her senses, I asked her outright how she felt about you and she said – she said . . .'

Toby grinned down at her and took both her hands in his own warm clasp. 'You always were a bossy kid, Evie Todd,' he told her. 'But I don't want to know what Seraphina said because I've known, oh, for ages, that she didn't care a button for me. And since we're being truthful for once, I'd better tell you that I don't care a button for her. It took me a long while to realise it because I got confused. Now, young woman, tell me the truth: who was it stayed with me all night when I came home after Dunkirk and had such terrible nightmares? It wasn't Seraphina, was it? I wanted to think it was, then, but now I think it was the same person who wrote me letters every week when I was in the POW camp, even though I could receive none of them. And it's my belief the lovely thoughts you put into those letters got through to me somehow, I don't know how.' He looked down at her, a painful question in his brown eyes. 'You seemed fond of

434

me and I believe fondness . . . no, dammit, love . . . can work all sorts of miracles. Sleep is something every POW craves, sleep and dreams of home. Is it too much to believe that you gave me those things by writing to me?'

Evie looked down at their clasped hands. 'Yes, I did stay with you after Dunkirk,' she said quietly. 'And I do love you, Toby. I think I always have. Only at first it was just kid's love, like you said. It was only later, when I started to dream about the prison camp, that it turned into something more. Only I *knew* that you loved Seraphina, so I just thought I'd be your sister-in-law and love you in that way.' Toby caught her in his arms and gave her an exuberant hug, then sat down with a crash in the chair by the fire, and began to kiss her. 'Stop it!' Evie squeaked. 'You – you're sorry for me, that must be it. You couldn't possibly love me the way you loved Seraphina.'

Toby nuzzled the back of her neck, blowing away the strands of soft brown hair as he did so. 'Little idiot, I never loved Seraphina,' he said reprovingly. 'I had a crush on her when we were both young, and when she rejected me my pride was hurt, so I determined to win her back. But all that had ended . . . oh, ages ago. I believe I was actually in love with you from the moment I came home after Dunkirk. Do you remember sending me five Woodbines? I kept them in the breast pocket of my tunic all through my time on the beaches. I was at a pretty low ebb, I can tell you, when I finally fished out those cigarettes, but when I handed them round to my mates, just for a moment, I felt like a king and I knew who I had to thank; it made me think of you, and even then, it was a good thought.' He turned her in his arms so that he could look into her face. 'Did you hear what I called back to you as the train left Lime Street station? I knew I shouldn't have said it, but it was the truth.'

'No,' Evie said. 'The train was kicking up such a racket . . . what did you say, Toby? And why shouldn't you have said it, anyhow?'

'I shouldn't have said it because I'm years older than you and don't have a marvellous job with wonderful prospects,' Toby said, his voice low. 'My face is scarred, but my mind is as well, though I'm beginning to come to terms with it. I'm not fit to marry anyone.'

'Oh, rubbish. What *did* you call to me as the train drew out?' Evie asked, stroking the scar which ran from brow to chin. 'And the scar isn't so terrible. I like it. It adds character, as my teacher used to say.'

Toby gave a crack of laughter, then began to kiss her, their mouths meeting with an urgency which might have frightened Evie once, but now merely made her give a purr of satisfaction. When they drew apart, her eyes were shining like stars, but she said, as steadily as she could: 'What did you say to me, Toby Duffy? If you don't tell me I'll – I'll not agree to marry you, so there!'

'I said "I love you, little Evie",' Toby said softly. 'And now I'll say the other bit. Will you marry me, sweetheart?'

Evie leaned up and kissed him gently. 'Of course I will,' she said. 'Oh, Lord, what was that?'

'It's our dinner, boiling over,' Toby said. He stood up, tipping Evie off his lap, then glanced towards the window. 'Oh, God, it's flaming well snowing again, and by the look of the flakes, the wind's changed direction. We could be stuck here for another three days!'

Evie giggled. 'That's the best news I've heard for ages,' she said, contentedly. 'Oh, I was feeling so bad on the way here, thinking I was going to break your heart, and now . . . well, it just goes to show it's true what they say: it's always darkest before dawn.'

Read on for an exclusive extract from Katie Flynn's next heartwarming bestseller

ORPHANS OF THE STORM

Jess and Nancy are nurses in France during the Great War. They have much in common for both have lost their lovers in the trenches, so when the war is over and they return to Liverpool, their future seems bleak.

Very soon, however, their paths diverge. Nancy marries an Australian stockman and goes to live in the Outback, while Jess marries a Liverpudlian. Their lives couldn't be more different.

When the second world war is declared, Nancy's son Pete joins the Royal Air Force and comes to England, promising his mother that he will visit her old friend. In the thick of the May blitz, with half of Liverpool demolished and thousands dead, Pete arrives in the city to find Jess's home destroyed and her daughter, Debbie, missing. Pete decides that whatever the cost, he must find her...

From the rigours of the Australian Outback to war-ravaged Liverpool, Debbie and Pete are drawn together... and torn apart...

Available from William Heinemann, February 2006

Willliam Heinemann: London

CHAPTER ONE
November 1918

Nancy Kerris bent over the young man in the bed and put gentle fingers around his wrist. Odd to feel such a tiny flutter in such a strong brown wrist – odd to see that his lips were purplish blue and that the tanned face looked suddenly yellow – almost as yellow as his hair. For one heart-stopping moment she did not know what to do, then previous experience, and her training, told her that she must get help – and quickly. She knew the patient had been badly wounded only a matter of a day or so before the Armistice had been signed and now, with a jolt of horror, she realised he was almost certainly haemorrhaging internally. But the gasp which rose to her lips never left them; if you panicked a patient, Sister Saunders said, he could die from fear. No, what she must do was get help and get it quickly.

She laid his hand down on the bed covers and smiled reassuringly into the bloodless face. 'You'll be fine, soldier, but I think maybe your bandage is loosening,' she said, in her most matter-of-fact voice. 'I'll just fetch Dr Amis...'

Nancy moved away from the bed, walking with a gliding, rapid step, which was the next best thing to a run, because Sister did not approve of her nurses running, or not on the wards at any rate. 'If you need help urgently,' she told her staff, 'then run as fast as you like along the corridors but not on the wards them-selves; is this understood?'

So now Nancy went out of the tent flap, because this was a makeshift emergency hospital from which the wounded men would presently be transferred to proper hospitals in England, and as soon as she was out of sight of the patient, broke into a fast run. A nurse coming towards her turned in her tracks to accompany her, saying as she did so: 'What's up, Nancy? Can I help?'

Nancy saw that it was Jess, her best friend, and spoke rapidly. 'Tent Three, fourth bed from the door, haem-orrhaging. I'm going to get a doctor; can you lay up a trolley, fetch instruments and so on?'

She did not wait for a reply knowing Jess was both skilful and competent, but ran on, hearing her friend's running footsteps fading in the opposite direction. Seconds later, she was gasping out her story to Dr Amis and turning to accompany him back to the tent she had just left. Obedient to the strictures laid upon them, both doctor and nurse eased their pace to a steady walk as they entered the ward. Already it was clear that Jess had got to work and had found a blood match between the patient and the young man in the next bed, and had obtained the necessary equipment to do a transfusion. Dr Amis nodded to Jess and moved to the bed. He spoke softly to the would-be donor, explaining the procedure he was about to carry out and the young man nodded. Before Dr Amis could ask, Nancy had leaned across the trolley and handed him the appropriate scalpel, then watched as the doctor inserted the tube into the dying man's wrist. Only after that was satisfactorily in place, did he make the long incision in the donor's arm. The boy went white but he grinned at Nancy then switched his gaze to the tubing through which his blood was now running steadily into the pint bottle which Jess was holding up. Nancy knew that the bottle contained a measured amount of sodium citrate solution to stop the blood from clotting and saw Jess giving the bottle a little shake every few minutes. The blood then ran down the other length of tubing into the patient's arm. The donor's arm lay on a board with a piece of rolled up bandage in his hand and the doctor gently reminded him to keep opening and closing his fist in order to facilitate the blood flow.

The young man nodded and Nancy averted her fascinated gaze from the five inch slit the doctor had cut in his arm and smoothed the damp hair from his forehead. He was only a boy, probably no more than seventeen or eighteen, yet he had volunteered to help another man without a second's hesitation. As she watched, he turned his eyes up towards her and gave her a beaming smile. 'Look at the feller's face,' he said, in a low whisper. 'He were yellowy-grey two minutes ago and to tell you the truth, I thought he were a gonner. But as soon as the blood started to flow, his colour began to come back. Ain't blood a wonderful thing, Nurse?'

Nancy, agreeing that it was, caught Jess's eye and they exchanged smiles. To save a life is always sweet and Nancy guessed Jess must know that their prompt action had probably saved this young man.

Presently the girls, who should both have been off duty, were dismissed and made their way towards their sleeping quarters. They were both extremely tired, having just worked a double shift and Nancy guessed that Jess, too, longed to get what rest they could before they were back on duty. Despite her tiredness, however, Nancy could not help remembering that other young man, the one to whom she had been engaged to be married. He had died two years previously when transfusing blood had been in its infancy; died in her arms, because no one had realised – until too late – that he, too, was haemorrhaging internally from a bayonet wound. She, who had loved Graham Peters to distraction, had knelt on the floor by his bed and held him in her arms whilst his life ebbed slowly away. He had looked up at her wonderingly out of tired blue eyes and she knew she would never forget his last words. 'You've grown so tiny my love,' he whispered. 'So tiny that I could hang you on the chain round my neck; then I would have you with me for always.'

Before she could so much as answer him, Graham's head had slumped forward on to his chest and she had felt the faint flutter of his heartbeat simply cease as though it had never been.

'Nancy?' Jess's voice interrupted her thoughts and Nancy saw the understanding there, the shared pain. 'Look, we need our rest; we'll feel better in the morning. And don't think I don't know what you're going through, because if they had known a bit more about blood and transfusions, Graham might still be here today.'

Nancy smiled wearily and gripped her friend's hand for a moment. 'I lost Graham and you lost Barney and it was dreadful for both of us,' she said quietly. 'But – but at least we had their love while they were alive and we have some beautiful memories. And – and we're still young, Jess. I know you think it won't happen, but we might meet somebody, get married, have children and be happy. I know Graham wouldn't grudge me being happy with someone else and I'm very sure Barney wouldn't grudge your happiness either; why, they'd both be glad of it!'

442

Jess was a pretty girl with a cloud of chestnut hair and large, dark blue eyes, but now her lips tightened and her eyes grew cold. 'I shall never marry,' she said bitterly. 'What chance would I have, stuck in a Liverpool slum with a fat, idle mother who wouldn't give tuppence for any of her kids? I suppose I'll have to put in for a training hospital and try to pass the exams but . . . oh no, I shall never marry. There's only ever been one man in my life and that was Barney. It's different for you; you're younger and you've a nice family.'

Nancy knew that in one way, at least, her friend was right. She was a vicar's daughter, from a parish in Devonshire, with loving parents and two older sisters. The Kerris family lived in a beautiful old vicarage, just outside the tiny village of Exham. True, there would be no work for her locally at home, but whatever she did, she knew she would have the support and help of a loving family.

Ten minutes later, the two girls made their way into the sleeping quarters. Nancy unpinned her cap and loosened her long, pale gold hair from its neat coil on the nape of her neck. Then she undid her stiff white collar from around her throat and removed the celluloid cuffs before casting off her stained white apron and the rustling cotton dress which afforded little protection against the extreme cold. She fished her thick woollen nightdress out from under her pillow and pulled it on over her underwear, for the tents were draughty and no one undressed completely before climbing into bed. As she slid between the blankets, she wondered about the young soldier who might with luck, now live. She did not flatter herself that it was only she who had saved his life, that had been done

443

by Doctor Amis and even by Jess, but she was glad she had played some small part in the night's happening. Then she snuggled her face into the pillow and put her hands, palms together, close to her chest. Until she had joined the nursing service, she had knelt every night on the cold linoleum of the room that she shared with her two older sisters and had said her prayers properly and respectfully as a vicar's daughter should. Now, in circumstances as different from those at the vicarage as could be imagined, she had long ago informed God, rather tartly, that he would have to forgive her for saying her prayers whilst cuddled down in bed.

But once she began, her prayers followed their usual course. She no longer had to pray that the war would end because it had ended. The Armistice had been signed, Victory Day had come and gone, yet still young men suffered and died for a war which she had long ago ceased to believe in. So now she prayed for the recovery of her patients, and for someone to come along and clean up the awful mess that wars leave in their wake, both for victor and conquered. She added a sort of postscript for the young soldier on Tent Three, realising as she did so that she did not even know his name, could scarcely recall his face. Then, at last, she slept.

'Well, Jess, we're back in Blighty at last! We've got a fortnight free before we start that intensive nursing course in the Liverpool Royal, which they promised us if we wanted nursing as our career. Are you still positive that it's what you want?'

The two girls were sitting in an uncomfortably crowded train heading for London, where they would part company, since each meant to go home to their people for a couple of weeks' break before they started their training. However, they intended to have a few days in the capital first so that they might buy themselves some warm clothing to replace their threadbare uniforms.

Jess pulled a face. 'What else is there for me?' she asked plaintively. 'I can't go back to living in a cramped little house in the slums with me mam, four sisters and two brothers; mind, they're all older 'n me, so they probably don't live at home any more . . . the boys don't, nor do me two oldest sisters, but Mam and me never got on. Oh, I suppose I might gerra job in a shop, or even an office, but the only thing I know anything about is nursing, and Sister Saunders said it were a good career with plenty of prospects for a girl who didn't mind hard work. Whilst we train, we'll have a room in the Nurses' Home and once we're qualified, we'll be able to afford lodgings. So . . . yes, I reckon I'll follow that part. But why do you ask? I thought we'd decided it betwixt ourselves. Why, we've even put in to go to the same hospital for our training, so's we can be together. Don't say you've changed your perishin' mind, our Nancy!'

Nancy smiled. 'When you mention Liverpool you sound more like a scouser every minute,' she said teasingly. She hesitated, knowing that what she was about to say could easily cause offence for Jess had changed since the death of her fiancé, Barney, more than twelve months before. Any mention of marriage seemed like rubbing salt into the wound and Jess was apt to answer sharply or worse, not to answer at all. However, it was no good beating about the bush; better to come straight out with what she was thinking and hope that Jess would at least listen to her proposal. Nancy fished in the pocket of her cloak and produced a cutting from a newspaper, then held it out to her friend. 'I saw this a couple of days ago and it made me think,' she said slowly. 'You and I are old friends, Jess, and we've both lost the men in our lives, but in one way I believe we are quite different. I would still very much like to be married and have a family of my own, whereas you seem to have given up any such thoughts. Oh, I know we agreed there's going to be very few young men to marry after the carnage of the trenches, so I suppose it seemed sensible to you to plan a career and to dismiss all hope of marriage. But then I saw this – this advertisement . . . well, read it for yourself.'

Jess took the small piece of newsprint and gave her friend a curious look. There was bitterness in that look and a sort of disillusion, but then Jess's eyes fell on the piece of newsprint and she began to read it aloud:

Wanted – wives for two white Australians
working in the Outback – return passages paid.
Apply Box No: 2046.

Nancy turned to peer in her friend's face. 'Well? What do you think? This would be as much a business proposition as a career in nursing.'

Jess snorted. 'They're after free housekeepers; someone to cook their meals, mend their clothes and manage their wages,' she said bluntly. 'What's more, it's half a world away. Anyone who goes that far isn't likely to turn around and travel all the way back to Britain again. And it's an awful long journey. You've got to live on whatever they send you for weeks and weeks and weeks. I guess that puts you under an obligation which would make it even more difficult to back out, say you'd made a mistake.' She tossed the newspaper cutting contemptuously into her friend's lap.

'Only a fool would answer that advertisement, Nancy Kerris, and if you want to be a fool, I can't stop you.'

Nancy sighed and tucked the advertisement back into her pocket. She had known in her heart what Jess's reaction would be but had hoped against hope that her friend might at least consider going with her. She supposed she could go alone, then dismissed the thought. After all, she had no idea yet what the hospital course would be like and how she and Jess would enjoy nursing in an atmosphere far more restrained and conventional than that of the makeshift hospitals in which they had worked for the past four years. So presently, when Jess had said, in a distinctly unfriendly voice: 'Well? Are you going to chuck all our plans out of the window and go off on this wild goose chase?' Nancy had replied, in her warmest voice: 'Don't be daft, of course I'm not; it was just an idea. Now let's talk about something else because I don't mean to fall out with my best friend over something which is probably just a leg pull anyway.'

She saw the look of relief which swept over her friend's face and was sorry she had caused Jess such misery, for she knew the other girl relied heavily on their friendship and was not anywhere near as self-reliant and independent as Nancy was herself. So she began to talk about the sort of warm winter clothing they would buy in London and about the show they would see at the London Palladium. At first, there was constraint between them but gradually this faded and by the time Victoria Station was reached, normal relations had been resumed.

But that night, when she was once more in her own little room in her parents' house, Nancy got out the advertisement again, then fished out a photograph of herself which she had taken from the big album on the kitchen dresser. It showed her in her nurse's uniform and it had been taken at the start of hostilities, but it was the only one she had so she penned a short, friendly letter, not saying much other than that she had read the advertisement and was interested in his proposition Then she popped it and the photograph into an envelope, wondering whether she was being a complete fool, as Jess had said. Yet despite doubts, next day after some more heart searching, she told herself that she was committing herself to nothing, squared her shoulders and sent both letter and photograph winging off to Box 2046.

Nancy enjoyed her time at the vicarage, and was sorry to leave at the end of her fortnight. Her eldest sister, Helen, had married her father's curate and had recently given birth to a baby boy, named Harold after his grandfather. Helen was still weak from the baby's birth and was happy to let Nancy take care of little Harry, and Nancy was enchanted by the baby. The warm weight of him in her arms, the sweetness of his smile and the soft, silky skin of him, awoke in her a strong desire for a child of her own. She did not envy Helen her marriage – she thought Samuel both pompous and boring – but she did envy her the child.

Anne, the sister nearest to Nancy in age, had also nursed in France, but had been invalided out in 1917 after a severe bout of pleurisy. Mrs Kerris assured her youngest daughter that Anne had made a good recovery, but Nancy thought her sister languid and weak still, content to carry out small household tasks such as dusting and arranging flowers, but spinning these jobs out so that they took all day. Nancy could not say much in front of the rest of the family but before she left, she persuaded Anne to walk into the village with her and cross-questioned her sister as to why she had changed so radically. She thought she could probably have guessed the answer, though in fact, she was quite wrong.

'I fell in love with a married man,' Anne said bluntly. 'He – he made all sorts of promises, said he would divorce his wife, swore he didn't really love her. I – I was every sort of fool, Nancy. I made myself believe him, told myself that divorce wasn't so bad, that love conquers all – that sort of thing, you know. Only then he – he mentioned his children and I knew I couldn't go through with it. So I had to tell him that we mustn't meet, that it was all over so far as I was concerned. He – he was a Senior Surgeon at my hospital, which made things difficult. When I was off duty, I tried to get as far away from the hospital as possible. I walked out one afternoon into a snowstorm meaning to go into the nearest village, only I lost my way and got benighted. A peasant family took me in but by then I was soaked to the skin and beginning to be ill'. She smiled tremulously at Nancy. 'The rest you know, as they say. I got bronchitis which turned to pleurisy and was sent home. I tell myself I've recovered from – from my love affair, but my health is poor and somehow nothing seems truly worthwhile any more.'

So Nancy left the vicarage regretfully, wishing that she could comfort Anne with the promise that things would get better as time passed, but she said nothing, because she knew Anne would have to learn this old truth for herself. She rejoined Jess in Liverpool, eager to begin the intensive training that they had been promised, but after only a month in her new position at the hospital – a month of being treated both as a nonentity and as a complete beginner – she began to long for something different, where she was not continually criticised or mocked. If only the Australian would reply to her letter! After all, there was no harm in exchanging correspon-

449

dence, she told herself defensively. Probably a score of girls would have answered the advertisement by now and the Australians might not even bother to reply to her own epistle. She had tried to make it lively, but the very fact that she was making some effort towards a life seemingly more rewarding than the one she lived at present, cheered her immensely and Jess commented on her friend's occasional bouts of optimism.

'I dunno what's happened, but you're more like the Nancy I first met when we both started nursing,' she said approvingly. 'I know you're feeling like I do – that the nurses here despise us – but they'll get over it once they see how hard we can work.'

Nancy smiled but said nothing and continued to watch for the arrival of the post every morning. She and Jess shared a room in the nurses' home but were on different wards and frequently on different shifts so they saw little of each other during working hours. Nancy was on a medical ward and Jess on a surgical one so even the staff with whom they worked were different. Jess liked Sister Evans though she was not fond of Sister Page who worked nights, but poor Nancy speedily realised that both Sister Frewin, and the rest of the staff on her ward, regarded her as some sort of threat. This was because Mr Myers, the surgeon in charge, knew her from France, where they had worked together, and was unwise enough to make it clear that he had considerable respect for the lowliest member of the nursing staff. Consequently, Nancy found herself emptying and cleaning bedpans, scrubbing floors and cleaning the lavatories. The patients liked her, appreciating her cheerful willingness to perform any task and teasing her by referring to her as Cinderella, much to Sister's fury. She was a middle-aged, weasel-faced woman, who disliked most of her nurses on principle, but truly detested Nancy. The older woman had a crush on Mr Myers, following him on his rounds with dog-like devotion and seeing her idol laughing and at ease with the newest probationer on the ward, filled her with spiteful fury so that it seemed to be her aim in life to make Nancy as miserable as possible.

So when in April a letter came bearing an Australian postmark, Nancy opened it with trembling fingers. Fortunately, she was alone in their room so was able to give her full attention to the missive but, first of all, she examined the photograph which fell out of the envelope as she extracted the letter. It was a picture of a very young man in army uniform. It was one of the posed pictures which most of the men sent home and showed him stiffly proud of his new uniform. He was half smiling, and the slouch hat which the Anzacs wore, could not quite hide the fact that his hair was as fair as Nancy's own. But this photograph had probably been taken in the early days of the war; Nancy flipped it over and read on the back the words: *Andrew Sullivan, 12th September 1914.* This was written in ink; beneath it, in pencil, were the words: *I don't have a recent photo but this will give you a rough idea; you will guess I am a good deal changed. Andy.*

Nancy nodded slowly to herself. She turned the photograph back and studied it intently; yes, he would be a good deal changed, as indeed she was herself. She knew that, before the war, a photograph of herself would show a conventionally pretty, innocent girl, still on the threshold of life, whereas now, the picture would be very different. She was not yet twenty-three but knew she looked a good deal older than girls who had not nursed men from the trenches. But it was impossible to guess from this photograph, over four years old, what sort of a man Andrew Sullivan was now. The boy had a nice face with guileless eyes. Still, the very fact that he had admitted he had changed meant he was an honest man who did not mean to deceive her.

Having studied the photograph for several more moments, Nancy turned to the letter:

Dear Miss Kerris,

Thank you for writing in answer to the advertisement. It was very brave of you, but then all the nurses I met during the war were brave; they had to be to do such terrible work. I have enclosed a photograph of myself, but I am much changed. No one could go through what we all went through and remain unaltered. However, now I am home again I would like a wife and family of my own but girls are scarce in the outback. I am Under-Manager of a cattle station, and I have a brother. I am twenty-seven years of age and my brother, Clive, is twenty-four. He works with me at the Walleroo Cattle Station in Queensland and is single like myself, with no commitments and he also is looking for a wife.

I have had one other answer to my advertisement but have decided that the lady would not be suitable. I will not deceive you into believing that life on a cattle station is easy for a woman. In summer, the heat can be intense and very trying if one is not accustomed, and in the wet, though it is not cold, it rains constantly and turns the station into a bog. Cattle stations are very large, so one's nearest neighbours are a great way off, which can mean a woman is lonely, though of course, we employ a great many native men and women. However, the native people do not always understand our ways and a woman in the Outback needs a friend which is why I decided to advertise. The other lady who wrote was very frank. She is a widow, forty-two years old, and has lived in cities all her life. I wrote back and explained how we live and she agreed it would not suit her. But you, Miss Kerris, might find the life almost easy after your work in France. You say in your letter that you have two sisters; would one of them not like to take up our offer also? It would be company for you, both on the long journey and, if we decide we are suited, on Walleroo Station.

I expect you can guess that this letter has taken me days and days to compose. I do not mean to give you information which may put you off, nor do I want you to see the Outback through rose-coloured spectacles. You say in your letter that you were born and reared in the country and this, more than anything else, leads me to hope we might suit. Horses are our main means of transport but, if you cannot ride, you can always drive the pony cart.

Clive and I have agreed between us that we will not urge marriage on anyone who comes over as a result of our advertisement, but will leave it up to you to either stay and marry one of us, or return home. I have not enclosed a money order since, until you reply, I cannot tell whether you will come alone or bring a companion – or whether you will simply decide that the Sullivan brothers, and life in the outback, are not for you. As soon as you let me know, hopefully, that you will give us a chance, I will set things in motion.

I am not a man who writes many letters and this one has taken me a mighty long while. I hope I've said nothing to offend you and shall eagerly await your reply.

Yours sincerely,
Andrew Sullivan

Having read the letter through twice and then, very slowly a third time, Nancy settled back in her chair and thought long and hard. If she took up Mr Sullivan's offer, it would be an adventure indeed, but the more she thought about it, the more convinced she became that it would be madness to go alone. She might find herself like a bone between two dogs which would be very uncomfortable and even if she discovered, upon arrival, that she did not wish to marry either young man, it would still be a difficult situation. She realised, of course, that this applied equally to the two young men, but even so, she found herself heartily agreeing with Mr Sullivan that two girls would find any situation easier to deal with than one woman alone.

She was still mulling the matter over when the door opened and Jess came into the room, untying her apron as she entered and saying, in an exhausted voice: 'Well, thank goodness that's over! I've been assisting Staff Nurse Smith in a dressings round and oh, Nancy, she's so clumsy and slow! But of course, I'm not allowed to say anything and when I told her that she had laid a dressing down on an unsterile surface and shouldn't use it, she was absolutely furious and ordered me off the ward to go and . . .' She stopped short, staring at her friend. 'What's happened? Who's the letter from? Oh, what a handsome young man!'

Nancy had spread the letter out on the table and propped the photograph against the milk jug. She went to gather the pages together, preparing an evasive reply, then changed her mind. 'The letter's from the fellow who put an advert in the paper weeks and weeks ago; remember, I showed you? And the photograph is the one he sent me.' She handed the pages to her friend. 'Go on, read it. Tell me what you think.'

For a moment, she thought Jess was going to refuse.

The other girl's colour heightened and her eyes narrowed dangerously, then she snatched the letter, plonked herself down in the chair opposite Nancy, and began to read. As Nancy had done, she read the entire thing through twice and then a third time, before pushing the now rather crumpled pages, back across the table. 'Anyone who takes up an offer like that is mad,' Jess said bitterly. 'Mad and sex-starved, if you ask me. Oh, I don't mean to insult you, Nancy, because I suppose you answered his advertisement as a joke, but he says one woman actually took him seriously, poor fool. What'll you do now though; you'll write and tell him it's not on, I suppose, or you could just not reply; perhaps that would be best, just don't get involved.'

Nancy stared, thoughtfully, at her friend. Jess had beautiful hair, a pretty face and a neat, though slender figure. She was an attractive girl but her looks were spoiled now by the strain in her eyes and the bitter lines about her mouth. Nancy gathered up the pages of the letter and thrust them into her pocket, then she picked up the photograph and stared at it, trying to imagine the changes which four years of that most dreadful war must have brought. He had talked about the nurses, which meant he had been wounded at least once. For all she knew, he might be crippled . . . no, of course not, if he were crippled he could not possibly be the under-manager of a large cattle station. Besides, she realised suddenly that she believed him to be an honest man, a straightforward man, the sort who would be likelier to tell the worst rather than the best.

'Well?' Jess's voice was sharp, almost spiteful. 'I'm tellin' you, Nancy, that if you go, you'll go alone. And if you ask my opinion, only a shameless hussy would go off into the blue, chasin' after a man she's never even met. So what are you going to do, eh?'

'I'm going to write to him again and I think I shall probably set off for Australia some time in the summer, like the shameless hussy I am,' Nancy said, quietly. 'I'm sorry you have such a poor opinion of me, Jess, my love, but I think I've discovered that nursing in peace time isn't for me. If Graham had lived, I would have married him and borne his children and been perfectly happy. As it is, I'm prepared to settle for something less. Perhaps I'll get to this cattle station and discover I've made a mistake but, oh, Jess, it'll be a new country, a new life! Even if Mr Sullivan and myself decide we aren't – aren't suited, as he put it, there may be somebody else. At any rate, I mean to give it a go and Jess, my love, come with me! I don't believe you're any happier with the present situation than I am. Think of it! A new country, new opportunities and young men; decent young men who want wives and families. Please Jess, give it a chance, don't turn your back just because it's a long way off.'

'It's nothing to do with being a long way off,' Jess said, her voice rising. 'I were in love with Barney and I'll never love anyone else, lerralone marry. You may forget Graham, but that's not my way. I'll be true to Barney till the day I die and I won't go chasin' after no bleedin' foreigners.'

'I'm not chasing after anyone, Jess,' Nancy said, coldly. 'I may get there and decide Mr Sullivan is not for me and come straight home. Or I may go for work in an Australian hospital, or do something quite different. And . . . I shall never forget Graham, but if he were here and able to speak to me, he'd tell me to seize any chance of happiness. After all, I'm only twenty-three; I might live another fifty years. Why should those fifty years be sterile ones? I told you how I enjoyed helping with my sister's baby whilst I was at

456

home; the truth is, Jess, I would very much like a baby of my own.'

'That's disgusting,' Jess said. 'Girls like us don't get married just to have babies; we know better. Anyway, there's no guarantee that you would have a baby. Lots of people marry and never have kids; what about that, eh?'

'If I can't have a baby of my own, then perhaps I could be a nanny and have charge of someone else's babies,' Nancy said, rather wildly. 'What's wrong with that, Jess?'

Jess snorted. 'You could be a nanny in this country,' she pointed out. She got up from her seat and went round the table, putting an arm round Nancy's shoulders and giving her a quick hug. 'I'm sorry I was horrible but you're me best friend and I can't bear to think of you going so far away. Nancy, just think! If you're ill, or very unhappy, you'll have no one to turn to. Not me, because I'm certainly not going with you, not your family, because they've got their own lives to lead. Why, you've only worked in this hospital for a month but you've half a dozen friends already who would do anything they could to help you.'

'I would hope to make friends wherever I went,' Nancy said. 'Jess, come with me! If there are two of us . . . remember, if I'm your best friend, you're mine! Don't let me down now, come to Australia as well and I'll make you a promise, if you hate it and want to come home again after giving it a try, then I'll come back with you, isn't that fair?'

Jess shook her head. 'I'm not going *anywhere*,' she said crossly. 'And nor are you if you've got a ha'porth of sense. Oh Nancy, say you won't go!'

Nancy sighed. She and Jess would be sharing this room and in each other's company for weeks, because she realised it would take time to arrange a passage to the other side of the world. Besides, she might change her mind, decide not to go after all, so she said slowly: 'I'm making no promises, Jess, except that I really will think very carefully before committing myself. I've already got several books about Australia out of the library, and I know a little bit about the heat and the sort of clothing and so on, which will be necessary if I do go, but I mean to write back to Mr Sullivan and ask him to paint me a picture of the sort of life a woman would live, and the sort of opportunities which children would have, because I understand folk on a cattle station can be pretty isolated. But, there are some farms on Dartmoor which are pretty isolated, so I'm not really worried by that, but I promise you, Jess, I won't do anything hasty. Will that satisfy you for now?'

'Not really, but I suppose it's the most I can hope for, if you're set on making a change,' Jess said sadly. 'Write back to him if you must, but remember, he wants a wife so he may not tell the truth, the whole truth and nothing but the truth.'

'There would be little point in his lying because, if I go, I shall see for myself what the true state of affairs is,' Nancy said, wearily. 'Besides, you've seen his photograph; he looks pretty straightforward to me. Why, you said yourself: *What a handsome young man*, when you first saw the photograph.'

'Handsome is as handsome does,' Jess said, rather obscurely. 'And now let's forget all about it because I've probably already said too much. I'm nippin' out to the shops to buy half a dozen eggs and a new loaf; do you want anything?'

Despite Nancy's hopes, it was not until the autumn of 1919 that she finally left the hospital and set sail for what she hoped would be the greatest adventure of her life. She and Andrew Sullivan had exchanged a great many letters, and the more she learned of him, the more she liked the thought of meeting him in person. She thought that she was unlikely to fall in love with anyone, for Graham's face was still clear in her memory; his voice sounded often to her inner ear. But Graham had been a generous and loving man and Nancy knew with every fibre of her being that he would want her to be happy.

Despite her hopes, however, Nancy was travelling alone. Not only had Jess proved obdurate, but a week after she had booked her passage, they had had the most dreadful row. It was over Nancy's intention to go to Australia, of course, and both girls had said things Nancy was sure they would later regret, though it was Jess who had hurled the most unforgiveable insults. It was fortunate that Nancy had handed in her notice at the hospital and was off to spend her last two weeks in England with her parents and sisters, for she did not think she could have so much as met Jess's eyes without remembering the terrible things her friend had said. She stood on the deck of the ship which would take at least six weeks to reach her destination and looked back at the coastline, fast disappearing as a light morning mist thickened. A tiny figure waving a white handkerchief was her sister, Anne, who had insisted upon accompanying her and seeing her safely aboard. Nancy had hoped that Jess might let bygones be bygones so that at least they could exchange letters, and had written a conciliatory note to her old friend, telling her both the port and the hour of her departure. She had scanned the crowds eagerly, but there had been no sign of Jess and when she had admitted her hopes to Anne, her sister had reminded her that Jess was scarcely likely to be given time off from the hospital merely to wave goodbye to an old friend. Nancy knew that it was true, but she also knew that if Jess had really wanted to make up their quarrel by seeing her off, she would have managed it somehow.

Nancy turned away from the rail and headed for the cramped little cabin she was sharing with three other girls. As yet, she knew nothing but the names of her travelling companions but guessed that they would grow to know one another well over the course of the long voyage. She had bought a thick notebook in which she intended to keep a diary of her movements and experiences and now she went and sat on her narrow bunk and fished the book out from her canvas holdall and began to write. She was halfway through her description of her tearful parting, first with her family and then with Anne, when another thought occurred to her. She was off on what was undoubtedly going to be an adventure, though whether good or bad she could not yet say, but poor Jess, who had stood by her through thick and thin during the war years, was left behind. The work she was doing was hard and could be satisfying, but it was only work. I'll write her a long, newsy letter, adding a bit each day and post it as soon as I get the chance, Nancy told herself. Of course I shan't be able to give her an address other than the Sullivan homestead, but I'll tell her to address her letters to the Walleroo Station and then her reply will be there to greet me when I arrive. Oh, what a marvellous idea; it will be the next best thing to being met by dear old Jess herself!

Jess had handed in her notice at the hospital a couple of days after Nancy left. She had already obtained a position as a private nurse to an old lady of eighty-two, who lived in a large house off Lancaster Avenue so she had no financial worries for the job was live-in. In fact she would be better off, for her employer, Mrs Bellamy, would provide all her meals and uniform. Despite her age, and the painful rheumatism which made it necessary for her to employ a nurse, she was a lively and intelligent woman and Jess had looked forward to starting her new job.

When she had received Nancy's note begging her to forget their dreadful quarrel and asking, somewhat diffidently, if Jess might like to journey to Southampton to see her off, she had been absolutely furious. How had Nancy dared make such a suggestion! As though she, Jess, would waste her time and money travelling all that way when she had much better and more important things to do. Besides, she told herself that she did not want Nancy's friendship; what was the use of a friend who lived thousands of miles away? Their letters would take a couple of months to reach their destination and Jess knew enough about Nancy to be pretty sure that, having made up her mind to go to Australia her friend would not turn round and come back to England without giving her new life a real chance. So she had not even replied to the note but had scrumpled it up and thrown it in the waste paper basket.

It was a fine, sunny day in spring. Daffodils danced in Mrs Bellamy's neat garden and Jess, who was growing fonder and more at ease with her employer with every day that passed, had put a tiny vase of violets on Mrs Bellamy's breakfast tray, before carrying it up to her room and placing it tenderly across her knees. 'It's a lovely day, Mrs Bellamy,' she said as she did so. 'If you feel up to it, you might enjoy a ride in the bath chair. You've not been down to the gardens Sefton Park since the Cheerfulness Narcissus came into bloom and their scent, when the sun is on them, is delightful. So if you feel like an outing . . .'

Mrs Bellamy agreed that it would be lovely to leave the house for an hour or so and Jess hurried downstairs and was turning into the breakfast parlour when the post came through the letterbox. There were four letters for her employer and one for herself which had been forwarded by the hospital and Jess did not even have to glance at the handwriting to know it was from Nancy. She thrust it into her pocket as a maid emerged from the kitchen with a tray carrying Jess's own pot of coffee and rack of toast. Jess took the tray, then handed her employer's mail to Gladys telling her to take it to her mistress, then turned into the breakfast parlour, sat down in her usual chair, and pulled out her letter. She was tempted to throw it straight into the fire, but perhaps because she was so happy in her present job, or perhaps because all women are curious, she slit open the envelope and pulled out several sheets covered in Nancy's clear, elegant handwriting.

Nancy's letter began with a description of her voyage and went on to describe several ports which she had visited in company with the three other girls who had shared her cabin. Then she described her excitement over reaching Sydney, the beauty of the big, modern city and her surprise and delight when, descending on to the quayside, she was approached by a tall, fair-haired man who introduced himself as Andrew Sullivan. *He had recognised me from my photograph and had come a great distance to meet me so that I should not feel myself a stranger in a strange land,* she wrote. *I know I should have realised what a huge country Australia is – Mr Sullivan had told me so in all his letters – but I had* not realised how long it would take us to reach the Walleroo from Sydney. First we had to catch a steamer which took us, extremely slowly, up the coast. Then we caught a train, which was also very slow. Dear Jess, I won't describe the journey to you because, to be honest, a good deal of the scenery, though strange at first, was also very boring. The heat on the train was intense, the food available of the plainest, and we were plagued by flies which descended on us in huge numbers every time the train stopped at a station, which was often. However, Mr Sullivan did his best to entertain me, telling me the names of all the trees, flowers, birds and animals which we saw whilst travelling and trying to put me in the picture as regards the homestead and staff at the Walleroo.

And now, Jess, I must tell you the most important piece of news. Andy – I must call him Andy now – and myself, were married before we left Sydney. Truly, Jess, Andy is a good man and I know you would like him. Neither of us pretend to be in love but we like one another very well and I am sure we'll grow even fonder as time goes by. Dear Jess, I can imagine your face, but please don't be cross, or think I acted impetuously, though I suppose I did. But it would have been very difficult to undertake this long journey as an unmarried woman, accompanied only by a bachelor; for Australians are every bit as conventional as English folk and would have expected me to have a female companion. Also, Andy says the Walleroo is very remote; we would have had to travel all the way back to this town – the one I'm writing from – in order to get married and Andy's brother, Clive, has already been in charge for far too long and Andy is obviously worrying in case his brother can't cope.

Andy manages the cattle station for a Mrs Briggs, who is very old and lives a great way away, down on the coast. She has one daughter, who is not in the least interested in *the Walleroo, so the arrangement is, that when Mrs Briggs passes on, the daughter will sell the property to Andy and his brother. So you see, dear Jess, that it is vitally important to keep the station in good heart, both for Mrs Briggs's sake and for the Sullivans' future.*

Oh dear, I do hope I've made you understand how difficult it would have been to delay our marriage until we reached the cattle station. Andy did not try to persuade me to marry; he simply set out how things were and left me to make up my own mind.

We are, at present, staying in a small hotel before starting on the last leg of our journey. Andy suggested that I should spend the day writing letters home since, if I were to leave it until we reach the cattle station, we would have to wait for the mail man's visit before the letters could be despatched. The mail is delivered once a week and any letters we may have written are collected at the same time. The pack horses cannot deliver parcels, only letters and small packets, so when a parcel arrives, someone from the Walleroo has to drive to the railway station to pick it up, which is almost a hundred miles away!

I am hoping there will be a letter from you, waiting for me, when we reach the homestead. You are such a generous person, Jess, so I'm sure you will forgive me for my part in our quarrel. I said some dreadful things which I certainly didn't mean, and I long to hear from you.

All my love,
    Nancy

Jess propped the letter against the toast rack and poured herself a cup of coffee. It was not fair! Nancy had not said one word concerning the intimate side of her marriage, so Jess hoped that there was no intimate side, that the young couple were behaving as they would have done had the wedding ceremony not taken place.

464

If only Barney hadn't died! She did not have Nancy's hunger for a baby but she was beginning to realise that, fond though she was of Mrs Bellamy, she did hunger for a home and a man of her own. But not badly enough to go to the other end of the earth, she reminded herself. No, no, she was not that desperate. Mrs Bellamy often suggested that her nurse should take an evening off and go out with her friends from the hospital, but so far, Jess had not done so. Slowly, she reached for a round of toast, spread it with butter and marmalade, and began to eat. It was not fair! Nancy was married to a man of some importance, who would eventually be the owner of an enormous cattle station. She would be mistress of the Walleroo homestead; the word homestead had already conjured up a picture in her mind's eye. It would be a long, low building, white-washed and roofed with cheerful red tiles. There would be roses round the door and the house would be set amidst trees and rolling hills. Every window would be framed by pretty curtains, the floors would be luxuri-ously carpeted, and there would be servants who would run to do Nancy's bidding and adore their beautiful intelligent mistress, with her ash blonde hair and big, blue eyes. Yes, Nancy had landed on her feet, there was no doubt of that.

If she, Jess, should do as Mrs Bellamy suggested and go to a dance, or some other social event, what sort of young man was she likely to meet? The war had left everyone weary and dispirited. Money was short – as were unmarried men – and jobs difficult to find. And anyway, she told herself briskly, you had a chance of a better life in Australia, the same as Nancy had, but she took it and you didn't. You said you'd never forget Barney, never love another. You were horrid to Nancy, now you really ought to eat your words, tell her you're sorry for the things you said. But Jess knew she would not. Nancy had abandoned her, left her to loneliness and spinsterhood; she would never forgive her old friend for that, not if she lived to be a hundred.

The Cuckoo Child

Katie Flynn

When Dot McCann, playing relievio with her pals, decides to hide in Butcher Rathbone's almost empty dustbin, she overhears a conversation which could send one man to prison and the other to the gallows – and suddenly finds herself in possession of stolen goods.

Dot lives with her aunt and uncle, the cuckoo in the nest, abandoned to these relatives after her parents died. She feels very alone ... until she meets up with Corky who has run away from a London orphanage. They join forces with Emma, whose jeweller's shop has been burgled and with Nick, a handsome young newspaper reporter who is investigating the crime. The four of them begin to plot to catch the thieves.

But Dot and Emma have been recognised, and soon both are in very real danger ...

A Long and Lonely Road

Katie Flynn

Rose McAllister is waiting for her husband, Steve, to come home. He is a seaman, often drunk and violent, but Rose does her best to cope and sees that her daughters, Daisy, 8, and Petal, 4, suffer as little as possible. Steve however, realises that war is coming and tries to reform, but on his last night home he pawns the girls' new dolls to go on a drinking binge.

When war is declared Rose has a good job but agrees the children must be evacuated. Daisy and Petal are happy at first, but circumstances change and they are put in the care of a woman who hates all scousers and taunts them with the destruction of their city. They run away, arriving home on the worst night of the May Blitz. Rose is attending the birth of her friend's baby and goes back to Bernard Terrace to find her home has received a direct hit, and is told that the children were seen entering the house the previous evening. Devastated, she decides to join the WAAF, encouraged by an RAF pilot, Luke, whom she has befriended . . .

arrow books

A Kiss and a Promise

Katie Flynn

Michael Gallagher is an Irish seaman, fighting with the British Navy. He comes ashore in Liverpool when his ship needs repairs and meets lovely young Stella Bennett on the quayside, searching for her lost kitten.

The young couple fall in love and want to marry but the Bennetts have other plans for Stella and when she gives birth to a baby, Ginny, Michael is dismayed by the child's ginger hair and convinced she is not his.

He returns to Ireland, leaving the sluttish Granny Bennett to rear Ginny. The child accepts her lot, expecting little from life but knows that, in order to escape from the slums, she must attend school. Granny Bennett prefers Ginny to skivvy for her, but when a sympathetic teacher, Mabel Derbyshire, comes into her life, Ginny decides she must better herself and the obvious way to do so is to find her father . . .

arrow books

ALSO AVAILABLE IN ARROW

Down Daisy Street

Katie Flynn

It's 1934 and Kathy Kelling is eleven years old. She has always
lived in Daisy Street in Liverpool, the only child of elderly parents.
Her best friend is Jane, who has half a dozen brothers and sisters,
and her worst enemy is Jimmy McCabe, who lives nearby, the
eldest of a large and penniless family. He calls Kathy spoilt and
posh because she goes to a private school.

The girls are forced to grow up fast when war breaks out in 1939.
But it has its advantages: Kathy is enchanted to meet Ned
Latimer, a handsome RAF pilot from Norfolk. He is delighted with
Kathy's wit and personality, but it is Jane who uses her good
looks to steal him away.

Broken-hearted, Kathy joins the WAAF, determined to do her bit.
But fate has not finished with her as she is thrown together with
Ned again, at Britain's most deperate hour . . .

arrow books

ALSO AVAILABLE IN ARROW

The Bad Penny

Katie Flynn

One wild night in the '30s, midwife Patty Peel is called to attend a birth on the opposite side of Liverpool. She pedals off into the storm and delivers a baby girl in a filthy slum dwelling, just as the mother dies. The drunk and violent father tells Patty to get rid of it, so she takes the child away, meaning to deliver it to the nearest orphanage.

But Patty has spent her entire childhood in an institution, except for the frequent occasions when she ran away, and cannot bear to hand the baby over.

However, she has few friends and despises the men with whom she comes into contact with, so how can she hope to bring up the child alone?

She has no idea how the baby will affect the attitude of those around her . . . nor how her life will change as a result . . .

arrow books

Order further Arrow titles
from your local bookshop, or have them delivered
direct to your door by Bookpost

☐	A Liverpool Lass	0 09 942999 3	£5.99
☐	The Girl From Penny Lane	0 09 942789 3	£5.99
☐	Liverpool Taffy	0 09 941609 3	£5.99
☐	Strawberry Fields	0 09 941603 4	£5.99
☐	No Silver Spoon	0 09 927995 9	£5.99
☐	Polly's Angel	0 09 927996 7	£5.99
☐	The Girl from Seaforth Sands	0 09 941654 9	£5.99
☐	The Liverpool Rose	0 09 942926 8	£5.99
☐	Poor Little Rich Girl	0 09 943652 3	£5.99
☐	The Bad Penny	0 09 943653 1	£6.99
☐	Down Daisy Street	0 09 945339 8	£6.99
☐	A Kiss and a Promise	0 09 945342 8	£6.99
☐	Two Penn'orth of Sky	0 09 946814 X	£6.99
☐	A Long and Lonely Road	0 09 946815 8	£6.99
☐	The Cuckoo Child	0 09 946816 6	£6.99

Free post and packing
Overseas customers allow £2 per paperback

Phone: 01624 677237

Post: Random House Books
c/o Bookpost, PO Box 29, Douglas, Isle of Man IM99 1BQ

Fax: 01624 670923

email: bookshop@enterprise.net

Cheques (payable to Bookpost) and credit cards accepted

Prices and availability subject to change without notice.
Allow 28 days for delivery.
When placing your order, please state if you do not wish to receive any
additional information.

www.randomhouse.co.uk/arrowbooks

a r r o w b o o k s